STORIES FROM THE STRANGE PLACE

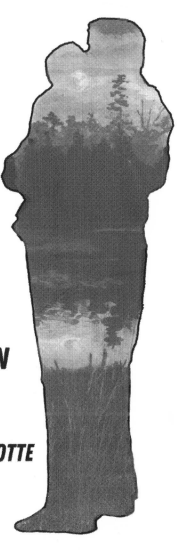

A COLLECTION OF SHORT FICTION

BY
MICHAEL JAMES RIZZOTTE

For Jamie,
and
for Nina and Lucas.

You have many years ahead of you to create the dreams that we can't even imagine dreaming. You have done more for the collective unconscious of this planet than you will ever know.

– Steven Spielberg

CONTENTS

FORWARD

Michael James Rizzotte was born on December 8, 1981. Just two months and four days before my birthday, February 12, 1982. As the story goes, our friendship was established when his parents brought him, still an infant, to visit me in the hospital. Our fathers had been lifelong friends, so it never seemed too outlandish to me that this story was based on fact. Nearly thirty-nine years later, Michael and I are still best friends to this day. I am honored to say our friendship has overcome all of the seemingly insurmountable challenges life throws at you as one grows out of childhood into adulthood. One thing which remained the same through all these years is Michael's ingrained ability to create a story.

Michael is a perpetual dreamer of the greatest type. Someone who fuses the imagination and reality in a way to enhance his audience's experience. This has been a characteristic trait before he ever decided to formally put down words on paper. I know this all too well growing up with him.

As children, he would convincingly tell me how he received communication bracelets from our favorite cartoon characters to stay in touch with them. Of course, whenever I asked to see the communicating device, he said he had to throw it out so no one would catch him. The disappointment I felt of not being able to talk with those cartoon characters, myself, was always overshadowed by the excitement I felt "knowing" my best friend was able to contact them. Sure, I had my doubts to the validity of Michael's claims, even as a five-year-old. Yet, it was something that brought me joy on a continual basis. Why spoil the fun?

Going through elementary school together, our curiosities expanded into supernatural and paranormal entities. The most popular of such was the story of the Jersey Devil. Raised in a town surrounded by the New Jersey Pinelands, it was impossible to escape this famous local folklore. There were re-enacted plays, books in our school library, and countless stories of close encounters with the famed beast. One story in particular involved Michael's father, David. As a young adult, he had gone out in the woods with his two brothers and left a sound recorder to record overnight. When they retrieved it the next day and played the tape back, there was an ungodly sound, not of this world. The way Michael always described it to me was a shrill shriek similar to nails running down a chalkboard. I would like to emphasize that it was Michael, not his father, who always told this story.

Is it not these types of experiences, though, which have forged bonds between humans throughout history? All supernatural beasts aside, there have been countless stories shared by mankind which ignite the wonder of the soul. Ordinary men taking down beasts three times their size, a sailor's recounts of a foreign land, or, more recently, unexplained objects flying through the sky that defy modern technology. It is natural for us to want to know more about those strange things which waver somewhere between reality and the imagination. Michael's enthusiasm and emotions exuded when recollecting tales of these kinds (whether experienced personally by him or not) can easily become contagious by his audience. There lies the purpose behind his work.

Stories bring a certain sort of connection to those willing to engage with the storyteller. It is this connection that Michael aims to bring us as a way of escape from our mundane routines. There are elements within his pages which most of us can relate to, and then there are those which we could only dream of experiencing. But who knows, maybe there are some small, granular truths embedded within those fanciful story elements of his. After all, if you were to ask me when I first met Michael James Rizzotte, I honestly could not give you a straight answer. It's as if we have been friends since birth.

-Jason Charles Garrison

JERSEY JABBERWOCK

The balcony of my studio apartment was a cramped perch, with just enough space for my bike and the lawn chair I was sitting on when my cell phone buzzed in my pajama pants.

"Yes, Mother," I said sarcastically, bracing myself for her usual hysterics. After a moment of hesitation, she said the three words that changed everything.

"Dad is gone."

"Gone?" I responded, as I rose to my feet, trying to shake off a sudden dizzy spell.

"He's gone," she said again, reassuring herself that the words were true.

"What happened?"

"They think a heart attack."

"They think? Who are they?"

"The medics. They're here with Uncle Beau. What are we going to do, Michael?" I steadied myself on the railing, as I looked up at the mansions. They were nothing more than drab Goliaths disappearing into shadowy hills, as they peered down upon the less fortunate occupants of the places below them. The allure of the balcony's view was no longer there. It was as if I was suddenly seeing the City of Angels for the smoggy, lonely place it really was. I had no answers for her. She continued to sob on speakerphone, fielding questions from the other people in the room, occasionally checking to see if I was still on the line. I went inside to wash down an Ativan with a swig of Captain Morgan, then flipped my laptop open to book an emergency flight to New Jersey.

A couple of hours - and one Uber ride later - I was sitting at an airport bar. The wayward traveler beside me was trying his hand at small talk, which I successfully evaded. I also ignored several calls from family members and friends. I'm sure they meant well but, as I stared blankly at the muted flat screen playing CNN, all I wanted to do was consume my chicken quesadilla and overpriced cocktail.

I was lucky enough to nab a window seat and immediately requested one of those awful pillows. As the plane ascended, I let the alcohol lull me to the dreary place between wakefulness and sleep. Fragments of memories danced with the muffled happenings inside the cabin.

4

The last time we spoke was two weeks before he passed. I asked him to send me some money. Again. During my stint out West, our relationship was defined by these pitiful requests for financial aid. Not much different from when I lived home, to be honest.

The Atlantic City airport was as cold and gray as I remembered it. My best friend, Charlie, was waiting for me in the parking garage.

"Hey, brother," he said, softly, as he hugged me. "I'm so sorry."

We awkwardly exchanged pleasantries on the drive home. A far cry from the two guys that used to chop it up on everything from interplanetary space travel to Kurosawa films. He was probably pissed that I had avoided his phone calls for a year but didn't hesitate to text him when I needed a ride.

When we arrived at the place I called home for twenty-two years, the familiar horseshoe shaped driveway was packed with cars. My parents' house was a long rancher, nestled in the woods off a busy highway. Although it was almost February, the outside Christmas decorations were still up. Not because of any extra holiday spirit, but because my father's workers hadn't had a chance to remove them.

The house was swarming with folks getting day drunk. Long lost friends and longer lost family shared stories over sandwich trays. I waded toward the master bedroom through a sea of condolences and "Welcome homes."

My mother was in a nightgown on all fours. She greeted me as if I still lived there, as if I hadn't moved to California five years ago, as if the house wasn't filled with people there to pay their respects. The reality of the moment was lost on her.

"I dropped my back pill," she mumbled. "Please, help me find it."

"I'm sure it isn't a back pill. Jesus Christ. Why are you in here, Ma?"

"Don't start right now."

"You have to clean yourself up and go out there right now."

"I can't. My back. I can barely walk."

In an instant, I was back to the life I retreated across the country from. But, I knew there was no time for a lengthy cross-examination about a feigned ailment and pills. The planet my mother was on was where she would have to stay, while I played host.

The rest of the evening was a whirlwind of drunken conversations about my father, with teary-eyed people who were practically strangers to me. At some point, as the crowd started to thin out, I found myself leaning against the kitchen counter, surrounded by three colorful figures from his life. There was the college teammate, the business associate, and the hunting buddy. Fifty-something year-old men, excited to speak to each other about their dead friend. Each one talked louder than the next, explaining how my father had become quiet in the months before his death. Reclusive even. Nothing like the man he was his entire life.

"So, was he sick?" I asked aloud, to no one in particular. After an uncomfortable moment of silence, the hunting buddy responded.

"I don't think so. Matter of fact, he was more active in the woods than I had ever seen him."

The college friend poured us some whiskey, then said, "Well, he was one of a kind. I'll miss the shit out of him, that's for sure."

He held his shot glass up and blabbered for what felt like at least thirty minutes. I helplessly clutched my own glass, pondering the last few conversations my father and I had on the phone. We usually kept our chats brief, but they had gotten shorter than usual. I felt like he had something important to tell me.

"Cheers to a great man," the college guy exclaimed at the end of his dissertation. I snapped out of it, took the shot, then made my way to the living room. My Uncle Beau sat on the couch beside me.

"How are you holding up?" he asked.

"I dunno."

"I hear ya. Well, we are going to try to get the safe in his office open tomorrow, see if we can find a will. You should be there."

It sounded like a lot of fun. I could hardly wait. Charlie was the last guest to leave. We embraced at the front door, as he told me he felt like he lost a father as well. Before I could apologize for being such a dick, he addressed the elephant in the room.

"You're my brother. Even if you don't want to take me up on it most times, I am here for you."

Something about losing a loved one helps those of us still here to cut to the chase a little quicker. A sense of urgency fills the air around us.

"I've been an asshole," I responded, somberly. "I'm sorry."

6

I went upstairs and wept in my old bedroom. It was a long, pathetic cry that stretched deep into the night. I wasn't wallowing in my sorrow, not by a long shot. It was more like a painful sadness engulfing every inch of me. At some point, my eyes fixated on a framed photo, centered between a couple of tarnished trophies. It was taken junior year, in my high school's gymnasium after a basketball game. I was in my uniform, sweaty and smiling, as my father wrapped his arm around my shoulders. I stared at the photo until the sun began to rise.

As guests returned to the house, my mother cleaned herself up and greeted them, giving me a chance to sneak out of the back door. I sauntered through a dormant blueberry field toward the packing house, with a frigid air whipping my face. It was oddly restorative. It let me know I could still feel something.

Everything in the dusty office was the same as it was since my earliest memories, with the exception of my cousin, Beau Jr., sitting at my father's desk. As kids, "Little" Beau would be out in the pickup with his dad, learning the ropes about planting and irrigation, while I would be in the packing house, hidden behind a wall of empty cucumber boxes, sketching superheroes. I knew the moment would come when the name on that desk would change, I just wasn't ready for it to be so soon.

I stood in the doorway while a crotchety locksmith worked on the safe. Little Beau wasn't the type to initiate conversation, so I spoke up.

"Wouldn't it be something if there was a mummified head in there?"

My cousin chuckled out of confusion.

The safe produced no will, just two thousand dollars in loose cash and a tattered marble notebook.

II.

My father co-owned a five hundred acre vegetable farm with his brother Beau, in our hometown of Cedarwood. He was the New Jersey Agricultural Board President who also competed in chicken wing eating contests and cut the meanest rug to Motown music you've ever seen. He was the smartest person in the room and usually the one with the most bedraggled appearance. He was sincere, thoughtful, and hilarious.

His services were of the Catholic variety, made difficult by the fact that I had to organize these strange rituals along with my mother. There was the meeting with the florist, then the funeral director, then the priest, then the nerdy guy who puts together highlight movies of dead people. No one ever tells you that burying a loved one is so much work.

The proceedings started with a viewing on a Tuesday night. The town anticipated an extremely well-attended event, so they took precautions, like police officers directing traffic in the church's parking lot. An eternal line of mourners stretched through the pews and out into the lot. Some waited as long as an hour in the light snow that was falling. It was a testament to my father and the impression he made on so many people. I received a million sloppy kisses and awkward hugs, from total strangers to people I had spent Christmases with. This all took place as my father laid neatly in a box a few feet away. A limousine picked my mother and me up the following morning. I concealed a flask of whiskey in the breast pocket of my suit jacket. We saw him one last time in the church, just the three of us. As I watched my mother cry over his body I could do nothing but stand there, helplessly placing my hand on her shoulder.

Mass was next. The priest rambled on aimlessly as I recalled a time when my parents were practicing Catholics, making me one by default. I remembered waking up early on Sunday mornings, CCD classes with Charlie, and the midnight masses on Christmas Eve. Somewhere along the road I started questioning all of it. From the virgins giving birth, all the way to the men living in whales. I guess you can say I lost my faith. Or, perhaps, I never had it to begin with.

I excused myself, then listened to the eulogy through the walls of the lavatory. The man spoke of my father's long list of accomplishments and the many times he helped those in need. I wondered how people would speak of me. The guy getting drunk in a stall at his father's funeral.

8

When mass was over, a ridiculously long line of cars followed the hearse to the cemetery. We drove by the farm, our house, and ended at his final resting place on the far side of the cemetery, along the edge of the woods. The priest said a quick prayer, then people began to place roses on his casket.

A few yards into the trees, I spotted an unfamiliar man watching the service. I didn't recognize his face from the viewing. He may have been at mass but my gut was telling me he wasn't. When his eyes locked with mine, he nodded then turned and walked deeper into the woods, until he was cloaked in shadows. A hand on my back startled me.

"You okay?" Charlie asked, softly.

"Did you see that dude over there?"

"Over where? The woods?"

"I dunno. Maybe I'm going nuts."

"We're all a little nuts, bro."

After a luncheon, my mother and I returned to the house. She escaped to her room and wept all night. Other than that, things were quiet. No guests - just week old hoagies and alcohol. I enjoyed the company of both.

III.

For the next few weeks, I got well acquainted with signing paperwork on fancy wooden desks. As co-owners, Uncle Beau and my father had set up a buy-sell agreement. It basically meant that if something happened to him, I would be bought out by my uncle. With the stroke of a pen, I no longer belonged to the family business. It was only right. I was a stranger to it anyhow.

The terms of the agreement left me with a substantial amount of money. More money than the guy living off Ramen noodles in Los Angeles ever anticipated.

"If I give this check back, will he be resurrected?" I asked his attorney. Tears were in both of our eyes.

"I wish," he responded. "But, this is what he worked so hard for. So, when this day came, you would be okay."

I was drinking heavier than ever, angry about squandering the freedom my father gave me to follow every foolish dream that festered in my brain. The freedom to write screenplays, songs, whatever. All along I was scrawling myself nowhere.

My mother was also compensated. One rainy afternoon we had a discussion rather than our usual profanity laced shouting match. To my surprise, she agreed that a woman in her condition should not have access to a large sum of money. So, I made a deal with her. I would take care of her finances and the house, while she completed a yearlong rehabilitation program. I was absolutely in no shape to accomplish any of this, but I kept telling myself I was the lesser of two let downs. I sobered up just enough to drive my father's pickup through a snowstorm to upstate New York.

"Some people said dad was acting weird. Did you notice?" I asked, as I clutched the steering wheel, struggling to drive in the inclement weather.

"He was caught up in something. I wish I could've been there for him. I was just...I'm lost," she responded, her voice trembling.

"Caught up in what, Ma?"

Before she could answer, I was cut off by some jerk in a sports car with custom Yankees plates.

"It's a blizzard and you're out here driving like an asshole!" I shouted, as if he could hear me. When I cooled off, my mother switched topics as quickly as she could.

"I'm so nervous about this place."

10

"Don't be nervous. This is a good thing you're doing. You'll be exactly where you need to be."

We reminisced about happier times for the rest of the drive. It was our longest and least volatile conversation in a long time.

The mountains of upstate New York made way for a refurbished mansion from the late eighteenth century. A philanthropist had purchased the building and surrounding land in the sixties, converting it into a safe haven for drug addicted prostitutes. It eventually grew into a recovery center that houses forty ladies at a time. Their motto was "Rebuilding shattered lives." I liked the sound of that when I found it online.

Our hug goodbye felt weird. I struggled to recall the last time I embraced my mother.

"For dad," she whispered.

"For yourself," I replied.

When I returned to the house it felt emptier than ever. People visited less every day. This meant I had to acquire my own forms of nourishment. The purchase I made at the liquor store was extraordinary. I didn't plan on drinking myself to death, but I wouldn't have been surprised if it happened.

Some loose ends needed to be tied up back in Los Angeles. My Les Paul and SLR camera went to the landlord to cover the last month's rent. I instructed him to donate the rest of my stuff to the homeless. None of my West Coast "friends" would be anticipating my return, so I didn't bother to inform them I wouldn't be doing so.

The couch still smelled like him. He had started sleeping on it many years before, most nights in his work clothes. It's where I slept now. I dreamt of being a child again, sleeping between them in their bed, nuzzled up against his broad back. He felt like a giant.

I was safe.

As time went on, his scent waned from the house. My dreams took on a darker tone. Disjointed images of monsters and the macabre. Unfamiliar visitors in the night. Strange beasts grazing in the yard. The days were no better. I spent them lost in the labyrinth of my own thoughts. I flipped every photo in the house around and did my best to avoid mirrors. I didn't want to see the sad, unkempt man staring back at me.

The doorbell rang one afternoon, as I was rummaging through the attic, exploring artifacts from a past life. I lurched downstairs and peeked through the curtains, expecting to see a random visitor with a bunch of flowers or a tray of lasagna. It was Uncle Beau, holding a shotgun in its carrying case and a bright orange hunting jacket.

My uncle was a man of few words but when he spoke, he sounded a lot like his older brother.

"How are you holding up?" he asked, to which I replied with the greatest lie ever told by man.

"I'm fine."

"Well, I can't stay long but I came to bring you this stuff. I know you ain't a hunter but I think he would've liked you to have it."

The men in my family were a long line of hunters and farmers, extending back to the 1800s. Real woodsmen. I was petrified of ticks. The thought of Lyme disease alone was enough to give me an anxiety attack. After he left, I felt more depressed than ever. Perhaps it was his kind gesture.

Perhaps I yearned for the company.

Perhaps it was the fifth of vodka.

That night, around the midnight hour, I sat on the couch with the heavy gun in my hands. It was the first time I had ever held a firearm. I contemplated the logistics of using it on myself. The barrel was long, and the trigger would be at an awkward angle, but what if I put it in my mouth and pulled it with my toe?

A noise came from the kitchen.

It led me to his jacket, which I had hung on the back of a chair. In the inside pocket, I was surprised to find the old tape recorder I used to log writing ideas back in my late teens. The button had been pressed, allowing a weird shriek to play from the tiny speaker. I had never heard anything like it in my life. I rewound the tape to discover the sound of someone trudging through the woods, followed by my father's deep, monotone voice.

"This is the spot I've been hearing it in for the last few days. It's like nothing I ever heard out here before."

I played it back, over and over, until the morning sun was creeping through the curtains. In the midst of incessantly Googling anything related to wildlife in the Pinelands, I noticed the notebook from the safe. I had tossed it aside, assuming it was just farm business. My father's distinct penmanship filled the pages. It was a daily journal, each entry filled with detailed descriptions of the woods. It also contained a folded map of the Pinelands that was marked up with coordinates and a trail in black magic marker.

A photo fell from the last page onto my lap. It was hoof prints in the mud. The date scribbled on the back was from a couple of months before he passed. Jotted down on the last page was the name *Ray* and a phone number.

Some quick internet sleuthing led me to a familiar place.

V.

A stiff Bloody Mary and a twenty minute drive later I arrived at the Pine Barrens Museum. I hadn't been there since I was a young boy. What it lacked in relevant technology, it made up in miniature models of forests and penny candy. They obviously relied heavily on charm. I helped myself to a stick of colored rock sugar and checked out a homespun exhibit about a headless pirate that haunts Barnegat Bay. I was startled when the stranger from the viewing stepped into the room. His attire looked like something a *Jurassic Park* employee would wear.

"Howdy. I thought I'd be seeing you," he said, as he extended his hand, then locked mine in a vice grip. "It's Monday morning and you stink like alcohol. Plus you just shoplifted."

"I'm sorry, I - "

"Don't worry about it. The lollipop is on the house. I suppose you're wondering how I knew your old man."

"I am."

"Follow me."

We entered the back room of the museum. A detailed map of southern New Jersey, thumbtacked into oblivion, blanketed an entire wall. Grainy photographs, newspaper clippings and sketches wallpapered the rest. Tracking and recording equipment was strewn about on tables; filing cabinets overflowed with paperwork.

"There's some serious Indiana Jones shit going on in here," I said, trying to bring some levity to the situation. Ray wasn't amused.

"I met your old man in the woods. We were pursuing the same thing when our paths crossed. I had always heard about him, what kind of man he was. It was all true."

I could see that he was getting choked up. This guy obviously cared about my father, which made me a bit emotional as well.

"What were you pursuing?" I inquired, with a lump in my throat. Before he could answer, someone shouted from up front.

"Anybody work here?"

"It doesn't matter. Your dad is gone and this place is getting shut down. Excuse me," he continued, before exiting.

I studied the room a bit further. It was mostly the investigative work of a lunatic, however, two photos caught my eye. The first was Ray and my father, standing side by side in the woods. They were dressed in hiking gear;

14

the setting sun gave the photo a beautiful, hazy glow. They looked happy. The second was from that same day, out of focus and off center. My father must've snapped this one. He wasn't much of a photographer.

Ray was in the same spot, with his arm around a younger girl. She seemed bookish but quite beautiful, with curly brown hair, glasses, and a contagious smile. I felt muscles move in my face that hadn't in some time.

On the drive home, the sky was painted in purples and pinks. Dusk was always my favorite part of the day. I pulled over by a lake, got out, then breathed in the last remnants of winter.

I knew what my father was searching for. I just refused to believe it.

Everything started to feel *off*.

Shadows danced differently. Unfamiliar noises rang out from the darkest corners of the house.

As a boy, I preferred sleepovers at my grandparent's. They lived in town, a couple blocks from Main Street. Not here, in this gloomy rancher at the edge of the Pine Barrens, with no neighbors and too many windows.

I stumbled from room to room spilling my drink, while switching on every light in the house. I was in my early teens again, the first time my parents went out and left me alone overnight. That anxious feeling was a recognizable one, but I had forgotten about it for many years. I stretched out on the couch, under my father's blanket, and began to listen to the distant burr of tractor trailers speeding down the highway. I eventually drifted into an alcohol fueled sleep.

The moon is high above a sandy clearing in the forest. There are a few tents set up. The last embers of a campfire glow softly. My buddies and I are sitting in a semicircle around my father. He's in his trademark Dickies, as youthful and animated as ever. Years before life beat him up.

He's narrating the story of Mrs. Leeds' thirteenth child. We've heard it before, from dozens of folks, but the way he tells it is the best. It always begins with, "A long time ago, on a dark and stormy night in the Pine Barrens..."

"Mrs. Leeds was in labor, weeping in pain, with her destitute family surrounding her. Long believed to dabble in the black arts, she cursed the child as it emerged into her eldest daughter's grasp. Her frail husband cut the umbilical cord with a rusted kitchen knife, swaddled his new son in a filthy towel, and placed him on to his mother. She looked upon her baby. A chubby infant drenched in bodily fluids, brand new to this world. Totally innocent."

My father clears his throat to continue. His voice begins to tremble. He clutches his chest.

"Dad, are you okay?" I ask.

My friends and I scramble to our feet. He's struggling for breath as he falls from his folding chair down to his hands and knees. When he looks up at me, his face has changed. His skin is gray and scaly and his teeth have begun to protrude from the gums. He looks into my eyes with his own, more

16

equine than human now. He attempts to speak to me but his words are replaced by the shriek from the recording.

It's deafening.

VII.

I awoke with a start. The strange noise still echoed in my head.

It was early afternoon. I needed to escape the house and I needed a friend. Charlie picked me up later that day. The sun was beginning to set as we drove to our local tavern.

"You okay, man?" he asked.

"No, man. Not at all," I answered.

Our fathers were best friends, making Charlie and me the same by default. Legend has it we met in the hospital the day he was born. He had a younger sister and I was an only child. Over time we became like brothers. He was somewhat reserved, a deep thinker, and physically fit. The antithesis of me. That's probably why we got along so well over the years.

As I spoke at length about the recent events, he simultaneously tried to console me and discern if I had finally lost my mind. His mood changed when I plopped down the journal and the tape recorder on the table in front of him. He played some of the recording while thumbing through the pages of the journal.

"Holy shit, bro," he said, with his eyes wide and mouth agape. "Was your dad looking for the Jersey Devil?"

"It sure as hell looks like it."

When you come from where we come from, you're at least somewhat acquainted with the legend. Charlie and I were especially fond of it. We were the children of Steven Spielberg and Stan Lee. But just as our comic books were stored in cardboard boxes, and Saturday morning cartoons made way for Saturday night scramble vision, folklore and myths were ushered to the back of our minds. Only popping up now and again during a hike through the woods or a trip down memory lane.

After dinner we relocated to the bar. We had chatted the night away. Both of us were fairly intoxicated.

"I have to go home and get to bed," he said, taking a last swig of his beer. I wasn't ready to go home. I was drunk and downright freaked out.

"C'mon, brother, one more drink. A night cap."

"I can't. I'm beat. Listen, man. The last couple of times I saw your dad, he was different. Distant. There's something to all this." Charlie could tell something took my entire attention away from him in an instant. "Someone catch your eye over there?"

"It's the girl. The girl from the photo."

"Go talk to her, stud."

I was never the type to approach an attractive lady at a bar, but this time I had a reason. She knew my father. Maybe she had some answers.

"Goodbye and good luck, my friend," he said, with a smirk.

Suddenly, I felt self-conscious about my appearance. This meant I would be invoking the recent unexpected loss of a father clause. It covered all lapses in hygiene, as well as the public inebriation. As I sauntered toward her, "The Promise" by When in Rome was playing from the jukebox. I imagined it providing the soundtrack to a photo montage at our wedding. Nothing better than 80's soft rock to bring the helplessly romantic side out of someone.

She was with two attractive friends. They were the three best looking people in the place, and it seemed like they were having a great time. This all would have easily been ruined by the sight of my beard alone.

"Hey," she said softly, as if she knew me already.

"Hi. I uh..." my brain suddenly malfunctioned. I looked insane; now I sounded like it.

"It's okay. I've seen your picture and your dad spoke a lot about you. I'm Penelope. Penny."

The chance encounter was made a lot less awkward by the fact that we were both drunk. She was introducing me to her friends as the bartender approached and asked how we were doing. I ordered a round for the four of us.

"I'm so sorry for your loss. I only met him a couple of times but he was so nice. And pretty hilarious. Well, I'm sure you know."

Her eyes got misty, as did mine. Her friends drifted further into their own conversation, while we got ingrained into ours. I sensed she was holding back though. The way she spoke about our fathers' friendship was either a cover or she genuinely didn't know what they were getting into.

"So my dad said you came by the museum the other day. I apologize. He tends to be a bit intense when he meets someone new."

"Nah, he was cool. He's got the adventurer thing down pat."

I made her smile. It was the kind of smile that could have crushed much stronger men than myself.

Eventually, I felt like I should let her get back to her friends. Not only because I was hogging all of her attention, but I was also teetering on the verge of weeping in front of three cute girls I had just met. We said our goodbyes, then I headed toward the exit.

It was an unseasonably balmy evening. Penny and I had chatted long enough that the sidewalk didn't feel like it was moving when I set down it. I only made it a few feet from the exit when I heard "Hey."

When I turned around, she was standing under a streetlight. Her dark curls were dancing in the light breeze.

"There's something you should see. Your dad would have wanted you to." Seeing her there, speaking about my father, stung my heart in a way that made the tears flow. There was no stopping them. "Can you meet me at the museum one day soon?"

"I have to check my planner," I responded, which made her smile. I was already hooked on making her smile. "Of course."

We made plans to meet the following day.

As I walked home that night I found myself looking up to examine the stars.

Like I did as a boy.

VIII.

I'm back at church for the funeral. He takes a seat in the pew behind me, wearing his work clothes, with a 7-Eleven coffee in hand.

"Ain't you supposed to be up there?" I ask, making a gesture toward the coffin.

"Ain't you supposed to be out there?" He points to the stained glass windows.

I woke up early the next day and examined my face in the bathroom mirror. I ran my fingers across the heavy bags under my eyes and looked closely at the plaque buildup on my teeth. I backed up, then jiggled my beer belly. My attention ended on the ghastly whiskers that had been ignored for far too long.

The beard had to go. It was time.

After going to war with shears, clippers, and finally a straight razor, I took a scorching hot shower. When I exited back into the steamy bathroom I almost felt human again. Under my care the house had become a wasteland of empty pizza boxes and emptier liquor bottles. I felt compelled to clean it up before leaving for the museum.

On the drive there it dawned on me that it was mid-afternoon and I hadn't consumed any alcohol yet. I had earned myself a drink; that much I was sure of. The dive bar en route was usually swamped with biker gangs and other assorted nomads. I figured it was a perfect spot to consume some liquid courage.

As I sipped my scotch on the rocks, I overheard a patron speaking with the bartender about a wave of dead livestock in the area. He looked frazzled and spoke quickly, as if someone or something was after him.

"What's up, boss?" he asked, when he caught me eavesdropping.

"Nothing," I answered. "I...I'm sorry about the cows."

I never thought I would utter those words, but these were strange times. He quickly polished off the rest of his beer and threw some money down on the bar.

"Be careful out there, kid. Something ain't right."

I quietly finished my drink and left for the museum. Whatever buzz I was working on had been expunged by the creepy guy at the bar. Thoughts of Penny, and whatever she had for me to see, filled my mind. The way things were going, it could have been anything.

There was a lone car in the museum lot. I parked next to it and made my way to the entrance. The door was locked with a **Sorry We're Closed** sign hanging in the window. Before I could knock, Penny opened it and greeted me.

"Hey."

"Hello again."

"Wow, you look different."

"It was getting itchy," I said, stroking my chin.

"I like it." She said, leading me back to Ray's investigation center. "Sorry for the mess, my dad isn't the neatest person in the world."

"I can relate." She went into the closet and wheeled out a television set and VCR. "Wow. I feel like I'm back in seventh grade."

"So, class, today we're going to be watching a movie about the dangers of smoking. Please act like you're taking notes." We shared a laugh as we realized we were on the same page. "My dad filmed this in 1998. Ever since then, it's been monster hunting 101 with Ray," she explained in a more serious tone.

After ten seconds of tracking itself, the VHS revealed tree tops in the twilight. I could hear Ray's heavy breathing. Through the graininess of the aged film, a shadow flew across the sky. Penny rewound and paused it. I moved in closer, almost pressing my nose against the screen. The image was mostly obscured by darkness, but I could decipher the bat-like wings, a thick forked tail, and horns.

"What the hell is that?" I asked.

"Ray calls it the Jabberwock," she answered. He thinks devil has a bad connotation."

I peeled my eyes away from the paused image and saw Penny smiling to herself.

"What?"

"Your dad was as excited as you are when he first saw this."

"I'm sure he was. He and I...," suddenly I was at a loss for words. I changed direction. "Has Ray been sitting on this footage all these years?"

"A few years ago the museum began to struggle. We thought about trying to sell it to a television show or something, but my dad is a simple man. A lot of attention makes him nervous."

"I understand, but this footage. It could be proof of the existence of something extraordinary, something people care a lot about around here."

22

We headed back out to the front of the museum to allow what I had just witnessed to sink in. She seemed to be getting more comfortable around me, as we sipped coffee between a display of colonial era tools and a stuffed coyote. She elaborated further on how the sighting had led them to stay in Jersey, how it had led them to purchase the museum and, eventually, their nearby house.

"After we lost my mom, I guess he just needed something to occupy his time," she explained. "I guess it takes his mind off the pain a little bit. He saw that thing in the sky just in time."

"Your mom? I had no idea. I'm so sorry."

"It's okay. I was five when she passed. A drunk driver."

Our watery eyes locked for a moment. Despite the extraordinary events in front of us, we were just two ordinary kids who missed their parents.

Day became night. It was one of those conversations that would have lasted forever if we let it, but I could tell she was tired. After all, she told me she was a nurse and had a twelve hour shift the following morning.

"Well, Nurse Penny, I should probably let you get home. You have a long day tomorrow."

After she locked up the museum, we walked out to our cars together. The thought of returning to my parents' dark, quiet house made me sad. I missed her already.

"So, can I text you in the next few days?" I asked. "Maybe we can get together if you're not too busy."

"Sure. Ray's monster movie isn't scaring you away?"

"It'll take a lot more than that to scare me away from you."

"Wow. Good line."

We hugged.

I hadn't had a girl in my arms in a few years. She gently nudged up into the crook of my neck. I rested my head on hers.

"You smell awesome." I whispered.

"Thanks for noticing," she whispered back. "I'm glad you got rid of that beard."

As we parted ways, she gave me a smile and a quick wave from her car. On the drive home I listened to When in Rome.

IX.

I visited the cemetery that next morning. The headstone had been put in place.

"Happy birthday, Dad," I whispered to the image of his face, carved into the granite. "So, Ma is in a recovery program in New York. I guess she's doing pretty well. She sounds different on the phone. I'm still struggling to sell the house. There's a few potential buyers but it's old. Needs a lot of work. You know."

It's weird, having a discussion with an inanimate object. On the flip side, it was the most I had spoken to my father in a long time.

"I met Ray. And Penny. She's awesome."

A familiar feeling in my chest was slowly making its return. The pain of losing a loved one wasn't just a figure of speech. For me, it was very real. "I should've been here with you guys."

Something caught my eye at the edge of the woods, almost in the exact spot where Ray had been standing at the funeral. I raced toward the trees as quickly as I could, not realizing how far I had gone until I was about twenty yards into the dark forest.

"Someone here?" I shouted through heavy breaths.

There was no response.

Just the snapping of twigs and rustling of leaves.

X.

Have you ever thought about being a cryptozoologist?

To my surprise, Penny responded *yes* to that text. I picked her up at her house. It was a quaint log cabin neighboring a beautiful lake. Ray came to the door.

"Hello, sir," I said.

"Are you equipped to take my little girl into the woods?"

"I have a bag. Uh. Bug spray, beef jerky. A couple of Gatorades."

"Jesus H. Christ, I knew it," he said, with an expression that looked like I just failed every warm-blooded man on the planet. "Take this." He handed me a bulky, tattered knapsack. "It's just the essentials, but it'll make me feel better if you have it."

Penny came trotting down the stairway.

"Daddy, don't scare him," she said, followed by a kiss on the cheek. "I'll be home later."

"I'll expect yas back for dinner. Venison," he said, as we exited the house.

"He likes you," Penny assured me as we drove away. "That's just his way."

We parked the pickup on a dirt road, about a mile into the dense forest. It was the starting point on my father's map. Thankfully, Penny could interpret it. The thing could've been hieroglyphic, for all I knew.

As soon as we made it far enough on foot that I could no longer see the truck, I began to panic. My backside hit a tree stump.

"Hey. You going to make it?" Penny asked, unfazed by our surroundings.

"Maybe this was a bad idea. I hate the woods." I said, sounding like a true coward.

"We still have a long way to go. It would be easier if we turned back now."

"No. Let's do this," I groaned, filled with foolish pride.

An hour into the hike, as our conversation died down, I found myself about ten feet behind Penny. I patted the flask against my chest, then reached into my pocket and jiggled my pill bottle. Out of embarrassment, I was trying to figure out the most nonchalant way to pop a pill and take a few swigs.

I watched Penny from behind. Because of the glorious invention of yoga pants, I could see that she was built quite well. I assumed this was the reason why she was able to traverse the rugged terrain like it was just another day at the office, while I lagged behind, clinging to life. Every now and again she turned around to see if I was still alive. Her dimples were perfect; her nose and cheeks were rosy from the cold air. I decided to ditch my plan of incognito substance abuse.

The forest was feeling colder and getting darker. Ray's footage was heavy on my mind as we surveyed our surroundings.

"So this is it," Penny explained. "This is where he must've found something."

"Maybe whatever that is?" I pointed at a metallic object shining in the setting sun. It was partially concealed by the surrounding trees.

We approached it.

Branches, rocks, bricks, and pieces of scrap metal were carefully wedged against one another. It was a carefully planned hodgepodge, reminiscent of a beaver dam, with an opening on one side. Our flashlights illuminated the entrance.

"It's a cave," Penny said.

"Do we go in?" I asked, hoping she answered with a no.

"We've hiked all day. It would sure be a waste if we didn't."

We entered and followed the narrow tunnel. The precision it must have taken to build it was truly remarkable. About fifteen feet in, we came upon a small lair. There was an array of everyday items. Some were antiquated, becoming one with the sides of the lair. Others, like a cell phone, looked to be placed recently.

"This is the most incredible thing I have ever seen," Penny whispered.

"Me, too," I responded, casting my light around the walls of the lair.

We discovered a fishing rod, a baby doll, an ornate vanity, a football helmet, pots and pans, and a tire. No two items had much to with each other at all. However, something stood out from the rest.

Off in a shrouded corner lay a pile of bones with chunky pieces of flesh still attached. The guy from the bar and his massacred cows immediately came to mind.

"Penny. We should go now."

"Come here, look at this," she said, ignoring me. Her flashlight illuminated partially faded boot tracks underneath us. "Your dad found this place."

There were also hoof prints. Freshly made.

"We're losing daylight. We should go," I said again, trying not to sound terrified.

Penny moved like a gazelle. I tried like hell to keep up with her, as the woods were getting darker by the second. It wasn't long until I tripped over a branch and went down hard. Penny stopped in her tracks, then turned back in my direction.

"You okay?"

"I think I twisted my ankle. Leave me. Go. I'm just weighing you down," I said frantically, only half-joking.

"C'mon, we're almost there," she said, as she helped me to my feet.

I limped the rest of the way. My ankle throbbed in pain with each step. When we finally reached the truck, Penny hopped in behind the wheel. I was sweating profusely, choking down vomit, and experiencing dizzy spells. As we sped back down the dirt road toward the highway, I managed to vocalize what was on both our minds.

"That was fucking insane."

XI.

Ray was in the smoky kitchen, tending carefully to the deer meat in the grill pan. It smelled delicious.

"How'd it go, kids?" He inquired as we entered, never taking his eyes off the meat.

"It was unbelievable! We found some kind of strange dwelling place. Something I never even imagined could exist." Penny beamed with enthusiasm. "You have to come back out there with us."

"I've seen it," Ray responded. Unimpressed.

"What?" Penny asked. Frustrated.

"Don't be mad. We found it a few days before your father passed," he nodded toward me as he set the table. "I was going to tell you guys when the opportunity presented itself, but everything happened so quickly."

Penny's eyes rolled to the ceiling for a second, then landed back on her father. It was the first I saw this look from her. I guessed it was because she was pissed.

"Sit guys, let's eat. Relax, Penelope. I knew you could find it on your own. Wasn't it more fun that way?"

Penny gazed over at me. My sweat was drying, making my clothes sticky. I mustered up an answer for us.

"I mean, except for the injuries I'm fairly certain I've suffered, it was pretty fun."

My ribs ached as the three of us shared a laugh. Because of the remains in the lair, the venison was hard to deal with at first, but I was starving. Ray served dinner with veggies that he harvested in the backyard and his own homemade wine. It had me feeling much better. Physically and mentally.

"I'm in awe of you guys," I said, feeling loose from the wine.

"How come?" Ray asked.

"I guess I got used to city life. Folks in Los Angeles are much different than here."

"I bet."

"I would love to visit LA one day," Penny added.

"Why?" her father asked. "To eat fish tacos and hobnob with celebrities? I'm fine right where I'm at."

"That does sound kind of awesome, actually. Don't mind Ray, his last vacation was with my mom. On their honeymoon a hundred years ago."

"Damn right. Only one I ever needed."

28

I was trying to grasp their dynamic. They shifted from lovingly agreeing, to sassing one another, then back again. All in a matter of minutes. So much different from what I was used to. The people in my family could go weeks, months, sometimes years, silently resenting each other. I changed subjects as I scraped my plate.

"Well, dinner was fantastic."

"Your old man made the best venison I ever ate. Breaded, fried - damn good!"

"Really? I guess I never noticed."

My eyes met with Penny's, as she flashed me a quick smile. Then her hand found mine under the table. Our fingers interlocked perfectly.

The rest of the evening we shared stories of Penny's mom and my dad. We chatted about Penny's long road to becoming a nurse. I shared embarrassing stories of my time out west. We laughed more and more as the night went on. I missed it. Or, maybe, I never had it to begin with. The family around the dinner table. The warm, comforting buzz from the wine. At some point in the night, our conversation drifted back to the unprecedented reason we were together in the first place.

"Do you think the thing in your video built that lair?" I asked Ray.

"That's not just any thing. That's Mrs. Leeds' thirteenth child. And yes, I'm sure it built that lair."

"How can you be sure?"

"I've spent the better part of my adult life in those woods. I have felt it. The Jabberwock is out there. I'm sure of it."

"You know, it's weird," I said. "I couldn't have been more than nine or ten. My father was driving my mom, myself and my friend Charlie home from some Italian restaurant about a mile from here. He took an unexpected turn and my mother started yelling at him. He ignored her, then informed us that we were in Jersey Devil territory. He had told the story many times before that but, on this night, he was especially excited to tell it. We drove around some back roads for an hour or so. My mother and Charlie eventually drifted off to sleep. I felt closer to him on that night than ever before."

"It was real to you guys. Even then," Penny said.

The midnight chimes of a grandfather clock sounded. Ray stretched and said, "Good Lord I gotta get to bed. You ain't driving. The spare room has cable."

I took a miraculous shower, then slipped into a pair of Ray's flannel pajamas. They felt like Christmas morning. Penny met me in the hallway as I walked toward the spare room.

"What a day," she whispered.

"What a day indeed. Thank you. For everything."

We hugged and our lips met for a moment. We both knew I was taking my life in my hands.

"I'll see you in the morning."

"Okay. Goodnight," I said, with a shit-eating grin on my face.

Despite the abundant taxidermy in the spare room, I drifted off into a fine slumber.

XII.

I awoke to the smell of coffee and the sound of chatting from downstairs. My clothes were waiting for me in the bathroom, washed and folded.

Penny was in dark blue scrubs with her hair tied back and glasses on. She looked quite different from the adventurer the day before.

"Good morning. I made breakfast," she said.

I shook Ray's hand and thanked him profusely. After breakfast, Penny followed me out to the truck.

"I'm going to be really busy the next few days at work, but we should keep in touch. Text me."

"Of course."

As the sun peeked over the lake and the birds sang their early morning ballads, Penny and I finished our kiss from the night before.

"Okay, go. Before Ray asks you to move in."

As she made her way back into the house, I texted her from the truck. I watched her remove the phone from her pocket and look at the screen.

My text read *Hi.*

She turned around, shaking her head and laughing.

My parent's house felt lifeless that night. I received a text now and again from Penny, but I could tell she was busy. Charlie was cross fitting, or whatever and I was lonely as hell. I decided to call my mother, who was ecstatic to hear from me. She sounded different. Lucid. I brought her up to speed with everything that was happening. To my surprise, she knew that my father was searching for something in the woods.

"He would come home late some nights and tell me these extraordinary things. I was so out of it. I couldn't tell what was real. The next day I would wake up and he would be gone again. Sometimes for days. Unless it just felt that way. But, I think I understand now. There's a woman here. You should come up and visit with us. She may have some of the answers you're looking for."

"What do you mean, Ma?"

"She found Christ, like we all have here. But it was only after she saw the devil - "

She was cut off by some commotion in the background.

"The next lady needs the phone. Please consider coming up. I have to go."

The next few days were dedicated to convalescing.

Liquor. Takeout. Netflix.

My mother's words haunted me. Eventually Penny sent me a text asking if I wanted to meet at happy hour for some three dollar Coronas and boneless Buffalo wings. It sounded heavenly.

And it was. It was so heavenly, in fact, I launched a "Hail Mary" and asked her if she wanted to accompany me on a trip to New York for Memorial Day weekend. To my surprise, she said yes. I suppose the promise of meeting my mother and further adventures in cryptozoology was too much to resist.

XIII.

We hit the road after an early morning discussion with Ray. Basically, he told me if anything happened to his daughter he would flay me alive.

The traffic was ridiculous, but it didn't bother us. We listened to mix CD's I found in my old bedroom. We explored every rest stop. In due course, we hit the mountains of upstate New York. Penny insisted on getting out. We pulled over at a lookout point. There was a crowd gathering, mostly young couples with hiking gear on, taking in the splendor all around.

"It's beautiful up here," Penny said, as I put my arm around her shoulders. "I can't wait to meet your mom."

"What a buzzkill."

"So, are you ready to tell me what the deal is with you and her?"

For the remainder of the ride I explained how my relationship with my mother had become strained.

"There was so much lying and manipulation that I couldn't take it anymore," I explained. "I couldn't watch my father exhaust every effort to get her help with her addiction, only to have her squander it every time. I finally fled to get away from it all."

"Well, she's here now," Penny said, "that means she is trying. Your dad spent a lot of time away toward the end but, according to Ray, he loved your mom. Very much."

"He must have. He stuck around," I responded, as we pulled up to where she was staying.

As we parked, my mother made her way out of the huge house, toward the pickup. Starting with the crucifix stitched on her sweater, she looked like a different person from the one I dropped off. She was healthy and present.

"Hey guys, I've been waiting by the window. I saw you pulling up," she said, hugging me and then Penny. "So happy you guys came. There are so many ladies waiting to meet you."

It was an all-female cast of characters. Women of every size, shape and color, each with her own eccentric personality and crazy backstory. The common trait was their newfound devotion to the Christian God. My mother was the oldest and compared to these ladies, she appeared to be the most sheltered.

The residents were permitted to leave the grounds for two hours, so Penny and I took her to a nearby restaurant that we Googled. The neighboring town where it was located had cobblestone streets and lanterns with real fires flickering inside of them. The kind of place Jack the Ripper would have felt right at home in.

As we forced down subpar Italian food, the main topic of conversation was how much she missed my father. She seemed physically incapable of speaking about anything else.

"Is she being annoying?" I asked Penny, after my mother excused herself to go to the restroom.

"Not at all."

"I wish she talked so affectionately about him while he was still here."

"Be nice. She's grieving."

"I guess you're right."

"I am right. How's your pasta?"

"I think it's SpaghettiOs."

After dinner we returned to the grounds. My mother gave us a tour. There was freshly trimmed grass, waterfalls, and even a few deer trotting in the distance.

"I guess this is God's country," I whispered to Penny.

Gods. Monsters. Life. Death. Love. Loss. All of it circled in my mind like a tornado.

Back inside the house, most of the ladies had turned in for the evening, with the exception of Sally. She was a tall, thin woman in her early fifties, with stark white hair. She was making coffee in the large foyer, where family members could sit and talk with their loved ones. After a pleasant enough introduction she clutched my hands and peered into my eyes.

"I watched you out there," she said softly. "You move like a man who has seen things he can't quite comprehend. Strange things. You look toward the trees differently, studying the dark places all around you. No need to worry, you're with kin now."

As we sipped bad coffee, Sally told us her story. She was on her way home after waitressing the closing shift at a diner, when her Chrysler LeBaron hit a patch of ice and slid into a tree.

"The highway was empty. The world around me was white. It was the worst snowstorm New Jersey had seen in years. The airbag did a number on me but I was okay for the most part. I was trying to get my wits about me when I saw it."

Silence filled the room.

"Saw what?" Penny inquired, as she clutched Sally's hand.

34

"The creature that has haunted my dreams ever since." She paused to gather her thoughts, then continued. "I turned to drugs and alcohol to rid myself of the image from that night. Only prayer has helped. Only Jesus. Let's pray together."

She kept Penny's hand, my mother took mine, then Sally's. The only link missing from this prayer chain was Penny and me. I dramatically grabbed her hand. Sally jabbered on for a few millennia. I believe she spoke in tongues at one point. I had a million questions for her, so I fired one out.

"What happened after you saw it?"

"It studied me with a tilt of its head. Then it flew upwards into the falling snow. I was in shock. I sat there for I don't know how long. Through his grace, the Lord sent me a trucker. He spotted me, pulled his semi over, and drove me to a nearby hospital. No one believed my story until the ladies here took me in. They believe it. They believe in me. Especially your mom."

After we said goodbye to Sally, my mother walked us to the pickup.

"I know you," she whispered through the driver side window. "You're going to try to finish what Dad started, I can't stop you. Just please be careful." She looked toward Penny, "Take care of him. It was nice to meet you."

"Very nice to meet you as well."

The Holiday Inn I had booked was in West Bumbleshit. We made up for the disappointing dinner by scarfing down room service on the balcony. There were fireworks over the Hudson River.

"So why is the museum closing?" I asked, with a mouthful of chicken finger.

"No guests, no donations, no museum," she explained, in between bites of crab cake.

"That sucks. I really like that place. Museums, video stores, the Walkman. We're losing all the magic in this world."

"I don't really remember a life before the museum. Just glimpses. Mostly of my mom. Doing my hair. Singing to me." Her eyes began to fill with tears. "My earliest memories are of that place. The best days were when we would find a neat bug or garter snake, then make an exhibit out of them."

"It's cool you and your dad have that. My father and I never bonded over much. Farming, and hunting and sports. They just weren't for me." I choked up. I was constantly choking up. "I guess maybe all we had in common was a fascination with this stupid piece of folklore."

"You know it's not stupid. Your dad spent the last months of his life searching for what's out there. It was very important to him."

"Something incredible was happening and my dumb ass missed sharing it with him because I was selfish. Because I ran."

"He loved that you were out there chasing a dream. Actually, the only reason why he wished you were back was so he could try to hook us up."

"It's funny how things work out."

"Indeed it is."

There was a stretch of silence. It wasn't uncomfortable or awkward, just different. We knew something could happen at any moment. Something that would change everything for us.

"So, I'm going to get in MY bed," she acknowledged it, much to my relief. "Don't try anything slick."

Of course I wouldn't. This girl was worth waiting for.

I stayed out a bit longer, watching a mist pirouette on the river. The scent of fireworks and distant cook outs lingered in the air. When I reentered the room, she was asleep. It smelled girly and fantastic from her shower. I removed her glasses and put them on the nightstand.

At some point in the early morning, as a soft blue light crept in between the hotel's heavy curtains, Penny asked if I was awake.

"I'm a little bit freaked out by all of this," she whispered. I was relieved to hear her say that, because I was scared shitless.

"Honestly that cave terrifies me, but I'm compelled to return to it. You don't have to come if you don't want to."

"Of course I'm coming," she insisted. "If it's really out there, if it's responsible for that cave, I have to see it. It validates my dad's work."

"Then I suppose when we get back to Jersey, it's on."

"Like Donkey Kong."

We decided to beat the traffic home, stopping again at the lookout point. This time it was just us.

We breathed it in.

Penny worked the following three days in a row. I called Charlie and told him to come by my parent's house. I had some stuff for him.

We hung out for a bit. I described the cave and told him about visiting my mother and meeting Sally. Mostly I spoke about Penny like an excited schoolboy. He helped me load up the back of his SUV with every drop of the alcohol from my parents' house.

"Don't go drinking all this at once," I joked, as I placed the last bottle inside the hatch.

"This is a huge step. I'm proud of you, brother."

"Thank you. I don't know how it got so out of hand. Listen, I am truly sorry for ignoring your calls for so long. I guess I was just embarrassed by my life. I love you, man."

"Don't worry about it. I love you too."

We hugged it out.

Back in the house, I remembered a lone bottle of vodka in the freezer. I removed it, went out to the backyard, then hurled it into the woods with all the strength I could muster.

Summer was closing in quickly. Penny decided that she wanted us to just enjoy each other for a while. She wanted a little bit of normalcy before returning to the cave.

We made the most of her hectic work schedule, spending her days off helping Ray close up shop at the museum. In the evenings we would go to the movies or out to eat. Sometimes we just stayed in at my parents' house. It was as if time had forgotten the place. We watched all the classics on VHS. Penny had never seen *Monster Squad*. We had battles with my old Nerf arsenal. Sometimes we'd take a dip in the Jacuzzi or play a midnight game of basketball in the backyard. It was the most fun I had sober since I was a kid. I made up for so much lost time at the house that I forgot I had to sell the damn thing.

My mother's king size bed was one of the first things I got rid of. I felt like it was probably cursed. My bed upstairs was a twin but there was no television in my old bedroom, so we camped out every night on the living room floor. It was more fun that way. We were two twenty-somethings who couldn't keep our hands off each other.

"It's been a long time since I've done this," she said shyly, as our bodies intertwined so tightly I couldn't tell where I stopped and she began.

"Same here, but I've heard it's like riding a bike."
"Shut up and kiss me."
That was a particularly amazing summer night.

XV.

"I started writing again," I told the headstone. "The other night, after Penny fell asleep. It felt good."

It was remarkable. The detail of his face in the stone. I imagined them doing it with a high-powered laser or something. With the tip of my finger, I followed the shallow crevice that made up the rim of his glasses.

"I'm taking Penny down the shore tonight. Mini-golf, maybe some rides. Should be fun." I glanced toward the woods. "It's out there. Ain't it, Dad?"

I was waiting for a sign. Something to let me know that my father was still with me, to tell me that things would be okay.

I got nothing.

Across the street, a farmer was tending to a field. His dark green John Deere tractor was kicking up dust as it went.

If the beast existed, if it was truly a cursed human being, lost in the Pine Barrens for three hundred years, it would render useless everything we think we know about the spirit world. Life and death would become bigger mysteries to us than they are now. Why would it be foolish, then, for me to think my father could communicate with me?

Perhaps I was a master of inter-dimensional telepathy and my powers hadn't been tested yet.

Maybe my father was floating right there above me in the cemetery that afternoon.

Or, could it be he never died at all? Instead he was taken by beings from a faraway place, his body replaced by a clone.

Or, maybe, I was just a guy alone in a graveyard talking to himself.

We coasted across the bridge to Ocean City, as the sun was beginning to set. The sulfury scent of the bay trickled into our open windows.

"We should return to the cave," I said, as I admired the Ferris wheel in the distance."

"Do you think you're ready?"

"As ready as I'll ever be, I guess. Has your dad figured out what he's going to do when the museum closes?"

"He's thinking about working part time at Home Depot or something. He's depressed. I've never seen him like this."

"I understand."

The boardwalk was bustling with people. Families rushed in and out of stores. Groups of teenagers hung on guardrails, taking selfies. After we ate a few slices of pizza, I purchased a cup of iced coffee for Penny, then we headed toward the beach. As we neared the ocean, the noise and light from the stores and amusement parks began to soften. We breathed in the salt air.

"You okay?" I asked, as I noticed Penny seemed a bit distant.

"Yea. Just tired," she answered, as she took me by the arm.

"So you wanna ride that Ferris wheel?"

"Sure."

We found ourselves stopped at the very top of the wheel. In one direction was the whole of the busy city, in the other, the boundless Atlantic Ocean. Its moonlit waves were softly hitting the beach.

"Quite the view," I said to Penny. Her head was on my shoulder. She was sound asleep.

The poor girl was trying her best, but between her work schedule, helping Ray at the museum, and hanging with me; she was exhausted. I spent the rest of the ride - two more times around the damn thing - contemplating just what the hell I was going to do with my life. I started to feel down.

Truthfully, I wanted a drink.

The first hint of autumn was in the air on the morning we set out for the cave. My former landlord was the proud owner of my old camera, so I dropped a pretty penny on a replacement. I felt compelled to document the events of the day, and since I fancied myself a photographer, I felt like I could at least contribute that to the mission.

The trek to the cave was cut in half this time around. Penny had a better grasp on where we were going and I was in much better physical shape. Penny was right about eating a healthier diet and exercising. It does, in fact, make you feel better. With the initial awe from our first visit out of our systems, we were able to thoroughly examine our surroundings. It was a trip to a strange, yet very familiar place.

"Hey look, this wasn't here the last time," Penny said softly from behind me.

An antiquated mirror was leaned up against a wall of the cave. Our flashlights illuminated the dusty reflection. We stood there looking at ourselves. These two people who had no idea what they were getting into. I snapped away; my flash lighting up the entire lair with each photo I took.

"Is that country music?" I asked, as a sound came in from outside and reverberated around the lair.

"It sure sounds like it," Penny responded. "We should check."

About eighty yards from the cave, we spotted a pickup truck. I took the binoculars from Ray's knapsack for a closer look. The vehicle's paint was barely visible under a coat of dry mud. A Confederate battle flag was draped across the rear window. Three drunkards were carrying-on around the bed.

"We have to get out of here as quickly and quietly as possible," Penny whispered.

"We'll just leave. If they see us, I'll tell them we were birdwatching or something," I said, like an idiot.

"Mike, they look dangerous. We shouldn't let them see us."

"Okay, I'll follow you."

We crept down low through the brush, trying to make a little noise as possible. As soon as we put enough distance between us and our discovery, one of the men spotted us.

"Yo! What the hell y'all doing over there?"

"We should approach them and try to divert their attention from the cave," Penny said.

"Good idea."

We walked through the trees in their direction. There was a big one and two skinny ones. They were hillbillies. Not like a few guys doing their best hillbilly impressions; these were the genuine articles. Their clothing was ragged and their mouths were full of chewing tobacco. I could tell the big guy was the ring leader by the way he was trying to make the other two cackle. He started right in on us with the insults.

I'm a pacifist, I could've taken it just fine. Shit, I've been called way worse than a "hipster from town." I kind of dug that one actually. It's when they set their sights on Penny that my mood started to turn from anxious to angry.

"I've seen you around," Big Guy spewed. "Ain't she familiar, boys?"

"That's the nut from the museum's daughter," Skinny chimed in.

"The fucking weirdo Jersey Devil guy?"

"Yea, that guy."

"I knew it. See, I told y'all. I never forget a nice ass. Shit, you're a cute little thing. You should be out in these woods with us. Not this snowflake," Big Guy continued, as his cronies laughed hysterically.

Now, I haven't punched someone in the face since high school, so it felt fantastic when my knuckles connected with this Neanderthal's jaw. He stumbled backward a few feet as one of the cronies blindsided me with something in my temple. I saw the cosmos, then fell into a heap of regret.

Skinny detained Penny as she tried to run toward me. I attempted, with all the strength in my wobbly arms, to push myself up to my feet. Big Guy saw my struggle and decided to drive his size thirteen boot right into my ribcage. Penny's shouting sounded further and further away as I collapsed back onto the ground. Warm beer rained down on my head.

A shriek cut through the forest.

The foreboding nature of the sound was disorienting at first. It seemed to be closing in from all around us. In an instant, the hillbillies second-guessed their senses, they questioned everything they thought they knew about those woods.

As unworldly as the sound was, it was familiar to me. It was the same one that emitted from the speaker of my tape recorder. I felt grateful to hear it again, as I watched their pickup truck kicking up a dust storm as they fled.

"I think I'm dying," I said to Penny, as she helped me up.

"There's a gash in your head and you may have a few broken ribs, but I think you'll make it."

"It's here."

"I know, but we have to go before those assholes come back," Penny said, as we scanned the trees.

XVII.

I was keeled over on the couch, clutching an ice pack to my ribs, as Penny cleaned the abrasion on the side of my head. The details on how we made it back to my house were still a thick fog in my head.

"I think you're okay, but you may want to see a doctor tomorrow. Just to be sure."

"I'm fine. I hate doctors."

"A hypochondriac that hates doctors? Interesting." She taped a bandage onto my temple. "Do you think you can make it to the shower? You smell pretty terrible."

"I know. I can't believe that fucker poured a beer on me."

"We are lucky they didn't do a lot worse to us."

Good point.

She was always making good points. She deserved a man who was accomplished, some tan and toned intellectual who could jog along the Jersey shore with her. The truth had slowly been revealing itself to me, never more so than in that moment.

Penny was too good for me.

She was too good for a clinically depressed college dropout pushing thirty. A schlep that was scared to death of commitment - scared to grow up. The sad truth is I took comfort in being a deadbeat, and because my father was gone, I had no one left to impress. I could be pathetic forever. I said these words aloud to her. I couldn't stop them, even though I wanted to.

"Wow. This really sucks," she responded, with an expression on her face that made my heart hurt. "I'm going to go."

I wanted to take it back. I wanted to propose to her. I wanted to light myself on fire and jump down a flight of steps.

"Wait, Pen-"

"It's okay. I understand."

I followed her out into the backyard. A light rain was beginning to fall. She turned around at the car door with tears in her eyes.

"I'm not even mad. I'm just really disappointed. I thought this was the beginning of something good. I guess I don't even know you."

"Penny, you do know me. Maybe better than anyone."

"Really? I didn't think you were the kind of guy who sleeps with someone and then comes up with some excuse as to why he can't be with her."

44

I had no response.

"You know, you have the potential to be a great guy," she continued, as she let her gaze linger on the woods for a moment. "Good luck finding your Jersey Devil."

Her taillights vanished into the strengthening rain. Old beer washed down my face. I walked past the tree line, using my phone's flashlight, and began to dig through wet leaves.

The full bottle of Grey Goose that I had chucked into the woods was unearthed right before my eyes. I took swigs from it right there in the woods, then polished it off on the back deck twenty minutes later.

The last place a man in my condition should've been that night was behind the wheel of a moving vehicle but, as I swayed from one side of the highway to the other, it was almost like I was begging to be pulled over. A night in jail may have been good for me. Somehow though, I didn't cross paths with a single police officer. I made it in one piece, back to the jump off point on my father's map. The spot where Penny and I had started from twice before.

I sat quietly for a moment, surrounded by nothing but the sound of the truck's engine idling.

Without further hesitation, I threw it back in drive and stomped on the gas pedal. I figured if those rednecks could get their truck back there, so could I.

The vehicle jerked me around violently as I struggled to put my seat belt on. Tree limbs smashed against the windshield and scraped across the side like nails on a chalkboard. I managed to avoid any large tree that my headlights illuminated and bulldozed over the rest.

A branch impaled the windshield, narrowly missing my shoulder, then exited out the rearview window. I slammed my foot on the break, just in time to stop the pickup from connecting with the large trunk of the tree. Shattered glass was everywhere. My ribs ached. The wound on my head had reopened. Running on adrenaline alone, I frantically opened the driver side door, got out, then screamed toward the sky.

I walked into the woods with nothing. No pack from Ray. No Penny to lead the way. Just a dying cell phone and rain soaked clothes on my back. Stumbling over branches, splashing across puddles of mud, I marched through the woodland, until I could no longer see the glow of my headlights.

Into the darkness. I kept walking.

XVIII.

The strength I needed to get to my feet was just out of reach. The sun beat down on my face. I had passed out at some point in the night. Still on my back, I reached for my phone.

It was dead.

Something began to stew in the back of my parched throat. I rolled over and lost the little food I had in my stomach. When I finally rose to my feet, it dawned on me how hungover I was.

As I took a seat on a downed tree, the world beneath me slid back and forth like the floor of a funhouse. My ribs and head pulsated with pain. There was a coating of dry blood, sweat, and beer congealed on most of my face. I had one option: try to find my way back to the truck and out of the woods, as quickly as possible. I began to walk in what I hoped was the direction I came.

I walked, then walked some more.

For hours, I lurched through the humid woods and got nowhere. I was lost. Hungry and terribly lost. I yearned for a Gatorade, a soft pretzel, and the comfort of my bed. I fantasized about wrapping up in freshly washed sheets, and burying my head in a cool pillow.

And Penny.

I missed Penny terribly. If I had the strength, I would've shouted her name into the heavens.

The sun began to set.

Damn Mike, you really got yourself into some shit here.

Soon it would be completely dark. I would be utterly alone except for whatever animal or mythical beast decided to take their best shot at me.

I crumbled into the brush below and cried hysterically.

An endless cry.

XIX.

On the morning of the third day, I had a revelation. The woods had eaten me alive. There was no way out. This would be the tragic end of my life.

I guessed it would be labeled a *missing persons* case until someone found my body. The news would refer to me as a "troubled" young man. They would be correct in that description.

Penny had started to teach me some yoga. I would always joke that the "corpse pose" was my favorite. I was in the corpse pose as I examined a cluster of tiny, red berries I picked off a tree. I deduced that they would kill me if I ate them. Not a bad way to go out.

How long can you even survive without food or water? I had no idea. I was never a Boy Scout. What I knew was those naked people on television went like twenty days. How about that rich kid that got lost in Alaska? Dude lasted like four months eating roots, until a bear finally ate him. I needed a bear to find me. A rare Grizzly bear in the Pine Barrens. I couldn't last four months.

It was chilly. Strange noises surrounded me. I had no idea what any of them were. None of the animals I had crossed paths with had killed me yet. A lot of squirrels and birds, a few chipmunks, a groundhog, and a deer. It was a doe, standing a few feet away from me, wondering what the hell I was doing there. I guess it could've been worse. I could've been lost in a wilderness filled with hungry carnivores. My main concern was poisonous plants and bugs.

I picked several ticks off my body and had a painfully itchy rash on my arm. It could've been a whole host of things but, for whatever reason, I was certain it was poison ivy. Not everything was bad, though. My ribs were feeling better and I could no longer smell the beer on my skin.

The sky was clear that night. The moon was full. I studied it. When there's nothing else around to distract you from the moon, it's a truly miraculous thing. It seemed closer than ever before. Just hanging there in space. Like me.

"Hey," Penny said.

I turned to see her and found nothing but trees, dancing gently in the soft lunar glow.

Was I losing my mind already?

I didn't think it happened that quickly. I could do nothing but a corpse pose, and ponder the journey that had led me there. To that spot.

Helpless.

As I dozed off, a shadow swept across the moon. Something big was in the sky circling me. Maybe a turkey vulture waiting for me to perish. Sleep paralysis set in. I could no longer open my eyes. I was trapped between a dreamlike state and the very real forest. The shadow was still hovering. Closer than before. Hot breath began to hit my face. I struggled to open my eyes again.

To no avail.

The shadow consumed me.

My eyes finally open to my dad standing over me. He's young and heavyset, like he was when I was a boy.

He asks, "Is this it?"

His deep voice echoes through the woods like my favorite song.

"You drop the ball with Penny. You mess everything up. Now you're lying here like a damn jackass. It's still out there. Show a little gumption and find it. Use your head this time." He pauses for a moment, then continues, softly. "Or don't. It's your choice."

I raise my hand toward him.

"Can you help me, Dad?"

He looks at me, tears in his eyes, and says, "Once more, just this last time."

His large, chapped hand takes mine.

When I regained consciousness it was morning. Uncle Beau was helping me to my feet.

"You okay, bud?"

"I don't know."

"It's okay. Help me get him up, son." Little Beau approached me from behind and assisted his father. "My pickup is right over here. Can you walk?"

"I'll try."

Three grown men squeezed into the cab of my uncle's pickup truck would've been extremely awkward at any other time, but I was happy to be with my family. And alive. I mustered up the strength to talk.

"How did you guys find me?"

"Nobody knows these woods better than us," Little Beau responded.

"You had a lot of people worried about you," Uncle Beau continued, "those folks from the museum weren't giving up, that's for damn sure."

After he said those words, the last bit of adrenaline from someone finding me wore off. Every single inch of my being collapsed on each other. I fell down a dark tunnel into nothing.

XX.

When I came to, I was in a hospital bed with the most beautiful nurse I had ever seen tending to me. And she looked kind of pissed.

"Penny I -"

"Shush. I don't want to talk about it. The doctor will be in shortly to give you the rundown. Are you hungry? Thirsty? Need anything?"

"I'm okay."

"Well, here's some ice water anyway. Hydrate yourself." She positioned the tray in front of me and placed the cup down. "I'm happy you're alive," she quipped, then exited.

The doctor informed me that I was suffering from severe dehydration and exhaustion, along with a bruised rib, some minor scrapes and bruises, and a poison ivy rash. I knew it.

He also said they were boosting up the dosage on my antidepressants and I should seek some cognitive behavioral therapy as soon as possible. I couldn't argue with that.

"Tracy will be in soon if you need anything."

"No more Penny?"

"Shift change. Let me know if you have any questions."

My stay at the hospital was a day longer than my time in the woods. I staggered aimlessly up and down the hallways, spending most of my time at the food court, hoping to see Penny again. I never did. She wasn't answering my calls or texts either.

Visitors came and went with gifts and cards. Uncle Beau and his family. My aunt, uncle and cousin on my mother's side. Even some buddies from back in the day. It made me realize that I still had good people in my life. People who cared about me. The way things turned out was nobody's fault but my own. I had pushed people away for a long time. I had become a recluse and I regretted it.

On my last afternoon there, Charlie came by with a pizza. We ate it in a waiting area while watching *The Goonies* on mute.

"Can I ask you something?"

"Sure."

"What the hell were you thinking, man?"

"I don't really have an answer to that question."

"Well, are you done now? Did you at least get whatever it was out of your system?"

50

I thought about that one for a minute.

"Yes. I believe I did."

"Good, bro. Now when you get out of here, go find that girl. She made you happy. Happier than I've seen you in a long time."

Charlie knew me. He already knew that's exactly what I was going to do. He just enjoyed delivering motivational speeches. When I was discharged, my first order of business was a shower. A long, scalding hot shower. Then it was off to find Penny. I had to drive my mother's car since the pickup was still lost in the woods.

I pulled down Penny's driveway in search of her car, which wasn't there. I attempted to do a drive by, but it was too late. Ray spotted me from the front porch. I envisioned him leaping from the steps and strangling me. To my surprise, he invited me to sit in the rocker beside his own, for a chat.

"When I was fifteen years old I ran away from home," Ray began. "I'm not talking down the street to the ball field. I'm talking the real deal. I hitched a ride with a traveling salesman. Two states over, I got a room at some seedy motel with money I stole from my old man's wallet. I became tight with the owner, Mitch. Nice guy. I stayed there for almost a month and he never asked any questions. Even bought some beer for me a few times. I befriended a prostitute and took in a kitten. I have no idea why I ran away, and, eventually, I ran out of money. Mitch politely asked me to leave. Told me I should go home."

"Did you?"

"I tried to hitchhike my way back. I failed. I made it half way on foot and finally called my father from a diner. When he picked me up, he smacked the shit out of me right there in the parking lot."

We sat there silently for a moment, both of us rocking gently. I had no idea what to say. Ray continued.

"What I'm trying to say is this. A man's heart is a mysterious thing. We don't know why we choose to do the things we do. Sure, you're a bit older than I was. Made yourself a bit dumber of a decision, but I hope you found yourself out there, in the quiet moments. Like I did in that motel room."

"Thank you," I said, for lack of anything else.

"Now, this situation with my daughter."

Oh boy.

"She told me some of the things you said. And hey, I get it. I've been down there before. Lower even. But she likes you. A whole lot."

Ray was handling this in a way I never would've imagined, but I understood instantly. This was a man who wanted nothing but happiness for his daughter. It didn't mean beating me up or threatening my life. It meant getting to the bottom of what the hell was the matter with me. I decided to speak directly from the heart.

"Ray, I made a big fucking mistake. I realized very quickly that I can't live without her. I was being selfish, but I'm ready to change. I'm ready to be the man Penny deserves."

"Watch your language. She's at the museum. Go see her."

"Thank you for understanding, Ray," I said, as he walked with me to the car.

"Listen. Your father and I were like best friends that met each other a bit too late. You remind me of him. You worry me sometimes, but I know people. You have a good heart."

"Thank you. I appreciate that. I really do." I said, as I extended my hand to him.

He took it in his trademark vice grip and said, "One more thing. No more drinking. It's no good."

"I know. Definitely. As of today, I'm back on the wagon."

"Good. Now go. Do right by my little girl."

XXI.

She was in a big sweatshirt, with her hair in a bun and her glasses on, as she cuddled up with a novel and a cup of coffee. Most of the museum had been cleared out, but the tool display and coyote remained. It's where she was sitting.

"Hey," she said. It was her usual greeting, but it lacked a smile. I needed the smile. "How are you feeling?"

I had to cut right to the chase, or else I may have spontaneously combusted right then and there.

"I'm okay but I need to say something."

I had rehearsed the next part for days.

"First of all, I am sorry. For everything. The fact is, I was depressed. I mean, I am depressed. I have been for a long time. I wake up every day and feel sorry for myself. It's kind of become my thing. The addict mother and the distant father, defeated by a life he didn't sign up for. Breaking his back at work, without his son. It gave me an excuse to be an underachiever. And a jerk. I relocated under the guise of being a screenwriter. I was a damn bartender who could barely afford rent. Honestly, I think I liked it that way."

I caught my breath, then continued.

"Things got even worse after I lost him. I escaped further into alcohol and pills. But then an unbelievable thing happened. The craziest shit in the world. It wasn't the very real possibility that the Jersey Devil exists, or even that we had almost found it. It was that I found something else. I found someone who made me want to man up finally and be a good person. I just needed help with that, and I was embarrassed to tell you." I stopped to gather my thoughts, debating whether or not to say the next part.

"I love you, Penny. I've loved you since the moment I first saw you."

I was so caught up in my speech that I hadn't noticed a young park ranger with a faux hawk and tattoo sleeve staring at me.

"Was that too much?" I asked.

"Nah, dude, that shit was perfect," the ranger chimed in as he slow-clapped.

Penny took me to the office to continue our conversation in private. She told me that I had hurt her. I made her a promise that I never would again. Although she was disappointed in me, she couldn't stand the thought of me lost in the woods, alone. I told her I wasn't alone. I had her. Also, I quite literally wasn't alone.

"It was out there with me Penny. I felt it. We have to go back."

"Go back? We have to be out of the museum in a month. You're not well. I don't think that's the best idea at this point."

"Listen. I have money. I want to help your dad. I don't want you guys to lose this place."

"What? I just - I think you're talking a little crazy! Let's just relax for a couple of weeks. See how we feel then."

"We don't have a couple of weeks. We'll find it this time. I'm almost certain we'll find it."

She looked confused, a little bit frightened even.

"I'll think about it. Okay? Let's sleep on it."

We slept on it. Penny was at her house; I was at mine. We spoke on the phone. She was being short with me still and I couldn't blame her.

"I'm going to see what my dad thinks at this point," she explained. "He's ready to give up."

"Give up? We are so close. We can't give up now."

"That's easy for you to say, Mike. He's been at this for years. He's tired. Tired of spending his days at a museum that no one seems to care about anymore. And, more importantly, tired of being the butt of people's jokes."

I understood where they were coming from, but I had a plan. After we hung up, I got right to work on it.

I didn't sleep that night. Instead, I wrote up a business proposal. Well, what a business proposal was supposed to be, to the best of my knowledge.

I started with the name, respectfully rebranding the Pine Barrens Museum as *The Jersey Devil Museum*, complete with a newly designed logo.

I compiled all of the elements in the existing building that were close to Ray and Penny's hearts, and wrote detailed descriptions on how we would freshen them up. In addition to that, I drew blueprints for a new building that would house a Disney World inspired "dark ride" complete with an animatronic monster in the finale. I packaged the paperwork together in a leather bound folder then headed to Ray's house.

He was at his usual spot in the kitchen, preparing eggs and jalapeño peppers. I spoke passionately, and at great length, about the plan.

"This all sounds good, and looks pretty on paper, but I don't have the money. You know that," he responded.

"My father left me a sizable inheritance. I can't think of anything else he would want me to do with it."

"I'm not the kind to take a hand out, kid."

"A hand out? It's not a fucking hand out, Ray. It's a business investment. I have faith in us."

"Language," he said, then continued after a long silence. "Jesus H. Christ, you're a crazy person."

"I've started therapy."

He chuckled, "So, what's the catch?"

"Nothing, really. Just one little thing."

Penny had informed me that Ray hadn't been back out since he located the cave with my father. He had lost his love for the woods, for exploration. He started to have doubts that the creature existed at all. He started to believe that his footage was just the distorted shadow of a Sandhill Crane. He even imagined that the cave was created by human beings, as a hoax to mess with his mind. She explained that after our encounter with the hillbillies, he was certain it was them who built it. So, my proposition had some weight to it.

"We go back out to the woods. We give it one more shot. Let's prove everyone that's ever doubted you, wrong."

He agreed. Then he began crying. I had no idea what to do next. He seemed like the type of guy that had his last cry when he entered into the world.

"You okay?"

"I'm fine. These damn peppers," he said, as his eyes connected with mine. "Thank you for this. Thank you very much, Michael."

We spoke enthusiastically about some of the exhibits we would open, and he explained how he would accomplish them in the most cost effective ways. I tried to sell him more on the ride and the new name. I had the feeling he was even starting to like some of my "batshit crazy" ideas, as he called them.

XXIII.

The three of us became an efficient team. Watching the command Ray had of the Pine Barrens was endlessly impressive. He recognized every sound, he could identify every plant. He was one with nature. Truly a man at peace.

Penny was slowly warming back up to me. The daily showering of gifts, flowers and massages seemed to be helping my cause.

We entered the third week of daily exploration. The refurbishing of the museum would take precedence soon. We were running out of time. Ray's video and my photographs of the cave's interior would be okay, but we needed more. We needed something to draw people in from far and wide.

I clumsily followed along with my camera, as Ray tracked its path through the woods. On her days off, Penny would join us. We heard it shriek several times in the distance. Penny was convinced that it was toying with us, fully aware that we were on toit.

It was late afternoon, somewhat chilly for a fall day. I was away from the group on a "bathroom" break. I closed my eyes and inhaled a breath deep into my lungs. As I exhaled, I felt a surge of emotions from somewhere deep inside. I was happy to be alive. The future finally looked bright again. When I opened them, I spotted it hunched over, drinking from the lake about fifty yards away. Its wings were folded behind its back, as its forked tail whipped slowly through the air.

I zoomed in, with my finger planted on the shutter button. Its hooves were dug into the sand. The tip of its long, serpentine tongue was scooping lake water into its mouth. The creature had a scaly upper body with mangy spots of gray fur on its upper arms and shoulders. Its head and face were goat-like. The eyewitness accounts I had read about - the sketches from my old books - they all became real in an instant.

I snapped away; crooked horns were now in the frame. I moved the camera down slightly to discover its eyes. They were locked on me.

The same eyes from my dreams.

I tried to shout for the others, but it swiftly launched itself upward. The sight took my breath away. I sprinted in their direction.

"Guys, it's here, it's fucking incred-"

Before I could finish, the creature swooped down and grazed Ray's head with a hoof. The rush knocked him off his feet. Penny shouted, as she dropped to one knee to check on him.

Ray was shook up but okay. He yelled at me to get more photos. I lost sight of it as it flew deeper into the forest. We regrouped. Ray told us to stay close and follow him.

They scanned the trees with their binoculars as I tried to keep up, stumbling behind them with my camera in my hands.

"There," Penny whispered, struggling to contain her excitement.

It had landed in the highest branches of a tree, shrieking at the sight of us.

"We're not here to hurt you. We are benevolent!" Ray shouted, as if it understood. "Twenty three years I've looked for you. I know who you are!"

The creature let out another sound, but this time it was different. It sounded more like a cooing of some kind.

Penny and I glanced at each other. We knew how much this moment meant to Ray. To us.

It cloaked itself in its wings then burrowed deeper into the branches. We could still see its eyes. There was something familiar to them.

Almost human.

"What do we do now?" Penny whispered.

"How much footage did you get?" Ray asked.

"A lot," I answered.

"We should leave. This is his home," Ray continued, with tears streaming down his face.

As we walked away, we kept turning back toward the tree. It watched us, as still as a gargoyle atop a building.

At once it sprang from a perched position, unfurled its wings, then flew in the opposite direction.

The golden sun was beginning its descent, as the evening's first few stars showed their faces. We watched the creature disappear under the horizon.

I thought of my dad.

XXIV.

"It could have hurt us that day, maybe worse. We will continue to study why it didn't."

It's a recording of my voice, usually playing for a theater full of guests in the new section of the museum. When crowds empty out from the exit doors of the dark ride, they are treated to a ten minute film narrated by yours truly.

The evidence from our explorations was the boost we needed. It didn't just rejuvenate the place, it turned it into a nationally recognized attraction. Guests do indeed come from far and wide. Some think it's all a clever ruse, but most immerse themselves in the experience. We even have certain groups that are trying to take us down. I spend a lot of time on Twitter tormenting them.

My mother completed her program and decided to stay in New York with Sally. They plan to ride out this wave of newfound interest by co-authoring a book titled *God vs. The Jersey Devil.*

At some point along this crazy road, I was able to sell my parents' house and move into a modest apartment with my fiancé Penelope. It's a bit tight and most nights we order takeout at 9 PM, but it has a beautiful view of a lake.

We are happy.

In the front lobby of the museum, between a display of colonial era tools and a stuffed coyote, is my dad's journal, framed alongside the photo of him and Ray.

XXV.

One morning not long ago, I spotted a skinny kid, maybe six or seven years old. He was checking out the "Reptiles of the Pines" exhibit.

The boy was dressed to impress and had lightning bolts shaved into both sides of his head, instantly making him the coolest kid I had ever met. I approached him and inquired about his interest in reptiles.

"I have two lizards at home," he replied, as if he made a habit out of conversing with total strangers.

Just when I was about to ask him where his dad and mom were, I heard a woman shout "David!" as she frantically approached us.

"What did I say about wandering off?" she asked, to which he rolled his eyes. "Sorry, this kid is so ornery," she said to me, as she took his hand.

I told her, "It's okay, we were discussing lizards."

He started to tug on his Mom's hand, "Can I ask him, Mom?"

"Fine, go ahead," she said, reluctantly. He was a bit bashful about it but asked anyway,

"Did you really meet the Jersey Devil?

Mom chimed in before I could get a word out. "Remember, it's all just a story, David. Make believe. Like *Star Wars*."

She shot me a look.

"Your mom is right. It's all just a really good story. Hey, even if he was real, I don't think he would ever bother you."

"So, he's sorta like a good guy?" the boy asked.

"Of course he is."

Mom thanked me, then I watched them as they continued on their way. The boy turned around and looked back at me curiously. I winked at him.

He smiled from ear to ear.

MISTER LEEDS

In the Northeast region of the United States, there are a million acres of woodland known as the Pine Barrens. What makes this place so unique is that, while it touches seven counties in Southern New Jersey, and plays neighbor to sprawling cities like Philadelphia and New York, it remains mostly undisturbed. The "Pines" are home to a wide range of plants and countless species of birds and mammals. But for some, it's most noted for a legend dating back to the mid-1700s.

It starts with the Leeds Family; the matriarch Mrs. Leeds, in particular. It wasn't rare to hear early settlers of the area speak about Mother Leeds' descent into witchcraft. On a dark and tempestuous night, she labored with her thirteenth child. Bellowing in pain, she cursed the child as it entered our world. His father and twelve siblings watched in awe as the midwives wrapped the baby boy in tattered towels and placed him onto his mother's chest. When the moon ducked behind the clouds, and the wind screamed like a phantom in the night, the cherubic infant began to transform. He stretched and convulsed, wailing in pain as every inch of his tiny body contorted into a hideous creature. Some variations of the legend say that he sprouted huge wings right there in his family's cabin, leaping from his newly grown hooves, up the chimney chute and into the New Jersey sky.

Since that fateful night, the tale of the "Leeds Devil" has been passed down from generation to generation; it's become folklore, woven into the fabric of the Garden State. Some people claim to have seen it, while others pass it off as simply a scary story. However, in these parts, it's doubtful that there's ever been a campfire-lit chat, when talk of Mother Leeds' thirteenth child hasn't been whispered through the trees.

Chapter 1

As curator of The Jersey Devil Museum, Michael Neary dedicates his days to the local legend. He's found that immersing himself in the mythology helps him make some sense of it, helps him make some sense of his experience five years ago. It was an encounter with the impossible, which caused a seismic shift in everything he thought he knew about the world.

As he makes his way through the shadowy museum, he surveys his surroundings a final time, making sure everything is in working order for the next day. Guests from all corners of the country will come early, trying to capture a small piece of the lore for themselves.

After he locks up, he drives home in his father's pickup truck. They found it years before, wrecked in the woods. He couldn't part with it; instead, he had it repaired and freshened up with a new paint job. When he arrives at his modest rancher, on a quiet street, the faces at the window are his most favorite sights, his constant sanity in this mad world.

"Daddy!" Josie shouts, as she sprints towards him. He scoops her up and swings her in his arms

"Hey, lady. I missed you today," Michael says to his daughter, as he plants a kiss on her forehead. "Where's Mommy?"

"In here," Penny shouts from the bathroom.

"Where are you going, all dolled up?" he inquires, looking his wife over.

"Tonight is the meeting with William Vaughn. Did you forget?"

"I knew it was sometime soon. I've had a lot on my mind lately. I'm sorry."

"Lately?" she says with sarcastic affection, as she kisses him. It's the kind of friendly sparring that develops when you live with somebody for half a decade.

"What's our plan?" he asks, as Josie trails them into the bedroom. No conversations will happen in this house that the four year old will not be part of.

"What plan, Daddy?" She asks as she opens her mom's armoire and uses one of her long necklaces as a lasso.

"Basically, my plan is to make sure my dad behaves," Penny answers.

"Pop Pop better behave or he'll get a time out," Josie replies.

"You're gonna get one if you don't stop messing with mommy's stuff," Michael says playfully, as he tickles her.

"Daddy, stop!"

They walk out to the car, Josie in her mom's arms. Although she's meeting a world-renowned businessman, Penny is cool and collected. After some negotiations about ice cream, Penny hands Josie off to her dad.

"Let's work on that bedtime. And no late night snacks, Daddy," Penny instructs as she enters her car.

"The pizzas are coming for ten o'clock though."

"I'm serious, Mike," Penny says, as her husband flashes her a big grin and dips into the driver's side window with Josie in hand. They share a family hug.

"We got this, Mama. Now go tell that guy we wouldn't sell the place for all the money in the world."

Michael is joking, but he means it.

Chapter 2

The meeting takes place at a well-known wine bar on the main street of Cedarwood, a small town in southern New Jersey. It's a typical Friday night. The place is crowded with young professionals washing down plates of risotto, with Cabernets and Pinot Grigios, while a jazz duo plays lightly in the corner. The banquet room toward the back of the building is reserved for parties of thirty or more people but, by a very special request, tonight it's been kept aside for just four.

The small talk is wearing thin on Ray. Penny feels it every time he checks his wristwatch. She knows her father, she knows this particular brand of torture has aggravated him for some time now. He's only there for moral support, which Penny insisted on.

"So, Mr. Carrol, may I call you Ray?" William Vaughn asks.

"Ray is fine."

"Ray, your daughter has done most of the talking tonight. I see that you're the old school, silent type. I can dig that. I would love to hear some of your thoughts about my proposal, though. I understand your reservations in the past, but I hope the updated figures are clearly stated in the latest package we sent out."

"They are," Ray grumbles, "and my answer is still the same one that I told the news. We have no interest in selling the museum. Now, or ever."

Vaughn glances toward his personal assistant, a hulking man in a black polo. A tattoo of a Bengal tiger starts at his elbow and travels down to his wrist, where he's wearing a heavy silver bracelet that's been tapping on the table all night, annoying Ray in the process.

"It's really an honor that you're interested in the museum and surrounding area," Penny speaks up, "these numbers you've presented to us are astounding. My father and I can't thank you enough for the offer. However, I'm afraid we have to officially decline at this time."

"Penelope, darling. Imagine, if you will, a rollercoaster, towering high above the treetops. You can see it from the parking lot as you arrive. Imagine a place where you can take a guided tour, perhaps a hunt, through the Pine Barrens, in search of mythical beasts. Imagine a beautiful resort, incorporating whimsy and a whole lot of adventure. For families with small children, for teens, for everyone. The business in this area would boom bigger than anyone could've possibly dreamed. Imagine it. We could rival Orlando."

William Vaughn, master salesman, smearing it on heavy.

"I think we need - ", he tries to continue but gets cut off by Ray.

"I'm sorry. Did you say hunt?"

"Yes, sir. A safe, contained hunt through the forest. Of course, only the guide would have a firearm, but we would give guests the idea that they were on the trail of something extraordinary. Make them think it's real. You guys have already laid the groundwork for it. Well done. I mean it. Penny, your husband's book, The Jabber Mouth, was it? Great storytelling."

"Mr. Vaughn, just what do you think you're dealing with?"

"Dad," Penny tries to interject.

"No, wait a minute. Do you think we're running a dog and pony show here? This is all very real. The museum shares the Pines with something special. Something we respect very much."

The assistant laughs aloud to himself.

"I'm sorry. Something funny?" Ray asks.

"Nothing is funny," Vaughn answers. "It's just...we were under the assumption that it was a very carefully planned fairy tale you guys were peddling out here."

"I think that'll 'bout do it for me," Ray exclaims, as he rises from his chair. "Thank you for traveling to New Jersey, gentlemen. I believe you have our answer. Penny, time to go."

"Our apologies," Penny says as she rises, "This is a very personal thing for him. Thank you for dinner."

Ray is already halfway out of the place. Penny is following him when Pauly positions his large frame in front of her. She's startled when she turns to see Mr. Vaughn a couple of feet away.

"I've spent a considerable amount of time wooing you folks. This kind of offer doesn't come along twice. Try to talk some sense into him," Vaughn whispers.

He nods to Pauly, who methodically makes way for Penny. She doesn't respond to Vaughn's parting words and continues on her way. Back in the car, Ray is stewing.

"Jesus H. Christ, that guy really thinks he owns the damn world. Don't he?"

"He does own it. Well, maybe like half of it. Don't let it bother you. That'll be the last we see of him," Penny says, trying to convince herself as much as her father.

Chapter 3

Lonnie slowly places a spoonful of chicken broth into the old lady's mouth. It's one of the only dishes she'll still willingly consume. The small television set on the kitchen counter plays the nightly news. Lonnie has been watching closely ever since it began to cover the negotiations between the museum and William Vaughn.

"You have to pick up my medication tonight, and some crosswords," the old lady instructs.

"It'll have to wait. I don't have the money this week," Lonnie responds, both eyes locked on the TV. "It's poison anyway. They want to keep you sick."

After supper, he pushes the old lady in her wheelchair from the kitchen table to her usual spot at the back window. The wheels fall perfectly into the indentations in the rug. She'll spend the rest of the evening staring at the edge of the woods that line their property. The floodlights on the dilapidated shack they call home illuminate the happenings in the backyard: a moth, a bunny, the occasional brown bat.

Out on the front porch, Lonnie smokes a joint. Customers come and go, mostly on quads or dirt bikes. They slip Lonnie some crumbled up bills in exchange for some weed, some pills. Tonight he's waiting for one of his regular customers, an eccentric miscreant named Ed.

"You headed to work?" Lonnie asks the man when he arrives. Ed bartends at a swanky hotel in Atlantic City.

"Yea, bro. They got me working these fucked up hours. That's why I need you, my man. You know? My pick-me-up."

"I hear ya. That big wig, William Vaughn, still staying over there?"

"He's been through the last few nights. Motherfucker has loot, bro. He must wipe his ass with hundreds, man. For sure."

"Do me a solid. Shoot me a text if he's at the bar tonight. Try to stall him until I can get there."

"You coming to the city? That never happens. Maybe we can link up in the morning when I'm off. Play some blackjack," Ed says, as he slips the baggy of pills into his back pocket.

"Doubtful," Lonnie responds. "Just give me a heads up if he's there."

"What you trying to do? Stick the guy up?" Ed chuckles.

"Something like that. Now, get the fuck off my porch."

Chapter 4

"I saw the monster out there," Josie whispers, as she points to the window in her bedroom. "Daddy's Daddy says it's okay because it's a nice monster."

"Did you see Daddy's Daddy again?" Michael asks softly, as he tucks her in.

"I saw him earlier. Just for a little while."

Josie's cherry blonde hair is slicked back and a bit damp. The room smells like all the magnificent ingredients that make up children's soap. Waves of blue light are projected from a stuffed sea turtle. They swim across the ceiling and walls.

"So what does this nice monster look like?"

"I told you already, Daddy, kinda like a dragon. Can we read another story?"

"Nope, we did five, boo. Bedtime." When he leans in for a kiss, she reaches out and puts her arms around his neck.

"Sleep in here tonight. Pleeease!" Josie begs.

"Josie, we talked about this. Big girls sleep by themselves, in their own rooms," he says as he makes his way toward the door. "Mommy and Daddy are right in the next room if you need us. I love you."

"I love you too, Daddy."

Michael often wonders what kind of dad his own was when he was just four years old. Sure, he has seen photos of his father hoisting him up to place the star atop their Christmas tree, or waiting with him at the end of the driveway for the school bus. Those are the big moments though. What was his gruff father like in their everyday life when Michael was getting used to the world, like Josie is now? Did he sit on the floor with his son and read to him? Did he skip around the backyard with a net, trying to catch butterflies? Michael can't remember. He can't recall much of his life at all before he was ten years old. Before he spent most of his nights sneaking out of his bedroom to the bottom of the stairwell, eavesdropping on his parents stomping around, shouting at each other.

The only light in the master bedroom is from the MacBook on Penny's lap. Michael kicks his slippers off and crawls into bed. He looks at the screen. Spreadsheet Mania.

"How are we doing?"

"Down some from last month. Ticket sales seem to be okay, but guests aren't buying at the gift shop. Memberships are starting to drop as well."

"These things happen. Summer is here; hopefully business picks up a bit."

"Hopefully."

"So, Josie is talking to my father again," Michael says, as he moves in close to his wife and reaches his arm across her waist.

"About the monster?"

"Yea. Should we be concerned?"

"Well, you've spoken a lot about your father to her, which is good. The talk about monsters worries me a little, though. Maybe you should tone down on the stories for a while. She's a four year old with a huge imagination."

"She has to know it's out there."

"Does she? It's been a long time, Michael."

"What does that mean?"

"It means we built our lives around something we saw in the woods one day. What do we really know about it? I'm just saying, it doesn't have to define us. It doesn't have to define our daughter."

"I guess you're right."

"I have to go to sleep. I have work in the morning. I love you," she says as she closes the MacBook then kisses him. "You should go to sleep, too."

"I will. Love you too."

Fifteen minutes later, Josie has planted herself in bed next to Penny, and Michael finds himself sipping herbal tea on the front porch. He originally wanted to purchase a house in the woods, similar to his father-in-law's cabin. Some deliberation later, Penny convinced him that after spending the day at the museum, he would want to come home to a neighborhood. It was the right decision. He enjoys it. The friendly hellos with the neighbors; the small talk across fences.

He sways on a wooden bench and scans the neighboring houses. They're mostly draped in darkness, except for some candles in the windows and flickering blue light from the television sets inside. There's no sound on the street, except for the occasional chirps of a cricket. He brings the cup of tea close, letting the lemony scent tickle his nose. He rocks gently, until the humid air lulls him into a deep sleep.

Chapter 5

The bass from the nearby nightclub vibrates through the restroom's walls. It's by far the fanciest restroom Lonnie has ever taken a shit in. That's precisely what was going through his mind as a huge man came out of nowhere and took him by the neck, swiftly pinning his spine against the mounted air dryer.

"Why are you following Mr. Vaughn?" the man calmly inquires, as Lonnie tries to break free from the grip. It's a futile attempt; the stranger is much too strong.

"I have to talk to him," Lonnie mutters.

"About what?"

"I have some info on the owners of the museum. Man, listen, I can't breathe."

Pauly examines Lonnie for a moment. The greasy locks, barely staying put by some strange hair product. The stench of cigarettes and the neck tattoo peaking up out of his sorry excuse for a dress shirt. The Confederate flag hanging from his back pocket. Part of Pauly's job description is to know people. He knows this sort of guy doesn't visit the Atlantic City casino scene very often. He unlocks his grip.

"I'll give you a minute with him. If I smell something fishy, you and I are going to have a big problem. You understand me?"

"Shit, man. Yea."

Lonnie fixes his collar and slicks his hair back in place. He removes a pack of smokes from his breast pocket, which Pauly promptly smacks out of his hand.

"No smoking. He don't like it."

William Vaughn is sitting VIP in the only corner of the club where the strobe lights aren't splashing. There's a bevy of scantily clad ladies mingling with a couple of sharp dressed goons. Lonnie takes it all in from the bar area with the commoners. He's been waiting ten minutes but the crowd and the incessant, electronic music has made it feel like a decade. The goons keep looking toward Lonnie and laughing. As he begins to second guess his decision to do any of this, Pauly approaches him with a grin on his face.

"Mr. Vaughn agrees to have a drink with you. Try to be decent company."

Lonnie takes a seat at a large glass table, across from a leather couch where Vaughn is spread out. There's a beautiful woman on each side of him. This is exactly how Lonnie pictured it. He's discovered a lot about William

70

Vaughn since the local news started covering the young tycoon's interest in the museum. He's heard about the crude business dealings, and how he managed to turn a large inheritance from his father into a billion dollar corporation. He's read about his parties with rock stars and his jet-setting with supermodels. What intrigues Lonnie most is Vaughn's penchant for thrill seeking: skydiving, big game hunting in Africa, and his latest foray into extreme motocross.

Vaughn immediately engages Lonnie in a full blown conversation about where he's from and what he's into. After a few Budweisers, Lonnie is buzzing and has almost forgotten why he's there in the first place. To his surprise, he finds himself taking a liking to this guy. At some point the ladies get up and join their friends at the bar. Pauly takes a seat next to his boss.

"Lonnie," Vaughn says, "we could bullshit like this all night, but let's get to it. What kind of information do you have for me?"

"Well, shit," Lonnie blurts out, then stares off into deep space for a moment. "Some years back I had a run in with the curator of the museum, Michael Neary. My buddies and I were minding our own damn business when the son of a bitch sucker punched me. Then he goes and writes some bullshit about me in his book - calls myself and the boys some rednecks."

Lonnie is getting louder and more animated with each word.

"About a year ago I got pissy drunk and bought me a ticket. When I was in there I made a bit of a scene. Broke some stuff. They had me arrested and they banned me from the damn place."

"What's your point?" Pauly interjects.

"My point is they was hiding something in the woods. But I found it. I just been waiting for the right time to expose it. That's when I saw you on TV."

Vaughn can tell that the disheveled man is speaking from the heart, with urgency, but also apprehension. As the tycoon takes the last few sips of a martini, he inquires about what it is that they are hiding in the woods.

"A cave. A goddamn cave, built by the Leeds Devil itself."

The music dies down at the most perfect moment, giving Pauly, and the other men who have crowded around, a chance to share a good laugh. Vaughn doesn't join them, however; he sits up and leans in closer to a visibly embarrassed Lonnie.

"Forget these people," he whispers. "Can you bring me to this cave?"

"You bet your ass I can. It's about a half a day hike, and it's gonna cost ya some money."

"Jesus, Lonnie, you're quite the businessman. Maybe there's room for you in my company after all this."

"We should've just stuck with the old one. This damn thing ain't been nothing but trouble since we got it!"

Ray is elbow deep in the circuitry of an animatronic monster. It's the second time in a month that the grand finale of the "Journey of the Jabberwock" dark ride has broken down. He and Michael can hear the aggravated chatter of guests, stranded in line, from the next room.

"We'll give out some free tickets and fix this bad boy later tonight," Michael says, fully aware that Ray needs a break. "Mack and the crew can handle the place for a few hours. Let's take a drive. We could both use it."

"There's at least thirty people in line out there. I gotta get this thing up and running. Hand me the parrot nose pliers."

Michael examines the array of strange, metallic apparatuses overflowing in Ray's tool box. He grabs one.

"That's a needle nose. The one right there, with the blue handle. Five years you've been fetching my damn tools, Mike."

"I know. I think it's a learning disability of mine. Math and tools. My brain just can't handle either."

Suddenly, the monster begins to swing its muscular arm, its large eyes glowing red. A piercing sound emanates from a small speaker in its chest, startling Michael.

"There you are, old friend," Ray whispers, as he closes the hatch on its back and lowers a pair of rubber, bat-like wings over it.

Ray decides to take Michael up on his offer. On the way out, Michael apologizes to the guests and informs them that the ride is back online. It's a successful dynamic that Ray and his son-in-law have built over the years. Ray takes care of the daily maintenance and makes sure the exhibits are up to standard, while Michael mingles with the guests and answers any questions they may have. Penny helps out on her days off from the hospital, and handles the business side of things. When an employee has an issue, Ray or Michael will often tell them to "see the boss", meaning Penny. The trio has established a reliable team of high school and college kids interested in science and nature. They are managed by a guy in his late twenties, named Macaulay.

"Mack" has worked for Ray in some fashion all the way back to the pre-rebranding days of the museum. Years ago, his great aunt won an RV on a game show, which she left for Mack in her will. He lives in it now and, as far as anyone can tell, all Mack does is read comics, smoke pot, and speak passionately about legendary monsters, or "cryptids" as he likes to refer to them. Michael took to his Mack's eccentricities instantly. He sees a little bit of himself in them.

"I got this, my good people," Mack assures them. "Don't even come back. Grab some brew, do some fishing. I'll close her up."

"Five and a half years sober," Michael answers.

"Aw man. I know I knew that. Congrats, dude. I have some cannabis. If you prefer."

"No thanks, bro. I'm good."

The windows are open, letting the scent of the bay fill the pickup. As they drive down Seven Bridges Road, "The Boss" is wailing from the speakers with his signature roughness. Ray never understood the name "Seven Bridges" since you only cross four, maybe five, when you travel it. What he's certain of, however, is that the early settlers built the bridges with a strong belief in the part of the legend that says "the Jersey Devil can never cross running water." Building several bridges connecting the marshland would ensure their safety from the beast. Ray doesn't look at these stories as legend; he looks at them as genuine, historical record.

"I believe your daughter thinks I'm obsessed," Michael says, as he watches the sun set over Atlantic City. They've been dancing around this conversation ever since Josie started speaking to her other grandfather - the deceased one - about monsters.

"She's worried about Josie. I understand," Ray answers. "This is a strange world for a child to inherit. Nonetheless, it is the world. We were witnesses to something incredible and now we are its ambassadors. For better or worse."

"You know, I agree. I must make a request, though. No more scary stories. Just for a little while."

"You can't shield her from the truth for the rest of her life." Ray laments, hesitates for a moment, then continues, "well you guys are the parents. As you wish."

They pull over and tie some crab traps to the pillars of the bridge. The steel wire traps open as they hit the water, exposing the bunker hooked in the middle. "Do you remember what it felt like that afternoon?" Ray asks, as he casts. His lure splashing in the water a few moments later.

"Of course. I'll never forget it." Michael responds, sitting on the edge of the bridge, chewing a tender piece of beef jerky.

"Maybe we're getting used to the photos and the footage in the museum. In a way, we're desensitized to the Jabberwock's existence. But that feeling of seeing it in the flesh. I want that feeling again. Do you think it's okay out there?"

Michael ponders the question. It's an odd question but, coming from Ray, it seems perfectly normal.

"He's been around, for like, four hundred years or so. I think he's fine. Maybe he just doesn't want to be bothered." Michael says, as he pulls a trap from the water. Three decent sized blue crabs are jostling about the cage. "Well, look at that. First pull."

Chapter 7

When William Vaughn was seven years old, his father, the entrepreneur Joseph Vaughn, took little William and his family, along with some business partners, to Virginia's Busch Gardens. The main attraction at that theme park at the time was "The Loch Ness Monster," dubbed the world's "fastest and tallest" roller coaster. William wanted no parts of it, but the other kids dragged him along. He held in tears as he waited in line. The sons and daughters of his father's business partners were older and, in William's eyes, much cooler than he was. They wore sunglasses and smoked cigarettes. He even spotted a couple of them kissing on the lips behind the bumper cars.

When the ride was over, William ran to his mother and sobbed violently. She tried to calm him down by taking him away from the group, but Joseph stopped them.

"You're going to have to toughen up to make it in this world, boy!" Joseph barked at his son. "I'll make you ride the thing until you like it."

William protested. Frightened and feeling ill, he vomited on himself and his mother. The partners, their wives, and the cool kids began to scurry in the opposite direction. What started out as a mildly amusing situation became an embarrassing scene once the chunks started flying.

"Real nice." William's mother hissed to her husband.

"Take him to the restroom. Clean him up." Joseph commanded.

The same group returned to the park a year later. In the time between the two trips, William had been forced into various situations to "toughen him up." Things like flying along as his father piloted a small plane over their endless property and accompanying the man as he went deer hunting, which also came with the added pleasure of biting into his first kill's warm heart. Over the years, there were a few beatings, mostly when Joseph would come home late, drunk from the whiskey he consumed regularly.

So when William rode the Loch Ness Monster again, three times in a row, it was just as much of a "fuck you" to his father as it was to impress the cool kids. Those fuck yous would continue all the way up to the day his father died. He bungee jumped at eleven; he went skydiving at fifteen. After he graduated from high school, he and a group of his buddies ran with the bulls in Pamplona.

After a yearlong battle with stomach cancer, Joseph Vaughn, withering away in a hospital bed, handed over majority stake of the company to his only son.

"Your sisters are much more capable than you are, but you are my son. My oldest child." Joseph grimaced, the mechanical opera of noises in the hospital room serenaded them, "Good luck, boy."

William leaned in close to his father. The scent of death was already in the air, as he peered deep into the ailing man's steel blue eyes and whispered, "Fuck you, Dad."

These were his parting words.

William Vaughn would go on to turn the company into a billion dollar enterprise before his fortieth birthday, mostly in spite of his father. His main focus for many years were theme parks brimming with thrill rides.

Vaughn has been in caves before; the one in New Zealand was his favorite. He was twenty-five and dating a young actress when he decided to commandeer a raft and take her across the underground Waitomo River. The grotto would've been completely dark if not for the galaxy of tiny glow worms, covering the walls, illuminating the inside. For a man who has seen amazing things, he always considered those glow worms to be the most amazing.

"Who knows about this?" Vaughn asks, as his flashlight moves across bent pieces of scrap metal, intertwined with one another, lodged perfectly against other pieces of discarded junk. Various items, some antiques, some modern technology, are carefully placed inside, lining the walls of the lair.

"Not many folks, far as I know," Lonnie explains. "I told ya, the museum keeps people away. They've managed to bring all the attention to their circus show across the way. This here, they keep to themselves."

There's a pile of animal remains. Fresh, half-eaten flesh was torn from its skin and placed on a slightly more decayed heap of meat. The bottom layer was dried out bones. Pauly is covering his nose with his shirt collar.

"I may be sick, boss," the big man grunts.

"You're fine." Vaughn snaps back. "The interesting thing to me is the notion that whoever crafted this cave, he wants you to also believe that the perpetrator feasts on animals in this barbaric way. This is clearly a sham. I'm willing to wager more people come through here than you think. The museum people probably give out maps to this place."

"Mr. Vaughn, I've spent most of my life in these woods. I've heard things. I've felt some shit. Shit I can't explain," Lonnie warns.

"Have you ever seen anything with your own eyes? No. You haven't. Nobody has. Well, except Ray Carrol and his friends. Pretty convenient, if you ask me. Nonetheless, I'm intrigued. I'm going to stay here. Whoever built this has to come back eventually."

This was Vaughn's plan from the jump. He had packed enough supplies to last two weeks. He instructs Pauly to take Lonnie back to town and wait at a motel. The idea being that whenever someone does return, they won't see any vehicles. They'll never think someone is crazy enough to bunker down, alone, in the pitch black cave.

"I don't think I can leave you here. This is the craziest shit you've ever done, and I've seen you do just about everything." Pauly objected.

"What? I have everything I need. It's a cake walk. Come back for me in fourteen days," Vaughn insists. "I'll be fine."

"I don't doubt you can take care of yourself."

"Then, what is it? Wait a second. I'm not losing you to this supernatural shit, am I? Pauly, my dear friend. You didn't even believe whales existed until I showed you them off the coast of Cape Cod."

"This cave, Billy. It's like nothing I've ever seen. No human being could possibly do this."

"Everything is fine. I'll see you in fourteen days," Vaughn boasts confidently.

Pauly shakes hands with not only his boss, but the man he's considered his best friend for more than two decades. Lonnie goes in for a handshake as well, then adds a parting word.

"I'll tell you something; you got a set of balls on you like I ain't never seen."

Vaughn laughs, then makes his way back into the cave with a battery powered lantern. His only source of light for the next two weeks.

Chapter 8

On the evenings that Penny gets stuck at the hospital, Michael leaves work early and picks Josie up from preschool. Usually they go back to the museum to see Pop Pop and the rest of the crew. They are mostly girls in their early twenties who adore Josie's every move. They take her around to each exhibit, or give her little tasks to complete. They frequent the dark ride, which Josie was a bit scared of at first, but has recently grown quite fond of, especially since she can pet the monster when the museum is closed and she doesn't have to ride on the guided vehicle. Tonight, they're going to the park instead. It's not as much fun, but it's a good change of pace.

It's cool for an evening in early June. As the sun sets, rays of light are showering the surrounding trees and colorful playground equipment. Michael is sitting on a bench watching Josie effortlessly scale a rock wall. She glances toward him and waves, smiling proudly. She gets her agility from Penny; it's one of the many ways she takes after her mother. Like Penny, from the day she began to formulate whole sentences, Josie was a realist. Sure, she enjoys princesses and unicorns, but as far as the stories her father and grandfather tell her, stories about magic and mystery, she's not buying it. She has way too many questions. Most of the time she'll exhaust you to the point where you can't make things up any further. It starts to feel like you're simply telling lies to a little girl. That's why the first time she proclaimed that she saw "Daddy's Daddy" was so alarming.

It was a Tuesday evening, no different than any other. Penny was in the kitchen fixing dinner, while Michael sat at the dining room table, laboring away at a novel on his laptop. Josie was playing with two dozen different toys, most of them scattered around the floor, as she bounced from couch to couch. Occasionally Michael looked up from his disjointed tale of outer space swashbuckling and made sure Josie wasn't adventuring too recklessly.

He spotted her leaning over the back of the love seat, peering out of the window and into the front yard. As he quietly snuck up close to her, he heard the whisper of her tiny voice.

"Are you going to have dinner with us? Mommy is a good cook."

"Josie, is someone out there?" Michael asked softly.

"Yes, it's Daddy's Daddy," Josie answered.

Ever since she was a little over a year old, because of the stories and photographs, and because she already had a Pop Pop, her paternal grandfather became "Daddy's Daddy." Michael surveyed the yard, expecting to see a man that looked like his dad walking a dog, or working in the street. Nothing. Just the front hedges, a bush swaying gently in the wind, the lamppost. She explained to her parents that he was out there and she was inviting him in for dinner. When Penny inquired if she was just playing make believe, Josie answered matter-of-factly.

"No mommy, I actually see him. He's pretty silly, too."

It was the first of many times Josie would speak of seeing "Daddy's Daddy."

After the park, Michael whips up his specialty for dinner, Kraft Mac and Cheese. When Josie is finished, he sets her up in the bathtub. As he folds clothes in the bedroom, he listens to his daughter singing and splashing in the water. She begins to snicker to herself, within a few seconds it grows into a full blown belly laugh.

"What is so funny in here?" he asks, poking his head into the door.

"Daddy's Daddy was here."

"Josie. Baby, are you kidding? You can tell daddy the truth."

"I just like to see him. Okay?"

Michael finds himself frustrated and broken-hearted within a split second of each other. It's likely that she is pretending, and that's fine. Who is he to stop a four-year-old from talking, and laughing, with her dead grandfather? Michael would probably do the same if other adults didn't judge him.

"Okay, boo bear, tell him I said hello." He's about to exit the bathroom and get back to the laundry, when Josie speaks again.

"Daddy's Daddy says the bad man is in the woods."

"What, baby?"

"Look, I could swim under the water like a mermaid. Wanna see?"

Michael is certain about what he heard, but doesn't want to press her on it and risk making her nervous. He decides to let it be for the time being, to see where it goes.

Chapter 9

On the thirteenth day of his stay in the forest, Vaughn called Pauly on a backup cell and informed him that there had been nothing whatsoever out of the ordinary. No museum workers, no ingenious woodsmen preparing for the apocalypse, no Dracula, and no Jersey Devil. He had no further clues about who or what constructed the cave. So he devised another plan.

He instructed Pauly to pick up Lonnie the next morning and have him direct them back to the cave. Pauly was to convince Lonnie that they needed his expertise in navigating the Pine Barrens. Schmooze him. Make him feel as comfortable as possible. When they arrived, Vaughn exited the cave and appeared frustrated at his two-week stay. He shouted and cussed, ordering Pauly to "Get the stuff from the Hummer and light this fucker up."

Pauly retrieved a canister of gasoline, then the men entered the cave. Lonnie informed them that with the dry spell New Jersey was having, lighting the cave ablaze would have severe consequences.

"This is a terrible idea," he pleaded, "there's a different way to go about this. Let's just get in the truck and talk about it."

It was falling on deaf ears. Pauly doused the interior of the cave, and the dusty collection of items gathered inside.

"Go, I'll follow you guys out," he said. As they moved toward the exit of the cave, Pauly lit the entire matchbook and tossed it back inside. Within moments, the lair was completely engulfed in flames.

They backed away and watched as it spread wider and grew higher. The fire gained strength as it consumed everything it touched. Vaughn rested his hand on Lonnie's shoulder.

"Sort of beautiful in a way," he whispered.

Pauly, wearing surgical gloves, crept up from the side of Lonnie and swiftly jammed a cheap revolver against his temple, pulling the trigger with no hesitation. Pieces of Lonnie's cranium splashed onto Vaughn's face and shirt.

"Shit, Pauly," Vaughn shouted, "you could've waited until I was a little further from him!"

The final part of the plan unfolded as Pauly effortlessly picked the dead man up and tossed him into the tunnel of the cave, placing the revolver in the corpse's hand.

Something - the men see only as a shadow - flies through the inferno. Quicker than a thought could formulate in his head; William Vaughn, a physically fit man in his mid-forties, is pulled from the ground and hurled against the trunk of an oak tree. The sun escapes behind a storm cloud, as the fire continues to grow at a rapid pace. The shadow is gone as quickly as it appeared. Pauly dashes toward his friend to find him barely conscious.

"Billy, it came out of nowhere, a bat or something." He scoops Vaughn up and makes his way to the Hummer.

"That was no bat," Vaughn babbles as he comes to. Pauly tries to toss Vaughn into the passenger side of the vehicle, but Vaughn kicks off the door jam and out of the large man's arms. He reaches under the Hummer's seat and removes a second gun. A Desert Eagle.

"Who's the better shot?"

"This is fucking nuts!" Pauly shouts. We don't even know what we're dealing with here and the whole damn woods is about to be on fire! We have to go!"

Vaughn spots the shadow again over Pauly's head, and fires into the treetops. It wails in pain, then falls into the underbrush. As it struggles to stand, it inspects a bullet wound in its left wing. Vaughn aims the gun at its leg, letting off a shot but narrowly missing, allowing it to trot quickly in the opposite direction. "Get in the truck, we'll run it down!" Vaughn exclaims.

The rough terrain is made more dangerous by the ever-growing smoke clouds. Vaughn is clutching the steering wheel, driving along the edge of the inferno, as he and Pauly ricochet around the cabin of the Hummer. They're tailing the shadow, about twenty yards behind it, as Vaughn pins the gas pedal to the floor.

The grill of the Hummer connects with the creature, sending its heavy body over the windshield, and back down to the forest floor behind them. Vaughn's surge of adrenaline dissipates, leaving the men stunned, covered in sweat and soot. When Vaughn finally finds the words, he begins shouting. "Element of surprise, gets 'em every fucking time!"

They exit the truck and make their way toward the rear, to find a twisted cocktail of a beast, curled up in a lifeless heap. Fawn legs connected to a muscular upper torso, arms with veiny forearms and sharp elbows, partially covered in fur. Ungodly large bat wings tearing through the flesh of its back. The most peculiar element is its head. The face and beard of a goat, but the horns of something else entirely. Long, crooked bones protruding from its head.

"Help me get it up into the bed of the truck," yells Vaughn.

"You kidding me?" Pauly asks.

Vaughn picks it up by the legs; Pauly hesitates, "I'm not picking this thing up near its head, look at those teeth."

"Pauly, it's barely breathing. Pick the fucking thing up and get it into the truck. We don't have much time!"

The men use their combined strength to hoist the creature up and into the trunk of the Hummer. It barely fits. Vaughn slams the tailgate closed and commands Pauly to take the wheel and retreat from the forest. When they're a safe distance from the flames, Vaughn begins to celebrate, grabbing Pauly by his sleeve and shaking him.

"This is incredible! Do you know what we can do? You don't need to visit a goddamn museum when you can see this thing with your own eyes. This will change the world. It's real, Pauly! It's fucking real!"

There will be plenty of time to raise the many concerns already on his mind, so Pauly lets his boss have this moment. They find a break in the woods, and come to an abandoned farm stand. Fully aware of the possibility of someone spotting the creature, they take a moment to regroup. There's a greenhouse behind the deteriorating market. Most of the Mylar tarp has been destroyed, but there is a big enough piece still intact. They tear it off and cover the creature, securing it with bungee cords.

"So what do we do now?" Pauly inquires.

"We take it to Fort Green. It's within driving distance and I've been looking to do something useful with the place. We get a skeleton crew together, get some people to nurse this thing back to life. Then we go from there."

William Vaughn prides himself on being ten steps ahead of everybody. He had this whole thing mapped out. They pull away from the farm stand and head down the highway, leaving the Pine Barrens burning behind them.

Sirens ring through town as the smoke plume rises toward the sky. You can spot it from every corner of Cedarwood and the surrounding area. The Neary family is making their way out of the grocery store when they notice it. Josie immediately has a thousand questions, so her parents try their best to explain the situation. After they enter their SUV, Penny calls Ray to see how close the blaze is to the museum. He explains that it's a good distance, but they are taking precautions and closing the place for the rest of the night. Much to Penny's dismay, Michael decides to head in the direction of the smoke. As they make their way across the familiar roads of their town, the scent begins to thicken. A line of police cars has formed across the street. A young officer approaches the family.

"Where are you headed, Mr. Neary?" The officer asks.

"Just trying to get a closer look. You know our place of business is out here."

"There are several fire companies already on it. It's pretty serious, but we're going to do everything we can to get it under control. You guys should head back to town."

"No problem. Thank you, sir."

On the drive home, Josie drifts off to sleep. Michael brings up the comment from the bathtub.

"It's weird," Penny says, "but it seems like a really big coincidence to me."

"This is all just really freaking me out."

"Well, we've had a pretty tumultuous few years. Perhaps we need a vacation."

"You or me going to tell your dad that?"

"You."

The sky is getting darker, allowing the fire to paint the woods with a reddish-orange glow. Michael pulls over on some undeveloped farmland. He and Penny hop out of the truck and peer across the vast field. A couple of news helicopters hover near the fire. They can hear the commotion, faintly in the distance. It's a strange but beautiful sight. Michael pulls his wife in close and leans against the truck. For a moment, they're the adventurous duo from five years ago, swashbuckling through the Pine Barrens in search of something extraordinary. They look through the back window of their SUV, upon the perfect little person they've created, sleeping peacefully in her car seat.

"We should go," Penny says, "there's ice cream in the trunk."

Chapter 11

The blaze was extinguished forty-eight hours later. In the weeks that followed, the typically quiet towns surrounding the Pines became hives of activity. The news ran an "official story" that was derived from the various investigations taking place.

The remains of Lonnie Wilkes were found in a primitive dwelling place in the woods. He was a thirty-five old man with a criminal record, dead from a self-inflicted gun wound to the head. He appeared to be a reclusive hoarder, spending his days away from civilization, collecting random items from the surrounding area. When his mother, Mildred Wilkes, was questioned whether she believed her son was capable of arson, or if he was suicidal, she repeatedly answered with "My beautiful boy was always so troubled." The authorities deduced that she was in the early stages of dementia and further questioning would most likely be fruitless.

Back at the museum, business spiked. Typically, summer was always the busiest season, but combined with the amount of attention brought to the area, the place was seeing record numbers. Curious folks from out of town caught wind of the strange circumstances surrounding Lonnie's death and the fire, which added to the overall mystique of the area. This all should be making Penny Neary quite happy, but something isn't sitting right with her.

The fire and the suicide seem to align perfectly with the total disappearance of William Vaughn. Since the meeting at the wine bar, Michael, Ray, and Penny haven't seen or heard a single word from him. No emails, no phone calls. This was a man who had no problem hounding their family at every turn. Penny didn't like the way he ended their meeting, and when she informed Michael about it, he liked it even less. Going below the radar didn't seem like the actions of a man who would die before he backed off a chase.

"He had no intentions of letting our answer go," Penny explains to her husband as she slices a cucumber for their dinner salad. "Like I told you before, he actually freaked me out that night - invading my damn personal space."

"Do you think he's behind something?"

"I don't know. It just feels off to me. The news reported that Lonnie Wilkes was responsible for the creation of the cave, which we know is wrong. There's something else, too. Vaughn had a guy with him, a big guy he called his personal assistant. I saw him floating around town a few times after our meeting."

"That *is* weird."

"Look at how Wilkes treated us five years ago. He and his friends harassed me, they attacked you. If it wasn't for, well, you know, they may have killed us. That, and the incident at the museum. I mean we banned him for life. The guy has a vendetta, that's for sure."

By way of the local news, Michael learned that the only living relative, and the last person Lonnie had spoken to, was his ninety year old mother. The authorities explained that she was sick and uncooperative with their investigation.

"Perhaps I should go talk to her," Michael says, as he gazes out into the backyard. Josie and her Pop Pop are sitting at a wooden picnic table, drawing with an arsenal of colorful crayons.

"What are you, a private investigator now?" Penny asks with a smirk.

"Old people love me. Maybe she'll open up a little."

A bit later, the family is finishing up dinner. Josie has relocated to the living room couch, where she's drifting off to sleep watching Mickey and the gang seek a cure for Donald's terrible case of hiccups.

"That spectacular cave. Our only true glimpse into the Jabberwock's world, destroyed by some suicidal heathen. I still can't believe it," Ray complains, as he spins the melting ice around in his tumbler of Scotch.

"Maybe we should have told someone about it when we discovered it. An organization, or some group that could've protected it," Penny says, as she refills her father's glass.

"That would've blown the top off this whole thing. We wouldn't have been able to save the museum. The damn government might have come for us."

"Or people that know much more than we do. Like scientists." Penny peers into the living room to make sure Josie is asleep. "Think about it. Maybe our monster," she lowers her voice, "isn't a monster at all, but an animal. An undiscovered species hidden deep in the woods. We were just lucky enough to catch a glimpse of it."

Penny's sentiment catches her dad off-guard. When she was younger, Penny was her father's biggest and, most of the time, only fan. Whenever chatter about "the crazy Jersey Devil guy from the museum" got loud enough to bother him, Penny was there with encouragement. A few times Ray even found himself ready to sell the place and move out of Jersey altogether. Penny would be there to convince him that "there is something still out there, something magical, waiting to be discovered. It's what mom would've wanted." With that, their journey would resume.

"This whole situation depresses me," Ray states, as he finishes up his drink and rises from the table. "I'm going home."

"I didn't mean to upset you, Daddy. I'm just saying."

"I understand. You make a good point."

Ray hugs and kisses his daughter, then they head toward the front door. Michael says goodbye to Ray, staying back to load the dishwasher and give them their space.

It's in these moments he thinks about his relationship with his own dad. The things they should've said to each other. The talks they should've had. Five years later and the death of his father is still heavy on his heart. Perhaps it will be until he, himself, is old and gray.

Chapter 12

The following morning, Michael drops Josie off at school and informs Ray that he's going to be late getting to the museum. He stops at a 7-Eleven and grabs a Slim Jim, a peach iced tea, and a cheap bouquet of cut flowers. As he pulls down the wooded, unpaved driveway toward the Wilkes' shack, it dawns on him that he has no idea why he's going there, or what to expect from Mildred, but nonetheless he's compelled to visit her.

He exits the pickup and approaches the porch door. It's swaying lightly in the wind; the screen is torn and frayed. He slips past it, onto the porch, as a rancid stank fills his nose. He glances around at the floor, barely visible under heaps of junk. After knocking heavily on the front door for a moment, he realizes that it's unlocked.

"Mrs. Wilkes, are you in here?"

The house should've been condemned years ago. It's depressingly murky, with a terrible odor present throughout. Michael half expects to come upon Mildred Wilkes' corpse as he gets deeper into the dump. He's shocked when she rolls out into the hallway in her wheelchair, appearing like an apparition.

"Hi. Uh. Mildred? My name is Michael Neary. I went to school with your son. I just wanted to come by and pay my respects." She stares at the young stranger standing before her, then motions toward the flowers in his hand.

"I can't tend to those. I don't have a vase."

"Oh. I apologize. I just thought it would be nice. I can take them back with me."

"Set them down somewhere. I'll see what I can do. You knew my Lonnie?"

Michael did know Lonnie, as a drunk and a bully. As someone who, along with his two lemmings, jumped Michael, then doused him with beer.

"He was a great guy. A good friend."

She stares at Michael suspiciously. Almost like a mother would stare at their six-year-old, lying about stolen cookies.

"My beautiful boy was a troubled soul."

A few minutes of awkwardness later and Michael was on his way out of the house. There was no further development about anything. Michael froze up; it turns out he's no private investigator after all. As he walks to the pickup he spots a Plymouth Barracuda flying toward the shack, kicking up dust. It comes to a stop a few feet away from him. A man jumps out.

"Howdy," he says to Michael and extends a hand. He's sweaty and twitchy. Michael knows an addict when he sees one. "You here to see Mrs. Wilkes?"

"Just leaving, actually. Were you a friend of Lonnie's?"

"Something like that. Yea, you could say a friend. You know. Yes. A friend. Ed," Michael looks on as the jittery man goes into the passenger side of the Barracuda and retrieves a couple of shopping bags. "I come by once or twice a week with some stuff for the old lady. I figure it's the least I could do." With that, Michael's prejudgment of the guy quickly fades.

"Well, you have a good day. Nice to meet you," Michael says as he enters his truck. He begins to pull a K-Turn to head back out of the driveway, when there's a rap on the passenger side window, startling him.

"Hey, uh. I know you're the museum guy. The author. I know about the issues you been having with William Vaughn and them."

Michael waits for a few seconds as Ed places a cigarette in his mouth and lights it, gathering his thoughts.

"Listen, I haven't told no one this, but the last time I saw Lonnie, he was asking me about William Vaughn. I work in Atlantic City. Vaughn was staying in the hotel I tend bar at. Lonnie wanted me to give him a heads up when Vaughn was there. He wanted to come meet with him or something."

"So, what happened?"

"I called him up that same night. He came by the city, met with Vaughn. Then they found him dead a few weeks later. I don't know, Lonnie didn't seem like a guy that would kill himself."

"Would he start a forest fire?"

"Nah, that's the thing. He was a damn hard ass most of the time. Far as I could tell he loved the woods, though. I don't think he would ever disrespect nature like that. None of it makes sense."

"I understand."

Michael exchanges another handshake with Ed, then pulls out of the dirt driveway. He glances in his rearview mirror at the nervous man, slouching his way into the Wilkes' house, with shopping bags in his hands. He feels an uneasiness like never before. His daughter's words... "The bad man is in the woods."

He can't seem to shake them.

Chapter 13

Standing in the watershed of the Connecticut River, in the "Northeast Kingdom" of Vermont, is the East Mountain. Unbeknownst to mostly anyone who wasn't stationed there, an abandoned military base known as Fort Green resides. It's a soulless, concrete facility circled by a small town where military personnel lived while the station was active.

For unknown reasons, the town and the base were abandoned in 1970, only ten years after their construction. In the years that followed, the only people who would come across the area were the most experienced hikers and skilled hunters; in turn, the place became a bit of a legend in itself. Theories on why the inhabitants suddenly deserted the place range from gas leaks to extraterrestrial visitors to werewolves. One traveler in particular came across the site in 2005.

On the fourth of July of that year, William Vaughn found himself needing a break from work, a quick getaway from his corporate headquarters. A business associate had told him about a surreal destination, somewhere along the Appalachian Mountains. It was then that he decided to drive up to Vermont and do some hiking. In his trek through the East Mountain, he stumbled across Fort Green. The eerie ghost town and concrete Goliath towering high in the middle peaked his interest. So much so that he acquired a huge chunk of land, and everything on it. For over a decade, he had nothing to do with his new property. Until now.

Inside the military complex is a labyrinth of cold, gray corridors of stone and concrete. Hallway after hallway, leads from one room of abandoned military equipment to the next. The only operational section in the compound is the main command center; that's where Vaughn ordered his team of engineers to construct a basic, glass enclosure. They filled it with an array of trees and shrubs native to the Pine Barrens, and set up a system of cameras to monitor the creature's activity. They are calling it the "Terrarium."

"They" are a team consisting of Vaughn and Pauly, along with a group of engineers, a small crew of wildlife experts led by a biologist named Lee Marvin, and a few young ladies ("friends" of Vaughn's) on hand for his mental health. All of them have taken up temporary residence in the homes that surround the base. Each has been sworn to secrecy, but Vaughn has taken the extra step and demanded them to stay on site until the project in Philadelphia is complete.

A small hatch was placed on one pane of the enclosure's glass. Dr. Marvin slides it open and places a tray of fresh venison inside on a ledge, quickly shutting it. The lights inside the Terrarium are dimmed as Dr. Marvin moves his chair close to the glass and adjusts his glasses. He's a sixty-year-old scientist, widely respected in his field, but here he sits, completely baffled by what's before him. William Vaughn approaches with his own folding chair, and takes a seat next to Dr. Marvin.

"Still no movement?" Vaughn inquires.

"Negative. It's been up there since this morning." Marvin points towards a tall pine tree in the corner. The creature has draped itself in its wings, barely visible behind them, except for its beady eyes glimmering red from the fluorescent bulbs above.

"It hasn't eaten since we put it in there. It barely moves. What should we do, doctor?"

"I'm not sure at this point. I need to examine it more. I need to do more tests."

"I told you already we don't have that luxury. You saw what happened when it regained some of its strength. It destroyed thousands of dollars' worth of medical equipment. If Pauly hadn't hit it with a tranquilizer when he did, that thing would've escaped. My entire vision would be destroyed."

"With all due respect, that's more of a reason to take our time, William. We have no idea what we are dealing with here. We don't know how dangerous this creature really is." Vaughn ignores the biologist's words and rises from his seat. He begins to knock on the glass.

Vaughn shouts, "Come on, you son of a bitch. Do something!" He waits a moment, then heads toward the exit. "I'm going back to the house; call me if there are any developments."

"Um, excuse me sir," Dr. Marvin interjects. "You brought me here with the promise of something extraordinary. This is indeed just that. I am simply asking for more time. The attraction can wait. Let me relocate the creature to my facility, where I can properly examine it."

"No. I'm flying to Philly in two days for a press conference. We're going public, no matter what. Figure out what's wrong with it." Vaughn once again walks toward the exit doors.

"You know, I see what's going on in the house. The women. The drinking. Whatever else you guys are doing until all hours of the morning. Do you think that's conducive to our work here?"

92

Vaughn swiftly approaches the biologist and comes within a few inches of his face.

"Dr. Marvin, you came highly recommended, and I think you've been fairly compensated so far. I would hate to have to terminate our working relationship."

With that, Vaughn exits the room, leaving only Dr. Marvin and the creature.

The biologist is slowly circling the Terrarium, as the eyes in the tree follow him. Judging from the size of the creature's teeth and claws, and its evolved, forward-facing eyes, it's a carnivore. Most likely a predator. The attack in the woods, and then again in the lab, shows that it's aggressive when it feels threatened. Dr. Marvin has been studying the way it gazes on the rare occasions it comes out from the tree and saunters, sadly, on its hooves. Although its head and face resemble the structure of a goat's, its expressions are most similar to a primate's. To ours.

Nothing else about the creature makes any real sense. It simply doesn't belong to our world. Dr. Marvin understood that immediately after he first saw it, lying unconscious on the examination table. The thing that's impacted the biologist most is the creature's intelligence. The keen awareness of its surroundings is like nothing Dr. Marvin has ever studied.

Chapter 14

Michael doesn't visit the cemetery nearly as much as he used to. He tells himself it's because he's busy and, while that's true, the main reason is because he began to find himself there too often. When his father's stone was first placed, Michael would go almost daily and speak to his old man. It continued through Josie's baby years, when she would sit in her car seat giggling, while she watched her daddy talk to thin air. When she hit her toddler stage, she began to ask questions, mostly of the heaven variety. These questions became a little too heavy for Michael. He wonders if those visits to his father's grave are the reason behind her hobby of speaking to her grandfather's ghost. This particular visit, Michael is alone, sitting on the grass near the stone, lunching on an Italian hoagie. They have some catching up to do.

"So, Ma is doing well. She moved out of the mansion and into the apartment complex where the counselors live. She's the second highest ranking lady there now. Five years sober. Penny is busy, between being a mom, a nurse, and basically the brains behind the museum. If there's anyone who can handle it though, it's her. You should see the museum. It's great. It really is." He takes a bite, then a swig of his Diet Coke. "Ray misses you. I catch him staring at the photo of you guys hanging at the museum. Then there's Josie."

The next part of the one way conversation is always the most difficult.

"I really wish you could've met her. She is amazing. And brilliant. I swear she's going to cure cancer or something. She loves to dance. She's doing ballet once a week. She and Penny watch old Julie Andrews's movies. Maybe she'll move out to LA and do what I couldn't."

Tears are streaming down his cheeks now; he wipes them and gazes away from the stone, toward the sweet potato field beyond the highway.

There was an autumn day, many years ago, when Michael picked sweet potatoes at his family's farm. It was a rare occasion that he did any farm work, and he hated every second of it, but he recalls his father driving by the field in his pickup, watching him. Smiling.

"She talks to you, Dad. Tells me she sees you. You want to let me know if that's true?"

He stares at his father's grinning face, etched in the granite. A warm breeze begins to fill the air. At that moment, his cell phone rings from inside the pickup. He gets up and retrieves it.

"What's up, Mack?"

"Yo, bossman. Have you been on social media in the last hour or so?"

"No...why?"

"There's something going down in Philly right now. Something that pertains to our friend in the Pines."

Michael puts Mack on speaker and checks his Twitter feed. The number one trend in the world is *#jerseydevil*. Michael's heart sinks into his gut.

"Mack, let me go. I'll see you soon."

"Okay, boss. Be well."

He clicks a live video stream of a press conference already in progress. William Vaughn is standing in front of the Academy of Natural Sciences, speaking into a microphone. He's flanked by the press as well as a large group of spectators. Behind him is a poster, illustrated with a nightmarish beast, and the words...

FACE TO FACE WITH THE JERSEY DEVIL: A Thrilling Encounter that will Change Our World!

"This is truly going to be a once in a lifetime experience, and I can't think of a better place to have it than right here in the city where I was born. Philadelphia!"

The onlookers cheer, as cameras flash and reporters blurt out questions. A tall woman's deep voice rises above the rest.

"Excuse me, Mr. Vaughn, is this exhibit connected to the very popular Jersey Devil Museum located in New Jersey, about an hour from here? The same museum that you famously have tried to purchase for some time now?"

"No ma'am. This is a totally separate venture. They have a cute thing over there. I could've taken it out of our stratosphere, believe me. But while I was there trying to negotiate a deal with those folks, I, myself, became quite enamored with this fantastic beast. So naturally I did something about it. I tracked it down and I caught it."

A surge of questions once again erupts from the mass of reporters.

"Listen, listen. I know you have a lot of questions about how I managed to capture this illusive beast. Perhaps some of you have safety concerns. I understand. What I can assure you is only this. When you purchase a ticket, you will enter a state of the art, fully secure exhibit. You will press your nose up to the glass, while a four-hundred-year-old monster does the same on the other side. You will experience a rush that you can't get anywhere else in the world. You think it's cool when you come face to face with those tigers down the street at the zoo? You people ain't seen nothing yet."

Michael presses the button on the side of his phone and the screen goes dark. He tosses it onto the passenger's seat, takes one last look at his father's stone, then peels out of the cemetery road, kicking up dust as he goes.

Chapter 15

It's nine PM. Like most evenings, Dr. Marvin has been alone with the creature for a few hours. Since Vaughn left for the city two days ago, the creature has been more active than ever. The head biologist has watched in awe as it has clawed down trees and gathered foliage and plant life, to construct a hut in one corner of the Terrarium. He's grown quite fond of the beast and after doing a considerable amount of research into its mythology, Dr. Marvin has decided to give it a name.

"We have something very special tonight for dinner, Mister Leeds. One of our guys killed a moose a few miles from the base. While I don't agree with hunting," Dr. Marvin explains softly, as he opens the hatch and places the tray inside, "I've heard the meat is delicious."

There's a rustle of leaves from inside the hut, as some of the branches begin to tremble. Mister Leeds rises up out of the entrance, then slowly approaches. He picks the metal tray up on both sides, like a freshman on the first day of school, then returns to his hut.

"You want to eat alone. Understandable. I'm going to sit here and have my dinner, too. If that's okay." Dr. Marvin removes a plastic wrapped sandwich from a brown paper bag. "Tuna fish on rye. Not as good as yours, I'm sure. My wife has me on a strict diet ever since my heart attack last year. I miss her. My wife. She's back at home in Maine."

Dr. Marvin listens closely, through the vent-like openings in the Terrarium. Sounds of tearing and chewing are coming from inside the hut. He continues to speak to Mister Leeds as they finish their dinners. At some point, while he's jotting notes down, Dr. Marvin drifts off to sleep.

He's a boy again, in his backyard, having a baseball catch with his older brother. The summer sun is setting; fireflies begin to rise from the freshly trimmed lawn. Their folks are sitting on the back porch by lantern light, drinking white wine. Something catches little Lee's eye by the man-made pond that lines the woods. It's a bullfrog. A big one.

"Look, brother!" he shouts as he tosses his glove off, and slides on the ground towards the frog, clutching it in his hands. It's a male, I heard his call just last night. It was beautiful!"

"Great," his brother says, sarcastically, "can we get back to the catch?"

Dr. Marvin awakens to see Mister Leeds standing at the glass with its clawed hand pressed against the pane. He can see the creases in its palm. Its lifeline is just like ours.

"Mister Leeds, you startled me. I was having a wonderful dream. I can't remember the last time I had one."

Dr. Marvin moves closer to the Terrarium. Without saying anything further, he places his own palm against the glass, directly aligned with Mister Leeds'. The creature's massive hand and clawed fingers dwarf the man's.

Something comes over him. A feeling that he's never experienced in his sixty years. A warm fusillade of otherworldliness. He's paralyzed at once, comforted and scared to death. Mister Leeds locks his eyes with Dr. Marvin's; the scientist is close enough to see them in great detail. They are very much like human eyes, only bigger. The iris is a deep shade of red, while tiny yellow veins protrude from the sclera. What Dr. Marvin finds most fascinating is that, while Mister Leeds' head most closely resembles a goat, its pupils aren't horizontal and thin like the animal, rather, they're round like his own. Without warning, Mister Leeds turns to retreat to its hut. Dr. Marvin takes a chance and shouts for him.

"Let's try something," the man says, as he grabs two Sharpies from a nearby workstation and removes their caps. He places one on a tray and slides it carefully into the Terrarium. The biologist slowly draws a circle on the pane of glass in front of the creature.

Mister Leeds ambles to the tray and picks up the other Sharpie. Not like it knows how to use it, more like a toddler picking up a stick. It puts it up to its nostril, which twitches a bit in return. It then places the tip of the marker firmly against the glass and leads it counterclockwise, drawing a sloppy circle next to Dr. Marvin's.

"My God," the scientist declares to himself quietly, trying to contain his excitement. "Truly remarkable, Mister Leeds. We will get you out of there. I promise."

Chapter 16

"I know you guys have been getting a lot of questions about the attraction opening in Philadelphia. Ray, Penny, and I have discussed it, and we've decided the best thing to do when a guest brings it up, is to simply tell the truth." Michael is speaking to the entire staff, thirty minutes before the museum opens. "We aren't affiliated with it in any way, and we have absolutely no info on it. Let's not bad mouth it, or get into whatever we may have found online about it."

A young employee raises her hand. She's sixteen and works a register at the gift shop.

"Mr. Neary," she says, nervously.

"Yes, Annie."

"I've been chosen by, um, like everyone, to ask a question."

Michael waits a moment for her to continue. She doesn't.

"Annie, are you okay? Do you have a question?" Penny asks.

"Well, some of us are nervous. If they really did catch the Jersey Devil, is this place going to, like...close down?"

Ray rises from his chair to speak.

"This place isn't going anywhere. Even if those people have caught the Jabberwock, they did it under illegal circumstances. They are holding it against its will. We are going to make every effort to stop them."

Michael and Penny glance at each other. They wanted to avoid this moment.

"What Ray is trying to say is - "

"I know exactly what I'm saying," Ray states, cutting Michael off. "I've put my damn heart and soul into this museum. I'm not going to let some rich pigs make a quick buck off the back of an innocent, beautiful creature. It belongs in those Goddamn woods out there!"

"Hell, yes!" Mack shouts from the back of the room.

"Mack, relax," Michael chuckles.

The staff start to speak to one another. They've been whispering about the Philadelphia attraction amongst themselves ever since William Vaughn made the announcement. Now that it's out in the open, there's a sudden buzz in the room. Michael is a deer in headlights. He looks toward his wife. She knows the look. Michael isn't good at being a boss, in the traditional sense of the word.

"Listen guys," Penny says loudly, over the chatter. The room falls silent. "It's almost time to open. Let's all just focus on today; if any of you have further questions don't hesitate to ask us."

"Does "us" mean me, too?" Ray inquires softly.

"Dad. Of course."

The museum opens as usual. It's a Saturday, so the entire staff stuck around to work, with one notable absence. No one has seen Ray since the meeting. Penny finds her husband speaking to a group of guests - children sitting on their parents' laps, teenagers filming him with their camera phones. They are glued to his every word as he tells them about the day he met the Jersey Devil. He infuses the story with humor, making sure he doesn't frighten the younger guests. When he's done, his audience cheers and moves on to other areas of the museum.

"Hey, maybe we should look for my dad," Penny whispers, "It's been a few hours. I'm starting to worry."

"Okay. I think I might know where he is." The couple leave Mack in charge, and hop in the pickup. They drive down Seven Bridges Road, and find Ray fishing off the last bridge. His usual spot.

"You left without telling anyone. We were worried," Penny says as they approach him.

"No need to worry. I'm a grown man who wanted to do some fishing." Ray continues tugging on the fishing rod, staring attentively at the bay, barely acknowledging his daughter and son in law.

"Daddy. Want to talk?"

"Those sons of bitches smoked the Jabberwock out of its home." Ray howls, as he tosses the rod down and turns to them. "They set fire to the cave. I know it."

"What about Lonnie Wilkes?" Michael asks.

"He was their Patsy, obviously. I refuse to stand by and let this shit go down. No way. They killed a man."

"Daddy, even if that's true, what can we do about it?"

"Alert the damn authorities. A murder has taken place. Mike, you know it's true. You talked to a guy."

"What guy?" Penny inquires.

"I went by Mrs. Wilkes' house and met a friend of Lonnie's. He informed me that Lonnie and William Vaughn had some kind of meeting. Maybe they were in cahoots. I dunno."

"Why wouldn't you tell me that?"

"I guess I was embarrassed. Everything is so weird right now. I don't know if I'm coming or going."

"Well, whatever. The fact is, there's been an investigation already. Without any real proof of what you're saying, we won't get very far."

"So that's it? We crawl under a rock and die?" asks Ray.

"Daddy, I'm not saying that at all. We don't even know if Vaughn is telling the truth yet. This whole thing may be a publicity stunt."

"Your daughter has a point, Ray."

"You shush. Since when did we start keeping secrets from each other?" Penny asks her husband.

"It wasn't a secret. I knew you would think it was silly and I was waiting for the right time to bring it up. That's all."

"You've done sillier stuff than that, Mike, but you've never kept things from me."

"Okay, guys. Nothing's biting," Ray interjects. "Follow me back to the museum. We have a lot of work to get done."

With just a quick look, the couple are back on the same page. They know that Ray gets nervous when they have an occasional squabble. It's because they understand that Ray would give anything to go back to the night he and his wife bickered over something meaningless he can't remember. It was on that night that she stormed from the house, got into her car, then was killed by a drunk driver - two miles from their home. Two miles from where their five-year-old daughter, Penelope, was sleeping peacefully in her bed.

On the ride back to the museum, Michael tells his wife that he sees where Ray is coming from, and believes that William Vaughn was responsible for Lonnie's murder, and the fire. Penny agrees, but doesn't think it's the smartest idea to engage in some sort of conflict with Vaughn.

"If he's capable of these terrible things, imagine what else he is capable of," she explains, "and he has unlimited resources at his fingertips. That's pretty scary."

"Very true. I should've told you about visiting Mrs. Wilkes. I'm sorry. Full disclosure from here on out."

"It's okay. Just remember we're a team. I got your back."

"Word."

Michael turns towards his wife and smiles, as they exchange a fist bump.

Chapter 17

The Terrarium's glass is covered on both sides with markings, reminiscent of cave drawings. It's the first thing William Vaughn spots when he returns to the base.

"What is all this?" He asks Dr. Marvin and his team, sitting in a semicircle around the work station. The excited biologist approaches Vaughn.

"We have made great leaps, Mr. Vaughn. Great leaps."

"Who built that?" Vaughn asks, ignoring the enthusiasm in the room. He points to the hut in the back corner. The creature is hidden inside.

"Mister Leeds did. His intelligence is far beyond what we first gathered. He is able to communicate. Look at this."

Dr. Marvin points to the shapes he drew on the glass, and then to the copies facing the inside of the Terrarium: a circle, triangle, square, and a peace sign, almost identical to the biologist's, only messier, like the work of a child. Vaughn quickly examines the drawings.

"I'm sorry. Did you say Mister Leeds? You gave the thing a name?"

"It's not uncommon to do so. I - ”

"Listen. I'm paying you to study this thing, not to make friends with it."

"With all due respect - "

"C'mon, cut it out with the politically correct shit and talk to me."

Dr. Marvin is a man that picks his words carefully. A soft spoken, thoughtful man. In his forty years of work in the field of science, he's never dealt with the brashness he's dealing with now.

"William, I understand it's easy to see that creature and conclude that it's an abomination. I admit, it took me several weeks to be able to really look upon him without the hair on my back standing up. But since you've been gone, I have come to know him a little bit. When you begin to look past his physical appearance, and examine his mind, it's a beautiful thing. Truly."

"So, what you're telling me is that you've fallen in love with it and the general public will as well?"

"No. I'm saying he simply cannot be thrown into another cage, in the middle of Philadelphia, for people to gawk and point at. He deserves better."

Mr. Vaughn stands silently for a moment. He glances toward the table of wildlife biologists and conservation scientists, all of them with their different backgrounds and experience, anxiously watching things unfold. He turns and looks at Pauly, as loyal as ever, waiting for his boss' next move, then finally his eyes land on the hut. He knows that he's gotten in over his head, but that's where he feels he does his best work.

"The exhibit opens in a month. You have until tomorrow, all of you, to decide whether or not you're on board with us. What I said at the press conference is true. We are going to change the world. It's up to you, whether or not you want to be part of it."

Mr. Vaughn and Pauly begin to make their way towards the exit. Dr. Marvin speaks up, loud enough to stop them in their tracks.

"You know, Mister Leeds was out and about this afternoon. He was scampering around the Terrarium, almost frolicking like. We all watched in amazement. He even spread his wings at one point. Then, about twenty minutes ago, he picked up the sound of your engine from outside. He retreated back into the hut. Been in there ever since."

"That's something. Really. You hear this, Pauly? Mister Leeds must not like us too much."

Vaughn moves in closer to Dr. Marvin, and rests his hand on the older man's shoulder.

"Why don't we see how close you and the monster are? It'll be the next step in our study. Pauly open the main door," Vaughn commands as he tightens his grip.

"I don't know about this," Pauly whispers to his boss. "We haven't opened that door since the examination."

Pauly pleads his case, but Vaughn ignores it, demanding his underboss to carry out the bidding. Pauly positions himself next to the lever that opens the main door to the enclosure. The other scientists begin to beg for the release of their mentor.

"This is the only way to truly see if this thing is dangerous," Vaughn says, as he drags Dr. Marvin toward the door by the sleeve of his shirt. "Pauly, are you ready?" Vaughn signals to Pauly to open the door, as he shoves the frightened biologist into the Terrarium.

A flurry of life suddenly emerges from the corner. In mere seconds, Mister Leeds is out of the hut, then colliding with Vaughn, who instinctively pulls Dr. Marvin to the floor with him. Another quick movement and the creature glides towards the rafters of the main building. He lets out a fierce shriek toward Pauly, who is running toward the tranquilizer gun mounted on the wall.

Mister Leeds lunges for Pauly. The big man manages to pull the trigger of the gun, ejecting a dart into the creature's chest, just as they fall on top of one another. Mister Leeds swipes his razor sharp claws across the side of Pauly's face. The hypodermic needle releases a powerful sedative into the creature's bloodstream. Another slash attempt fails, as a bewildered Mister Leeds suddenly goes limp, crumbling into a heap. As Vaughn rushes to Pauly's aid, Dr. Marvin gathers himself and slips out of the Terrarium towards his team. They are anticipating his command.

"It's time to go. Gather your things and meet me at the van in ten minutes."

Chapter 18

The house is quiet. The summer's setting sun casts shadows on the living room floor. Because of their hectic schedule, the Neary family only gets an hour or so each evening to enjoy one another's company. Penny and Michael are admiring Josie as she lies on the carpet, scribbling in one of her drawing pads. She's lost interest in coloring books, preferring to create her own pieces of artwork now. She draws an abstract set of shapes inside of a green square, sitting on top of an upside down V.

"That's really good, baby girl," Penny says. "Can you tell us what it is?"

"It's the monster. The bad man has it locked up in the green castle. On top of the mountain."

"That's a cool story," Michael adds. "Did you see it on one of your shows?"

"No. Daddy's Daddy told me."

Later that night, Josie is on her pink stool at the bathroom sink. She and Penny are brushing their teeth.

"Can Mommy ask you something?" Josie nods, with a mouth full of toothpaste. "I love your stories. I hope you always tell them. They are make-believe though. Right?"

"No, Mommy," Josie answers, spitting into the sink. "I told you already. Daddy's Daddy really talks to me."

Michael is listening in from the next room.

"Is he here now?" Penny asks.

"No. Not right now. He went back to the green castle."

Penny finishes up story time and tucks her daughter in. Not long after, Josie migrates from her bedroom to her parents', planting herself firmly between the two in their bed. It's a nightly ritual, which Penny and Michael allow to happen. After the girls snuggle and drift off to sleep, Michael quietly slips out of bed and across the hallway to the office. He turns on the MacBook and enters words into the search engine.

Green - Mountain - William Vaughn.

He comes across a blog titled: *Stories from the Trail*. One entry in particular, along with accompanying photos, catches Michael's attention.

Today I hiked the East Mountain, all the way up to Fort Green. I've been to this eerie place twice, but this afternoon was way, way different. Instead of the abandoned military base and ghost town I stumbled upon before, I spotted a landed helicopter, with a group of people around it. They looked like suit and tie types, but when I approached them, I immediately recognized the one guy that was doing all the talking. He was none other than a personal hero of mine. Billionaire and all around badass, William Vaughn. They were surprised to see me at first, but when I got to talking to William, I could tell he liked me. He informed me that he hiked this place once before, and loved it so much that he decided to buy it. The whole damn area. The base, the town, everything.

A chill rushes down Michael's spine; his mouth goes dry. He slams the Mac closed and hurries back into bed, pulling the sheets over him. Josie is sleeping soundly, nuzzled up against her mother's back. The light from the television is painting her a pale blue. She's telling the truth. Michael is sure of it.

For the first time in years, Michael senses the presence of his father in the room. At first he's frightened, but the feeling soon melts away, and is replaced by a warm, familiar emotion. He reaches his arm across his family, pulling them both closer to him. Penny stirs and asks if he's okay.

"I'm fine. I love you," he answers.

It took a week to sell Penny on the idea. A week of tense conversations and awkward silences. She believes that there is something to the conversations that Josie is having with Daddy's Daddy, something that none of them would ever truly understand. The way her stories and drawings match up to the information Michael discovered couldn't be happenstance. It's her husband's idea of traveling to Vermont, on a rescue mission that concerns her. She was adamantly against it at first, but then a revelation hit her like a ton of bricks.

On her way home from work one night, she glanced at the impossibly large moon, glowing silver through the pine trees, following her. She thought about five years ago, how determined her future husband was to return to the woods, even though he had just been hopelessly lost in them. She recalled his promise to Ray and herself that, if they went back, if they worked together, they would find the creature. It was in that moment, five years ago, when she felt like Michael was at his most unhinged, that she put her faith in him.

She decided, on that drive, to put her faith in him once again.

Chapter 19

Dr. Marvin and his team managed to flee Fort Green, leaving the rest of the crew behind. Most of Vaughn's employees are in Philadelphia, working diligently to ensure the exhibit is ready for its grand opening in two weeks. The workers have been pulled from various projects from around the country, and relocated to the city. They are working on a second, more advanced Terrarium, with no idea of what it's going to contain. The only insight into their jobs are blueprints and designs that they've received from the engineers at Fort Green. The designs - sketches for signage and marketing materials - depict a snarling, unearthly beast.

For seventy-two hours straight, Vaughn and his engineers have filled the enclosure up with a chemical compound that mimics a dense fog floating through the display of trees. The chemical is supposed to act as a pheromone, stimulating the aggressive side of an animal. While Dr. Marvin was still there, he had reluctantly agreed to use the gas as a last resort, and only after he tested it on house flies. It's causing severe side effects in Mister Leeds. Instead of exiting his hut and moving about the Terrarium like they had hoped, he's gagging and retreating further underneath his wings.

"Billy, we're going to kill this poor bastard. It's not working," says an engineer named Robert Elliot, a loyal employee of William Vaughn, and former creative director of his theme parks.

"Two weeks. Two fucking weeks until we are live, and this thing won't move," Vaughn complains. James, another engineer, this one fresh-faced and eager to impress his superiors, speaks up.

"Mr. Vaughn, perhaps we should go a different route."

"What route?" Vaughn asks the young man.

"Well, I'm just saying, maybe we try to coax it out without the gas," James whispers to his boss. "I watched Dr. Marvin while you were gone. I saw the interaction. Let me try to communicate with it."

"No. Fuck that. I've been lucky twice now," Pauly adds, the wounds on his face concealed by bandages. "You try anything that gives it a chance to escape again, I may not be as lucky the third time."

"Pauly is right. We can't take another chance at this point. If this thing is as smart as you think it is, then it'll realize that it can't withstand much more of this. Everything has a breaking point. Wait an hour. Gas it again."

The RV barely fits in the driveway of the Neary's house. Ray is helping Mack stock it with enough food and supplies for the next couple of days. The inside of the vehicle consists of the main sitting area along with sleeping quarters with two sets of bunk beds, a kitchen with a small dining area, and a bathroom. Ray is both impressed by the features of it and confused by its decor. It looks less like the traditional living space of a recreational vehicle and more like the inside of a fun house. Shelves are covered with models and action figures and vintage sci-fi movie posters are framed on the wall. There's a Pac-Man arcade machine, a life-size stuffed Sasquatch, and Christmas lights strung about. Ray can only imagine that the inside lights up like a pinball machine when the sun goes down.

"So, you're telling me you live in here?" Ray asks.

"Yessir."

"Mack. I pay you pretty well. Let's get you a little apartment somewhere."

"Huh? I love the Falcon. We are a part of each other now."

"The Falcon?"

"Yessir. Like the Millennium Falcon." Ray looks at Mack confused. "Star Wa - "

"I know what it is."

Negotiations are in progress inside the house, as Michael tries to convince Josie that it's just a boring business trip he and Pop Pop are going on. She is stomping around her bedroom and demanding to join them.

"Josie, I promise, I will bring you home the coolest toy you have ever seen. It'll be a special toy, just from Daddy. Whaddya think?"

"A big toy?" Josie catches her breath and inquires through tears.

"A huge one. I may not be able to get it through the front door." Michael glances toward Penny, who's standing in the doorway, smirking. "What is it?"

"Are you bringing me something home?" Penny asks, playing on the fact that since she is allowing this trip, her husband will be forever in her debt.

"Of course. What would you like?"

"I would like my husband and my dad to return home safely," she says as they embrace. "You do know this is absolutely crazy. Right?"

"I do. But I also know that my father is communicating with Josie. That sounds impossible. It does. But so does everything we've been through." They look toward their daughter, who has composed herself and refocused her attention on a wooden dollhouse.

"Listen," Penny says softly. "When I was growing up, I questioned everything. Maybe it was like an armor I wore after my mom passed. The only thing I never questioned though, was my father's search. I watched him dedicate his life to finding something that I didn't even believe was real. Then your dad came along, then you came along, then Josie. I know I said it doesn't have to define us. But who am I kidding? It does define us. It brought us all together. So yes, it's crazy. But it's us."

"Thank you. I couldn't do this if you weren't in my corner."

Michael is the last to board the Falcon. His girls follow him on so they can say goodbye to Ray. Much to Mack's dismay, Josie begins to rummage through his stuff.

"JoJo Bear, those actually aren't toys," the man says, nervously.

"By definition, they absolutely are toys," Ray answers. "Go for it, sweetheart." She moves on from the action figures and scoops up a porcelain dragon, pointing it toward Mack. He's sweating.

"May I have this?" she asks. Michael intervenes and takes it out of his daughter's hands before Mack can answer.

"How about this? I'll bring you home a dragon. A much better one," Michael says, as he winks at Mack, then hands him the sculpture.

"Okay, Daddy."

After some hugs and kisses, Mack backs the Falcon out of the driveway. Penny is standing at the front door with Josie in her arms. A somber look washes over their faces as they wave goodbye. Michael imagines being an astronaut rocketing into space, helplessly watching his world get smaller and smaller as he drifts away in his ship. The RV turns off the street; Michael can no longer see his home. A jolting pain tears though the pit of his stomach. His thoughts are whipped into a cyclone. He hasn't felt like this since he was lost in the woods. The suffocating fear. The looming uncertainty of what's to come.

"You okay?" Ray asks, snapping him out of it.

"Just nervous to be leaving them."

"I understand, but we will be back in Jersey before you know it."

Their plan is simple, but reckless. It starts with them trying to talk some sense into William Vaughn. They've predicted that there will be no reasoning with him, so their next step is to break the creature out. A long shot in Michael's opinion, but Ray believes that the Jabberwock will remember them. After they free it, they will transport it home in the RV

"Ray. Have you thought about what we do if this trip doesn't work out like we intend?"

"We go on. We get up every day and go to work."

"What if there's no work to go to?"

Ray turns away from his son-in-law for a moment and glares out of the Falcon's window. They are heading north on Route 206, passing Michael's childhood home.

"Do you ever miss that house?" Ray inquires, changing subjects. The question throws Michael off, jogging a part of his memory that's lain dormant for some time.

"Once in a while. Not so much the house, as my life there. My father. You know."

Ray clutches Michael's forearm and gives it a gentle shake, "I miss him too," and then gets up from the sitting area of the RV and heads toward the cockpit.

"How are we doing, Mack?"

"Wonderful, sir. Moving right along."

Ray has a way of calming people's nerves. He speaks in a straightforward manner, with thoughtful, reassuring words. Michael inhales a breath deep into his lungs as he sits back on the leather sleeper sofa. Just in time, the interior lights of the RV turn off, and are replaced by the string lights. A rainbow of color fills the cabin and for a moment it feels like Christmas - even in the middle of summer, traveling down the road in a recreational vehicle.

The colorful, beautifully sculpted glass fills up with smoke. Mack places the mouthpiece up to his lips and pulls the slide; the bubbling increases as the smoke exits the bong and enters his respiratory system. He coughs violently for a minute, while Michael laughs hysterically, then composes himself and continues his comparison.

"So, I'm just saying. All things considered, Ray would most definitely be Chief Brody. You're Quint, leaving me as Hooper."

"I just don't understand why you're so sure that you are Hooper," Michael responds. "By your logic, it's because of your extensive research into cryptozoology, but I have seen it. All the books about Sasquatch and the Skunk Ape, they can never truly explain what it was like to actually see something like that."

They've parked the Falcon at an RV camp, about ten miles from the base of the East Mountain. Ray has gone to bed, leaving the younger guys in the sitting area with a busload of junk food and *Jaws* playing on the flat screen television in front of them. The characters they are discussing are drunkenly crooning "Show Me the Way to Go Home" in the cabin of their ship, the Orca.

"I'm saying. I'm saying," Mack continues. "You're focusing too much on Quint's grumpy disposition. Of course that's not you. You're the jolliest bastard I know. It's the experience, my man. No one on that boat had the experience with sharks that Quint had. Just like you with our Leeds Devil."

Michael ponders Mack's assessment and concludes that he's probably right. They've worked together for five years and, although they enjoy each other's company at the museum, they've never really gotten to know each other outside of it.

"What got you into all this?" Michael inquires, nodding toward the stuffed Sasquatch in the corner.

"Well, I was a chubby kid. And sweaty. Like a sweaty mess, all the time. You know kids, man, they picked on me. I became a bit of an outsider. One Saturday afternoon, my old man was watching a documentary. You know that footage of Bigfoot from the sixties? The one where he trots across the edge of the woods, turns toward the camera, then kind of darts into the trees?"

"The Patterson film?"

"Yes. That one. Impressive, bro. For a long time that footage haunted me. Not because I was frightened by it. It was because I related to Bigfoot. I saw the way he walked, swaying his arms in this sort of frightened way, scurrying away from the strangers filming him. He just wanted to be left alone. I guess my interest in monsters and other weird shit just grew from there." Mack hits the bong once again, then begins to hack up the remainder of his lungs. "Shit. I'm done."

"Jesus, man. I'd say you are," Michael laughs. "You know, I'm technically your boss. This seems inappropriate."

A bit later, as the credits begin to scroll over Chief Brody and Hooper's return to the beach, Michael turns to find Mack passed out with a bag of Cool Ranch Doritos in his hands. He slips out of the RV and into the cool Vermont air. Most of the other campers have turned it in for the night, with the exception of a few night owls chatting underneath retractable awnings and circling around fire pits. He strolls through the makeshift city of motorhomes, speaking softly to Penny on his cell, nodding his head to the friendly people he passes. He tells her about the drive and explains that they've parked for the night so they can head out early in the morning, well-rested for their hike up to Fort Green.

"Please be careful, Mike. I'm really nervous."

"Me, too. I can't believe we're here. We're actually doing this."

"If things aren't going well, if the trek up the mountain is too dangerous, or you guys aren't permitted access to the damn military base, or whatever, just come home. Josie and I need you back here with us."

"I know. I better get back to the RV and get some sleep. I love you."

"I love you too. Goodnight."

James stumbles through a dark corridor. A gooey substance is draining quickly from the vents above the young engineer's head. He lifts his hand to catch some in his palm. Examining it closer, he discovers that it's thick, with a greenish tint - something vile, resembling swamp water. As he makes his way down the inclined floor of the corridor, the liquid is rising, about shin deep now. He hears splashing up ahead but can't make out what's causing it. The fluorescent lamps above him are flickering, malfunctioning from the moisture in the room.

He's closer to the splashing now, droplets of water are hitting his face, landing in his mouth. The taste is sickening. Bathing in the flashing lights ahead, thrashing around the dark water, is an octopus. It's huge, too big for the shallow water. As it scans James with a pair of peculiar eyes, a tentacle suddenly wraps around the man's leg, from his ankle up to his mid-thigh, and yanks him towards the water. He falls through it, completely submerged. An impossibility, since he was standing in knee-high water just a moment ago. But, the tentacle doesn't stop pulling him down, deeper and deeper, into the abyss. The lights from the fluorescent lamps become pinholes, obscured by the surface of the water.

James jolts awake. He's alone with Mister Leeds, in the main room of the base. They've been taking shifts staying with the creature through the night. Since they started gassing the Terrarium, Mister Leeds has barely moved. James is shocked to discover the creature standing near the glass, with its palm pressed against it. Staring at him. The startled engineer asks Mister Leeds if he's okay, not expecting an answer.

He gets one anyway.

The creature lets out its signature bellow. James has heard it once or twice before, but this time it's loud, and in his direction. The force almost knocks him off his feet. He frantically unclips the walkie talkie from his belt.

"Mr. Vaughn." He waits a moment and tries again. "Mr. Vaughn. Are you there? Come in."

Mister Leeds' eyes are locked on James. The terrified man feels pulses of electricity throughout his body, a sensation the likes of which he's never felt. The assistant architect of the Terrarium has a brilliant mind for engineering but, for his entire stay at Fort Green, he's been on edge. Nothing could've prepared him for Mister Leeds.

"James, what's up?" Vaughn's groggy voice blurts from the other end of the radio.

"Mister Leeds is up and moving. He's acting weird. Aggressive, even."

Vaughn tries to say something else but his voice is distorted. They've been using the walkie system for months; this is the first time there's loss of signal. The pulses travel from different areas of his body and congregate in his hand, with enough strength to make him drop the transceiver.

Mister Leeds begins to whip the glass with his tail. Large, clubbing blows. The sound rings through the base. James picks up the walkie and tries to alert his boss again but gets nothing. It's completely fried.

The creature starts rapping the glass quicker, steady shots with its tail and claws. The two layers of thick, laminated glass that are supposed to resist the heaviest impact begin to crack. James watches on, terrified, as the creature unfurls its wings, and flies towards the back of the cell. For a moment, there's silence. James looks at the Terrarium, the structure he helped to create. The glass is smashed; the inside is filled with the smoky remains of the gassing trials.

Instantly, Mister Leeds slams into the same spot he was striking. The entire side of the Terrarium disconnects from the steel corners, crashing to the floor. James struggles to his feet and bolts toward the exit doors. He barrels through them at full speed, almost hitting Vaughn on the other side.

"What the fuck is going on?"

Before he can get another word out, Mister Leeds flies in the men's direction. The powerful beast swipes the jagged edge of its wing across Vaughn, slicing him from the sternum to his hairline. A flurry of crimson fills the hallway. It takes the men a few seconds to realize that it's Vaughn's blood that has drenched them. James goes into a paralyzing shock, as Vaughn makes his way into the main room. He looks upon the broken Terrarium; his biggest fear has come true. His prize is on the loose.

Vaughn swipes the tranquilizer gun off the wall, steps over a helpless James, then moves quickly down the hallway towards the main exit of the base. Pauly is just arriving at the outside of the building.

"Did you see it?" Vaughn shouts.

"No. I just got here. You're bleeding all over the place! How the hell did it get out?"

"I'll be fine. It smashed right through the glass. Exactly what these people guaranteed me it couldn't do. Grab the Hummer. We're going to have to track it down."

"Billy, you're hurt bad. It's the middle of the night and we're on a fucking mountain. This isn't the Pine Barrens out here. "

"So, what the fuck do we do?"

"You need medical attention, man. I think we need to go inside and regroup."

"No. You're right, this isn't the Pine Barrens. The fucker is lost and vulnerable. We can't waste any more time. Get the Hummer."

Vaughn and Pauly drive through the mountainous terrain for close to an hour. It's a perilous search and Vaughn has bled through several towels. He's starting to doze in and out of consciousness.

"Billy, I'm turning around. It's over."

"It can't be over," Vaughn splutters.

There is nothing but trees and darkness. One false move, one wrong turn of the wheel, would lead to the Hummer spiraling down a slope. Vaughn drifts off with his head jammed against the passenger side window. Pauly turns the vehicle around, to the direction he was coming from. He drives slowly, clutching the wheel, for what feels like an eternity.

The forest eventually thins out. Feeling like he's getting closer to the parameter of the town, the big man picks up speed, narrowly missing a patch of trees, then takes the Hummer right into a shallow ditch.

"Fuck!" he yells, and throws it in reverse, pushing down on the gas pedal as hard as he can. Vaughn's bloody body jolts around lifelessly as he mumbles gibberish. "Come on, you fucker!"

Something lands hard on the top of the truck, causing it to shake. Pauly immediately knows what it is. There's hammering above him, followed by a terrible clawing sound. The Hummer's wheels finally manage to climb out of the ditch. Mister Leeds' face appears upside down in the windshield. He stares at a frozen Pauly, too terrified to drive.

"What the fuck do you want from me? I'm sorry," Pauly cries. "Let me get him back to the base and we will leave you alone. I promise you!"

Mister Leeds drinks the man in, then leaps off the Hummer, making it tremble once again. Pauly sits, questioning if the creature is truly gone. Questioning *everything*. He looks at his friend's bloody face, then puts two fingers under his chin in search of a pulse. He's alive.

He manages to return to the base, helping his barely conscious boss into the main room, where the engineers and the girls have gathered. Robert Elliot is brandishing a rifle, with the frightened group huddled up behind him.

"Where the hell did you guys go?" Robert snaps.

"We went looking for it," Pauly answers.

"You left James here in shock. You didn't think to inform any of us that Mister Leeds has escaped. This is a disaster."

"It is a disaster, because of your shoddy enclosure," Vaughn angrily interjects, finally coming to.

"Excuse me? I told you, before I ever signed on, that we knew nothing about this creature. Not how strong it is. Not what it can do. Nothing. How in the hell would you design something for a situation like that?"

"We'll discuss it later. I need you to address these wounds in the medical lab."

"Medical lab? It's an empty room with a first aid kit. Have Pauly take you over there. We're done."

"Done?"

"Yes. We were waiting here to tell you face to face. We are leaving, all of us. It's too dangerous. We are taking the van, and getting the hell off this mountain."

Robert, with the group following close behind him, heads towards the exit doors, keeping the rifle trained on Pauly and Vaughn.

"I will stick that gun up your ass," Pauly sneers, as they slide by him. Vaughn begins to shout at the group as they exit.

"You people will never work again! You hear me? You're all finished!"

Robert is the last of the group left in the room; he turns and quickly advances toward Vaughn and Pauly. He shoves the rifle into the big man's chest, relinquishing it to him.

"Billy, listen to me," Robert asserts. "Call this thing off. It's not too late. You'll take a loss, but you'll still be in a good spot."

"Fuck you, Robert. I don't quit. This is a minor setback."

"A minor setback? That...that fucking monster is gone! It's nothing but mountains for hundreds of miles. You'll never find it. Call the project off. Get your name as far away from that thing as you can. Before it starts killing people out there."

"Maybe he has a point, Billy," Pauly adds.

"No. We will find it. Then after the project takes off, you'll hear from my lawyers about your bullshit designs. Now get the fuck out of here."

Robert takes one more look at Pauly's bandaged face. He knows that the big man is scared, but desperately loyal. Robert knows by their history together, if a corpse was the work of William Vaughn, it ended up in the ground because of Pauly's work with a shovel.

"Good luck," he says, then continues on, out of the building.

Penny is in the office, looking over figures. She's surprised to see that it's the most profitable thirty days they've had since the reopening, as well as a record-breaking month for new memberships. The surge of interest in the Jersey Devil from the buzz around the exhibit in Philadelphia, has brought people to the museum in droves. She picks up her cellphone, excited to tell her husband and father the news when the cashier, Annie, enters.

"Hey Annie. What's up?"

"There's a guy out here looking for the owners. An old guy."

"Did he say what he wants?"

"No. He seems nervous."

The man is admiring the poster size images on the wall. They are the photos Michael took on the afternoon of his encounter with Leeds Devil. The biologist has only seen the beast in a glass cell, defeated. So to see it basking fully in its own environment is confirmation that he's made the right decision to visit the museum, to speak to the Nearys. Penny approaches him.

"Hello, sir. May I help you?"

"Penelope. Correct?"

"Yes."

"Hi. It's wonderful to meet you. This place is phenomenal. A proper representation of an amazing creature."

"Why, thank you."

"My apologies. I'm Lee Marvin," he says, with a chuckle, extending his arm out for a handshake.

"The scientist?"

"Yes, ma'am."

"It's an honor to meet you," Penny responds, taking his hand.

"And you as well. Unfortunately I am here about a dire situation. I was a special consultant to William Vaughn and his dreadful project. I studied the Leeds Devil. I grew quite fond of him."

"I'm sorry," Penny politely interrupts. "Let's continue this conversation elsewhere."

Back in the office, Dr. Marvin speaks about the couple of months he was on board with the project. The infighting and the terrible living conditions of Mister Leeds. Penny also describes her dealings with William Vaughn, especially the last meeting, when he tried to intimidate her into a deal.

"He's a man capable of wicked things," Dr. Marvin continues, "even murder."

"Murder? Do you know for sure?"

"Yes, ma'am. You see, about a month into my stay at Fort Green, I started to hear whispers about a man from around here named Lonnie Wilkes. I looked him up. I pieced events together. I even began to hit "record" on my cell phone and leave it behind, in hidden places. Well, it paid off."

The biologist places his cell down on the table in front of them.

"There's a recording on here of Vaughn and his right hand man Pauly. They're terribly intoxicated and discussing the killing of Wilkes. All the evidence we'll ever need to take him down."

Penny's blood turns ice cold. She quickly rises from her chair to retrieve her own cell phone. Dr. Marvin is startled by her sudden move.

"Are you okay?"

"My husband, Michael, and my father. They left for Vermont yesterday. They're in more danger than I thought."

Ray was right about everything. As soon as it was confirmed by Dr. Marvin, Penny immediately realized how painfully obvious it was all along. In a way, she was in denial about it. She knew that if what they all believed to be true - was in fact true - her father wouldn't rest until he brought William Vaughn down. Now that there's proof, it could make things simpler. Perhaps she can convince them to call off the ridiculous rescue mission, come home, and get the authorities involved. She just needs to reach them. She tries her husband first. The call goes right to voicemail. Then her father. Nothing.

"Penelope. There's absolutely no cellphone service once you reach the base of the East Mountain. We communicated at Fort Green with a system of walkie talkies."

"Fucking shit!" Penny shouts, then slams her cell down on the table. "I'm sorry. I just don't know what to do."

"I never met these men, Penelope. But when I walked through this museum, I felt their spirit. Their energy. I believe they'll be okay." Dr. Marvin says, trying to convince himself as much as Penny.

"This is the end of the line," Ray says, as he scans the terrain.

There are gaps in the trees that a smaller vehicle may have been able to weave through, but the massive RV would be impossible to maneuver. They came prepared for a hike, and they've got one.

"Listen, Mack you should hang back with the RV, in case any kind of law enforcement comes sniffing around."

"I beg your pardon, boss, but shit, no. If this is my chance to see the Jersey Devil, I'm taking it. The Falcon will be okay."

"And if they see us parked over here? If they tow us?"

"I guess we will cross that bridge when we get to it, sir."

"Fine. Let's pack up. It's time for a walk."

They gather their backpacks and begin their march up the East Mountain. The air gets thinner as civilization gets further away. There is nothing but thick woodland on all sides, as far as the eye can see. A little over an hour into their hike, Mack stops in his tracks.

"I should've stayed with the RV. I don't think I can make it."

"Let's take a breather," Michael says, as he takes his pack off and retrieves a Gatorade from inside.

"You have an extra? I'm dying."

"Where's your water?"

"I drank it all. Back in the Falcon."

"What's in your backpack then?"

"Some snacks. Some weed."

"Jesus H. Christ, Macaulay." Ray growls. "Take this one, make it last." Ray grabs an extra canteen from his own pack and tosses it to Mack. They find a small clearing in the underbrush and take a seat. Ray unfolds a map and examines it.

"You know, it's a trip that you're actually using a physical map right now," Mack says, as he packs a psychedelic glass bowl with marijuana. "How were you even able to locate this place?"

"I contacted a high-up in the National Park Service. She contacted someone else, and so on. You can do these things when you're a responsible adult."

"I resent that," Mack says, as he takes a hit from the bowl.

They continue on their way, until they come across tire marks on a narrow dirt road. The marks stretch through another dense patch of trees, in the opposite direction from where they are headed.

"These are fresh," Ray explains. "Someone must've left the base in the last day or so. We're getting close."

They follow the tracks for another mile and find a large hill lined with a fence. The tracks lead right into an open gate. Beyond it, they set their eyes on a plateau, where the military town is located. Fort Green is towering high above.

"We made it, boys," Ray says with a sigh.

He removes a pair of binoculars from his backpack and eyes the base. There's no movement, no sign of life at all, except for a black Hummer. The same one parked outside of the wine bar the night of Ray's meeting with Vaughn.

"They're here."

"How do you know?" Michael asks.

"That black truck, New York plates. It was in town the night I met with them," Ray explains, handing the binoculars to his son-in-law.

"Well, gentlemen. Let's do this thing," Mack chimes in.

A main strip of homes leads up to another wire fence, surrounding the main building. The men carefully traipse through the abandoned town. It's an eerie experience. They can feel the ghosts of yesteryear in every house, around every dark corner. It's as if life stopped at the drop of a dime and never resumed. They continue to follow the tire marks, through the fence and up to the yard that circles Fort Green.

"Maybe they're expecting us," Michael says, pointing to the large entrance doors. They've been haphazardly left open, swaying slightly from the strong gusts of wind, grating on the concrete. Right on time, Pauly exits the doors, removing a pack of smokes from his back pocket.

"What the fuck?" The big man is shocked by the sight of strangers on the East Mountain, until his eyes land on Ray's familiar face. "What the hell are you people doing here?" Michael is about to answer when Ray angrily speaks up

"We are here to stop this madness, to take the Jabberwock home."

"Yea? Well keep looking. It isn't in here."

"You're lying."

"Why don't you come see for yourselves?"

They follow Pauly down the main corridor to the command center. Since the engineers and the girls fled, it's been only Pauly, nursing a wounded, depressed, and drunk Vaughn. Pauly knows firsthand what the creature is capable of; he knows that it's lurking on the mountain, vengeful. He's actually relieved to see other people. William Vaughn, however, not so much.

"You people came a long way. What was your end game, exactly?" he asks.

"We were going to take the Jabberwock with us. Whether you liked it or not," Ray tells Vaughn with authority.

"Really?" Vaughn laughs, "So this was like a rescue mission? You folks from New Jersey really are crazy."

"You can insult us all you want," Michael adds, "but we felt that you weren't prepared to properly care for the creature. Judging from the mess in here and those wounds on both of you guys, we were right."

"And you're the expert because you saw it one time? Judging from your own words in that stupid book, you're nothing more than a pill popping drunk."

"You know, there was a time when I'd probably punch you in the face for that, but I have a family waiting for me back home. Plus, your henchman looks pretty scary."

"Personal assistant," Pauly inserts.

"Got it," Michael quips back.

"Well, I would love to have this stand-off with you boys all day. But, to me, it looks like y'all are trespassing on private property. So, I would pissoff," Vaughn says, taking a swig from a bottle of whiskey.

"One last thing," Ray demands. "What do you know about the murder of Lonnie Wilkes? The forest fire? The cave?"

In an instant, the air is sucked from the room. Michael and Mack glance at each other with worry in their eyes. The expression on Vaughn's face changes, as well as Pauly's, who reaches toward the back of his belt and runs up on Ray. He wields his Desert Eagle, pressing the muzzle against Ray's forehead.

"I suggest you mind your own business, old man," Pauly says harshly.

Michael plants himself between the two men, using his own head to nudge the gun away from Ray's. He shoves his father-in-law back a few feet, and locks eyes with Pauly. He recognizes something in them. Something that only seeing the impossible can bring out of a man. Pauly removes the muzzle from Michael's head, then drops the gun down to his side.

"My good people," Mack announces, "no need for all these dramatics. As of this moment, we are outie-five-thousand. My boss, god bless him. He's a wonderful man, but easily susceptible to ugly rumors."

As Michael leads him to the exit, Ray battles with every inch of his being to stop himself from telling Mack to shut up, then physically assaulting the bastard who just jammed a gun into his face.

"We're basically back in Jersey already," Mack adds. "Good luck, Godspeed, and all that."

They hit the exit doors, rush down the corridor, and back out into the yard. Ray shouts, asking Michael what the hell he was thinking by getting in front of the gun like that.

"He wasn't going to pull the trigger. That guy is fed up with Vaughn. I could feel it," Michael answers.

"Are you a damn psychic? That man would've made my baby girl a widow, without another thought on the matter."

"Then what the fuck were you provoking them for?" It's the first time Michael has ever raised his voice to his father-in-law. Ray can't deny his point.

"Language," Ray says. "I suppose you're right though. It was a bad move. What do we do now?"

"I say we make our way back to the RV and go home."

"Then why the hell did we come here?"

"I don't know. Perhaps we regroup, come back another day. We found him once, we can find him again."

"The Jabberwock belongs in New Jersey."

"So do we, Ray."

Mack looks towards the pale moon, high against the blue of day. Soon it'll be dark, nothing to guide them back to the RV but a few flashlights.

"We're losing daylight fast, and we've pissed off crazy guys with guns. I gotta side with Mike here. We should go, like now, Ray."

"Okay. We will follow the tire tracks to the base of the mountain. It's where we parked, the only road out of here. Plus, we're moving downhill; it should cut our hike time in half. Can you keep up, Mack?"

"I'll try like hell, Chief."

"Good. Let's go."

Penny spent the rest of the morning, and most of the afternoon, with Dr. Marvin at the police station. They explained the situation and presented the evidence.

Come to find out, the FBI has been building a case on William Vaughn for the better part of five years. Some shady business practices here, tax evasion there. Typical slime ball stuff. The recording on Dr. Marvin's phone will be enough to do Vaughn in. Not even his personal team of cutthroat lawyers will be able to stop this one.

Penny absorbed as much information as she could, but her mind was elsewhere. Every few minutes she placed her cell on her lap, under the police chief's desk, and pressed her husband's name. It's next to a photo of him and Josie hugging on a carousel, huge smiles on their faces. She never got a response; still, she kept pressing.

"Where will you go now?" Penny asks Dr. Marvin as they leave the station.

"I have a room at the motel. First thing in the morning, I'm heading home to Maine. I miss my wife something awful." The biologist senses that his words hit Penny harder than he intended. "I'm so sorry. Still haven't heard back from them?"

"No."

"I wish there was something I could do."

"It's okay. I'll be fine."

"Well, you have my number. If you need me tonight, please don't hesitate."

"Thank you, Dr. Marvin."

"Please. Call me Lee." Penny extends her hand, but Lee pulls her in for a hug. "I would love to meet your husband and father one day. Perhaps I'll treat for dinner. We can chat about Mister Leeds over some Surf and Turf."

Penny laughs through her tears, then watches the old scientist walk to his beat up Saab, double parked in the officers' lot. She leaves the station and heads to school to pick up Josie. On the ride home, Penny tries her hardest to shield her emotions from her inquisitive daughter. It's not working.

"Mommy, what's wrong?"

"Nothing, baby, just allergies."

"You miss Daddy, don't ya?"

124

"I do. He'll be home really soon, though."

"Yep. With my dragon!"

"Hey, Josie. Have you talked to Daddy's Daddy lately?"

"No. He told me was going to the green castle for a while."

They stop at a red light. Penny is scared, and frustrated. She's frustrated with this world of mysterious forest monsters, and ghost-in-laws. She's almost frustrated enough to ask her four-year-old daughter to summon the dead, to see if Daddy's Daddy has any intel on her stubborn-ass husband and father, when her phone rings.

It's Michael.

Chapter 26

Mack is trudging across the forest floor, stomping on branches and leaves as he moves. His eyes are locked on the RV's brake lights.

How could they leave me?

They were supposed to be in this thing together. He stops for a moment, trying to catch his breath, his heart beating heavily. He looks toward the ground at his bare feet. They are huge, covered in a mangy layer of thick hair. His nails are long and jagged. He lifts his hands up; his fingernails are the same. He doesn't have time to ponder it; the lights are getting away from him. He starts to move quicker than ever, swinging his arms to and fro, a deep rumble emanating from his chest. His chase is not enough. The brake lights vanish. Mack hears the snap of a twig to his side. He glances over his shoulder at a man with a camera, a huge telephoto lens pointed right at him.

"Mack, wake up. Wake up, man."

Mack opens his eyes to Michael hovering over him. They're somewhere around Albany, half way through their ride home. They've pulled the RV off the highway to a picnic area neighboring a rest stop.

"Where the hell are we?"

"Upstate New York. You need to come out here."

Mack follows Michael out into the picnic area. The only light in the area is across a large parking lot, gleaming from the rest stop. There's a row of semi-trucks idling in the lot; on top of the closest trailer, basking in the soft glow of the moon, is the Jersey Devil.

He's hunched over, blanketing himself in his large wings, peering towards the men. His eyes glow red each time a headlight from the highway catches them.

"Holy shit," Mack says softly, in a state of complete wonderment. "Is that him?"

"That's him," Ray responds.

"We were walking out of the rest stop when we noticed something big in the sky," Michael explains. "We circled around to this picnic area, trying to keep an eye on him - trying not to bring any attention to ourselves. We parked out here, and he landed up there."

"Do you think he's following us?" Mack asks.

"Sure looks like it," answers Michael.

126

A husky truck driver exits the cabin of one of the nearby semis. The creature doesn't move an inch, as the trucker gazes over toward the trio of bewildered men, trying their best to act normal.

"Howdy," Michael says to the man. "Beautiful night. Huh?"

"Not bad," the trucker answers. "What y'all doing over there? Having a picnic?"

"Yea, you know. Why not take in this lovely evening?"

The trucker looks them over again. It's a sticky situation. It'll get much stickier if the man decides to gaze up towards the top of the trailer.

"That's a beautiful RV y'all got there. I'd love to look inside, if you'd have me."

He's lingering a bit too long.

"No can do," Ray answers. "Kids are asleep. If they wake up it's going to be a long ride back to New Jersey."

"Shit, you got that right," the man scans the RV one last time. "Well, you folks have a good night. Safe travels."

He walks across the lot, towards the rest area. The creature moves his head slightly to watch. His tail whips for the first time since the stranger came onto the scene.

"We should go, that was too close for comfort," Michael whispers. "Mack, you good?"

"I don't know. I think I may puke."

"I know the feeling. Let's get back in the Falcon."

They cautiously make their move back to the door of the RV, never taking their eyes off the creature. Ray and Michael enter, while Mack stops and looks towards it.

He recalls a coloring book he received on his seventh birthday. Each page was dedicated to a state, and the legendary monster that resides there. "The Lizard Man of Scape Ore Swamp" was South Carolina, "Chessie" was Maryland, and so forth; but, it was always the devil from New Jersey that Mack kept flipping back to. The image in that coloring book stuck with him. It wasn't far off from the very real thing staring at him now. Mack smiles and waves in the direction of the creature. He acknowledges the man's gesture with a slight tilt of his head.

Ray takes the wheel and turns the Falcon around, toward the exit ramp. Mack and Michael are peering out the side windows, keeping watch. As they exit onto the highway, they spot the creature unfurling his wings then leaping into the air. He zigzags through a line of trees, then ascends until he's bathed in darkness.

"We lost him," Mack says excitedly.

"I don't think so. He's there," Michael assures him.

"How do you know?"

"Just a hunch."

Ray has insisted on driving duty for the remainder of the trip. He says it's because he's "in the zone" but really he wants the younger guys to have this moment. Ray has seen the creature again and now, for him, it's good enough knowing that the Jabberwock is on its way home.

They continue down a long stretch of highway. The monstrous structures of industry make way for trees and lakes as they near New Jersey. Now and again, they wonder if the occasional spot in the sky is the creature, trying to keep pace with the RV. They pass a sign welcoming them back to their home state and soon after, merge onto Route 206.

"I'm gonna get high. It's a celebration," Mack proclaims.

Within minutes, the man is passed out. Between the hike, the marijuana use, and the shock of seeing the Jersey Devil, Michael is surprised Macaulay made it this far. He gently removes the bong from the sleeping man's grip and places it on a table near him. He makes his way toward the front of the RV.

"We did it," Michael says, as he places his hand on his father-in-law's shoulder, and looks through the windshield. "The Jersey Devil is home."

"Indeed he is," Ray says, "I want to thank you, Mike."

"For what?"

"Getting in front of that gun."

"You would have done the same for me. It's all good; soon those assholes will be in prison."

They follow a road of sugar sand circling a small lake. The moon is peaking through a line of tall oak trees, reflecting off the water. Ray and Michael exit the RV and inhale the scent of the Pine Barrens, as cicadas serenade them with a familiar tune. The men wait, instinctively looking towards the sky, hoping to see the creature a final time. Perhaps a fly-by, some acknowledgement of the journey they've been on. After a few minutes, and no sign of the creature, Michael turns to Ray and asks him what he thinks.

"I think it's time to go home. You have some girls that are missing ya."

Josie's princess night light has been relocated from her bedroom to the foyer. Its soft pink glow greets Michael as he enters, along with a handwritten note.

There's spaghetti and meatballs in the fridge. We tried to stay up. Love, Mommy and Josie

He follows the sea turtle's waves, to find Penny sleeping with Josie in her bed. He stands in the doorway and absorbs the moment. The adrenaline rush of the day wears off, as he tries to focus his tired eyes on his family, amidst the cavalcade of blue light.

How could any of this be real? Did he fall asleep one night in Los Angeles and dream all of it? From the moment his mother called him with news of his father's death, to this moment, now. A father himself, standing over his family, in the warm, safe place he calls home. What he knows for sure is that if it is a dream, he's going to ride it out. See where it takes him. New Jersey devils, guardian angels. He welcomes all of it.

He removes a fluffy, teal dragon from his backpack, and places it near Josie. She stirs slightly and wraps it in her arms, pulling it close. Just then, Penny's eyes open.

"You're home," she whispers.

"I'm home."

Michael crawls slowly under the comforter and reaches his arm across his girls. Penny's hand finds his.

"I love you," she says.

"I love you, too. Very much."

Chapter 27

A few months ago, William Vaughn's company headquarters in Manhattan was teeming with life. Employees on every level, rushed around, excited about the project opening in Philadelphia.

Now, it's desolate.

Hip, abstract paintings hang on the walls in the lounge area, with no one there to admire them. A fluorescent sign, bearing the company logo, glows brightly, pointlessly.

Samantha, a twenty-five-year-old secretary, makes her way through the place with a bag of Japanese takeout in her hand. She's the only employee who still comes to the building. She and Vaughn had a romantic relationship a few years back. She still cares for him; she's possibly still in love with him. After a few knocks on the last door, at the end of a long hallway, an exhausted voice shouts, "Who is it?" from the other side.

"It's Sam. I have dinner."

He lets her in. The place is a disaster area. Even more so than the last time she was there, two nights prior. Worse, it appears all the alcohol from the mini bar has been consumed. Vaughn is in nothing but a Turkish bath robe, with a monogram of his initials stitched in the breast. He stands with his back towards her, at a floor to ceiling window. It's nighttime; the city looks beautiful from the twenty eighth floor.

"Billy," she says softly, "the attorneys have been trying to reach you. Paul was arrested this afternoon. They say you don't have much time."

He stares blankly at the sea of lights. His chiseled jaw, once his defining feature, is cloaked by an unkempt beard.

"Billy - "

"They're getting much worse."

"The night terrors?"

He turns to her. There's nothing going on behind his light green eyes. "Yes," he sobs, "I don't know when I'm dreaming. When it's real. Lonnie Wilkes came here today."

"Who?"

"The man I...the man who they say I killed. He had a hole in his head. He bled all over the office." She looks around her, confused and frightened. "Do you see the blood?

"No, Billy. It's just a nightmare."

"Leave me be."

She feels a sadness tearing at her chest. A sadness for the man she once adored.

"Please, just eat with me. I got you all your favorite rolls. And some seaweed salad."

"Seaweed salad," he says with a chuckle, then continues to gaze over the city.

"Okay. Forget this. I have a boyfriend wondering why the hell I still come here. I tried, William. Can't say I didn't try." She darts toward the doors.

"Samantha."

She stops and whips around. "What?"

"Thank you."

She leaves, closing the door behind her.

Vaughn looks over the city one more time. It's where he has stood night after night for many years. Whether it was with Pauly, or a business associate, or one of several women like Samantha, it's always been about contemplating something that resembles world domination.

He takes a seat on his throne-like chair, looking at the only framed photo on his gigantic marble desk. It's of him in Africa, a long rifle in his hands, kneeling behind a slain male lion. He closes his eyes.

A knock on the door.

"Samantha, go home!"

The knock again. This time louder. It continues. Again and again. He springs up from his chair and approaches the door, swinging it open when he gets to it.

It's his father.

But, not really. It's a deformed, misshapen version of his father. The abomination begins to scream. It's the same bellowing Vaughn heard many nights at Fort Green. Vaughn is so frightened by what's before him, he flies backward, slamming the door shut, and launching himself over the desk, back onto the chair. He jerks open the drawer near his lap and removes the Desert Eagle, shoving the barrel into his mouth and pulling the trigger.

Samantha hears the gunshot from the lounge area and rushes back to the office. She finds William Vaughn slouched in his chair. The back of his head is still smoking. His brains are on the window pane.

For the remainder of summer, and well into autumn, large crowds continued to flock to the Jersey Devil Museum. The Nearys had to up their staff and expand their hours. Mack was given a raise but still lives in the RV. They've started construction on another addition to the building, which will house a new exhibit.

Dr. Lee Marvin, along with his wife Betty, did end up having dinner with the Nearys and Ray. They chatted for hours, through the night, long after Josie went to bed. With several bottles of wine finished, they mulled over pages and pages of Dr. Marvin's notes, compiled during his work at Fort Green.

The idea behind the new exhibit, 'Science and Mister Leeds' was born that evening. It's being billed as "A unique look into the biology behind a one-of-a-kind creature."

It's a week before Christmas. The first snowfall of the season has dusted the cemetery. Michael, Penny, and Josie are visiting Daddy's Daddy. Josie makes her stuffed dragon, now named Mister Leeds, climb up and down on the headstone. Michael is holding his wife's hand, speaking quietly, in his mind, to his father. There's so much to tell him, but Michael can't help feeling like he already knows.

"Hey Josie. Have you seen Daddy's Daddy lately?

"No. He had to go someplace else," she answers, flying Mister Leeds off the stone, then spinning him in a circle.

"Where did he go?" Penny asks.

"He doesn't tell me everything, Mommy."

Michael and Penny look at each other and smile.

"I think I want to leave Mister Leeds here with him," Josie says, placing the stuffed dragon on top of the stone.

Michael asks, "Are you sure, baby? You take it everywhere with you."

"I'm sure."

The family makes their way back to the SUV. Michael lifts Josie into her car seat, then straps her in. As he makes his way around to the driver's side, he stops for a moment and looks toward his father one more time.

The fluffy dragon is perched perfectly on the stone. Behind it, a string of colorful lights decorate a front porch, as the sun sets in the purple sky.

A BAD MOON

I.

The day before a bad moon is the worst.

The stomach pain, the twisting and turning of my insides. It doesn't matter how much I've eaten during the lunar phase, I usually find myself curled up in a bed, sick with hunger.

Today is no exception.

Other than a strip of the afternoon sun creeping in under the heavy curtains, the only light in the room is from the television set. I crave the darkness. The slightest bit of anything brighter than the TV and the world's most terrible migraine will ensue, followed by a puking fit that could rival a college kid, after an all-night bender. A pretty brunette is on the screen, breaking the news about the President and his unsavory connection to a porn star. This is music to my ears. The more the twenty-four hour news cycle resembles a circus, the better I feel about my particular affliction.

In preparation for the struggle of the day, I usually gorge myself the evening before. Last night I ventured across the highway from my motel and had dinner at a sports bar. A cheesesteak, twelve Buffalo wings and French fries seasoned with Old Bay. I washed it down with a few beers and a tall rum and coke. The bartender was a muscle-bound guy named Chad.

I shit you not. Chad.

He was the star of the show happening exclusively inside of his overgrown cranium. Most of the patrons seemed to be used to him, with his unsettlingly squared jaw and ugly forearm tattoos. The group consisted of regulars, with the addition of three college girls and myself. Chad seemed thrilled to have some people to serve besides middle-aged couples and lonely bachelors. He chatted us up about a litany of stuff you're not supposed to talk about at a bar. I guess Chad didn't read his job description.

As the night progressed, he became more comfortable with attempting to get a rise out of the trio of young ladies, at my expense. Standing a couple of inches over six feet, with a stocky build and lumberjack's beard, he wasn't necessarily wrong about my "scary" appearance. He definitely wasn't wrong about the inordinate amount of food I was eating either.

Fair enough.

I smiled and laughed through it all. Even as the girls stopped humoring him and began to retreat into their own thing, I gave Chad the benefit of the doubt. If it ceased at the jabs against my looks and my meal, I may have even given him a pass. But at some point he got it into his head that I was some old, washed up poser trying to be down. I had mentioned to the girls that I dabbled in rap music back in high school. From there, it became "homie" this and "homie" that. He even brought up Vanilla Ice.

Grave mistake.

I continued to converse with him, never hinting at the fact that his shtick had started to wear thin. "So, you work here every night?" I asked.

"Nah, man. A couple of nights a week. Just to pay the bills. Like I told these ladies, my food truck is about to take off. Fish tacos, couscous. Real food, not like the garbage we serve here," he said, nodding toward my empty plates.

Every remark he made felt designed to insult me in some way. It was likely because the ladies were interested in the hungry stranger sitting next to them, rather than the loudmouth bartender. The more he vied for their attention, the more they whispered to me, genuinely interested in the little I had to say. Chad was my main focus of concern, though. "I'm in town for the next few nights. I may want another cheesesteak tomorrow. You here?"

"Yessir. I get here for the night crowd, work until close. Same as today."

"What time is that?"

"Usually around six. Damn, homie. You trying to take me out on a date? I'm not usually into white rappers."

I feigned a laugh as he glanced toward the girls. They were no longer paying the poor bastard any mind. I said my goodbyes to the girls as they playfully jeered my exit. The outgoing one shouted from her stool.

"You sure you don't want to join us? We're going dancing!" Unfortunately, cutting a rug was not in the cards for me.

Before I headed back across the highway to the motel, I strolled over to the employee lot to take a peek into the window of a souped-up Honda Civic. The gym bag and comically large tub of protein powder gave Chad up instantly. It appeared that we would be having that date after all.

My throat is starting to dry. For many years, I tried to combat the dryness by a continuous consumption of liquid. Anything I could get: rain, lake water, the last few drops in discarded fast food cups. Nowadays I let it come. I let it all come, even the stomach pain. I no longer try to numb it with marijuana or alcohol or pills. I learned that welcoming the pain is the only successful approach.

Before the hunger takes over completely, I try to gather the charred remains of my humanly thoughts. They're being replaced by a surge of amplified scents and sounds, a kind of sensory overload.

I used to bellow in agony and tear at my skin, flailing my body around as if some invisible force had me locked in a wrestling ring, fighting a very one-sided bout. Now I'm able to lie almost entirely still as the transformation takes place. I chalk it up to the strand of years in my twenties when I practiced mindful meditation; although, I can't be sure.

When the transformation is complete, I lunge to the door of my room and head out; an unforgettable image for whoever's headlights catch me sprinting across the highway.

I circle the place with the good cheesesteaks and crouch behind the dumpster in the back, along the edge of the woods. Right on time Chad pulls up in his Civic and approaches the back door of the building. The waitress I met last night welcomes him. A short, sweet girl with a nose ring and streak of purple in her dirty blonde hair. She lights a cigarette for Chad. Wow, Mr. Couscous smokes, interesting development. They share a laugh about something, most likely one of Chad's terrible jokes.

C'mon girl, go back inside.

Although I'm several yards away, my bowels make a thunderous noise, loud enough that I'm afraid they've heard me. The hunger continues to grow. There is nothing but the hunger. It's about to get really messy, really fast, if this girl doesn't go back inside and wait on her goddamn tables. She flicks the smoke to the ground and steps on it. Chad is still working on his.

Finish it up, Chad. Savor it.

The waitress opens the door and lets the kitchen noise spill out for a moment, before closing it behind her and leaving Chad by himself.

Time to bring the ruckus.

I dash toward the man and see his face. The face I've seen many times before. The face of unparalleled fear.

Chad instinctively throws a right hook, God bless him. I clutch him by the forearm and strike, the jagged edges of my nails puncturing the flesh of his thick chest. He attempts to scream but I take my free hand and jam it into his mouth, ripping downward and dislocating his jaw. I pick him up off his feet and toss him about half way toward the dumpster. Time is my enemy.

This has already taken longer than I planned. If someone were to come out of the kitchen, or from around the side of the building, that would mean more eyewitness accounts. I'd get away, but I can't afford anymore eyewitness accounts.

Chad struggles the entire way as I drag him by his head a mile or two into the dense forest. He's a tough son of a bitch, I'll give him that. When I feel like I'm far enough away from the highway, I snap his neck and begin my feast.

It's better than any sex I've ever had. Any high. Every fleshy limb, every organ. Even the junkies I've devoured, their pieces had a bitter taste to them but still, miraculous. Chad is especially delicious. It takes a bit longer than usual to finish off the big guy, but when I'm done, there is nothing left but his skeletal system on the forest floor.

When I'm back to my common form, I'll bury his bones. But for now, I sleep - drenched in blood with a full belly. Under the beautiful moon, I sleep.

1997. Summer in New Jersey.

A new Wu-Tang Clan album has dropped and a flu-stricken Michael Jeffrey Jordan just scored thirty-eight points on the Utah Jazz, winning game five of the NBA Finals. Jack Sharpe, legal driver for a mere seven days, clutches the wheel of his 1989 Dodge Daytona, hugging the shoulder of the road, as he drives to his best friend Robert's house.

The windows are open, allowing the sticky summer wind to invade the car. Jack's head unit is newly installed, his CD booklet has reached maximum capacity. School is out and he barely made it through.

On the other side of town, Mrs. Valentini shouts, "Rob, run down to Wawa and get me a frankfurter and some cigarettes!"

"What the fuck?"

"What was that, sweetheart?"

"Nothing, Ma." Rob tosses his PlayStation controller down on the bedroom floor, then smacks Christopher's out of his hands. "Let's go. Maybe she'll give me a few extra bucks. We can get some snacks and shit."

"What about Jack?" Christopher asks.

"He'll see us on the way. It's hot as shit out there, I can't be walking that far anyway."

Jack spots two familiar figures under the streetlight up ahead. He knows exactly who they are when he hears Rob's familiar voice, "Pick us up, bitch boy!"

Jack swerves the Daytona to the curb and lets the boys in. Rob calls "Shotgun!" as the new Wu-Tang is playing low from the speakers. He immediately grabs the dial. "Gotta turn this shit up, son!"

"What's going on, man?" Christopher asks, over the bass heavy production. Jack extends his arm over the back of the passenger seat, exchanging a pound with his friend.

"MJ just threw down forty points with a temperature of one hundred and four," Jack answers.

"That's bullshit," Rob says. "Total bullshit. I bet he had a stuffy nose and that's it. You should probably think about removing his dong from your mouth."

"I have something to tell you guys," Jack says, as he adjusts the volume.

"You're gay. I knew it. He's gay." Rob jokes.

"This is important, bro."

"Okay. We have to hit up Wawa for Ma Dukes though. Turn this piece of shit around and tell us on the way." Jack pulls into the apartment, then follows the lot back out to the street.

"I'm kinda talking to Wendy," Jack says.

Christopher has been there every step of the way for his friend's unrequited love affair with Wendy Pierce. Every glance in the hallway, every shared drink at a house party; the tiny moments that seem so huge in this type of situation. He is sincerely happy for his boy. Rob, not so much.

"What the fuck, bro? This was supposed to be our summer!"

"It will be, man. Chill. They're just talking," Christopher insists. "This is a beautiful thing."

"Yea, beautiful. What about finishing an album? What about doing some open mics? Women weaken legs, bro. Haven't you learned anything from Rocky?" The Daytona is idling in the Wawa lot as the boys continue.

"Rob, dude. I am a white kid from the sticks, recording on a dual cassette deck. C'mon."

"Well, I guess that settles it. We give up."

"Jesus. The drama. Let's just go in here and get a few slushies, maybe some Hot Fries. We'll hit the video store on the way back. It'll be a nice night," Christopher says.

"Let him rent something with his new bitch," Rob says, as he exits the vehicle, "I'm gonna go in here and kill myself."

Christopher leans over the passenger seat's headrest. "He's just being stupid. Man, I am so stoked for you. Didn't she just go to the prom with Matt Moretti though?"

"That shit was arranged. Their dads are friends. She told me she can't stand that guy."

"Well, he is the biggest douchebag on the planet. I can't believe you finally nabbed her, bro."

"She's not mine quite yet. We're just talking."

"Wendy Pierce," Christopher says to himself, with a hint of jealousy.

"I know. Right?"

III.

"We've been following you for a long time," the familiar stranger says to me as I come to. "You're getting sloppy. Two miles from the highway?"

I've spotted his bun of receding silver hair from a distance these past couple of months at places like truck stops, campgrounds, and motels. This time however, he's up close and way too personal.

"Who are you?" I'm barely able to ask. I'm barely able to do much at all. The soreness in my limbs is unbearable and I have what feels like the work of a concrete mixer in my stomach.

"My name isn't important. What's important is that you're with friends now," he answers.

Judging by the two goons behind him clutching rifles, each with their fair share of face and neck ink, I assume he's lying. There's a big, flushed face guy, and a short, pale one.

A real life *Ren and Stimpy.*

"As you can see, I'm in no condition to entertain company right now," I say, as I attempt to get to my feet, falling ass first onto a tree stump. "Please let me get on my way."

"Come on, boss. Our van is just over here. We have some fresh clothing and a pillow and blanket. It's a two hour drive but you'll be comfortable. Then, when we get to where we are going, you'll have a shower and a bed. It'll be much better than whatever plan you have in mind."

"That sounds great," I answer, "but no thanks."

"Oh, are you under the impression that this is a choice?" Ren and Stimpy brandish their firearms. "Did he have a choice?" Man Bun motions toward the remains of Chad, lying beside me in the underbrush. "You're coming with us."

I've been in some sticky situations before, but not quite as sticky as this one. I take another look at the men, totally at ease with their rifles, grins on their tattooed faces. Beyond them, through a thick patch of trees, is what I assume is their van. I lock eyes with Man Bun, damn near hovering over me.

The fact is, I don't have anywhere to go. If half of what this guy says is true, it probably is better than whatever I had planned. I agree to follow them to the van and I'm fairly shocked to find exactly what the man promised in the back. He informs me that the three of them would be sitting upfront and that I should use the ride to rest. He also explains that he understands the

140

situation that my bowels are in and "one of the boys" would accompany me to a rest stop if need be.

"Just knock, and we'll pull over. Don't shit back here. I've heard bartenders are a mess coming out."

"How do you know?"

"Like I said, you're getting sloppy."

My digestive system is in chaos. The worn out pillow and blanket are doing nothing to ease the ride. Every bump in the road hits me like a shotgun blast. The day after a feast is always hell, but this is a brand I've never experienced. I'm about to knock on the wall of the van when it stops moving and the engine turns off. The back door swings open to reveal the three men.

As I exit and scan the surrounding trees, I get a sudden feeling that we are in the middle of nowhere. The ride changed about thirty minutes in, from somewhat smooth with the occasional bump, to the herky-jerky ride of a dirt road. I come around the front of the van and look upon a nondescript, warehouse-like building.

"Welcome to the Silver Compound," Man Bun says, while the goons keep their rifles trained on me.

Inside, it's like a church vomited in a pristine waiting room of an asylum. I sit on a leather sofa and wait to meet Mr. Silver, as an extremely detailed Jesus hangs on the wall before me. Thin canals of blood flow, from where the thorns of a crown pierce his head, down to his ankles. Nails travel through the chunky flesh of his feet, straight into the wooden cross.

I have to take a shit. And fast.

Stimpy instructs me to follow him to the laboratory. I barely make it onto the pot before there is an eruption of flatulence, followed by what can only be described as the sound of cannon balls falling into a kiddie pool. I imagine the goons are sharing a good laugh just outside the door. I give a few courtesy flushes, and a few more, so I don't clog the damn thing with toilet paper. There's a knock on the door.

"I'm almost done," I shout. "A little privacy!"

"Hurry the fuck up!" Stimpy responds.

After I wash up, I gather myself and open the door to find Man Bun, the goons, and another man I recognize from TV. His face looks even more doll-like in person. Shiny and tight from years of facelifts and whatever other surgeries they make reality shows about.

"Hello," he says. "Please, take a seat. You must have a lot of questions."

I sit back down on the sofa; *Wayne Newton face* takes a seat across from me. The rest of the guys stand around him like sentries, as he asks if I know who he is.

"Teddy Silver. The televangelist," I croak.

"I don't really like that term. I would say I am a spiritual leader. The country's foremost Christ Warrior, to be exact."

Besides the fact that I've been kidnapped, and this jackass seems to be behind it, his botched plastic surgery and general smugness is not very endearing. He asks if he may tell me a story, and I imagine if I declined, it wouldn't matter a damn bit; so, I give him a shrug.

"I was born Theodore Drake and, as a young man, I was chosen by the Lord to be his servant. It wasn't until my thirties, however, that I would find my true purpose in this world," he continues, folding his legs and taking a sip from his water bottle. I could tell this guy enjoys pontificating. "You see, it was then a woman named Hannah came into my life. She was the most adventurous and beautiful soul I had ever met and I was going to make her my wife. A week before our wedding day, Hannah and her two best friends went on a hiking trip. I would later find out that the area they were making camp at was known for a legend; a legend about werewolves. Can you believe that? Werewolves."

Something lurches in my stomach.

"In the middle of the first night of their trip, they were attacked. The following morning, another group of hikers discovered them. There was nothing much left of Hannah's friends but, as they searched the site a little bit further, they heard something. They followed the noise to find my darling Hannah, with most of her lower body missing. The rest of her was twisted and bloody. By the time the authorities arrived, she was gone."

I manage to utter "I'm sorry" as he dissects me with his unfeeling blue eyes.

"It's quite alright. I bet you were only a boy back then. You see, it's not personal. This world has gone awry. The gays and the transgenders. It was only a matter of time until something like your kind came along. And when you did, oh man, you left people in your wake." He stands up, takes a last swig, then tosses the empty bottle into a nearby trash can. "Not anymore. That purpose I mentioned, that purpose is to rid this world of Satan's creation. Rid it of you."

I think about July Fourth a few years back. Swimming in a lake somewhere, by myself, the reflection of distant fireworks on the dark water. Or the Christmas Eve I spent with milk, cookies, and a suicidal stripper named Cashmere, in a motel room overlooking a beautifully lit spruce tree. Ah yea, all of the dusty motels I've rested my head in, all the prostitutes and nomads I've met. It all makes me laugh.

"Is something funny?" Silver asks.

"Just my life," I answer.

"I'm glad you can laugh about your life. The remainder of it may not be as funny."

"Listen, man. If you plan on killing me, get it over with. I've dealt with much worse than death." Silver turns to his henchmen and shares a chuckle. I'm at the whim of these zealots and it really starts to piss me off. "I see a lot of religious shit around here. Is it very Christ like to hold people against their will?"

"People? You are no person. You are an abomination, and I do plan on killing you. Just not yet."

"When?"

"In about twenty-nine days. When the moon is high in the sky. See, I like to watch it happen. The thrashing, the tearing at the skin. So much pain and suffering. I can only imagine what it's like for you. Then, just about when there is no human being left to be found, I'll put a silver bullet right between your eyes."

There was this primetime special a few years back. It covered the questionable ways Teddy Silver built his empire. Manipulating God-fearing people, preying on those fears of damnation and using their donations to fund his own personal interests. I decide to start hitting back for no other reason than fuck this guy.

"This isn't some big arena, Teddy. It's just you and me and your boys. You can keep it real. Do you even believe all this Christ Warrior nonsense you spew? Or do you know, deep down, it's all just a farce?"

His taut face manages a joker's smile. That didn't land like I anticipated. Let's try another.

"I feel bad about what happened to your fiancée, I really do. However, judging from the very short time I've known you, it seems like the pack saved her from a lifetime of misery."

The last thing I remember before the lights go out is Teddy standing up, snatching the rifle from his goon's hands, and smashing me across the bridge of my nose with the buttstock.

"What are you into?" Jack inquires, as he and Wendy shuffle through the New Releases section of Sam Goody.

"I like all kinds of stuff," Wendy answers.

"Yea, but what are you really into? I'm a Hip Hop guy."

"I know, Jack. You and your friends play it, really loudly, at every party. That kind of music is a little too aggressive for me."

"Well, what should we play next time?"

"I like No Doubt, TLC, Janet. My sisters and I rock out to the Spice Girls."

"The Spice Girls? Oh man."

"Don't judge."

"Do you like this?" Jack points to the overhead speakers playing "Name" by the Goo Goo Dolls. Wendy nods her head and sings along.

"...you could hide beside me, maybe for a while, and I won't tell no one your name, I won't tell 'em your name...,"

She shares a bashful smile with him, just enough to expose her dimples.

"Yea, I like it too," Jack says.

Later on, while sharing a few slices in the food court, Wendy notices Jack studying her face.

"What is it, creeper?"

He's watched her across classrooms and from the stands at her field hockey games. He's even made her smile a time or two while they were amongst friends at a party. But here, while it's just the two of them, he starts to notice things he never has before. The splash of hazel every time the light reflects off her eyes - the different things her face does when she laughs.

"You're really pretty."

"I know," she says, playfully, as she shoots the wrapper off of her straw, hitting Jack in the face.

"Ouch. That could take out an eye."

"Shut up."

"So, want to catch a movie or something?"

"I can't. I need to get home. I was shocked my parents let me come at all."

Wendy's father, John Pierce, is the CEO of Pierce Construction, which allows her mother Margaret to commit to her full-time job of meddling in

Wendy and her sisters' business. Since they were very young, they've been pressed on their grades and whether they liked it or not, being involved in all things at school. Wendy is the middle child, between the oldest, Meryl, and Abby. She's also the natural overachiever of the trio, which allows her to do things like secretly convincing her mom to let her go on a mall outing with Jack Sharpe.

Jack's family life is a bit more unconventional. His dad, Marvin, is a jack of all trades and master of none. His mom, Gail, is a starving artist-slash-waitress. They've managed to make ends meet and provide for their only son, but it hasn't always been smooth sailing.

On the drive home, they chat about their aspirations after high school. As if Jack didn't feel out of his league already, Wendy informs him of which colleges she's been thinking about, and the constant debate in her mind on whether she wants to be a doctor or a civil rights lawyer.

"My main goal is to help people, but I also want to make enough money that I can travel," she explains. "My father isn't really into vacationing, so I've never really seen the world outside of Cedarwood, New Jersey."

"Man. I am such a freaking loser," Jack responds.

"Hey. Don't put yourself down."

"I mean, it's true. A rapper? Really? Rob and I have had these stupid plans for so long. When I hear about your plans, I realize how big of a joke mine are."

"They are not. I heard you rap at a party once. The way people were yelling out random words and you were going off of them, making a whole verse, right on the spot. That is an amazing talent."

"You were paying attention to that?"

"How couldn't I? You aren't exactly the quietest rapper in the room." He's been complimented a few times before but, coming from Wendy, it means something.

"We have like forty-five minutes left," Wendy says as she checks her wristwatch. "Want to get some ice cream?"

Jack turns the Daytona off of the turnpike and into the lot of Custard Kingdom. Tonight, like most summer nights, the place is jumping. Wendy and Jack make their way toward the end of the long line and discuss their options.

"It all sounds pretty good to me," Jack says, looking over the menu. "What are you thinking?"

"I kind of want a frozen chocolate banana."

"Something long and hard. Just the way Wendy Pierce likes it," the voice says from behind them. It belongs to Franky "Fats" LaRusso and he's getting punched on the shoulder by his best friend Matt Moretti.

"Hey Wendy," Matt says, ignoring Jack's presence.

"Hi," she says unenthusiastically, as she takes Jack by the arm. It's the first they've made contact, and it catches Jack off guard.

"I haven't seen you since the last day of school," Matt says. "What have you been up to?" He gazes at her arms, locked with Jack's.

"Just hanging out," she answers.

"On the wrong side of the tracks, by the looks of it," Fats chimes in.

"The wrong side of the tracks?" Jack chuckles. "What is this, the fucking Outsiders?"

"Watch your mouth, Sharpe," Fats snarls. Wendy tugs Jack by his arm and spins them away from the uninvited company.

"Let's just ignore them until we order. Then get out of here as fast as we can," Wendy whispers.

"That's not cool, Wendy," Matt says. "Come the end of August, I leave for Villanova. I was hoping we could hang out."

Cold shoulder.

"Wow, okay. I see how it is."

They polish off dessert back in the Daytona, as Jack asks Wendy what happened on prom night. "Let's just say guys like Matt don't hear the word 'no' too often," she explains.

The Pierce residence is a French Colonial sitting atop a hill at the end of a long, lantern-lit driveway. Jack and his friends refer to the area as "Mount Richness" on their bike rides, so it's surreal to him as he coasts up the driveway and parks in front of the large home. The DJ on the radio station says, "Here's one by the Goo Goo Dolls," as "Name" begins to play. They can't help but laugh.

"I guess this is our song now," Wendy says.

"I guess so."

Like many sad sacks before him, Jack contemplates the moment a bit too intensely and lets it vanish in the summer air.

"Well, thank you so much for tonight. Call me tomorrow," she says.

"Of course."

His new favorite song plays, as he watches to make sure she gets into the house. Her sisters come to the door in their pajamas, as a freshly groomed Golden Retriever makes its way onto the front porch. Wendy gives it a pat on the head, then turns to wave at Jack once more.

"Bye, Jack!" Abby shouts from the doorway.

Wendy shakes her head, laughing and shoving her little sister back into the house, closing the door behind them.

The Sharpe house sits back in the woods off the highway, a modest bungalow that "needs some work" like Marvin Sharpe always says. Marvin dropped out of community college to care for his father until his passing, then inherited the house. In 1980, he met an eccentric painter named Gail. A year later they had a shotgun wedding, welcomed Jack into the world, and have lived in the house ever since. Jack pulls up to find his father swinging on the front porch bench, sipping a beer.

"How's the Daytona running?" Marvin asks his son.

"Not bad. Shakes a little bit when I'm at a red light."

"That's all right. Something working itself out, is all. You'll be able to buy yourself a Mercedes Benz when your rapping takes off." Jack takes a seat on the bench next to his father, who reaches into the cooler next to him and removes two beers. "You in for the night?"

"Yea."

"Fantastic. Have a beer with your old man."

"Where's Ma?"

"Inside, asleep."

Marvin was somewhat of a functioning alcoholic for most of Jack's childhood. When the liquor wasn't making him miserable, it made him vibrant and talkative. A year ago, after a car accident almost killed him, he decided to cut back to a beer or two a night. He's been introverted and soft-spoken ever since.

They rock, sitting silently and taking in the balmy evening for about twenty more minutes. Jack occasionally sips his beer, wondering how his father drinks the revolting beverage so often.

"I'm going to bed. You can kill that last beer in the cooler if you want."

"Hey," Jack says, stopping his father at the front door. "How did you know Ma was, like, the one?"

"Oh man," he pauses for a moment to contemplate the question. "I guess it was when I realized there isn't nobody that could compete with her. When you find a gal like that, don't shit the bed."

"Thanks. Good advice, Dad."

"Anytime. Goodnight, bud."

V.

Four walls and an unforgiving cot. A toilet, smack dab in the middle or the room. Nothing to occupy my time but a Holy Bible that they were kind enough to throw at me two weeks ago. Three times a day, one of the goons brings me in some schmutz that vaguely resembles a meal, while the other stands in the doorway, keeping his rifle aimed at me. Man Bun lied about the damn shower. I still have Chad's dried guts stuck to my skin.

This has been my life for a month. To say I'm happy to see the full moon rise is a first, and an understatement. That said, I've been dreading this final day. The day of unrelenting hunger.

Stimpy brings me a peanut butter sandwich on a tray, along with a rotten apple and a glass of lukewarm water. Just like always, Ren is behind him, playing soldier.

"I need something more. This shit ain't cutting it today," I utter through the agonizing pain my insides are in.

"Sorry, we just finished the last of the pizza," Stimpy chuckles, then digs into his pocket. "Here, have a Tic Tac," he says, shoving a bunch in his mouth, then tossing the empty container at the floor in front of me. I'm in too much pain to be angry.

The hunger grows, until I can do nothing but curl up in the fetal position and sob. Before long, the torment becomes too much to bear and I pass out.

When I come to, I'm in the middle of an operating room. There's an upper tier with shadowy figures behind a pane of glass. It dawns on me that the Silver Compound is actually an old medical facility of some kind. The room I'm in must've been where surgeries took place, and the shadowy figures used to be students observing the procedures. That was a different time.

A different world.

I begin to feel the change take place. It starts in my finger and toe nails; they grow long and jagged, pulling my hands and feet with them. One by one, my limbs begin to stretch, my body hair spreads, becoming thick and coarse. My only hope is to stay as still as possible. Silver wants a show, but I ain't giving him one. The final, and worst, part of the transformation is my face. My mouth and jaw protrude into a snout-like shape, spreading my now incredibly sharp teeth almost out of their gums. Still, I lie on my back in silence, allowing it to come. Two of the figures disappear from behind the glass, I anticipate that they'll be checking if I'm dead.

I stay still. A six-foot-five lifeless wolf man.

Ren and Stimpy come rushing into the room, wielding their firearms. I haven't budged. Stimpy stands over me. I've studied this pudgy king of insults for a month. The way he gets off on having a rifle and being able to torture me because of it. The back acne and heavy perspiration. He's either on juice or, judging from some new found flab, used to be.

I doubt he has ever had one of us from the pack clutch him by the testicles and tear them away from his midsection, in one fell swoop.

I do just that, then bend my legs up toward my head and kick the ever living shit out of his rifle. It goes flying out of his grip as he bellows in pain. Ren, the younger, more timid of the duo, fires off a few shots; one narrowly misses me. I back roll to a standing position.

Before it can even register in his brain that he just watched his comrade's nuts sail across the room and he's staring down certain death, I charge in his direction, falling on top of him with my full body weight. I hear the snap, crackle, and pop of his spinal column, then smash his head against the concrete floor.

There's a couple more scumbags on my mind as I barrel through the doors. I hit a long corridor at full stride and follow the scent of cigars and aging, Caucasian body odor. Superhuman strength, speed, and senses; there are upsides to this affliction.

The trail leads me to a large window that looks out into the surrounding yard. I spot red taillights slicing through the night and continue to pick up speed in their direction, smashing through the thick pane of glass and into the chilly air. The car hits the dirt road and reaches a clip I can't possibly keep up with. About two miles away from the compound, I spot light pollution and begin to smell a whole host of new things. I deduce that civilization must be nearby and decide to give up on my pursuit, turn around then head back toward the compound.

When I return, Ren is already dead, while Stimpy is sitting against the wall, pressing a blood soaked towel against the spot where his man parts used to be. "I'm sorry," he cries. "Please. I have a son. Let me go. Please."

I could put him out of his misery, but I decide to eat his friend and make him watch the entire thing. When I'm done, I methodically approach him, as he begs for his life.

"Please. It was nothing personal. I just fell on some hard times. Mr. Silver took me in. He helped me. I can't die. My son. Please." I crouch down in front of him, my muzzle grazes the tip of his nose. I let him smell his friend on my breath. He turns his head away from me, crying like a baby.

When he finally finds the courage to open his eyes, I'll be gone. His life; my parting gift. He's a little less of a man now, so I hope it changes his wretched personality. Especially for his son's sake.

VI.

When Jack was five years old, Marvin mounted a backboard above the garage door. Through the years, they would play pick-up games when Marvin got home from work, or find themselves shooting around, debating the greatest baller of all time - Marvin's guy, Wilt Chamberlain or Jack's hero, Michael Jordan. Sometimes their discussions would turn a bit more serious - grades or financial struggles - but still, they would pass the rock to each other and talk it out in between jump shots.

Organized sports, however, were never Jack's thing. He loathed the idea of practice every night or competing in front of bleachers filled with rabid parents. Eventually, Marvin talked him into joining his school's team. Jack was never the star, but what he lacked in skill, he made up in toughness. A lot like Marvin, back in his day.

Marvin did his best to make it to games, but they were usually scheduled right around happy hour and after a long day of whatever job he had at the time, happy hour took precedence. Rob and Christopher, on the other hand, never missed a game. They had a front row seat to see how much it hurt their buddy every time he looked up at the stands and didn't see his father.

It was Jack's sophomore year, a couple of weeks before Christmas, when Marvin made a little too merry at the pub, tried to swerve around a deer on the drive home, and flipped his pickup truck. He was extremely lucky, escaping with only three cracked ribs, a broken arm, and a gang of scrapes and bruises; the accident took a bigger toll on Jack. He began to spend more time with his boys, his grades dropped, and he never tried out for the basketball team.

As time passed, Marvin began to heal, and it was the last night of his hospital stay when Jack broke the news. After school he walked to the hospital, like he did every day his father was laid up. In an attempt to soften the blow, he swung by Luigi's Pizza and picked up a pepperoni Stromboli, Marvin's favorite, and a two liter of Coke. When he entered the room, his mother was there with an easel set up. She was working on a picture of her husband in the bed.

"Hey Jacky," she said. "Did you bring dinner for us? How nice."

Jack wanted to be alone with his father when he told him, so he was annoyed that his mother was already there. He was also baffled by the painting.

"What is this, Ma?" He asked, nodding to the artwork.

"I wanted to capture the moment. A strong man, lying helpless in a hospital bed. The medical equipment juxtaposed with the shadows in the room. It's strangely beautiful. Don't you think?"

"Sure. Hey, Ma. Do you think I can be alone with Dad for a minute?"

Gail headed to the cafeteria to grab some coffee, giving the two men in her life some space. Jack placed the Stromboli on the tray and began to try to cut it into pieces.

"What is it, man?" Marvin asked.

"Dad, I uh. I never went out for the team."

"What? Why?"

"I'm not really feeling it this year."

"What? I thought you loved playing basketball."

"I do. In the driveway, with you or the guys. I'm just over putting in all this work. For nothing."

"It's not for nothing. It's a team sport. You're learning a lot of valuable lessons. Honestly, I'm a little disappointed in you, man." His father's reaction irked him, as he struggled to slice up the cheesy mess that the Stromboli had become.

"Yea, well, I'm disappointed in YOU," Jack snapped back, slamming the useless plastic knife back down on the tray. "How many games did you come to last season?"

"A bunch."

"Two, Dad. Two freaking games."

It was at that moment Marvin realized how much he had let his boy down. He sat quietly, as tears welled up in his eyes.

"I'm sorry that I'm getting bent out of shape," Jack continued, as his voice cracked and some tears of his own streamed down his face.

"No, I'm the one that's sorry. I'm out of control. I have been for a long time. This accident has put everything back in perspective for me. I'm going to do better, buddy. Starting right now, I'm going to do better."

They wiped their faces and without another word spoken to each other, began to eat the Stromboli. Gail got back to the room and immediately felt the tension.

"So are you boys going to tell me what I missed?"

154

Marvin repeated his words, "I'm going to do better," and that was it. They finished dinner, Gail went back to her painting, and Jack walked to Rob's.

The following day, Jack got home from school to find his father sitting on the porch. "Take a seat, bud. I got something for you," Marvin said, as he reached his good arm into his pocket, removing a sterling silver chain with an anchor pendant. "As you know, this was Pop's. I was going to wait until your eighteenth birthday to give it to you, but I decided now was as good a time as any."

"You wear this all the time, though," Jack said, as he moved his thumb over the pendent.

"Yea, well, now you can. Have I ever told you what Pop told me about the significance of the anchor?"

"I don't think so."

"Well, there's going to be rough seas sometimes, especially in this family. Wear this and remember you got people to hold you down through it. Or something like that. Pop was a lot more philosophical than I am."

The boy unclipped the chain, and put it around his neck. "Thank you, Dad. I appreciate it." Jack made his way through the house, quickly greeting his mother, who was putting the finishing touches on the painting from the hospital.

He tossed his black Jansport onto his bed, grabbed the stereo remote off the dresser, and pressed play on Gang Starr's *Hard to Earn*. DJ Premier's boom bap production spilled through the room as he stood before his mirror, checking out his new piece of jewelry. His father's son staring back at him.

VII.

The last thing anyone expects to run into on their early morning jog is a half-naked man with most of his body painted blood red. But that's exactly what the athletically built Hispanic girl, with a colorful shoulder tattoo and sea of curly, black hair, runs into when I rise from the woods.

I'm wearing nothing but a towel I managed to snatch on my way out of the Silver Compound. "You're not in any danger," I say softly, keeping my distance. I expect her to flee but, to my surprise, she just backs away a few feet. "I need to use your cellphone."

"Are you hurt?" She asks, wide-eyed, at the intersection of confused and terrified.

"No. I'm okay actually," I say, almost laughing.

Her dark brown eyes meet mine. There's something to her. Military, maybe? Rough upbringing? She's young and beautiful, and I wish more than anything I had time to get to the bottom of it.

"I'll dial and put it on speaker for you. Okay?"

"Of course. I don't know how to use one of those anyway." That confuses her even further, but she asks me for the number, then stands as far away as she possibly can while holding the phone up.

"Roger," the voice from the phone.

"It's Sharpe!"

"You don't have to talk so loud," the girl interjects.

I lower my voice. "Okay. I'm sorry. It's Sharpe," I say again. "I need you to get me."

"What's your location?"

"Where am I?" I ask the girl.

"You're on Oldpond Road. In Springdale."

"What state?"

At this point, the situation is so absurd that she manages a bemused smile. "Pennsylvania." Roger hears all the information and asks for a landmark. "Um, there's nothing much outside of some houses," she explains. "A couple of farms. There's a liquor store."

"Got it," Roger says. "Go to the liquor store, Sharpe. Lay low. Expect my arrival in two hours."

I thank the girl and ask her about how far the liquor store is from where we are. "About a mile north," she answers, then starts to put the weird little nuggets back into her ears. She notices my stare.

156

"What are those called?" I ask.

"They're earbuds."

"Ah. That's right. We had headphones in my day." A smile runs quickly across her face. I decide to take advantage of the momentary levity. "What are you listening to?"

"Um, Drake," she answers, with trepidation.

"I only heard him a couple of times. I thought he was wack."

Awkward. Moment. Of. Silence.

"I'm going to go now. I have work," she says.

I thank her again, then watch as she resumes her jog in the opposite direction. I'm entirely grateful to her for handling our bizarre meeting with such grace. I feel compelled to know her name, so I shout in her direction. She stops in her tracks and removes an earbud. "What's your name?" I ask.

"It's...," she hesitates for a moment. "It's Ola. What's yours, again?"

"Jack."

"Well, Jack. I hope you find some clothes out there."

We share a smile, then continue on our much different paths.

One hour and fifty-eight minutes later, Roger's black Cadillac pulls into the liquor store parking lot. I spot him from the surrounding woods, and make a beeline for his passenger side door. I hop in and find a duffle bag full of fresh clothes, a protein bar, and a bottle of water.

"You smell terrible," the seventy-something year old Englishman says. "Really. Quite awful."

"I haven't bathed in over a month," I tell him, as I wrestle with the clothing, trying to get dressed in the seat. "I'm fucking frozen."

"Here," he reaches into the backseat and grabs a thick blanket. "Warm up. Get a little something in you. Then sleep. I'll wake you when we arrive. Mr. Steels is waiting for us."

I thank him and, before I can even unwrap the protein bar, I fall into a deep sleep.

VIII.

The Pierce sisters have long outgrown the weathered trampoline in the backyard. They use it solely to discuss secret matters now, like throwing a party while their folks are out of town. Wendy sits and listens, while her older sister Meryl, stretches and bounces, swimming in the rapture of her young, fit existence. They're both extremely pretty, but Meryl has an easier time flaunting it. Makeup, skimpy outfits. Wendy has always admired her big sister's confidence.

"We do it Friday night. We keep it smallish, nothing too crazy. Then we use Saturday to clean up. Mom and Dad get home on Sunday, none the wiser," Meryl explains.

"Do you think this is a good idea?" Wendy asks. "You know, since they just remodeled the kitchen and all?"

"Just keep people out of the kitchen. We'll use the fridge in the garage, hang out back here, on the deck."

"I suppose there is going to be alcohol at this party?"

"Duh," Meryl says, as she tosses a rubber ball at her sister, catching her off-guard. "That's where you come in."

"Huh?"

"I know that boyfriend of yours has connections."

"Jack? I feel a little bit funny asking him to do that," Wendy says, tossing the ball back with a bit more force. "We've only been talking for a couple of weeks."

"It's been like a month, Wendy. I know his friend Chris has the hookup. His big brother, he's like in his twenties I think. So hot. He can stick around after he buys it," Meryl says, as she throws the ball again. It immediately gets chucked back at her.

"Ew, Meryl." The sisters continue to mull it over until their mother calls them inside.

Margaret Pierce whips up a picturesque dinner every evening; her husband, John, wouldn't have it any other way. He sits at the head of the table and delivers a homily in between bites of a medium rare slab of meat.

"It's Fourth of July weekend, Meryl. So I don't think I need to tell you that driving at all is probably a bad idea. Your mother is going to fill the refrigerator and pantry with enough food to last the weekend. If you must go

158

out for anything, please be careful," John says. "You ladies may each have two friends over. Absolutely no boys," he continues, glancing over to Wendy. He's recently caught wind of the Jack Sharpe situation.

"Daddy, I have it under control," Meryl says, winking at her sister.

"I think they're planning a party," Abby chimes in. She's two years younger than Wendy and, although her sisterly telepathy isn't as sharp, she's on to them.

"Abby, shut up," Meryl snaps.

"Be nice," Margaret instructs.

"Mom, she's being a brat because she has to come with you guys."

"Okay, well, let's all try to get along until it happens," Margaret says softly, glancing toward her husband.

She has mastered the art of diffusing a situation before John can stomp around the house acting like he's made the biggest mistake of his life. When dinner is over, he retreats to the study to wash down *Crossfire* with Glenlivet, while Margaret plays Yanni on the kitchen stereo system. The older sisters clear the table and fill the dishwasher quicker than usual, anxious to get to their bedroom phone and engage in some party planning with Jack and the boys.

I've arrived at the mansion in bad shape before, but not quite like this. Wilson is waiting at the front door, the smoke from his pipe dancing around his face. "Good lord, Jack," he says, as I struggle to exit the car.

"We have some things to talk about," I mumble, collapsing into his arms. He embraces me and I'm surprised by how fit he manages to stay for an older guy.

"We'll talk but, for now, you need to clean yourself up and rest. The guest chambers are vacant," he explains, as he helps me into the mansion, Roger following close behind us. "It's been quiet around here lately."

Wilson has been on several expeditions around the globe; you can tell by the treasure trove that the refurbished, Victorian-era mansion has become. Artifacts from his journeys are displayed in orderly fashion, completely free of dust. Roger will have it no other way. The place is cold and lit only by candles, but the Ella Fitzgerald spinning on the record player lets me know I'm home.

I close the guest room door behind me, immediately stripping down to nothing and hitting the shower. The stream of scalding hot water brings me to the Promised Land and I get lost there for almost an hour.

"Master Sharpe, I left some fresh clothes out here," Roger says from outside the door. "When you're ready, join us in the dining room."

Most of the pack members I've encountered throughout the years have had questions about Wilson Steels' background. How did someone with our affliction manage to accumulate such wealth? How is he able to trek around the world unnoticed? How did his relationship with Roger come about?

Some believe that he hasn't consumed a human being in twenty-five years. Instead, with every full moon, he sits at his dining room table fully transformed, while Roger serves him a fresh kill from the surrounding forest.

Others speak of a legend that says Wilson's transformations no longer depend on the lunar phase at all, that he's able to will them into existence whenever he wants. Full moon or no full moon.

I've never paid any of it much mind. I certainly never brought it up. What I know is this; he took me in. He took us all in. When we were scared, hurt, drugged out, suicidal, homicidal, Wilson Steels took us in, and never asked for anything in return.

I follow the scent of something delicious downstairs to the dining room. Roger is sitting at the end of a boundless, wooden table. Wilson is at the head. Behind him is a painting of Russian folk hero Ivan Tsarevich riding his fearsome Gray Wolf through the woods.

My meal awaits me across from Roger. He stands and I imagine he's coming to remove the ornate, stainless steel lid from my plate. "I got it, Roger," I say.

"My pleasure, Master Sharpe. Tonight we have filet mignon with garlic and herb buttered baby potatoes and bacon-wrapped asparagus bundles. We've also opened a '97 Shiraz. Would you like a pour?"

"Sure, man. This is great. Thank you."

As we dine, I speak in detail about my kidnapping, and the operation that Teddy Silver is running. To my surprise, both Wilson and Roger are already aware of it.

"He's a pawn in a game that we've been playing for many years. The thing is, Teddy can't blow his cover. The real way he makes his millions. If he starts to spread the word about Lycanthropes, people will think he's more insane than he already is. His phony church will crumble in no time. So he is forced to move in the shadows. A lot like us. He's thorn in our side, but we've managed," Wilson says.

I want to tell him that it felt a lot worse than a thorn in my side, as he and his goons held me against my will and damn near murdered me, but I bite my tongue. I've never contested Wilson and, as the wine starts to work its magic, I decide that I won't start tonight.

"We've wiped out most of his operation through the years. They run on a skeleton crew now. They've killed their share of the pack as well, but I believe this shadow war is nearing its end. That's why I decided to keep you in the dark. It's only when one of us really lets our guard down that they are able to strike. Which begs the question, Jack. How did you let your guard down?"

"I fucked up," I answer, tentatively. "I had gone almost three years without feasting on a human. But there was this dude. A bartender. I did him no more than two miles from the damn highway. I passed out after. Never even buried his remains." Wilson glances over toward Roger. I take some comfort in knowing that they've seen and heard it all before. "The worst part is, I did it in anger."

"Why were you angry?" Roger asks.

"Fucking guy called me Vanilla Ice." A fleeting moment of silence fills the room, followed by Wilson's huge belly laugh. "Is it really that funny?" I ask, looking over toward an extremely confused Roger.

"Vanilla Ice," Wilson says to no one in particular. "Now that's one helluva name for a rapper." It dawns on me that this could be the first time Wilson has heard the name. He gathers himself and continues. "So you've broken two of our sacred rules so far. Any more you want to talk about?"

There is a rudimentary list of rules, maybe ten or so, which I believe Wilson Steels created himself. I rack my brain trying to remember them, until Wilson addresses the most important one. "When was the last time you used your claws on someone?"

"I don't remember," I answer.

He leans in closer. "Try to," he says, as his pair of deep-set, onyx eyes lock with mine. His beard and head of balding, curly hair have both turned gray long ago. He's distinguished and quietly intense. Incredibly difficult to lie to. It doesn't stop me from doing so.

"It's been a long time. I've lost track." During a transformation, our nails take claw-like shapes and gain some kind of mystical property that allows us to transport the Lycan gene to whatever unsuspecting man or woman we choose to lacerate. I've never done it.

Not once.

"If we don't use our claws, our species cannot continue," he says.

"I'm not sure I want our species to continue," I respond, understanding full well that I'm the only person that can say something like that between these walls. "Thank you again, gentlemen. Now, if you'll excuse me, I'm going to go upstairs and pass out."

"We wanted a keg, bro. What is this shit?" Rob asks, as he and Christopher attempt to hook a tubed contraption up to a disco ball full of Coors Light.

"This beautiful thing is called a *Party Ball*. I told you, we didn't give my brother enough funds for two handles of liquor and a freaking keg, dude."

Meryl has been sitting on the kitchen counter observing the boys' struggle. "You guys have never done one of these in your lives, huh?"

"What? You trippin' girl," Rob says. "I been doing these for mad long. It's just, I think they forgot a piece or something."

"Sure. So um, Chris, do you think your brother will be coming back later? "

Before Christopher can answer, the doorbell rings. Meryl runs to the front window and is shocked to find Matt Moretti, Fats Larusso, and three guys she barely recognizes at the doorstep. Beyond them, a fleet of cars is pulling up her driveway. "Shit," she says to herself. "Shit. Shit. Shit."

She dashes back through the kitchen, paying no mind to Chris and Rob, hurdles an overflowing laundry basket, then crashes through the back door where Wendy and Jack sit on the outdoor sofa, curled up under a blanket.

"What the hell, Meryl? You scared the shit out of us!" Wendy shouts at her sister.

"Can you two keep your hands off of each other for two minutes? We may have a situation here."

"What kind of situation?"

"Matt just showed up. And Fats. And like, a shit ton of cars."

"What? How did they even know about this?"

"Well," Meryl contemplates lying about it, as she watches the love birds rise from the sofa and gather themselves. "I may have invited Matt."

"Are you kidding me?"

"I just didn't want this night to be lame. That's all!"

"Yea, well, we agreed on smallish, and did you ever stop and think about how I would feel about Matt coming?"

"I'm sorry, Wendy. I honestly did not think they would show up."

"Hey," Jack says. "We all know these guys are a bunch of assholes, but some of them are a good time. Let's get them back here, away from the house, and have a nice night. Wendy, if we turn them away, there will be all sorts of drama. You know that."

"Yea, I guess so," Wendy sighs.

Fifteen minutes later, Biggie Smalls is rapping, "Hugs from the honeys, pounds from the roughnecks...," from the stereo system as Rob has finally decapitated the Party Ball with John Pierce's hacksaw.

Chris, Jack and Wendy are taking turns scooping the beer out with a ladle, then chugging it. The rest of the party is mostly in the backyard, much to the relief of Wendy.

"Fats is passing around a bong out there." Rob says, as he returns from running a reconnaissance mission. "Then there's this weird guy by the trampoline, in some beat JNCO jeans, talking about being abducted by aliens. They're playing Tool. Maybe it's Tool, I dunno, but it's definitely some *Butt Sweat* music," he explains.

"I'm sorry. What kind of music?" Wendy asks.

"Butt Sweat. Anything as depressing as that shit is Butt Sweat music." He grabs the ladle out of Christopher's hand and dips it into the beer. "I made it up. Anyway, this is where the real party is at," he says, as he takes a swig.

Jack and Wendy share a laugh as she pushes the backside of her body up against the front of his. It happens more frequently as the night gets longer and the Party Ball gets emptier. Now and again, Jack presses his lips against the crook of her neck. Whenever the others aren't looking, they kiss. It's a kind of deep, urgent kiss that only teenagers engage in.

"Do you want to go up to my room?" She whispers.

"Yes. I think I would love that," he answers, the scent of beer, hot on their breath

They hold hands and scramble through their friends, toward the stairs. "Well you guys have a nice night," Rob says, then turns to Christopher and motions the ladle toward the Party Ball. "We're finishing this shit."

Jack has no idea what he's doing other than feeling all the parts of Wendy that he's been dreaming about for three years. Wendy lets herself get lost in the haze of the alcohol until she begins to shiver. It could be that they're down to nothing but their underwear, or it's more likely the reality of the situation is starting to sober her up. "Let's get under the blankets," she whispers.

Pillows and stuffed animals spill to the floor as they clumsily relocate to beneath the bed set. Wendy's eyes catch a glimpse of a pennant she bought while visiting Yale. "I can't wait until you're here with me next year," her friend's voice rings through her head.

Wendy underestimated the mass of cotton on top of them and they've started to sweat, their skin sticking together from the perspiration. The pennant is hung right next to a poster of Rosie the Riveter flexing her bicep, exclaiming, WE CAN DO IT!

She suddenly finds herself feeling claustrophobic and uses all of her strength to roll Jack over and straddle him, tossing the stuff off of her and toward the foot of the bed. "I don't think we should go any further, Jack."

He was savoring every second, not only because it was amazing, but because he also knows what kind of girl Wendy Pierce is. He knows that she's in the driver's seat in this situation and could've hit the brakes much earlier in the night if she chose to.

"Of course," he whispers. "What do you want to do?

She climbs off of him and lays in his arms. "Just hold me for a while."

The noise from the party sounds like it's miles away, as the huge, silver moon positions itself in the arch of Wendy's bedroom window. It doesn't happen often but, right now, high school feels perfect.

Wendy's hand finds the anchor pendant lying on his chest. "What's up with this?" She asks.

"My dad gave it to me about a year ago. It was my grandfather's."

"That's why you never take it off, huh?"

"That's why."

"You're lucky it's cool-looking. It could've been something really weird." They laugh and kiss once more. "You know, I really want to be with you," Wendy whispers. "I'm just not quite ready."

"Hey. You don't have to explain yourself to me," he says, looking into her eyes. "Ever."

She kisses him again, for a long time. It feels different. Jack can't put his finger on it, but it's definitely different.

There's a knock on the door, followed by Meryl's voice. "This is my room, too. Let me in, punks!" The couple hop out of bed and frantically throw their clothes back on, as Meryl continues to rap on the door. "Come on, guys!"

Wendy swings the door open to find Meryl with Rob and Christopher. "We're heading to the Pine Road railroad cars," Rob says.

"What? We haven't gone out there in years," Jack responds.

"Yea, well, we drank all the booze and it's boring as shit down there. Railroad cars it is. Let's go."

"Where is everyone?" Wendy asks.

"Word spread that Alex Helton was having a party too. Fucking bitch," Meryl says.

On the way out, the friends throw on some hoodies and windbreakers and grab a couple of flashlights from John Pierce's workstation. They head across the backyard where Matt and Fats are loitering.

"Um, why are they still here?" Wendy asks her sister.

"Damn, that's cold. When did you become such a bitch?" A drunken Fats Larusso asks.

Jack, still stewing over the frozen banana comment, and a bit inebriated himself, approaches Fats. "Why don't you shut your fat fucking mouth for once?" he says loudly, right in Fats' grill. Fats volleys it back even louder, "Wanna go right now, you punk bitch?"

Matt steps between the boys, then shoves Fats back a few feet. "Knock it off. Let's all just chill out," he says. "We heard you guys were going out to railroad cars and thought we should join. Our parents are friends and we don't want anything happening to these girls."

"Oh, please. What the hell are you going to do out there? Offer a murderer a thousand dollars not to kill us? Give me a break," Wendy says.

"Yea, that's pretty funny coming from the Princess of Cedarwood," Matt responds.

"Okay. I think I've heard enough. Go home, Matt," Meryl says.

"Huh? You invited me here."

"Well, all this name-calling is getting to me."

"Fine. Alex's party is probably more fly than this shit anyway. Let's dip, Fats."

The friends exit the back gate and follow the edge of the woods. Behind them, they hear the distant sound of Matt performing a burnout in the Pierces' driveway. "What a great idea it was inviting them," Wendy says to her sister.

It's unseasonably cool for a midsummer's night in New Jersey. The full moon is partially cloaked in dark clouds; it seems to follow their every move. They make it to the woodlot, where the back end of the Pierces' street meets Pine Road. From there, they pass the only life on the street - farmhouses with their accompanying greenhouses and fields. Beyond that, the streetlights end, and a darkened stretch of the road takes them to the fabled railroad cars.

It could be that it's one in the morning and Wendy has been drinking since eight. Or it could be that she hates horror movies, still sleeps with her closet light on, and would never dream of visiting abandoned railroad cars in the middle of the night. Then again, it just may be, that she saw something that resembled "a really tall, hairy man," a few blocks back.

"I'm telling you, Jack," she whispers, clutching his arm, both of them trying to keep pace with the others. "I thought it was a stray dog at first, but then it stood up."

"So, it's like Bigfoot or something?"

"Who knows what it is, but I know I saw it. It looked like it was following us."

"Why didn't you say something?"

"I don't know. I guess I froze up. I'm just really freaked out. Let's go back to my house. Please." Jack stops the others and tells them that he and Wendy are turning around. Meryl rushes toward her sister.

"Wendy, come on. We're almost there. We'll look at the cars for a second, then leave. I promise."

Wendy wants to tell her sister about the figure she saw in the woods, but she starts to second guess herself. It has been a long night, maybe it is just her mind playing tricks on her. She feels safer as a group, anyway, rather than just she and Jack hightailing it back to the house.

"Okay, Meryl. One second, then we leave. Deal?"

"Deal."

They walk another half mile and come upon a dead end where the four graffiti-laced passenger cars reside in darkness.

"So, ladies. Are you aware of the little boy that haunts this place?" Rob asks.

"Yes, Rob." Meryl answers. "We live in this town, too."

Christopher shines his flashlight across the towering cars, illuminating the effects that Father Time has had on their condition. He walks up a short flight of rusted, iron steps and enters.

"Dude, you're nuts," Jack says to his friend.

"I've been here so many times with my brother. I know this place like the back of Rob's mom's ass."

The wind picks up, carrying a symphony of otherworldly sound. It whips through the cars and causes the surrounding trees to sway in the moonlight. Christopher jumps from the railcar quicker than he entered it. "Did you guys hear that?"

"Yea, bro," Rob answers. "It sounded like wolves or some shit."

"Wolves?" Jack ponders. "In Cedarwood?"

Meryl comes up from behind her sister and wraps her arms around her waist. "Okay, guys. This was fun," she says. "Time to wrap it up."

The five of them start running down Pine Road, back toward the brighter end. The glow of their lanterns slice through the dark of night. They spot the front lamps of two dirt bikes up ahead. Meryl, the fastest of the bunch, turns and shouts toward her friends, "Who the hell could that be?"

"Fats has a dirt bike," Rob answers, "it has to be those pricks!"

"Let's hit the woods, they won't be able to keep up with us," Chris says.

They make a sharp turn and follow a dirt road into a patch of trees. The bikes continue to follow in their direction until the woodland becomes too thick. The riders double back and hit the dirt road again, kicking up a dust storm. The dark undergrowth of the forest proves too much for the friends to navigate. Against their best efforts, they begin to separate from each other. Meryl tries to raise her voice over the thunderous sounds of the dirt bikes. "Wendy, where are you guys?"

"Over here. I'm okay, I'm with Jack. Rob is with us too."

"Okay, good. Chris knows how to get back to our house. Will you guys be okay?"

"Yes. These fuckers are just messing with us. Go, fast. We'll meet you at home."

Jack, trying to hold on to Wendy as tight as he can, as well as keep an eye on the assholes on the dirt bikes, trips over a large branch. It causes him to jerk forward, lose Wendy's hand and his flashlight, then tumble down a shallow ditch.

Wendy shouts for him, but he doesn't respond with her name. Instead, it's a painful yelp from the darkness. Rob retrieves the flashlight from the ground and points it in Jack's direction, only to find his friend curled up in a heap.

His hoodie has been torn down the front.

His chest is gashed and bloody.

When I was twenty, I found myself slumped in a leather chair in Wilson's study. The blaze in the furnace warmed me as I sipped from a tall glass of ice water. Wilson heard me out as I explained that I had started using drugs, and I was determined to ride the bullet train, ridding myself of the nightmare I was living in. He never tried talking me out of it; instead, he began to remove books from the surrounding shelves and read passages from them about our affliction.

I learned much that night about the history of Lycanthropy. How it traces back to the Middle Ages, its ties to the witch purge of Europe, the integral part it plays in much folklore around the world. Wilson wanted me to know that I wasn't just a helpless wolf man lurching around the Northeast. He wanted me to know that there was more to this - that I wasn't alone.

I find myself in the same chair tonight - the fire, just as warm. It's my third night at the mansion and, while I'm starting to feel better physically, my mental state is a different story. I explain to Wilson that I feel like the walls are closing in on me; that I'm damn near forty and I'm uncertain if I can manage this condition much longer.

"You're strong, Jack. You've made it this far. Most end it after the second or third transformation. You're in it for the long run. Like me," he says, in between drags from his pipe.

"Yea, but you have this place, and Roger. I have nothing. No one." Wilson doesn't acknowledge my statement. Instead, he rises from his chair, approaches the serving cart Roger had wheeled in earlier, then pours some Johnnie Walker over rocks.

"I have a story," he says, as he hands me a glass. "I've never shared it with anyone. When I was a young man, working the docks in New York City, I would get off work and walk a few blocks over. It was one of the only black nightclubs in the city at the time, and the gal that sang there was, well, she was gorgeous. With a voice like Nina Simone, I wouldn't lie to ya. I sat at a table by the stage, sometimes with a friend or two, most times by myself. I would have some food, some drinks, but it was mostly her that I was ingesting. One Friday night, feeling really good off the white lightning, I decided to talk with her when she got done her show."

He takes a seat across from me, like so many times over the past twenty years, only this time it's about him. He puts his feet up on an ottoman and continues.

"Those nights in that club, chatting with her, they were the best nights of my life. Then I ran into one of the pack. One of us. I saw her three more times, but I knew what was coming. I knew the bad moon would rise and it scared me. Scared me to death. I had to flee. Never even said goodbye to her."

I didn't think Wilson Steels had tear ducts, but I see them starting to fill. He kills his scotch, then heads to the serving cart to pour another.

"If I could go back to the night you were clawed by that rogue and stop him, I would do it. It's no damn fair that your life was stolen from you when you were barely a man." The sudden switch from his story back to mine rattles me. "That's why we have rules. It's a damn shame they're broken sometimes." He sits back down and stares beyond me for a moment. "What was her name?"

"Who?" I ask.

"The gal you used to tell me about when you first arrived here."

I had gone so long without thinking about her that his question awakens a sleeping giant in my brain. Memories come rushing back. Memories of a time before. A pure, unpolluted time. I'm surprised Wilson was even listening to me back then.

"Wendy," I answer. "Wendy Pierce." It feels good just saying her name. I hear myself as a seventeen-year-old again.

"Ah, yes. Wendy. Like *Peter Pan*."

"Yeah. I guess so."

"Well, Jack," he says, killing another scotch. "I'm turning in. Finish your drink, enjoy the fire. I'll see you in the morning."

And just like that, I'm alone in the study with a cold drink, a crackling fire, and a head chock-full of memories about Wendy. About Cedarwood.

Memories of a life that I had convinced myself was nothing but a dream.

XII.

Dr. Cheung is the best in town. He's the son of "the old" Dr. Cheung, who was one of the most loved and well respected doctors in New Jersey. He was groomed to follow in his father's footsteps ever since first grade, when he and his buddy, Marvin Sharpe, stole a frog from the science lab and dissected it in the cafeteria to impress a girl.

He enters the waiting room of the hospital, where the Sharpes, the Pierce sisters, and Rob and Christopher are waiting to be informed about Jack's condition. Marvin and Gail anxiously approach him. "What's the word, Doc?" Marvin asks.

"The wound is pretty deep," Dr. Cheung responds. "We cleaned it up and stitched it. We're still waiting on results from a few tests. Animal-borne disease and what not."

"Oh my God!" Gail exclaims.

"He does have a considerable amount of alcohol in his bloodstream."

"Well, shit. We always did. No?" The doctor is not amused by his old buddy's ill-timed joke.

"Can we see him?" Gail asks.

"Sure, sure," Dr. Cheung says, as the friends jump from their chairs and rush past him, toward the patient room doors. The doctor clutches his friend gently by the arm to stop him. "Marvin. Your boy has no idea what did this to him. Chalk it up to the dark, the drinking. I have no idea. But the way his skin was torn, the size of the wound, the width between each laceration, it's peculiar to say the least. When the sun rises, there will be cops and animal control people in and out of here. Be prepared. Also, Jack's girlfriend. That's John Pierce's daughter, were you aware of that?"

"The construction guy? My son don't tell me shit," Marvin answers.

"Yea, well, I know the man. This thing can get ugly if he finds out his girls were gallivanting around the woods in the middle of the night with your son and his friends."

"To hell with that rich bastard."

"Okay, Marvin. Just keep your guard up is what I'm saying. You don't want trouble with the Pierces."

A hospital room is a cold, bleak place. The kind of place that should be reserved for the sick and the old. It's difficult for his friends to see Jack lying helplessly in a bed, surrounded by wires and monitors. They are huddled around him. Wendy is clutching his hand while his mother strokes his hair. Marvin walks in on the somber sight. "Guys, I just had a chat with Dr. Cheung. He's going to be okay," he announces quietly.

"His chest is mangled. He'll never be quite the same after this. I just can't believe you kids were fooling around out there in the woods," Gail cries.

"Gail, honey. Relax. No one died." The Sharpes have always been a stark contrast in crisis reaction. "We'll talk about stuff later. For now, you kids should get home and get some rest. Who drove?"

"That was me, Mr. Sharpe," Meryl answers. "We basically carried Jack back to our house, then I drove us here."

"Thank you. I appreciate all of you guys for standing by your friend. I'm sure he appreciates it as well, but he's just going to sleep it off right now. No sense y'all hanging around."

"Uh, Mr. Sharpe," Meryl says, as the friends begin to gather their belongings. "Are you going to tell our parents about this?"

Gail attempts to answer but is cut off by her husband. "No. Your secret is safe with us." If Gail were able to fire deadly lasers from her eyes, Marvin would be incinerated at this very moment. "Y'all have been through enough. Get home, clean up that house."

"Dad," Jack mumbles, catching everyone off-guard. He's mostly communicated with hand gestures and head nods to this point. "I want Wendy to stay."

"Okay, buddy. I guess that's okay."

"Can we be alone for a minute?"

The kids take turns hugging their injured friend, then follow his parents out. The sun is rising, coloring the room a pale blue. Now that they're alone, Wendy feels comfortable enough to totally embrace Jack. They wrap their arms around each other.

"Climb in," Jack whispers.

"Are you sure I won't hurt you?"

"I'm okay."

She cautiously climbs into the bed, curling up beside him, then rests her head on his shoulder, just above the wound.

"It was the thing you saw in the woods that did this," he says.

"What?"

172

"The Bigfoot thing. My flashlight caught its eyes for a second. I think I smelled its breath, or something. I don't know. It all happened so fast."

"Jack," Wendy gasps. "Are you sure?"

"I'm positive." She begins to cry into his shoulder. "Hey, hey. You okay?"

"No. I'm really scared. We need to tell somebody."

"I know. It's just a lot to process right now. Let's wait until things calm down."

"I'm so sorry, Jack. I shouldn't have listened to Meryl. If we'd turned around when I wanted to, maybe this wouldn't have happened."

"Don't be sorry. The only people that should be sorry are Matt and Fats. Fucking assholes."

"Well, Matt actually came by the hospital. He wanted you to know that he had nothing to do with it. It was Fats and Jeremy. The kid from the party with the nose ring and ugly pants."

"He's probably trying to save face. I don't trust him."

"I don't either, but I think we have bigger things to worry about now."

"Yea. I guess so."

The young couple lie in the soft glow of the morning sun. The only noise in the room is the rhythmic beeping of the heart monitor.

XIII.

Wilson doesn't allow a pack member to leave the mansion until Roger has taken him to the mall about an hour up the road. He encourages us to spend however much of his money we want, on stuff we'll need when we set back out into the world. In the early years, it took me a handful of times, coming back with nothing but a toothbrush and some socks, to understand that Wilson means business when it comes to this ritual.

"You got everything you need?" he asks as he looks over the two overstuffed duffle bags sitting at the foot of the guest room bed. I tell him I do, and thank him for the eighth time. "I also put a grand in the side pocket of your bag."

"Wilson, I ca - "

"Don't bother protesting. I won't listen. So, where are you heading?"

"I think I'll head out to the West Coast. Beat the cold weather around here."

"How about Cedarwood, New Jersey? I hear it's beautiful there during the holidays."

We hung out on Main Street around December first of every year, to observe the lighting of the town's Christmas tree. I sipped hot chocolate and admired my father as he mingled with the crowd. I haven't heard someone speak the name of my hometown in almost two decades. "Why Cedarwood?" I ask.

"Well, because Wendy is there and you owe it to yourself to see her again."

"It's been eighteen years, Wilson. She may have moved, she may have gotten married. Maybe she has kids. Maybe she's dead."

"She's very much alive. She's Wendy Moretti now and, yes, she has a five-year-old daughter."

Wendy fucking Moretti.

All these years later and hearing that particular merging of names, and the fact that they've procreated, makes my insides churn. It's so cruel to make me hear it, I almost think Wilson is torturing me on purpose.

"No, Wilson. Forget that. Thank you. But no."

"Relax. According to her page, she is separated."

"Her page? What, do you have, like, a private investigator following her?"

"Facebook, Jack. Facebook."

174

I keep hearing about this Facebook. A couple of people I've met on my travels even let me look at theirs. It's a mystery to me and I don't have the patience to begin solving it.

"I don't know. They had a funeral for me. If I go waltzing back into town, it could become a thing. We don't need that kind of attention."

"I'm not saying to throw yourself a parade in honor of your return. Go to her. Just her. Do it like I've taught you. No tracks."

For the majority of my life on the road, I pined for Wendy. Especially the early years when I was still a virgin. The first few times the full moon rose, when I descended into a nightmare world of physical transformation, I could still cling to the memory of the night in her room. Our young bodies tangled together. The silver moon peeking through her window, so far away. So harmless.

After countless flings, with so many different ladies of the night, I was able to forget about Wendy almost entirely. All of the tiny details that I held on to for so long faded away. Wendy became more a feeling, a misty representation of my life before I was clawed.

But, the way my mind and body reacted to the mere mention of her name, makes me know that Wendy Pierce was never very far away to begin with.

"Okay, Wilson. I will go to Cedarwood."

"Tremendous. It's the right move. A second chance, perhaps. Most of us never get one."

He gives me a pat on the back and leaves me alone in the guest room. I take a look around. The king size bed and the adjoining washroom, the window overlooking a koi pond. I am lucky to have Wilson Steels in my life.

As I'm washing up and preparing to take off, I hear commotion from downstairs. I look down from the landing and watch, as an unstable girl I've seen at the mansion once before is confronting Wilson.

"Someone is fucking following me," she shouts. Her hair is thin and windblown; she's wearing dark, days-old makeup that's run down her face and dried like war paint. "Is it someone working with you, Mr. Steels?"

"No, Alice. We've discussed this. I employ no one. It's just Roger and me here."

"Well, I need money."

"Okay, we will talk about it. How about a shower and a hot meal first?"

"Money first. Please."

There's a sound. An unholy sound out of nowhere. It racks me.

The flesh from Alice's scalp tears back; the walls and ceiling are painted with her blood. I duck behind the bannister and watch as a masked figure appears from the room directly underneath me. He's brandishing a familiar rifle, donned in black from head to toe. On the other side of the grand foyer, two more gunmen smash through the double doors. They open fire on everything, their bullets dismantling all of Wilson's meticulously well-tended to belongings.

Wilson attempts to run in the opposite direction of the attack, but a shot lands in his shoulder. The momentum takes him over the back of the sofa.

Roger, with a katana, sneaks up on the first guy's blindside and takes the blade across his forearm, causing him to drop the gun. In the same movement, he changes the direction of his swing and slices the man across his throat.

Kills him dead.

The assailants focus their fire on the old Englishman. He anticipates the bullets and manages to dodge a couple of bursts, then zigzags and gets within striking distance of one of them. The second gets lucky and hits him with a string of bullets, causing him to lose grip of his sword and crumble to the floor. They remove their ski masks to reveal the sweaty faces of Teddy Silver and Stimpy. I let the man live and this is how he repays me.

Wilson crawls on his hands and knees toward the stairwell. Stimpy puts a boot against his ass, cracking himself up. They stalk him, taunting him with the rifles. I don't hear a word they're saying, I only hear Wilson.

And I'm seventeen again.

"When I acquired this mansion, I had it refurbished with a quick escape in mind. There are several points throughout this place that will lead you to a system of underground tunnels. The most vital to you will be the trapdoor in the main guest chambers, behind the bookshelves."

Anger, adrenaline, but mostly, fear propels me through the hidden door and across a narrow corridor, leading to a flight of steps. I take them down to another door; this one opens to an intersection of tunnels. I have abandoned my friend, my mentor. A man who saved my life on more occasions than I can remember. And, as I hear the faint echo of rifle fire in the distance, I realize that I left him to die.

It's what he would've wanted. That's the thought that keeps me moving down the dark passageway. Wilson wanted the pack to live on, to thrive, long after he was gone. He wanted me to see Wendy again. If I was having any doubts about returning to Cedarwood, they were destroyed the moment those sons of bitches opened fire in the mansion.

When I rise from a hatch, hidden deep in the woods, night has fallen. I've been a drifter longer than I was a normal kid from some small town in New Jersey; but it's only now, as I look up toward the sickle moon, that I feel totally alone.

XIV.

It's Jack's last day in the hospital. His week has been a constant struggle to stay awake long enough to speak with his visitors. The press, police and animal control officers, classmates, even a few teachers. Christopher, Rob, and Wendy have been there around the clock, as well as his folks. His wound is healing on schedule and all of the tests came back negative. The boys have arrived this afternoon with Mickey D's and talk of a get together.

"The pool looks like a swamp, but my father gave us the green light for tonight," Christopher says, tossing a whole McNugget into his mouth.

"Pool party, bro. By ten o'clock tonight I'm going to be Tupac in that video, surrounded by all the honeys," Rob adds, dancing with a French fry in one hand and a container of barbecue sauce in the other.

"More like the bee girl from the Blind Melon video," Christopher jokes, chucking a fry at him.

"Another party so soon? Are we even in the clear yet for the last one?" Jack asks.

"It's not a party. Think of it as a small soirée. Just us, your girl, Meryl and my brother. Those two have been talking all week. It's kinda weird, but awesome too. We can all hang out together. All summer long," Christopher exclaims.

There's a tinge of excitement in Jack's heart but it's quickly displaced by a different sensation. A feeling that he has never experienced before. He chalks it up to the lingering uncertainty about the thing that did this to him. His boys feel his apprehension.

"What's going on, dude? We're breaking you out of here today. Summer awaits. Wendy Pierce awaits that Johnson of yours," Rob jokes.

"I know. It's just...I won't be able to go in the water. I'm still on pain meds."

"Yea, so what? You'll get drunk quicker. Listen, you dip your feet in the water, and listen to some good tunes while Wendy rubs your booboo. Sounds like a nice night to me."

Jack gives his friend an insincere laugh. That alone makes him feel depressed, even angry.

He should be laughing. He should be happy.

He should have the world by the balls.

That thing in the woods. Why did it pick him? Why did it rob him of a carefree summer with his best buds and new girlfriend? The attack skips in his mind over, and over again, like a broken record. Each time, it takes his breath away.

It scares him to his core.

He tells them that he wants to sleep for a bit before his mother returns to bring him home. They leave, bummed out and confused. Jack finds himself alone, no longer hooked up to any monitors. No more guests, or nurses in and out. The room is quiet. Still.

Walls crumble to pieces. Trees invade the room, their branches growing, wrapping around everything they touch like a boa constrictor. Jack springs from his bed and into the ever-growing forest. He runs, a suffocating tunnel vision leading the way. He's unable to turn his head, but he can feel his brothers and sisters. They are running alongside him, breathing, snarling. He cuts away from the pack, as the trees begin to thin out and lead him toward the Pierces' backyard. He slows to a creep as he makes his way across the backyard, then through the sliding door. He's in the house now, barely making a sound. Up the stairs. Into Wendy's room. She's asleep. He slips underneath the covers, spoons her. The moon is in the window. She stirs, and takes the beast's forearm into her grip. He sinks his teeth into her, tearing every muscle and tendon in her shoulder. There's nothing but screaming. And blood.

Jack springs awake to his mother leaning over him. "Hey, are you okay? You're all sweaty. You must've been having some dream."

"I'm fine," he answers, lying.

"Hey," she says, her voice softer than before. "There's a man in the hallway waiting to see you. He's friendly, says he's the new basketball coach, but I don't think we know him."

"Okay. Send him in."

She leans in closer, "He's a black man," she adds, even softer.

"Okay, Ma, send him the fuck in!" Jack snaps, surprising both of them.

"Wow. Fine, Jack. You didn't have to cuss at me," she says, as she exits the room.

He's uncertain why he lashed out, and too exhausted to apologize for it. Gail comes back in, followed by a man in a top hat and trench coat. Jack has never seen the man before in his life, but immediately feels an odd, warm connection to him.

"Hello Jack," the stranger says, somberly, as he removes his hat. "May we have a minute or two, Mrs. Sharpe?"

Gail looks toward her son for affirmation. He nods. "I guess so then," she says. "I'm going to pull the car around."

The stranger slides a chair up to the bedside and says, "Hey, champ," as he places his hand on top of Jack's. "My name is Wilson Steels. I'm not going to get into how I found you, but I want you to know something very important."

"Okay."

"I know how you're feeling. I have been there. All of us have. I say us, because I want you to know that you are not alone. I want you to keep that in mind for the next few weeks, because it will help get you through them. That's the good news. I'm afraid there is some bad news, however. Some terrible news. I won't sugarcoat it. The next three weeks are going to be hell. And there is no light at the end of the tunnel. Only pain and suffering that is hard to imagine."

Jack begins to cry. Every one of Wilson's words sting, because he knows they are true and in some strange way, he knew they were coming.

"When the full moon rises, you will want to be with us," Wilson continues. "This is how you can reach me," he places a white business card, with nothing but the phone number embossed in gold, down on the tray table. "Please call. Anytime within the next three weeks. It could be three in the morning, doesn't matter. We will come and get you, wherever you are. Jack, in your heart, you will want to tell your family and friends about this meeting, but your instincts will tell you not to. Follow your instincts. Your loved ones can't help you. They'll only make this situation more complicated, I'm afraid."

"Mr. Steels," Jack sobs. "What is going to happen to me?"

"A transformation. That's all I can say. Come stay with us and I will explain everything. I am sorry, Jack. So very sorry."

Gail reenters the room, "Is everything okay?" She asks.

"Everything is just fine. It was my pleasure, Mrs. Sharpe," Wilson says, as he puts his top hat back on. "We're going to have a heck of a season next year. Jack, we'll be in touch."

Main Street is nothing like I remember it.

The corner bodega and stationary store have been replaced by a café. The Chinese restaurant, where Rob drowned a Ninja Turtle in the fish tank, is now a children's boutique. Even Pete's "Cosmic Comics" has made way for a clothing store with fiberglass hipsters mingling in the windows.

Yoga studio? Check.

Juice bar? Check.

The abandoned buildings that used to make up the rest of the street have become swanky storefronts, most of which are dressed up for Halloween. There's corn stalks, pumpkins, and well-disposed monsters in every direction.

I have my hood over a baseball cap, hoping no one will recognize the Sharpe boy who went missing back in 1997. I'm sitting on a bench across from a quaint coffee shop; string lantern lights decorate its front window. There's a couple of tables set up out front. The owner flips the sign on the front door from OPEN to CLOSED, then follows a group of sharply dressed young people out. She smiles and waves goodbye as she locks up. Her face is fuller, and she's curvier than she used to be; other than that, she looks exactly like I remember.

The sun is setting, and the lampposts are turning on one by one. I haven't felt these kinds of nerves in a long time. When I get close enough, I remove my hood and say "Wendy" as my voice trembles.

"Yes," she answers, slowly looking up from her cell phone. When her eyes meet mine, I see a wave of familiarity wash over her face. "Jack?"

"Hello again."

"I um. I don't feel so hot," she says, as she staggers. "I have to sit down." She takes a seat at one of her tables. I do the same, and give her a minute while she searches for words.

"This is really strange. I thought you were dead. We...we all did."

"I know. I'm sorry."

"Twenty years. It's been almost twenty years."

"I know. I'm so sorry."

Say something else, you jackass.

"I have to go. I have to pick my daughter up from ballet," she says, as she rises and moves quickly toward her car. To make sure I don't freak her out more than I already have, I try not to make any sudden movements toward her.

"Wendy. Please. I understand that this is crazy, but I can explain everything. I'm staying at the inn. Room 12. Please come there. Bring Chris and Rob if you can."

"Chris and Rob? What the hell are you talking about? I haven't seen those guys in a long time. What is even happening right now? I have to go." She unlocks the door to her Jetta and starts to get in.

"Wendy," I say, a bit louder this time. "Just consider it. I can explain. I have to explain. Please."

She pauses for a moment, but doesn't look up. I watch as she slams the door and pulls away from the curb as quickly as she can. A horn blares as she cuts off an oncoming car. I adjust my cap and toss my hood back on. That didn't go exactly like I've pictured, but I guess it's a start. I'm hungry and exhausted. Some food and a bed at the inn sounds like a dream, but I have one more stop on the way there.

I walk my old bike route, cutting through the carnival grounds, then past Luigi's, down Broadway, and finally come to the highway. Night has fallen as I move quickly along the edge of the woods, the glow of headlights zipping by me.

When I was ten, my father and I spray painted the words SHARPE ROAD on a piece of wood and nailed it to the tree closest to the highway. The sign has vanished, along with most of the opening to the dirt road that leads to the house. It's been swallowed up by the forest, leaving just enough room for a car to fit through. The surrounding driveway is even worse. I recall the way my father used to stay on me about keeping a good-looking yard and get a feeling that something is definitely wrong here.

I gaze upon the old basketball hoop, and my adrenaline wears off for the first time since I fled the mansion.

What the fuck am I doing?

What are my parents going to say?

What would any parent say when their only child comes back from the dead? I'm about to turn around, find the nearest phone and call Roger, when it hits me like an eighteen wheeler.

Roger is gone. Wilson is gone.

The people that gave me life, however, are ten feet away, in my childhood home. I approach the front door and knock.

Nothing.

I knock louder, for about ten seconds straight.

Nothing.

I sneak around to the side of the house and peer through a living room window. There's light from a television coming through the curtains.

I come to the front door again and give the knob a forceful turn. It's jammed but unlocked, so I let myself in. Noise from the television fills the house as I examine the shitshow before me. My mother would never allow this.

He's in his recliner, passed out. The coffee table in front of him is barely visible underneath pill bottles and empty beer cans. On a closer look, there are spoons and bottle caps scattered about, along with a few hypodermic needles. I turn to my father and find his forearm wrapped tightly with a rubber hose. I continue into the filthy kitchen. Just as I begin to think that my mother no longer lives here, I see her face. It's young, just like I remember it - on a Mass card, pinned by a magnet to the refrigerator door. I take it in my hand and flip it over, to read everything I already knew and the one thing I was looking for.

She died three years ago, with her husband by her side.

I walk back out into the living room and shout at him. He stirs slightly, and struggles to open his eyes.

"Who's that?" He asks; his voice sounds like it's coming from some bubbling abyss.

"It's Jack."

"Jack, my boy," he mumbles. "You coming to see me again? You bring me something? Something to eat. For me and Mommy?"

"What the fuck, Dad?"

He says something else that I can't decipher then nods out. My knees get weak, and I collapse to the floor. Crying.

I cry for Wilson and I cry for Roger. I cry for this place. Mostly, I cry for myself.

The monster that I am.

When I rise, he's still unconscious. I clear off the coffee table, throwing every bit of paraphernalia in a trash bag, then heave it into the woods about a hundred yards out. I discard the rotten milk and fly infested meat from the fridge, along with the roach infested slop in the pantries. Before I leave, I place a hundred dollar bill on the kitchen counter, along with a note that reads:

Dad, I am truly sorry for the way things turned out. I love you. Jack

It's midnight by the time I get back to my room at the inn. I take a shower, then scarf down some beef chow mein as I watch a movie about a group of guys having a bachelor party in Las Vegas. They've lost the groom and can't remember shit from the night before.

I wonder if this is the sort of life that normal guys in their twenties and thirties lead. I think about what I've missed. I think about Wendy. The look she gave me. She hates me and I don't blame her. Tomorrow I plan to hit the road and never return to Cedarwood. I have no idea what the future looks like with no Wilson Steels to guide me, but my immediate plans couldn't be clearer.

I am going to find Teddy Silver and his fat henchman and I am going to murder them both.

XVI.

Jack never made it to the pool party. He's not answering phone calls either. It's been a week since Chris and Rob have heard from him at all, so they're peddling their Diamondbacks with purpose, primed to give their boy hell when they arrive at the Sharpe's house.

"Hey, guys, come on in," Marvin says, when he answers the door. "You boys want a soda or something? I know it's a long ride from town."

"We're okay," they answer.

"Wendy is up there with him. He ain't been himself lately. I dunno."

"He hasn't answered his line all week," Christopher says.

"Is he laying pipe up there, Mr. Sharpe?" Rob asks.

"Yo, Rob. Mrs. Sharpe is in the next room. Watch that talk, dude."

"Sorry, Mr. Sharpe."

Marvin yells up the stairs. "Jack. Wendy. Your buddies are down here. Join us, I'll make some lunch!"

Jack comes downstairs a few minutes later. He's in a pair of dingy pajama pants and a tattered white tee. He's pale, his hair is matted to his head. The most noticeable difference is the patchy facial hair beginning to sprout from his face.

"Jesus Christ. You look like shit," Rob blurts out.

"Rob. The language," Marvin says.

"Shit, sorry, Mr. Sharpe."

Jack takes a seat at the kitchen table with them. "Where's Wendy?" Chris asks.

"She's asleep," Jack answers. His voice sounds different. Deeper. Marvin examines the three friends. Jack is the oldest by a few months, but now it looks like a few years.

"You hungry, buddy?" Marvin asks his son. "I got some salami and provolone. Them banana peppers you like. I'll make up some hoagies."

"I'm not hungry. Actually, guys, I'm not feeling all that good. Thanks for coming by, but I have to go back to sleep," Jack says.

"Wait a sec. We need to talk bro," Rob says.

Marvin rises from his chair. "Okay, you boys talk it out. I'm gonna go see what my wife is working on. Looked like a still life or something." Rob leans in closer as Marvin exits the kitchen. "Dude. What is going on with you?"

"What he's trying to say is we're worried about you, man," Chris adds.

"I'm fine. It's just my chest. You know? It's still bothering me."

"That's bullshit. Even if your chest is bothering you, that's no excuse to ignore us," Rob laments.

"Rob, chill," Christopher says, smacking his friend on the bicep.

"Nah. I'm not gonna chill. Maybe you're the one that got hurt, and that sucks. But we all went through that craziness together. Fats and that other psycho chasing us on dirt bikes. Meryl Pierce speeding to the hospital, with you in the backseat bleeding all over like Mr. Orange from Reservoir Dogs." Chris chuckles at his friend's comparison. "This shit ain't funny, man. We waited there all night. We visited you every day. Then you get released and it's like we don't exist."

"I hear what you're saying, and I apologize," Jack snaps back. "It's just...there's some things you wouldn't understand. Nobody will. I just need to be alone right now, to sort it all out."

"You aren't alone, though. Wendy is up there with you," Christopher says.

"That's because he's a pussy-whipped little bitch."

Jack grabs Rob by the collar of his tee shirt and pulls him from the chair. He swings him toward the floor but Rob pumps the brakes and uses his forearms to unlock Jack's grip. He overpowers his friend and puts him in a headlock.

"Guys, what the hell is happening?" Christopher shouts, as he puts his body between them. "Stop this shit!"

Christopher manages to break the hold and separate them as Jack cries out, "I will kill you!"

"You ain't killing shit, you little bitch!"

By now, Wendy has come running down the steps, and Marvin and Gail stampede in from the next room.

"Boys, let's break this up," Marvin demands, as he grabs his son from behind, restraining his arms. Jack wriggles from his father's grip, and heads towards the stairs, snatching Wendy by the hand on the way and pulling her with him. "We need to sit and figure this out."

"Forget that, Dad. Make some hoagies for them, I don't care. I'm going back upstairs."

186

"What the hell was all that about?" Wendy asks, as Jack stomps around his bedroom, throwing punches at shadows. "Jack, please calm down."

"Fuck him. Always acting like some tough guy."

"He's your best friend."

"No, he's not. He's a punk."

"Okay, just sit. Relax." Jack sits on the edge of the bed as Wendy massages his shoulders. "Listen, I have to get home. I'm like an hour late already. My father probably has the FBI looking for me." Jack desperately wants to tell her about the unexpected visitor in the hospital. It's now or never.

"Wendy," he whispers.

She saw something in the woods. Perhaps it's connected to whatever Wilson Steels was talking about. He owes it to her - to let her know about the stranger that came to see him. Then again, Wilson said in no uncertain terms that it will only make this situation more complicated than it already is. He not only hears Wilson's words; he could feel them. In some impalpable way, he knows they are true.

"What is it, Jack?"

"Nothing. Just, thank you for staying with me so much. For listening."

"Thank you as well," she says, as she hugs his head, bringing it close to her chest. "Something really weird went down that night, and I'm just glad I experienced it with you. I mean, I hate that you got hurt but we're in this thing together. That makes me feel better."

Her words almost break him in two.

It's almost noon when there's a knock on the door, which means I slept way longer than I planned to.

I stumble over and open it to reveal Christopher Hammond and, about ten feet behind him, Robert Valentini, leaning on a Lexus, sucking on some high-tech contraption.

"Well, I'll be goddamned. It is you," a balder, much heavier Christopher says. He extends a hand, and I take it in mine. To my surprise, he pulls me in and hugs me tightly, pounding my back a few times with his fist. He lets go, backs up, and looks me over. "Man, this is a trip."

I'm embarrassed by the empty liquor bottles and fast food debris scattered about my room, so I ask if they'll give me a few minutes to get dressed, then walk over to the diner for some lunch. On me. They agree, much to the very visible dismay of Rob.

"How's it going, man? Have you heard any good Hip Hop music lately?" An absurd question, I know, but a decent attempt to break the ice.

"I don't listen to that stuff anymore," Rob answers, stoically. He looks much different. Gone are the baggy clothes and backward cap. Instead, he's rocking an awkward side part, and wearing a blue Under Armour polo tucked into a pair of nut-hugging gray slacks.

After a moment of silence that's probably still lingering somewhere over the North Pole, I go back inside and change out of my basketball shorts and cutoff tee into something presentable. Ten minutes later, we are walking to the diner. Rob is following about twenty feet behind us, nervously taking hits from the thing that's too hi-tech to be smoking from. I ask him what it is.

"It's called a vaporizer. They didn't have these wherever you were?"

"I've seen them before, I just didn't know what it's called, or what's inside."

"Tobacco. I gave up cigarettes."

"Look at this guy, Rob," Christopher interjects. "He's in better shape than you are. You been working out all these years?"

"Something like that," I answer. At my request, we take a corner booth, away from the crowd, and put in our order. Rob isn't feeling lunch, so Christopher jokes, "More for us."

I learn that Chris started delivering pizza for Luigi senior year. He stuck around long enough that when the old man was ready to sell it, Chris took out a loan and bought the place. He's married to a girl that was a few grades below us, and they have four children. The youngest, his first boy, was born a year ago.

"It's chaos at my house. Seriously, man. Four kids, two dogs. I get one day a week away from the pizzeria and, by the time it's over, I'm ready to get back to work," he explains, as he makes bacon sandwiches out of his syrup-drenched French toast and shovels them into his mouth. "I had a heart attack last year. You believe that? Thirty-five and I got a bum ticker already."

"I bet he never would've guessed," Rob says, gesturing toward Chris' meal.

Besides the obvious hostility Rob has toward me, it seems like there may be some tension between him and Chris as well. Either that or the guy is simply a big douchebag nowadays. I once again try to bring some levity to the situation. "So, Rob. Did you ever bang that redhead from forensic science? I forget her name."

"Her name is Lexi Bell. She moved to Maryland. Has a nice family. Wrote a cookbook, actually. And the funny part is? No mystery. No investigation. We stay in touch on Facebook."

His attitude is starting to rub me the wrong way, but I try my best to keep it light. "Chris has told me all about himself. What is it that you do?

"I'm a teacher."

"Cool. What subject?"

"Physical education."

"Awesome."

"I also coach high school football. Only two losses since I took over."

"That's fantastic, man."

"I was married to an out- of-town girl, you probably don't know her. We divorced three years later. Hot-headed bitch said I abused her. It was this big ordeal. I almost lost my job. Since then, I've had some of the finest pieces of ass you could ever imagine. Sometimes I bang 'em two at a time. I like to lift weights and shoot guns. Anything else you want to know?"

"Nah, I think that covers it."

After another moment of suffocating silence, Chris speaks up. "What's your issue, man?"

"To be honest, I have a lot of issues with this whole situation," Rob answers.

"I could tell."

"What did you expect? I'm not going to sit here, stuffing my face. Acting like this ain't some fucked up shit."

"Then why did you agree to this? You didn't have to come," Chris says, glancing toward Jack.

"Because I wanted to hear it, face-to-face. I wanted to hear where this guy's been for the past twenty years."

I understand his frustration. The three of us had been inseparable from preschool to a few weeks before I left Cedarwood. These men deserve the truth. "Okay. He's right, Chris," I say. "I owe you guys an explanation."

I understand how crazy what I'm about to say will sound, but I figure it's not nearly as crazy as actually living it. This world is a truly bizarre place. My childhood friends should be made aware of that.

"The night of the party. The thing that attacked me. It was a Lycanthrope."

Chris asks, "A Lyca-what now?"

"A Lycanthrope, it's something like a werewolf."

They sit across the table. Totally dumbstruck.

"It sounds nuts. But it's true. The affliction, my affliction, is spread when a Lycan's claw comes in contact with a human being's blood. So after I was attacked, I had until the next full moon to find the only man that could help me. Obviously, I was scared shitless. I had to leave. It killed me to do so, but I had to."

Rob's reaction is not one I expected. He starts to laugh. An exaggerated belly laugh, made to draw attention to the fact that he thinks this whole thing is ridiculous. He gets up from his chair and says, "Fucking werewolves. Unbelievable," then bolts toward the exit. The waitress approaches and asks if we are okay.

"Actually, I think we need some Mimosas. What do you think, Jack? Some Mimosas sound good?"

"Sure," I say, relieved that Chris is taking this in stride.

We talk about my story, as we finish off a few more Mimosas and shoot a couple of Kamikazes. Chris is hearing me out, without any doubt or judgement. I feel a tinge of regret, and sadness, that I've missed out on a friendship with this man. He's practically a stranger to me now. We share a good laugh when the manager approaches the table to tell us that we should think about heading to a bar or another establishment better suited to serve our needs. Basically, we've been flagged.

"It's all good, Tim," Chris seems to know him. "So much catching up to do. We got a little bit lost in the moment. We'll pay the check and be out of your hair."

"Thank you, Chris. Hey, do I know you?" Tim asks in my direction. My attempts to look away from him every chance I could have failed.

"Nah, I don't think so," I say, staring down at my empty glass.

"Dude, I do know you. I can't fuc...I can't believe it. Jack Sharpe."

Shit.

"Sweet baby Jesus on a stick. I thought you were dead!"

"Well, here I am."

"I was a grade below you guys. I tried out for the freshman b-ball team when you were already starting junior varsity. This is nuts. Where have you been, man?"

I ignore him, abruptly standing up and tossing enough cash on the table to cover everything. I tell Tim it was nice to see him, and Chris to meet me outside. When Chris exits the diner, he's got a shit eating grin on his face.

"Well, our old buddy Timmy is in there telling everyone that's willing to listen, that Jack Sharpe is back."

"Shit, man. This is exactly what I didn't want to happen."

"Eh, don't sweat it too much. Tim is easily excitable, but also a pretty huge pothead. By six tonight, he'll forget he even saw ya." He checks his phone and continues, "I got an hour or two before the wife starts calling. Where to next?"

"This is your town."

He decides to drive us to a dusty, old tavern known as the Foxhole. I would sometimes find myself at this place with my father, eating mozzarella sticks while he got drunk and flirted with the bartenders. We're the first people here besides the servers, which pleases me. Chris orders us a couple of beers and I address the elephant in the room.

"So, Wendy didn't want to join you today?"

"I'm afraid not. Listen, man, you did a number on her. I mean, we all were affected by it to some degree. The investigation, the constant news people in our shit. But, Wendy? She was messed up good."

"I understand."

"It had been like a year since I heard from her, outside of social media. I'm not big on her overpriced coffee, I'm a Dunkin' Donuts man myself. So, you know, I was shocked when she called me last night. Even more shocked to hear that she had seen you and that you wanted to meet up. Crazy shit, bro."

"I want to thank you."

"For what?"

"For this. For today. It means more than you can imagine."

"Hey, that's what friends are for. Even long-lost ones."

I pick up my bottle, he does the same. We toast to long-lost friends.

We get back to the inn as the sun is setting on Cedarwood. He asks me what I'm going to do now, to which I lie and say hang out for a few more days. I wasn't about to tell him of my immediate plan to kill two human beings.

It's going to be hard to leave him, like it was two decades ago, but I must. We hug it out by his car and he says, "One last thing. Wendy wants me to let her know how today went. Like what I think of you, and if you're safe to be around."

"And?"

"Of course you are, bro. I'm just saying. She told me to tell you, that is, if the day went well..."

"Spit it out, Chris. Shit."

"...That she's open to having dinner with you tomorrow night."

"Isn't she Wendy Moretti now? How will Matt feel about that?"

"Well. They've been on the outs. For a long time. Never should have gotten married in the first place."

"Wow. I didn't think I would see her again before I left."

"There's history there, man. Hey. Listen. I'm drunk. It's a few days before Halloween. Today has been wacky. I'm just going to put it out there. Once or twice a year, we used to get together to shoot the shit. We'd forget about our jobs, our family problems. Just Wendy Pierce and me reminiscing about, shit, I dunno. That summer. The nineties. You. Mostly you. Wanna know something else?" I can't be sure but I think Chris is beginning to cry. "I thought I had a shot with her. I was ready to risk it all. My beautiful fucking family." He stops himself. "She loves you, bro. I love you too." He pulls me in for another bear hug, and rests his big head on my chest for a moment, soaking my shirt. Yep, he's crying. "I love you."

"I love you, too," I say, for lack of anything else. It looks like Silver and his goon will live to see a few more days.

192

I pay for another night at the inn, and get the feeling that the old lady working the desk is starting to develop a crush on me. When I hit my room, I order an unjustifiable amount of Domino's Pizza as *Close Encounters of the Third Kind* plays on the flat screen.

I think about my mother. My father. It's like I've lost them both, all over again.

I think about Wilson and Roger. When I woke up this morning, the only thing in the world I wanted was revenge. I was going to use everything within my power to locate the scumbags who took them from me. Once I found them, I would play the shadows. Wait it out, until the bad moon was high. Then make my move.

Now there's Wendy.

As Richard Dreyfuss erects Devil's Tower in his living room, I ruminate over what I'll say to her. What she'll say to me. I start to wonder if any of the clothing I have in my duffle bags is acceptable attire for a date. Then again, who said this was a date? Christ. I've become the hopelessly romantic wolfman of New Jersey.

When I'm done gorging myself, I lay down and remove the folded piece of paper with Wendy's cell number scribbled on it. I place it on the nightstand against the clock radio and, as the little gray men lead Dreyfuss into the mothership, I fall into the best slumber I've had since Clinton was in office.

XVIII.

Three days until the full moon, and Jack's condition is deteriorating. His thoughts are like scattered pieces of an impossible jigsaw puzzle. No matter how much he scrambles to place them together, they simply will not fit. It has made him agitated and, at times, even mean. The more his parents try to console him, the more he pushes them away.

"He needs to talk to someone," Gail says, as she paces the kitchen.

"I don't know what that means," Marvin snaps back.

"It means a psychiatrist, Marvin!"

"No. Hell no. He ain't seeing no headshrinker. Forget it."

"Then what are we going to do? Because I'll tell you what, I don't even recognize him anymore. Do you? Do you recognize that boy up there?

"He's going through some shit is all. It runs down my side of the family. Gloom and doom, and all that. It'll pass."

"Marvin, listen to me," she says, as she takes her husband's face into her hands. "There is something not right with him."

"I ain't listening to this," he says as he backs away from her and grabs his keys off the counter. "I'm going for a ride. I'm gonna think about the best way to help our boy. I'll figure it out."

"You're leaving right now? He hasn't been out of his room in days. He doesn't even see his girlfriend anymore. He needs us."

"And I need to drive so I can approach this situation with a clear head. I'll be back in an hour with some pizza."

"Pizza isn't fixing anything."

"It's a start," he slams the door on the way out.

Jack listens to his parents' words echo through the house as he crams his Discman, and as many CDs that'll fit into his Jansport. When it's full, he tosses it on top of his suitcase, already packed and in the shrubbery below his bedroom window. With his father gone, it's time to make his move.

"Oh my god, Jacky. You startled me," Gail says, when her son appears in the doorway of her studio, shaved and showered. "You're looking a little better."

"I'm going to Wendy's house," he says.

"Okay, that's great," she takes him into her arms. He's been taller than his mother ever since he turned twelve. "I'm just so happy to see you out of your room. Do you want to talk about anything before you go?"

194

"No. I'm fine."

"Okay. Your father is getting pizza. Will you be back in an hour?"

"I don't know, Ma. Save me a couple slices."

"Okay, honey. Please be careful. Say hello to Wendy for us. We miss her."

As he steps out of the back door of the only home he has ever known, he turns and looks toward his mother. She's leaning on the kitchen counter watching him thoughtfully. He nods his head at her and she returns it with a teary eyed smile.

Their song plays low from the Daytona's speakers as he rehearses what he's going to say to her. There's no right words. Knowing that he had to leave her, he simply couldn't stand seeing her anymore. He parks and approaches the house. Before he can ring the bell, Meryl opens the front door.

"I didn't expect to see you," she says.

"Hey. Is Wendy home?"

"Yes. She's really pissed off at you."

"I know, and I don't blame her. I just need to tell her something."

Besides the obvious fact that he looks like he's aged ten years in two weeks, Meryl senses something isn't right with him.

"I guess I'll get her," she says, noticing beads of sweet starting to drip down his forehead. "Are you okay, Jack?"

"I'm fine," he answers, wiping them with his sleeve.

"Come in, nobody is here but me and Wendy. Chill for a minute on the couch while I go up and get her."

Jack takes a seat, as the Pierce's Golden Retriever cautiously enters the room. She gets down low on her front paws and begins to growl.

"Lucy, it's okay. You know me."

At the sound of Jack's voice, the dog starts to scamper back and forth from the bottom of the stairwell to the entryway where Jack is sitting. Meryl comes running down the steps, followed by Wendy. They try all the tricks: patting, scratching, massaging, nothing is working.

"I'll take her for a walk," Meryl exclaims, as she retrieves a leash from the front closet.

"Have you ever seen her act like this?" Wendy asks.

"Never. She's being a crazy bitch," Meryl answers, as she frantically clips the leash on. They go thundering down the hallway and out the front door, leaving Wendy and Jack alone. They're standing at opposite ends of the living room. Jack can barely look at her.

"Are you going to say something?" Wendy asks.

"I um, I am. I have to."

He continues the staring contest with his sneakers.

"Jack. I'm not going to wait all day."

"I hate that I have to say it but I have no choice."

"I knew it. You're breaking up with me." Her words snap him out of it.

"What? No. Absolutely not. I would never break up with you. You're like the best thing that has ever happened to me."

"Okay. So what is it?"

"I um. I have to go away. Just for a little while."

"Go away? What are you talking about?"

"I can't talk about it right now, but one day I will explain everything. I promise."

Wendy tries to hold back tears, to no avail. She had convinced herself that Jack was going to break up with her. That he was going through some stuff and, like so many guys before him, he was going to use the "It's not you, it's me" spiel. Whatever this is, however, has her genuinely perplexed.

"I don't understand, Jack. You're seventeen. You're going into your senior year of high school. Where are you possibly going away to?"

"It sounds nuts, but I don't even know, Wendy," the waterworks have started for him as well. "Here," he unclips the chain that holds his anchor pendant. "I want you to hang on to this until I come back."

"This is your special thing. I can't take this."

"You have to. Please."

He places it into her palm, then closes her hand with his own. For the first time in a while, he looks directly at her. She notices that the whites of his eyes have developed a shadow of amber, and his pupils have become smaller. It sends a chill down her spine. She pulls her hands free and backs away.

"Jack."

"Yes."

"Does this have anything to do with what happened in the woods? The thing I saw?"

"I don't know. Maybe I'll find out."

"Okay. So that's it. You better go now, my parents will be home soon." She sits down on the couch, wiping the tears from her face, waiting for Jack to leave.

"Wendy - "

"Go."

He walks toward the front door, trying his hardest not to turn around and say anything else. He understands that this is the way it has to be. As he turns the handle, he looks back once more. He hopes to see her come into the foyer, to tell him that she'll miss him.

Nothing.

He exits, walking as slowly as possible to the Daytona. Maybe she'll come running from the house, into his arms. He'll scoop her up, they'll kiss passionately as he stumbles back against his car. He looks for her.

Nothing.

He gets in, turns the ignition and puts it in drive. He coasts down their driveway, looking in the rear view mirror, praying to see some sign of her.

Nothing.

XIX.

Our phone call is short and to the point.

We agree to meet a few towns over from Cedarwood, at a quiet place called The Lighthouse. She's still a bit suspicious of me, so she wants people around, but she also wants to keep any curious townsfolk from meddling in our business. Her voice sounds just like it did when we used to stay up all night and chat. I would march around my bedroom aimlessly, getting tangled in the telephone cord, trying to make her laugh so I knew she wasn't asleep.

I get dressed at the inn. I opted against going out and doing any risky clothes shopping, so I don a white tee and a pair of blue jeans that I had packed.

The bar at The Lighthouse is a dimly lit, rustic affair. I grab a comfy seat at the end, by a flat screen. The Birds are up by seven and the bartender is determined to pick my brain about it. "I haven't really been very much into sports lately," I tell her.

"No? A big guy like you? I imagined you played some in your day."

"Some basketball in high school, that's about it."

There was a sunny afternoon when my father spent a few hours trying to teach me how to sink a left-handed layup. I believed he was so good back then that he could've been playing in the NBA. I guess that's how all sons see their fathers. That's how they should, not like I did - shot out and defeated by drugs. I guess I blame myself for the way things turned out.

With him, with my mother, with everyone.

I fled and destroyed my parents' lives. I led Teddy Silver to the mansion. I put Wendy through hell. She's supposed to be here in five minutes, and I battle with the urge to pay my tab and retreat. What good is meeting her going to do, anyway? As I reach for the cash in my pocket, I hear my name whispered.

She's wearing glasses, with raven black hair straight to her shoulders. Her form fitting black dress shows off her hourglass shape. A tiny silver crucifix hangs from a necklace, just above her cleavage. She's gorgeous and smells amazing, but I was expecting someone else.

"Can I help you?" I ask.

"You can. If you follow me outside to my car, it would help me a great deal," she says softly.

"Excuse me?"

"Jack. We have Wendy. It would behoove you to follow me out to my car. Right now." Her words almost knock me off my stool. We have Wendy?

"Who the fuck is we?"

"Lower your voice, Jack. You want to avoid a scene. I'm only going to say it a third time. Pay your tab and follow me outside, or something bad happens to Mrs. Moretti."

"If she is so much as breathed on wrong, bodies will drop. Starting with yours."

I toss enough cash down on the bar to cover my drinks, and leave a hefty tip for the talkative bartender. She may be the last kind soul I meet in this progressively fucked existence of mine. I follow behind the imperious stranger and I'm willing to bet that the sleeveless dress was a conscious decision to showcase her beautifully sculpted arms, and the fact that she could probably best any man in the place in a fair one. We hit the parking lot and I continue to follow her to the far side, where a black Escalade is parked. She opens the door, and orders me to get in.

Stimpy is behind the wheel with Teddy Silver riding shotgun. In the far back is a sweaty, reptilian-looking man, pointing a handgun at a bound and gagged Wendy. It takes every bit of strength in me not to attempt some Jackie Chan shit on these motherfuckers when I spot her, but it's too risky. I'm once again at the mercy of these people, and this time so is a totally innocent woman. I take a seat in the middle row, along with their female companion. Stimpy puts it in drive and pulls away from the Lighthouse.

"So, Jack. Here we are again," Silver says.

"Let her go. It's me you want. She has absolutely nothing to do with any of this. Let her go and I'll do whatever you need me to do," I plead.

"I'm afraid it's not that easy anymore, Jack. You see my friend back there? You ate his brother a few weeks back. You ate his brother, without a second thought about it."

"And you did it right in front of me, after you mutilated me and left me for dead. You fucking monster," Stimpy growls.

"Your pal, Roger, murdered another one of our associates as well. With a ninja sword," Silver continues. "I must say however, Roger Brown and the King Wolf himself were bigger scores for us. I imagine, without them, you're all just a bunch of scared puppy dogs. Oh, my apologies. Did you know that, Jack? Did you know that your friends are dead?"

"Yes, because I watched it happen. You should try looking up when you're slaughtering people."

"And Steels should have tried erasing the history on his computer. It led us right to Cedarwood."

"Okay, it's over then. Kill me. Just let her go. Please."

"We are gonna kill ya," Reptile Man hisses. "Right after I have a go with Wendy here and make you watch. She's hot, man. I reckon I'll enjoy every second." He moves his tongue up the side of her neck, and she cries through the thick piece of material tied around her head.

I make a quick move for the gun, when I feel something shock my back, followed by an intense current through my body. I sink back into the seat and see Teddy Silver wielding a cattle prod.

"Don't try that shit again," Reptile Man says, as he jams his gun's muzzle against the back of my skull.

She slipped on a gray sweater and black leggings, did her hair and makeup, then drove twenty minutes to meet a man that she hasn't seen in eighteen years - only to be kidnapped in the parking lot by these scumbags, and I'm responsible. I hear her sobbing behind me and my heart shatters into a million pieces. She has a daughter, a coffee shop, a life. At any moment, these people can rob her of all of it.

We drive in silence for what feels like hours. I spend it gazing from the window, watching as we move past the trees that line the highway. Occasionally, I turn my head and try to see Wendy; instead, I get Reptile Man's gun in my face. We eventually take an exit and follow a service road to an abandoned industrial park. The area is blanketed in darkness; buildings loom over us like shadowy giants watching our every move. The Escalade slows as we approach a warehouse. Stimpy presses a button on the controller clipped to the sun visor. We enter through a huge steel door.

He hits the button again, closing the door behind us, then parks the vehicle. Silver hops out and, thirty seconds later, the light fixtures hanging from the ceiling turn on. It's like we instantly go from midnight to high noon.

"Let's go, pretty lady," Reptile Man says as he yanks Wendy by her arm out of the Escalade. "You, too," he gestures toward me with the handgun.

I'm outmanned and I'm forced to succumb to this creep's every command. They lead us into the corner of the massive room, to an area surrounded by iron bars. These people love cages.

"This is where you two will wait. My father should be here soon," the woman in the black dress says.

"Who is your father?" I ask, as they slam the door shut and secure it with a chain.

"You wouldn't know him," she answers. "Let's just say he has a vested interest in watching your kind go extinct. This war is bigger than you know, Jack."

Silver comes up from behind the woman and puts his arm around her shoulders. "Did you think I was the man behind the curtain?" He asks, as they share a quick kiss. "I'm flattered."

They exit the main room, leaving just Wendy and me in the cage. I instinctively check the heavy padlock on the chain and give it a forceful tug. The door barely budges.

We're not going anywhere.

Wendy is leaning against one side of the cage, as I pace the opposite side. Eventually I slide down the bars and take a seat on the concrete floor across from her. She has her head turned away from me. Streaks of mascara have dried on her face.

"I'm not going to let them hurt you. I promise."

She chuckles, then turns to me. "No more promises, Jack."

"I am so sorry, Wendy."

"For what? What exactly are you sorry for?"

I'm sorry for everything. For not telling you about what the thing in the woods did to me. Maybe we could have figured it out. Together. I'm sorry for leaving and never returning to Cedarwood. For going eighteen years without finding the courage to come back to you.

"For getting you into this shit," is all I manage to say.

"I got myself into this shit. I went against my better judgement. When every inch of my being was telling me I didn't know you anymore. That I had no idea what kind of shit you could be into. I'm the one that decided to call my mother, last minute, to watch my daughter. I'm the one who lied to Matt about going out with my friends."

"Don't blame yourself. This is on me."

"Well, it doesn't matter now. Does it?"

"I guess not," I scan the place, taking mental notes. "So, what's her name?"

It's not the question she expected. "Audrey," she says with a faint smile, which quickly turns into a cry. Then, a resounding cry, from somewhere deep inside. One I could never understand. A mother's cry. "I have to see her again. I can't leave my baby alone. I have to get out of here."

Her despair enrages me. I look out from our cage again, around the huge, insipid room. Our only hope is to try something when one of these bastards comes back into the cell. At least if I can fight them off long enough to give Wendy a head start or something.

Fuck. I don't know.

Reptile Man comes back in through the door they left from, carrying something large. Bigger than him. It takes a second for it to register that he's towing a filthy mattress into the room. Stimpy is following behind, with his trusty rifle in hand.

"I know it ain't a honeymoon suite or nothing like that," Reptile Man says, as he tosses the mattress down on the unforgiving floor, "but we gotta get this in before the bossman gets here." Wendy and I stand up and naturally drift toward each other. I plant myself in front of her.

"Well, look at that. Chivalry ain't dead after all," Stimpy says.

"This is going down whether you like it or not, Hoss," Reptile Man says, nearing the door, hand resting on the gun in his belt strap. Stimpy aims the rifle at my head, as his partner inserts the key, slowly, into the padlock. "Move. Now," he says. "Either you let this happen, or you get shot and it happens anyway."

"Fuck you," Wendy bellows from behind me. "You're going to have to kill me for this to happen!"

They look at each other and then charge in. I pounce as quickly as I can toward Stimpy's rifle, grabbing it by the barrel with both hands, then yanking it with all my strength. Reptile Man sneaks up behind me and lodges his forearm across my throat. I can feel my windpipe start to collapse as Stimpy overpowers my grip and pulls the rifle from my hands. Wendy grabs Reptile Man's face from behind, digging her nails into his face.

He shouts, "Bitch!" then whips around and delivers a backhand, sending her to the floor. It gives me just enough time to square up with the skinny man, and throw a blind haymaker at his jaw. It connects perfectly, causing him to stumble backward and collide with the bars. As I turn to Stimpy, he swings the rifle like an Easton Ultra Light. I attempt to duck, but the stock grazes the top of my head.

202

I see splashes of light. Reds and blues.

Like fireworks.

I feel another impact on the back of my head. My thoughts are muddled, but I imagine it was the floor.

I've failed Wendy once again. She's screaming. At the top of her lungs.

Begging them to stop.

XX.

It's nine in the morning when Marvin knocks on the front door of the Pierce residence. When Margaret last saw him, he was cleaned up for parent-teacher night at the high school, so she doesn't immediately recognize the unkempt man at her doorstep.

"Hi. Can I help you?"

"Hello there, Mrs. Pierce. I'm Marvin Sharpe, I think we've met once or twice before."

"Oh, yes, Marvin. Of course. How are you?"

"I'm fine. Jack didn't come home last night. He told my wife that he was coming here."

"Oh no. Okay, let me get Wendy, see if she knows anything. We didn't get in until late last night. The girls were already in bed. Come in."

He follows her through the foyer, trying to walk as straight as he possibly can. For the first time since before the accident, Marvin got good and drunk. He spent the night in Jack's bedroom, finishing a bottle of whiskey as he thumbed through his son's sketchbook. Page after page of drawings, depicting a hairy humanoid lurching through the trees.

He examines the palatial abode and is surprised by how well adjusted the Pierce kids are, because the parents are just as he thought, a couple of rich snobs. Lucy trots in and begins to sniff him out.

"Hey, girl, he says, scratching behind her ears. "You're a beautiful girl. Ain't ya?" The dog soaks up the affection then plops down at the man's feet.

"Hi, Mr. Sharpe," Wendy says as she enters.

"Hey, Wendy. Call me Marvin. Please."

"Okay," she says, taking a seat on the couch across from where Marvin is sitting. "I told my mom I needed to talk to you alone."

"Is everything okay?"

"Well, the thing is..." she hesitates for a moment, nervously twirling a strand of her hair.

"Wendy. Please."

"Jack did stop by last night. But only for a minute. He told me he was leaving. He said, he, like, had to."

"He had to leave?"

"He didn't tell me anything else. He couldn't. He doesn't know anything else. But he said he'll be back. He promised."

"I don't understand."

"He gave me this," she removes the anchor pendant from underneath her Cedarwood Field Hockey tee shirt. "He said he'll be back for it."

"That was my father's."

"I'm sorry. Do you want it back?"

"Of course not. Jack wanted you to have it. I want you to have it. My boy keeps his word. If he said he'll come back for it. He will."

Tears begin to roll down Wendy's face, she's been fighting them back since she walked in. Marvin approaches her and rests his hand on her shoulder. She stands, and catches him off-guard by wrapping her arms around him.

"It's going to be okay," he says, as he rubs her back. "He'll come back to us."

He follows Wendy to the front door. They exchange phone numbers and say their goodbyes. Marvin removes the keys from his pocket and heads toward his pickup.

"Mr...Marvin," Wendy says. "There's one more thing. The night Jack was hurt, we saw something in the woods."

"A strange...animal, or creature, of some kind?"

"Yes," Wendy says, in quiet shock. "Did Jack tell you?"

"Maybe he was trying to," he answers, peering beyond his truck, across the road, and into the trees. He turns back toward Wendy and looks into her rheumy eyes.

"Keep your head up. It's going to be okay," he assures her, even though his gut tells him that nothing is going to be okay.

Ever again.

XXI.

The pond has frozen over. Snowflakes fall all around us.

"The koi survive all winter. Right there underneath the ice," Wilson explains, between draws from his pipe. I look down and notice orange silhouettes of the many fish.

They're still. Dormant.

"I want to tell you about a place. A place where you can coexist with the beast," he continues. "It's quite the journey to get there, and most never do. You, Jack. You, my friend, will. And, when you do, the power you'll possess is truly remarkable."

His words confuse me, as I continue to examine the immobile orange splotches underneath the ice.

Suddenly one flutters. Then another.

As they begin to move, whipping their fins, their true forms take shape. The ice begins to crack.

Like a tidal wave, it hits me. But this time it feels different.

It's like I've harnessed it.

I stand up, relieved to see the shadow of the beast.

It falls over Reptile Man, who hasn't been able to overpower Wendy. Her leggings are pulled down, and her sweater is torn, but she's okay. Wide eyed, paralyzed upon seeing me in this form.

"What the fuck? How is this happening?" He screams, reaching for his firearm. I leap toward him, one foot lands on the gun, the other, on his calf. "Fuck!"

I grab him by his neck and peel him away from her. I sense Stimpy behind me and turn to catch him raising his rifle. I leap again, landing right in front of him. Before he can let off a shot, I shove the barrel of the rifle into his nose, then take my claw and swipe it across his face, tearing most of the flesh from his skull. It never ceases to amaze me how easily a human being can be mangled by the beast.

My beast. Me.

I make sure to finish Stimpy off this time and puncture his chest. The tips of my claws tickle his heart. Wendy is crippled with fear, but this is better than what they had in store for her

Reptile Man hits me with a shot from behind. It stings a bit, but the crushed bullet bounces off my back. He fires again, this one bounces off my chest. He quickly learns that lead ain't getting the job done tonight.

I approach him slowly, giving him a chance to contemplate what's coming. When I'm close enough, I grab both sides of his head and twist his neck like a bottle cap. He collapses to the floor.

Wendy gets to her feet and bolts toward the driver's side of the Escalade. I watch as she retrieves her purse from the backseat, then frantically searches for the vehicle's keys. No luck. She presses the button for the door. As it opens, Teddy Silver and the woman in black appear in my peripheral vision. Silver, with the cattle prod in hand, makes a beeline for Stimpy's rifle. I cut him off.

"Listen. Let's talk about this," he shudders. "I know you can understand me. I know more about your kind than you think. Let my wife and me go and we'll never bother you again. I promise you that."

When I'm close enough, I swat the cattle prod out of his grip and wrap my hand around his neck. Wifey screams as I lift him off the ground; his face turns veiny, a beautiful shade of maroon, as his legs dangle in the air. I've never had this much control. Before, I would've crushed his throat, but I decide to drop him when he's seconds away from death. He hits the floor like a sack of potatoes as his wife sprints to him, dropping on her knees to check his pulse. I grab a handful of hair and yank her close to me as she begs for her life. I trace her cheekbone with the claw of my pointer finger, then take it and perforate her bicep.

A few nights from now, when the moon is high and her perfect shape shifts, both her father and husband will have a change of heart about us Lycans, or they'll put her out of her misery.

The scent of Wendy's perfume leads me to where she's hiding, crouched behind a pallet of gas barrels about fifty yards from the building. The area is pitch black; I'm surprised she made it that far. She calls my name when she feels my presence. I want to respond, but I'm physically incapable of doing so. Instead, I sweep her up and cradle her close, then dash through the darkness as quickly as I can.

We move with the leaves, getting lost in the night. The air carries the first signs of winter as it whips our faces. Wendy is in shock, this much I know. She mumbles "Is this a dream?" under her breath, before nodding out.

I follow the backroads, running in the woods alongside them. Eventually, I come to something that seems like civilization: a liquor store, gas station, and motel. It's midnight and the area is as seedy as they come, ideal for the situation we are in. I catch a glimpse of myself in the window of the liquor store, the hair covering most of my body is beginning to recede, my human attributes are starting to show themselves again.

Inside the office of the motel is a crotchety old man sitting back on a recliner, watching soft porn on a relic of a television set. When he spots us, he barely flinches, just continues sipping on a Corona. It's almost as if he's seen a man carrying an unconscious lady into his establishment a time or two before.

"I need a room."

"No shit? I thought maybe you were running for president."

"Excuse me?"

"It's sixty bucks. No more continental breakfasts."

"I didn't think so."

"Room number two," he says as he hands me a key, connected to a keychain that reads: I'm not a gynecologist, but I'll take a look. Surprisingly, the room isn't as filthy as I imagined it'd be, but I'm not going to take any chances. I lay Wendy down on top of the covers as she begins to stir, then head back out to the vending machines. I grab two bottles of water, two Gatorades, and an array of junk food. When I return, she has regained consciousness, sitting up against the headboard of the bed, holding her legs to her chest.

"You must be starving," I say as I drop the stuff on the bed. "It's all they had out there." She looks at me. Almost through me.

"It's all true," she says. "All of it. You're not insane."

"Did someone say I was?"

"Christopher. He was already researching the best psychiatrists in Jersey." We laugh. In spite of everything, we laugh, and it feels cathartic in some way. "I can't imagine what it's been like for you. I'm so sorry."

"I'm the one that's sorry. I got you wrapped up in this mess. Did that fucker hurt you?"

"No. He ruined my new sweater, but I'll be fine. He certainly got what was coming to him."

We laugh again. Each time, we feel closer to the edge of sanity, but there's some unspoken agreement between us that we'll ride it out, see where it takes us.

I explain everything.

Wilson. Roger.

The last couple of months, and how they led me back to Cedarwood.

The recent development in my affliction.

"So that was the first time you were able to control it? All these years, it's just been happening with every full moon, and you've been white-knuckling it?"

"Yes."

"My God, Jack. I am so sorry."

"Will you stop saying you're sorry? You have nothing to apologize for."

"I mean, I sort of do. I saw the one in the woods, the one that attacked you. What is it, again? A Lycanthroat?

"Thrope."

"Lycanthrope. I should've made us turn around that night."

"How do you know I would have listened?"

"Jack. I could've made you do anything in those days."

"Yea. I guess you're right. So, a coffee shop? I was expecting to find Dr. Wendy."

"Well, I attended medical school. I was almost finished, actually. Then my father passed away."

"I'm so sorry."

"It's okay. I moved back to Cedarwood to be with my mother, mainly because Meryl and Abby suck. Matt and I started dating, got married. He never wanted me to go back to school. He liked the idea of the little wife being at home."

"That figures."

She tosses an empty Gatorade bottle at me.

"We opened the coffee shop a few years ago. He thought I was unfulfilled."

"Were you?"

"I don't think that's any of your business. Is it?"

She opens a bag of Doritos and begins eating them, taking one at a time and breaking it into tiny pieces. Just like in high school.

"You still do that. With your chips. That's unbelievable."

"What? Eat them like a human be...," she stops herself, realizing what she was about to say. "I'm sorry."

"That's quite alright. Can you toss me the Oreo's? They're not quite as tasty as human beings, but they'll do for now."

We laugh once again, at the absurdity of this whole situation.

"It wasn't a total loss," she says. "We have an amazing little girl." She starts to cry. "I have to get home, Jack. Where the hell are we?"

"I smelled the salt air outside. We're near the ocean. That's all I got."

She reaches into her purse and retrieves her cellphone, pressing the screen a few times. "We're right outside of Atlantic City. About an hour from Cedarwood."

"Awesome. I can get that friendly gentleman in the office to call you a cab."

"Don't sweat it. I can get an Uber on here," she explains, continuing to press the screen.

"I don't know how any of that works. It's like sorcery to me."

"You never had a smartphone?"

"Nope. Does that make me dumb?"

"Kind of," she smiles at me, then places it back in her purse. "Just kidding. Paul should be here soon to get me."

"Who is Paul?"

"The Uber driver, Jack. Try to keep up."

I guess Roger was my personal Uber driver. I won't have him this time. I'll send Wendy on her way, and I'll be stranded at some shithole on the outskirts of Atlantic City. Maybe, in time, I'll become one of these homeless drifters with a cardboard sign. It's not like I haven't lived on the streets before, but I was never homeless. I always had the mansion to go back to. Wilson and his koi pond and soul records.

Wendy senses my sadness.

"What's wrong?"

"Nothing," I say. "Just thinking."

"Hey, Jack," she reaches into her purse again. "I believe this belongs to you."

"Wow," I gasp, moving my finger over the anchor. "My grandfather's pendant."

"You told me to hold onto it until you came back. I guess better late than never. Huh?"

"I can't believe it. Thank you so much for keeping it safe," I unclip the chain and put it around my neck. "Still fits."

Her phone buzzes.

"Paul is here."

"That was fast. What did he do, teleport?"

"He was in the area."

"Ah. I see."

"Thank you, Jack."

"For what?"

"Saving me."

"Don't mention it."

We embrace. It starts out a bit stiff, but we quickly melt into each other's arms. The hug seems like it may go on for the rest of time.

"I should go," she says, burrowing her head into my chest.

"I know."

"Do you think those people will come back for you?"

"I have no idea, but if they do, I'll be ready."

"Do you think they'll come back for me?"

I don't know Silver enough to know how personal this thing can get, how vindictive he truly is. It hurts me to know that Wendy will have to live in fear now, for herself, and her daughter. I do my best to comfort her.

"They want me. They want my kind wiped off the face of the earth. You were in the crossfire, but as long as I stay far away, you should be safe."

"Okay. I really should go now."

I walk out of the room alongside her, needing to see Paul for myself. I have reservations about this Uber shit. He's fresh-faced, with a mound of curly hair, wearing an unbuttoned flannel over a Nirvana tee. I figure he was just a baby when that band was around so at least he doesn't settle for the overproduced tripe from his generation.

"Hi guys, let me get the door for y'all," he says nervously, as he hops out and opens a door to the backseat. Wendy gets in.

"You coming, sir?"

I'm not sir. My father is sir. I'm just a kid from Cedarwood, who jams out to Das EFX and loves curly fries.

"Listen, man. Get her home safe. She has a little girl waiting for her."

"Of course. I have five stars, sir."

Wendy rolls her window down, and says "Goodbye, Jack."

"Don't worry about a thing, Wendy. You're in good hands with the General here."

She laughs, but there's a quiet sadness to it.

I watch as they pull away, leaving me standing in the lot of the motel, examining my tattered, bloodstained clothes. A cold drizzle begins to fall from the sky.

When I raise my head, I notice the malfunctioning neon sign for the first time. It reads, THE MOONLIGHT MOTEL and, like everything in the past twenty four hours, well, eighteen years actually, it makes me laugh to myself, like a madman in the rain.

XXII.

Jack drives the Daytona over the bridge that connects Somers Point to Ocean City. Eddie Vedder sings, "Isn't it something? Nothingman..."

He ponders the lyrics. Like most Pearl Jam songs, the words are mostly a mystery to him, but he can't help to think that he's something of a Nothingman himself now. Drifting away from his home, unaware of where he is headed.

Slow. And sinking.

He gazes across the bay, at one of his most favorite places in the world. The place where he had his first kiss, under the boardwalk with a cute blonde named Erin. The place where he, Rob, and Christopher took their Boogie Boards and rode the huge, dark waves under the distant glow of stores and amusement parks. The place where he plans on washing down a couple slices of Mack's with a large birch beer, then dial a stranger's phone number.

He arrives in the busy town, and pays five bucks to park by Wonderland Pier. The Ferris wheel towers high above, shining its dancing lights down upon the lot. Families walk back to their cars, high on caramel corn and the salty air, hands filled with stuffed animals.

His head starts spinning. His heart races.

This was a huge mistake.

He had a romantic sendoff planned for himself, but now he's nauseous, sad, and alone. A Nothingman, in the midst of a million shiny, happy people. There will be no pizza and birch beer. His only plan now is to find the nearest payphone.

There's a row of them by Wonderland's restrooms. He fetches the card from his Jansport, inserts some change into the phone, then dials.

"Roger."

"Hi, uh. This is Jack Sharpe. Wilson Steels gave me a card with this number on it."

"Of course. Jack, I was waiting for your call. Where are you?"

"I'm in Ocean City, down at the end of the boardwalk, in a parking lot by Wonderland Pier." There's a moment of silence on the other end. Jack panics, thinking that he said something wrong. "Roger, are you there?"

"I'm here, Jack. Wilson and I will be there to get you in two hours. Can you make it that long?"

"I think I can."

"Good. Sit tight and, when it's time, be in that lot, looking for a black Cadillac."

"Okay. Got it."

He stretches out on the sand, using his backpack as a pillow. The Goo Goo Dolls are in his headphones. It's almost midnight and, even at the height of summer, people turn it in early here. Except for the occasional knucklehead being loud up on the boards, the only sound is coming from the waves crashing against the shore.

He stares at the vast, dark sky. The clouds occasionally make way for the moon. It's nearly full; in just a few nights, it will be.

He's more frightened than ever.

The black Caddy pulls up, five minutes early. Jack is waiting in the parking lot, wearing his Jansport, suitcase in hand.

"Master Sharpe," Roger says, exiting the vehicle. The name catches Jack off-guard but makes him feel like Bruce Wayne. "Let me take your bags." He hands the Englishman the suitcase but keeps the backpack.

"I'll hold onto this. If that's cool," Jack says.

"Of course."

"What about my car?"

"We'll take care of it."

Wilson is waiting in the backseat when Jack gets in. "Hello again, Jack. I'm so happy you called."

"Hello Mr. Steels."

"Just Wilson. Please. Get comfortable, it takes about two hours to get to where we are going."

Jack removes a Discman from his backpack and puts the headphones on. Q-Tip and Phife Dawg trade rhymes over a jazzy instrumental.

"Who is that?" Wilson asks, gesturing toward the Discman.

"A Tribe Called Quest."

"I'd love to hear it. Can we put it in the car's player?"

"I guess."

"Roger, put this in the player. What number is your favorite?"

"Uh, eight, I guess."

"Roger, number eight."

214

The music fills the car; it's familiar, yet totally new to Wilson. He starts to nod his head to the beat. "This is nice," he says, "good groove." Jack has never seen an adult dance along to Hip Hop music, much less compliment it. "Ronnie Foster comes to mind. You ever hear any Ronnie Foster?"

"No."

"Any jazz at all? Rhythm and blues? Motown?"

"I mean, I guess I'm familiar with some of it."

"Have you ever heard anything on a record player?"

"My grandfather had one back when I was a kid. I listened to some of his records, Frank Sinatra and stuff."

"Ol' Blue Eyes. Okay."

"My father had Thriller on vinyl. I must've spun that a million times."

"Now we're talking. Jack, you and I may have some fun yet." Roger attempts to lower the volume. "Roger. What are you doing?"

"I thought it was a bit loud, sir."

"It was just fine. Turn it back up," Wilson says, winking at Jack. He returns it with a smile.

Jack's future couldn't be less clear but, for the moment, he feels like he's made the decision to journey into it with the right man. And, as Wilson gets more and more into the music, tapping on his knee and snapping to the beat, Jack can't help but to feel like joining along with him.

XXIII.

They're going to need someone.

Most of them are lost, scared to death of the bad moon. Living on the run, addicted to drugs and alcohol. Chalk it up to our heightened senses, or simply the smallness of the world, but whatever the case may be, eventually we all find one another and end up at the mansion.

The motel's cold water rinses over me as I realize my new plan. Wilson and Roger need to be buried, the place needs to be put back in working order. The pack needs me.

I'll miss Wendy terribly, but she has a life. What could a man in my situation do? Hang around Cedarwood? Take her to dinner once a year like Chris? Transform into a werewolf and occasionally fend off Teddy Silver and his death squad? It's an impossible situation.

I hear a noise. It sounds like someone coming into the room.

Could it be Silver and them?

"Hello?"

No response. These fuckers found me.

"That door probably should've been locked. There are people trying to kill you."

Wendy.

She swings open the shower curtain and steps in. She's wearing nothing.

"God damn this water is cold," she says, laughing nervously.

"Wendy - "

She grabs my face and pulls it close. Before I can finish whatever the hell it is I was going to say, we're kissing.

Our bodies meet.

She wraps her legs around my waist and I carry her out to the bed. We are no longer kids, with body parts that we don't know how to use. We are two people getting lost in each other, until the morning light washes over the room.

"Jack," she whispers, lying in my arms. "Do you remember our song?"

"I was at a rest stop once, somewhere just outside of New York City. It was late. I was just kinda sitting at a table, watching people come and go. College kids. Truckers. I did that a lot back then. It started playing on the

216

overhead speakers. It brought me right back to Cedarwood. I had heard it once in a while before that night, but the rest stop was the last time. I think I stopped listening for it. It started to hurt. Going back."

"Wow. That's a lot more romantic than it popping up occasionally in my phone's shuffle. Want to hear it now?"

"How?"

"The phone, Jack. More sorcery."

It starts to play from the tiny speaker in her phone. About halfway through the song, we make love again. This time it's different. Slower. Gentler.

"Jack," she whispers when we're done. "I could really use another one of those Gatorades."

I throw my clothes back on and float out of the room, buzzing off the last few hours. The sun has just begun its ascent, there's noise from a big rig passing by on the neighboring highway. A chill is in the air. As I'm dropping the last of my change into the machine, I feel a shock. A familiar shock.

The shock of a cattle prod.

I go down hard, face first into the vending machine. Another shock. Followed by another. Each one longer than the last. Before I can gather my thoughts, Teddy Silver is on top of me, his hands are around my neck. His blue eyes are like a shark's, glazed over and soulless.

I can't breathe.

"Where's your wolf now?" He asks. "Where is he?"

I was expecting a frenetic montage of my life to pass before my eyes. Like a movie in fast forward. Instead, it's more like every moment meshes together as one. Everything happening at the same time. No beginning. No end.

My eyes close.

There's nothing. Darkness.

I feel the shock again, only this time it's from some faraway place.

My eyes open to the red sky of morning. Silver is attempting to get to his feet as Wendy stands over him, wielding the cattle prod. I crawl over, climb on top, and begin to strike him in the face. Each blow drains more of the little strength I have left, but I keep swinging.

For Roger.

For Wilson.

Every time my knuckles connect, more blood squirts from his nose and mouth. As soon as I hear Wendy's voice, my anger dissipates. "Don't kill him, Jack," she says softly.

I stand up, rubbing my neck, dizzy and exhausted. Silver is a bloody heap under my feet. If Wendy never came back, I'd probably be dead.

"Thank you."

"Well, we're even now in the rescue department," she says. "Come back to the room. Let's get you cleaned up."

"He killed my only friends in the world."

"And what? Will vengeance make you feel better? Probably not. Be the bigger man here, Jack."

His face is barely recognizable. A contorted mess. All that nipping and tucking for nothing. I imagine this is a fate worse than death for the pretty boy.

I decide to heed Wendy's words.

This time around, I get in the Uber with her. It's Paul again, wholly confused about the situation. We decide to have some fun at his expense, explaining that we're cage fighters working on our marriage. He actually buys it.

The Pierce house is as picture perfect as I remember it. Paul pulls up the hill and parks in front. Wendy lights up when she sees her daughter through the front window, painting pumpkins at the kitchen table.

"That's her," she says. "That's my Audrey."

"She's beautiful."

"Do you want to come in? My mother will probably faint."

I laugh and tell her "I'm spent, perhaps another day."

"When will I see you again?"

"I don't know. I have a couple things I have to do."

"This feels a little like deja vu."

"Don't say that."

We wrap our arms around each other once more, breathing each other in. Wendy whispers into my ear.

"Happy Halloween, Jack."

Paul and I watch from his Prius as Audrey dashes toward her mother, getting scooped up in a bear hug. They're spinning around in the foyer when Margaret appears in the doorway and glances toward me. Just in time, I turn my head in the opposite direction. When I look back, the front door is closed.

The first thing I notice when we pull up is that the trees have been trimmed. You can actually see the entrance to the driveway.

"You can leave me off here," I tell him.

"You sure?"

"Yea. I know Wendy paid you already, but take this as well." I hand him two hundred bucks.

"I can't take this. It's too much."

"Thank you, Paul," I say, ignoring him. "You're all right, bro."

I exit the car and walk up Sharpe Road. About halfway along, I hear the engine of a riding mower.

My father is behind the wheel, coming around the side of the house. He's freshly shaved and as full of life as I can ever remember seeing him.

XXIV.

Winter was rough. The house and coffee shop sold and the divorce was finalized. They moved into Mom-Mom's house and spent the holidays there. It was a stressful time, and all very confusing for Audrey. But it was worth it.

Now she sits in her booster seat, windows down and radio on, as she and Mommy make a beautiful life on the wide open road. They've spent the entire spring traveling the Northeast, stopping everywhere from LEGOLAND to Jell-O Museums. They've driven the Kancamagus Highway, and taken a boat out on Lake Champlain. Their destination is along the bay in Belfast, Maine. Aunt Jane's summer house, where she promises there will be long days of eating lobster rolls, and even longer nights catching fireflies. But they're in no rush to get there. Wendy prefers to keep moving. It makes her feel safe.

On the side of the road, somewhere in New Hampshire, she gets out and glances through the window. The curly-haired little girl is clutching her stuffed bear, soundly asleep in the backseat.

The White Mountains are basking in the glow of late afternoon as the moon hangs high. She leans against her Jeep, then adjusts the anchor pendant so it sits just right on her chest.

She closes her eyes and breathes deeply.

And, for a moment, she swears she hears the song of a wolf.

THE INCREDIBLE NIGHT OF
NOISE AND WONDER

Chapter 1

There was less than a week until Christmas.

I was heading out for my eighth night of work in a row (yes, that's eight nights in a row; my goal was to work away the holiday season) when I bumped into Glen, the old man from across the hallway. He continued his careful cultivation of an inside joke between the two of us.

"Good morning, neighbor," he said, alluding to the fact that he had never seen me rise from my apartment before six pm. "Just a friendly reminder, my family will be in and out for the next few days. You may hear more bells and whistles than usual."

This was a reference to his trains. I had yet to accept his invitation to step inside and check them out but, from the noise and the few glimpses I caught from the landing, I gathered that he was a serious collector of model railroads. I mumbled something about it being no sweat, then continued on my way.

While en route, I swung by Rite Aid to pick up my prescriptions. Prozac. Xanax. Fritos. The shelves were overstocked with animatronic Santas and electric foot massagers. The girl on the radio was rapping about meeting the love of her life over some forgotten cranberries or something. I wasn't in the mood to sort it all out.

When I arrived at the Foxhole, my place of employment for the better part of a decade, I found that the waitresses had snapped. One of them was wearing oversized plastic ears connected to a green and white striped elf hat. The other girl, a seizure-inducing light up necklace. The third was wrapped in one of the most ridiculous sweaters I've ever had the misfortune of setting my eyes on. It was Jolly Old Saint Nicholas, inexplicably mounting a unicorn in front of a rainbow. That's when Rusty sprang from the kitchen doors sporting a sweater of his own. This one was Jesus Christ in a party hat, holding a balloon. Jesus' shirt read BIRTHDAY BOY.

"Dude. Where's your sweater?" Rusty asked, prompting me to glance down at my monochromatic polo. Upon closer examination, I saw that they were all wearing some variation of a knitted nightmare. "It's the ugly sweater party. Did you forget?"

"Yea, I guess I did. It's okay. Really."

"Listen to me, man. I can't have you moping around behind the bar tonight. I need your A game. I want to see some Christmas spirit out of ya."

222

The last thing I wanted was another spat with the sixty-year-old former Hells Angel, so, as much as it pained me to partake in a ritual of wearing an article of clothing ironically, I decided to be a good sport about it. "Do you happen to have an extra lying around somewhere?"

The blonde haired, perpetually upbeat Elf Girl chimed in from across the dining room. It's like the ears were fully operational. "I have one in my car. There were so many good ones at Target, I couldn't decide between them. Let me go get it."

She returned with the abomination that was a moose, with ornaments hanging from its antlers. I told her that there was no way I was wearing it.

"It's beautiful," Rusty insisted. "Put it on." Besides the offensive design, the sweater was a few sizes too small. Rusty and the girls shared a good laugh when I squeezed my paunch into the damn thing. "Aye," Rusty wasn't the type to let a light-hearted moment linger for too long. "Come to the office, I gotta talk to ya."

It wasn't so much an office as it was a shrine to the female anatomy. Posters of scantily clad ladies, life-size cardboard cutouts of scantily clad ladies, framed photos of Rusty standing with scantily clad ladies. I took a seat at his desk while every bikini model on the Eastern Seaboard stared at me.

"You know any mulattos? One came by here looking for you yesterday," he said, as he sipped from the old-fashioned tumbler he carried in with us.

"I don't think you're supposed to use that word anymore," I replied.

"What are you now? The PC police? I believe he was of mixed ancestry. Is that better?"

"Yes. A little bit. And no, not off the top of my head. I don't get out of Cedarwood much these days."

"Well, I just wanted you to be aware, is all. He definitely wasn't from around here. Looked like he may have been on drugs. Asked a lot of questions."

I asked him what kind of questions but, before he could answer, one of the cooks popped his head in and informed us that the onions were missing from the food order.

"Son of a bitch! We'll chat later." With that, he bolted from the room.

The night went as they all did. Drinks were poured, small talk was made. The itch from my sweater was unendurable. Through the years, I found that patrons are generally in good moods around the holidays. You would think that with all the gift buying, tips would be down, but they actually go up. I guess all the moms and dads are hunkered down at home, baking cookies and watching Clark Griswold on an infinite loop, while the sad sacks that have no one to buy gifts for are sitting at the bar, throwing ten dollar bills at people like me.

The stranger Rusty spoke about was on my mind all night. My regulars could sense I was more distant than usual. Anymore so and I would've floated from our solar system.

After my shift, the neon glow of Wendy's red locks comforted me, as I devoured a spicy chicken sandwich underneath her sigil. The sounds of some trippy ambient music filled my car. It was like a warm, electronic serenade just for me. After my divorce, I stopped listening to music with words. Something about musicians and the pieces of their lives, crumbling perfectly to create beautiful songs of heartache and second chances, started to annoy me.

I thought about the stranger and how I had a couple of buddies back in college that fit Rusty's extremely general description. Those were brief friendships though. If you put a gun to my head, I couldn't have told you their names. I doubted that they had any reason to come looking for me.

The more likely possibility was that it had been Macy's new boyfriend. About a year after our split, I started hearing rumblings that my ex-wife, Macy, was seeing some big shot personal trainer known for designing a newfangled exercise plan for middle-aged women. Something like CrossFit for lonely cougars. I went on a two-day, alcohol fueled mission and became the world's greatest social media sleuth in the process.

When I finally located him, I stole a pic from his site and put my amateur Photoshop skills to good use. He was in crisp workout gear. The sweat on his sculpted arms was shining under the gym lights, while his clients stretched out their leathery, fifty-year-old bodies behind him. In one of his hands was a water bottle with his logo on it. In the other, I placed a *neon green dildo*.

Sure, it was childish, and my profanity-laced tirade that accompanied the photo on her Facebook wall was in bad taste, but I was in a dark place. I thought he looked Dominican. Like a less handsome Alex Rodriguez. Combine that with the fact that Rusty gets confused with any flavor of human being that isn't vanilla, I was almost certain it was him.

224

In my apartment, I mixed myself a White Russian. Then another. After I made a third, the strongest yet, I swiped to Macy's number. It was still the first one in my *Favorites*.

"What is it, Daniel?" She asked sleepily, after three rings.

"Did he come looking for me?"

"Excuse me?"

"Did your boyfriend come by the Foxhole the other day?"

"Daniel, it's after midnight. You're lucky I answered. No one came looking for you."

"I know he still wants to kick my ass for last year."

"He doesn't, Daniel. If he did, he would've by now."

"Oh really?"

"I'm hanging up. Please don't call me again."

"Where is he now? I know you wouldn't be answering the phone if he was around."

"He's away on business."

"Cougar CrossFit going national?"

"Yes, actually."

Nothing worse than a real answer to a sarcastic question. She said goodbye then hung up. I stumbled to the kitchen to whip up another White Russian (mostly just vodka this time) and chased it with my nightly ritual of ruminating about everything I've done wrong since I was fourteen years old.

My apartment complex was a refurbished 1800s mansion. Joe, the owner and landlord, lived on the first floor with his wife and three young sons. Me and Glen were on the middle level. One floor up from us was Pedro, a painter from California. All of us were connected by a staircase in the middle of the building. Off the back there was an addition that Joe added when he acquired the place. This part housed two tiny apartments that belonged to the token cat lady, Janice, and a young couple who seemed to do nothing but order takeout and fornicate. I'm the only tenant that used the rocking chairs on the wraparound porch, which was odd because it had a nice view of Cedarwood Lake. It was an unseasonably warm night in December, so I decided to throw on a hoodie and head out for some fresh air.

As I scanned the brightly lit homes that sandwiched my house and beamed on the other side of the lake, I realized that I was probably living in the town's only dark spot. Pretty fitting, to be honest. My buzz started to reach its crescendo as I drifted around to the back porch. I almost jumped out of my slippers when I ran into another person. She was sitting cross-legged on one of the rocking chairs, with a sketchbook on her lap.

"I'm sorry, I didn't expect anyone else to be out here," I said, turning to flee.

"Hey, where are you going?"

"I don't want to disturb you."

"You live here, dude. Chill."

I'd seen her floating around the house twice before. She's quite attractive, so I remembered both times vividly. Christmas Eve, the year before. I was returning from a particularly intense night of drinking when I crossed paths with her in the driveway. She was leaving Glen's place, arms locked with some guy. They were both dolled up, practically skipping to his car. She looked like a Christmas angel, in a brown trench coat over a purple blouse, billows of dark curls dancing in the frosty air. He looked like an asshole in a turtleneck.

"Happy holidays, boss," the guy said, as I imagined murdering him in a jealous rage.

The other time was a few months before this. She was leaving Glen's again as I was getting home from work. In the hallway, she shot me a pensive smile, and I couldn't help noticing that she looked like she had been crying.

Back on the rocking chairs, I asked her what's up, as I sat two over from the one she was occupying.

"Do I smell?" she asked, sniffing underneath her arm. She was wearing a baggy gray sweat suit, with a faded Cedarwood High logo on both the pants and top. "I'm only messing with you," she added, sensing that I was taken aback by her forwardness.

"Are you in high school?" I nodded toward the logo.

"These are ancient. They're sort of like my pjs now." It dawned on me just how drunk I was when I found myself kicking my feet and rocking back and forth like a five-year-old watching a parade. "So, you must be Daniel," she said, unfolding her legs and mimicking my sway.

"My reputation precedes me."

"Pop talks a lot."

"Shit."

"Don't sweat it. He likes you. All things considered."

"What things?"

226

"Just things."

Her face was like one of those "Magic Eye" pictures from back in the day. The more I looked at it, the more I discovered. The flecks of green in her almond-shaped eyes, the dimples trying to come out of hiding. It all came together to make her even prettier than I initially thought. I think she knew it too, as she swayed on the rocker, getting a kick out of herself. I asked her what she was working on.

"A sketch for my blog."

"You're a blogger?"

"Yes."

"What do you do for a living?"

"I sort of do that."

"There's a living in that?"

"If you're good."

"Are you?"

"I'm phenomenal."

I told her that I had majored in biology at Temple once upon a time - explained that my goal was to become a veterinarian or a zookeeper. "That's cool," she said. "You like animals, I take it?"

"They generally talk less than people. I like that part about them."

"So, what happened?

"I took a fifteen-year semester off. I may go back soon."

"Right."

"So, Glen is your grandfather?"

"Yep."

"Do you mind filling me in on these things he considered?"

"Well..." She placed the pencil down in her sketchbook, then closed it. "There was that night he found you passed out against his door. He helped you into his place and made you some soup and grilled cheese."

It's a scary thing, not remembering a single second of something like that. I immediately felt like an asshole for failing to thank him or even acknowledging the incident.

"I was in a dark place." I could've elaborated on my situation from there, told her how nice of a guy Glen is, maybe sent some apologies his way. But, I was reeling from the conversation with my ex. The sound of her voice was still ringing in my ears, polluting my better judgement. Plus, old Glen painted an awful picture of me to his hot granddaughter. "That was none of your business anyway."

"Right. Well, it was a pleasure to officially meet you, Daniel." She rose from the rocking chair then zipped past me.

My next words bullied their way out, even though I tried to stop them. "What happened? Did that douche in the turtleneck break up with you?" She stopped in her tracks. Tears were welling up in her eyes when she turned to face me again. I initiated damage control, muttering something about it being a joke.

"Yea, hilarious. You should know that there was some lawyer here looking for you tonight," her voice got sharper. "Are you in trouble? Did you pass out behind the wheel this time?" Before I managed to muster up my coveted last word, she turned the corner of the house.

Across the lake, the multicolored string lights turned off, leaving the water dark and still.

Friday nights were the best nights. My father would bring Alan and me to the video store and allow us two movie rentals each, then we'd swing by the pizzeria and pick up some pies. Dad never failed to grab three Slim Jims, one for each of us, for the ride home.

After dinner, we would view what would usually turn out to be a pretty filthy horror movie, then gather up all the pillows and blankets that we could find in the house and "camp out" on the living room floor. Around four o'clock in the morning, there was what Alan referred to as a "Sasquatch Sighting". It was our huge and fairly hairy father, donning nothing but his tighty whities as he trekked through the living room. We suppressed our laughter and pretended to sleep as he stepped over us and made his way to the utility room closet, where he kept his work clothes.

I have no idea why, but that's where my mind traveled when Alan's attorney informed me that my big brother had passed away from a rare form of cancer. The wicked kind that could kill a forty-year-old man in just under a year.

The lawyer was a soft-spoken, gray-headed white guy in his early sixties, who I met out on the front porch after he rang my buzzer. He hit me with a ton of medical jargon but, because of the severe hangover I was experiencing, I couldn't digest any of it. As the chilly morning sliced through my pajama pants like a knife through hot butter, I cut to the chase.

"Do I have to plan a funeral or something?"

"No, Daniel. His wishes were for a small ceremony with his wife and children, and for his ashes to be scattered at sea."

"What do I have to do, then?"

"You don't have to do anything. I know you guys weren't very close but he always spoke highly of you. I have a couple of items in my trunk that he left for you in his will."

I was seven years younger than my brother. A mistake, born in the shadow of a child prodigy. When I was eleven, I watched him give the valedictory speech at his high school graduation. Then he gave another one at Stanford. At our parents' service, I couldn't shake this funny feeling that most of the attendees were there to hear him eulogize the dead, rather than pay their respects. The astrophysicist waxing poetic about his blue-collar father. I'll never forget it.

As I followed the lawyer to his parked Lexus, I asked him the question that had been nagging at me since my buzzer rang.

"Was there another guy looking for me? A young guy. Maybe, biracial or Hispanic?"

"Alan was pretty well known. It's just someone trying to pay their respects, I'm sure." He removed a two- foot long, white storage box (which I immediately recognized as Alan's comic book collection) then set it on the ground. "So, there's this," he said, "and there's this." Out came a wooden watch box, about twelve shiny pieces in all. With a quick glance, I spotted three Rolexes. He placed it on top of the comic book box. "And finally, there's this." Another box, in perfect condition. This one contained a cherry red Tasco Refractor Telescope. A Christmas gift from our parents, so many moons ago. The telescope was Alan's prized possession for many years.

"So that's it," he said, as he shut the trunk then removed a heavily soiled tissue from his pocket and added some more bodily secretions to it. I was cold and hungover and now I had three heavy items to truck upstairs to my apartment. I thanked him and told him to take it easy, as I bent down and attempted to lift my brother's belongings. "Daniel, I just want to say I am so sorry for your loss. He was a great man."

A great man.

What makes a man great? I'm sure you could spin the wheel of my brother's life and find plenty of things. I never paid much attention. Figured I'd read about it in National Geographic someday.

"Honestly, I wouldn't know. I've only seen him a handful of times in the last decade. I'll take your word for it though," I repositioned the stuff in my hands and feigned a grunt. "Later."

Alan's boxes loitered in the corner of my apartment and taunted me for a few hours as I rested on the futon. Day became night, and it started to feel like the stuff was growing. Pretty soon there would be no room left for me. My neighbors would watch in awe as the end of a telescope shoved me from the second story window and out into the lake. I had to get out. I needed a drink.

My place of employment was out of the question; Rusty would never let me get as drunk as I needed to be. So, I decided to travel a town over, to a dive bar I've visited a few times before. A drab, quiet place with a few flat screens and some pool tables. Upon entering, I made a beeline to the far end

230

of the bar, where a chubby, middle-aged lady in a Santa hat approached to take my order.

"Hello there, handsome," she said, as I noticed the head of a tiger sticking out of her V-Neck. I imagined that the whole of the animal kingdom lived on the rest of her gigantic breasts. To sidestep any attempts at small talk, I quickly placed my order of twelve Buffalo wings and a tall vodka and cranberry.

A week or two after my divorce, Alan called with an invitation to his house in the Poconos along with his wife, Kate, their daughter Gabrielle, and newborn son, Jack.

"I need this break from work and you need to be with family. C'mon man. You haven't even met your nephew yet." I could hear Gabbie screaming "Uncle Dan!" in the background, like a lunatic shouting at the wall of an asylum.

After dragging my feet for thirty minutes, he finally won me over with the promise of obscenely expensive cigars and a Jacuzzi. I was living between motel rooms and my Jeep Wrangler at that point, so it sounded like a nice change of scenery. Plus, my stuff was already packed.

On my way there, I stopped for a drink. Alan texted me and told me how excited he was that I was coming. And I can't lie, I was excited myself. Perhaps this trip could've been what it took for us to find each other, to be those kids camping out on the living room floor again. As I reached into my pocket to pay for my drink, an old buddy from high school plopped down on the stool next to me. We got to talking and, to make a long story short, I ended up following him back to his house and getting shitfaced.

I never made it to the Poconos.

A week after I moved into my apartment, a couple of months after what was supposed to be our trip, Alan showed up at my doorstep. I tried to meet him on the porch but he insisted on coming in. I guess I owed him that much. The place was nearly empty at the time. Nothing to speak of other than my newly purchased futon, a flat screen television, and a couple of suitcases vomiting up my garments all over the floor. Oh, and a fridge full of booze. I sat in a wife beater and boxers as my big brother reprimanded me.

"That fridge is a disgrace. And I know if I look hard enough, I'll find some drug paraphernalia in here. But I don't even care about that. What I care about is having to explain to my three-year-old why her uncle isn't coming to spend time with her." He wasn't shouting, but he wasn't so quiet either. I didn't know what to say, so that's what I told him. We sat in silence, him on the cast iron radiator, me on the futon, for what felt like hours. He finally spoke, in more of a whisper this time.

"You know, forget the fact that you have a sister-in-law and niece that you barely know and a nephew you've never met. I'm on the precipice of something huge, Daniel. Something that could change the world. I would love to be able to share it with you."

"That's just it," I snapped back. "I don't care about what you're doing. I just need a brother, that's all. Not a guy whose mind is off in space every time I see him."

"I'm here, man. I've always been here. That's why I invited you to the mountains."

"Why? So I could play with your kids and look at Kate's Pinterest while you jerked off with a telescope?"

More silence. He looked pissed. I could tell that he wanted to punch me in the face, but that's a move that would've always ended badly for him. He knew it. Alan was all brains. As for me, I've been in my share of scraps.

"Macy was the best thing that ever happened to you," he said, as he made his way to the door, "and you fucked it up because of shit like this."

"Any more brilliant insight, Professor Trembly?"

"No. I think that's it for today."

That was the last time I saw my brother.

My wings sat uneaten on the plate and my fourth cocktail had just slid down my throat in record fashion when I saw a familiar face enter the bar.

It was Elf Girl, trailed by a couple of cute girlfriends. I turned my head away as she passed me, and watched as she exchanged greetings with a trio of boys at the pool table. These guys had been annoying me since I sat down. They were oily faced loudmouths, wearing the traditional garb of the millennial, and speaking in the native tongue. At least a dozen selfies were taken in the first five minutes of their contact with the females. One of them hit the jukebox and played Bruce Springsteen's song about Santa Claus. You know the one, in which he scolds his band for not practicing enough and tells them they're getting *fuckall* for Christmas. It's obviously the only song you're permitted to choose in a New Jersey dive bar in December.

My attempt to pay the tab and sneak out failed. Elf Girl approached me with her usual bop, clutching a Corona. She asked me why I wasn't wearing her sweater.

232

"I burned it, actually," I answered. "Did you want it back?"

"It's all good. Why don't you come chill? We never hang outside of work."

"With your friends over there?" I nodded toward the boys. "I'd rather not."

"They're not really my friends. Just some guys." I didn't hear her. Instead, I saw one of the boy's mouth *something* to his buddy. I made my way toward them as Elf Girl followed anxiously. When I was within arm's reach, I asked him what he said.

"I didn't say nothing."

"I could've sworn you said something about the 'weirdo at the bar'."

"Nah, bro, I didn't say that shit."

"Don't call me that."

"What should I call you then? Asshole?"

I knew that if I punched this kid, there would be a high probability of a serious injury occurring, so, I settled on an open-handed slap. The kind his daddy never gave him. He fell to the floor upon impact. The largest member of the trio seemed like he might've wanted to avenge his friend's honor. He was a foot taller than me and looked to be no stranger to the gym.

"Hey there, big guy. You next?" I squared up with him. Elf Girl grabbed me by the arm.

"Daniel, stop," she said, as an inked up, bald-headed bouncer approached. This guy made both me and the big kid look like we were in the wrong weight class.

"Y'all better knock this shit off," the world's largest head of bar security demanded, as he pointed to a nearby chair. "Take a seat while we sort this out." Fuckboy was finally to his feet, with a pale pink mask covering one side of his face. It made him look like a bitch ass Phantom of the Opera. I had to laugh at the sight of it. "You feel like a tough guy beating up little kids, bro?"

What was it with this bro shit? I had one brother, and from the looks of it, none of these guys were on the precipice of changing anything but their shitty underwear.

I lunged at the gargantuan bouncer as quickly as I could. He blocked whatever the hell I was trying to do, swung me around like a *Wrestling Buddy*, then planted me up against the wall. His catcher's mitt-sized hands were wrapped around my throat.

"Let him go, he lost both his parents." Oh, sweet Elf Girl, you could've told him that my brother was dead as well - that I was the last of the Tremblys. I was like a *Dugong*; a truly endangered species.

"Is this true?"

I couldn't bring myself to answer the big oaf, so Elf Girl provided the details.

"It's true. A car accident. It may not seem like it right now but he's a nice guy. He's just in a dark place."

It warmed my heart to hear her wield my go-to phrase, in a way that I might have. To my surprise, the bouncer freed me from his grip.

"You guys finish up your game," he said to the boys, "and you, walk on out of here. Be thankful I don't put you out on your ass."

Elf Girl was nice enough to take me home. "Thanks for the ride," I told her as she lowered the volume on the Carpenter's downer about getting horny over a Yule log.

"No problem. You need me to bring you back to your car tomorrow?"

"No, that's okay."

"Will you need a ride to work?"

"I don't think I'm coming. I've had a death in the family."

She looked puzzled. All she knew was that it had been ten years since my folks died. I wanted to tell her about Alan but, instead, I let her confusion linger in the air for a moment, then let myself out. She rolled the window down.

"Hey, Daniel. Are you okay?"

"Never better. I didn't really burn your sweater. Do you want to come upstairs and get it? Maybe we can watch a movie or something."

She looked at me like Jane Goodall might look upon a slain chimpanzee.

"I have to get back to my friends."

"Okay, well I'll see you later."

I ascended the steps to my apartment, each one felt harder to climb than the last. I knew what was waiting for me up there. The stuff that my brother felt compelled to leave me. Useless crap meant to torture me. Well, except the watches. I planned to sell the shit out of them and make a pretty penny.

Right after I slept for a few weeks.

Chapter 3

I didn't sleep for a few weeks. It hadn't even been a few hours when I awoke to Rusty standing over me with breakfast. I asked him how the hell he got in.

"You gave me the code to the front door. And a key. Remember? I would imagine for mornings like this. C'mon, sit up, give me some room." He gave me a gentle shove and plopped down on the futon next to me, tossing three bags of McDonald's on top of the coffee table. I think he hit the drive-thru and asked for one of everything. In a matter of seconds my apartment stunk like a grease trap. "I'm sorry about your brother, man. Nobody can say you ain't been dealt a pretty shitty hand."

I asked him how he heard, as he scarfed down an Egg McMuffin. Every time he moved, the futon sounded like it was begging for its life underneath his girth.

"Front page of the *Cedarwood Gazette*. Something about losing a hometown hero."

It's funny, Alan left Cedarwood and never looked back. "Hometown hero," I mumbled. Rusty sensed my aversion to the notion.

"Ah, c'mon now. He was your brother. Have a hash brown."

"I can't. I'll puke."

Rusty took in his surroundings, mainly the empty liquor bottles making the floor their permanent residence. "You're fucking up, kid. I ain't saying this as your boss, I'm saying it as your friend. You're fucking up." I told him I was fine, lied about how much I had been drinking. Frankly, his presence was beginning to annoy me. "Well, some good old-fashioned work will keep your mind off things for a while. We got two holiday parties tonight, on top of the Sunday night gravy crowd. I'm gonna need you a bit earlier."

"Yea, about that," I said. "I was thinking I need a week or two off."

"That ain't gonna happen, Daniel. I need you there. The next two weeks are our busiest all year. I ain't gotta tell you that."

"What about Franky? Or Doc?"

"Franky is a damn invalid and Doc is getting old, man. He can't keep up."

"Well, I need off. Mental health."

Remember in the old cartoons, when a character had a fever and the mercury in the thermometer would rush to the top and explode? Rusty's big, balding head was as red as that stuff, and appeared like it may have been on the verge of exploding as well. I've seen it like this, usually right before he tells an unruly patron to get the hell out of his bar. He stood up and kicked an empty bottle of Crown Royal. It spun a few times on the carpet then crashed into the baseboard.

"How many times have you run down your brother in front of me? Shit, man, you've worked for me for eight or nine years now and I ain't never met him. You realize that?"

I hadn't realized that until he told me. I also realized that there was no way that this unannounced visit was going to end on a high note, so, the next thing I said was ill-advised, but a long time coming.

"I quit."

"What? Are you fucking kidding me right now?"

"No. I'm not, actually."

He paced around for a minute or two, while I stretched back out on the futon, fluffed my pillow and fixed the blanket on top of myself.

"You know, one of these days you're going to have to get out of your own damn way," he said, holding back what I imagined he really wanted to tell me. "But if this is how you want it to go down, then fine. You're done."

His words, particularly the "get out of your own damn way" part, hit me like a truck.

"My father used to say that to me," I said, not really to him, just sort of to the ghosts in the room.

"Well, you should've listened," he tossed the spare key on the carpet, then left.

The sun was setting over the lake, casting long shadows throughout my apartment. I hadn't had the strength to get up and turn on any lights. I did nothing since Rusty's visit that morning but lay on the futon, stare at the ceiling fan, and switch back and forth between regretting my decision and feeling like it was the best move I've ever made in my life.

I lurched toward the kitchen like an undernourished two-toed Sloth, and discovered what I already knew. The fridge contained nothing but empty liquor bottles and a quarter pound of Genoa salami that went bad three months prior. I made my way back to the futon, with plans to sleep off the hunger, when my buzzer rang.

"Rusty, I'm in no shape to have you come up right now," I said, pressing the talk button on the intercom. "I'll call you tomorrow. We'll figure stuff out from there."

"This isn't Rusty," a man's voice said from the other side.

I asked who it was, then resumed a comfy position back on the futon when I received no answer. I chalked it up to a lost delivery guy seeking out the fornicators in the back apartment, or neighborhood kids playing Ding Dong Ditch. The cool embrace of a late afternoon nap was lulling me to the Promised Land when it rang again. I sprang up quicker than I had moved in years and struck the intercom.

"I swear to God, do it again and I'm coming down there to smack the shit out of you!"

"Daniel. I was a close friend of Alan's," the same voice. "It's imperative that you allow me to come in and speak with you."

If I stretched out from my front window, I was able to see across the portico, catching the very top of a visitor's head. The stranger had an unkempt mound of tight, brown curls and wore a baggy black hoodie. That was about all I could make out. I shouted, trying to get him to back up so I could see exactly who I was dealing with.

"Hey, Daniel," he answered, when he spotted me hanging out of the second story window. He was around my age and had a yellowish brown complexion. My first thought was the stranger Rusty told me about. "May I come up? It's awfully cold out here."

A few months before my parent's accident, Alan left NASA. I remember there being a lot of confusion surrounding his decision. He had worked himself up to the forefront of astrophysics, but there were rumblings that he had started to devote his time and energy into a very controversial science. My father didn't even like to talk about it. For a while there, I felt like the good son. The following twelve years, I heard less and less about my brother's work even though, during the handful of times I saw him, he seemed more preoccupied than ever.

The "very controversial" part is what bothered me. What if he was involved in some wild government conspiracy? I've watched enough History Channel to know that most of the time that kind of shit doesn't end up all that great. People get hurt, and killed. Innocent people. People like the brother of a renowned scientist that decides to up and quit on everybody.

"Are you here to murder me?" I asked him, feeling like it was the only appropriate thing I could ask in a situation such as this one. He laughed until he coughed, then it started to sound like he was choking. "Shit, man. You okay?"

"No, Daniel, I'm not. And I'm not here to murder you. Actually, I'm the one that's going to be dead soon."

As his words registered, I suddenly saw him differently. I'm comfortable enough in my manhood to say that he was a good-looking guy, but there was something off about him. His face was gaunt. His eyes were a striking light blue, but they looked tired, lifeless. I almost trusted him, but I needed a little bit more. I employed one of the oldest tricks in the book.

"If you were a close friend of Alan's, what was his favorite movie?"

He was thrown off by my question, and couldn't help but to laugh again. "Shit, man. I know we talked about this," he stroked his chin.

From my vantage point I could see most of Main Street and the houses that make up the southern end of Cedarwood. Night had fallen and the endless string lights were like the cosmos themselves. Galaxies, asteroids and dancing nebulas. For a second, I almost understood what my brother saw in it all.

"*Titanic*," the stranger said from below. "He loved *Titanic*."

I couldn't believe it. He got it.

"I'll buzz you in."

Since I had existed solely in the area surrounding the futon up to that point, asses were introduced to my IKEA dining room set for the first time in history. "Sorry I have nothing to offer you," I said to the man who had introduced himself as Neil.

"It's quite alright. I've been cutting back lately." His words were tongue-in-cheek, obviously hinting to the fact that he was nothing but skin and bones.

"So, how long did you know my brother?"

"We met at NASA, but I was the first to join him in his new venture"

"Which was?"

"Have you heard of the SETI Institute?"

"Search for extra, something or other."

"Extraterrestrial intelligence. We piggy backed off their work. And the world. The work. The...The optical telecommunication and the radio..." His words trailed off and he began to massage his temples. It seemed like he may

238

have been practicing this oration for a while but was fumbling it. "I'm sorry. We refined the technology. Your brother, myself, and a few others. And then the night. The incredible night of noise and wonder..." He trailed off again as he held his head in his hands. He was perspiring heavily and rubbing his temples more intensely than before. "It's these headaches."

I fetched a glass and filled it with cold water from the kitchen sink. "Get some water in you, man," I said, placing the glass on the table in front of him.

"Daniel. I have to tell you something. But it can't be here." I told him that I didn't understand. He leaned in close and whispered. "They could be listening."

The controversial science. The government conspiracy.

I knew it.

Everything became crystal clear. This was my brother's payback. For all the fights and all the times I let him down. His parting gift was to mix me up in some dangerous espionage.

"Neil, listen. This is as far as this is going to go. I can't be wrapped up in it," I approached the door. "I'm sorry about your situation. I really am. But, you need to leave."

"Alan told me you might react this way. So I've come prepared," he reached into the front pocket of his hoodie and I braced myself for the gun he was going to retrieve from it. "I'm going to leave this with you. Please release, please re...consider your stance on the matter. I'm sorry. It's a terrible thing when you can no longer find the words. If you change your mind, I'll be staying in room twelve at the Traveler's Lodge. Take care, Daniel."

He walked past me, then headed down the stairs and out the front door. I followed, to the front door window, trying to catch a glimpse of his vehicle. I was surprised as I watched him throw the hood over his head, plant his hands into his pockets, then walk around to the back of the house. I sprinted back up the stairs, perching myself at the window overlooking the lake. Sure enough, he appeared again, passing the back porch and continuing through a break in the wooded area that surrounds the water. A trail that leads right into the parking lot of the Traveler's Lodge.

Glen startled me when he popped his head in my door. He was dressed as sharp as I had ever seen him, with a double-breasted jacket and matching fedora. He smelled like an old man with plans to get laid. "Everything okay? I heard a lot of commotion and saw your door open." In between heavy breaths, I told him everything was fine. "You sure? You're sweating pretty heavily."

"I'm good. I'm good. Where are you headed looking all snazzy?" When I'm nervous I use words like snazzy. I followed him out to the landing.

"Just a little Christmas shindig down at the VFW."

I should've known Glen was a veteran. He probably stormed the beach at Normandy just to end up sharing a hallway with some young punk who failed to thank him for a grilled cheese sandwich. I swear I was about to apologize for my general rudeness when he spoke again.

"Well, you have a nice night, neighbor. And Merry Christmas to ya."

"Happy Christ Days," I stuttered back to him. I was going for Happy Holidays, then I remembered midway that old people like to keep Christ in Christmas. Basically, I failed miserably at a response.

Back in my place, Alan's stuff was still in the corner. The cherry on top was the envelope Neil left behind. I picked it up and saw my name written on the front.

It was my brother's handwriting.

Clifford Smith was the biggest bully in middle school. He swaggered around the halls with his two shit heel cronies, Bobby and Dennis, terrorizing everyone. They'd steal our classmates' Hot Fries and Jolly Rancher Stix (the two hottest commodities back in those days) and, eventually, they started stealing our lunch money. They were bigger than the rest of us and had facial hair. There was even a rumor that Cliff kept a switchblade on him. This was all pretty scary stuff for kids in the seventh grade.

For my birthday that year, Alan gave me a North Carolina Tar Heels baseball cap. In place of their usual logo, read the word Tar Heels in graffiti.

It was the coolest shit I had ever seen.

And made even cooler by the fact that it was a gift from my big brother, who was away at college, doing all the coolest shit I could ever imagine. I didn't take it off for weeks.

Me and Elliot, my best friend at the time, found ourselves in a bit of a pickle at the Little League Park that same year. We should've been involved in a game but, since we both quit earlier in the week, we were hanging out at the tire park and getting fat off of sodas and mozzarella sticks from the concession stand. As the sky turned dark and a light drizzle started to fall, Cliff and his cronies approached us.

"Cliff, look at the little fags playing with themselves," Dennis said.

Elliot and I were sitting up high, in one of the towers or the tire castle. He was already tearing up, so I kicked him and mouthed the words, *Don't be a pussy.*

"Danny boy, I like that," Clifford said, gesturing toward my hat.

"My brother got it for me. I can ask him from where. Right after you kiss my ass." This wasn't the first time, nor would it be the last, that my mouth got me in trouble.

"You know who you're talking to, bitch?"

"I know exactly who I'm talking to and I also know I ain't afraid of you like everybody else." This was a lie. I was pretty afraid of him, but I'll be damned if I was ever going to show it.

He reached into the back of his belt and with a flick of his wrist, there *it* was. A switchblade, shining under the lamps that illuminated the tire park. He waved it around for effect. To make everything scarier, it had started to pour.

"Give me the fucking hat, kid," he demanded.

I turned toward Elliot, who rose and leapt over the side of the tower before I could get a word out. He landed on his feet, then took off running. I followed. "Get those fuckers!" Bobby shouted from behind us. We made our way to the crowded area by the concession stand and found a dry spot under an awning where the picnic benches were located. The players fled from the fields and jumped into vehicles with their parents; kicking up dust as they whipped through the dirt parking lot.

"It looks like we lost them," I said to Elliot, as I surveyed our surroundings.

"This is nuts," he said back to me. "This place is clearing out like it's the end of the world." We took a seat at one of the tables, our clothes soaking wet. "Danny, my parents aren't here, they didn't even know I was coming."

"Same here, bro."

"What are we going to do?"

"I guess just wait under here, then walk home. The rain can't last all night like this."

As if it took my words as a challenge, the rain started to fall heavier. Lightning crashed, blanketing the whole park in an electric silver. It was followed by an unholy thunder. The wind was trying to tear the shingles off of the awning above us. Elliot looked like he was about to piss his pants. In a matter of minutes, the park was deserted. We took comfort in the fact that it was just us, until three shadowy figures appeared in the distance. They were moving fast, heading straight toward us. "Shit, Elliot. Look"

"Oh no. We have to go. Now!" my friend cried.

"No way, man! We'll get struck by lightning out there. We're safer under here. Cliff ain't gonna use that blade."

"They'll jump us though."

"Shut up. Just shut up and let me handle it."

I underestimated Clifford Smith and his goons. As soon as they hit dry ground they started in on us. Cliff and Dennis threw a flurry of punches at my face and stomach. I blocked a few and managed to get Dennis with a quick jab, causing him to fall back and trip over a bench. Cliff hit hard, though. One of his right hooks connected with my temple and I fell to my knees, grasping at his waist. My attempt to tackle him to the ground failed miserably. As I held on to him, his knee connected with my nose and I saw the most beautiful display of fireworks imaginable. At that point, I thought it'd be best to curl up in the fetal position. I managed to catch a glimpse of

242

Elliot, my buddy since kindergarten, retreating through the pouring rain. I'd later find out that he got lucky with a kick to Bobby's balls.

Dennis stood back up, then Bobby joined the party. They formed like *Voltron* and began to kick the sweet blue hell out of me. I figured their size nine Nikes could do more damage to my brain than anything else, so I shielded my head. Each time a kick landed against my back or my ribs, I could feel the wind exit my body. Just as I thought they might kill me, headlights cut through the dark rain and lit them up. They looked like some kind of blood thirsty, pale-faced goblins that had their meal cut short.

It was a black Chevy Silverado. My brother's truck. They left as quickly as they came.

"We need to get you to a hospital," Alan said, steering his truck through the lingering drizzle.

I was leaning against the passenger seat window, "I just wanna go home," I said, as I watched lightning through distant clouds. Alan explained that he had just gotten home for the weekend when Dad and Mom told him that I hadn't returned from the game yet. I asked him how he knew to look by the concession stand.

"You got lucky, I guess."

I thanked him, trying like hell not to cry, even though every inch of my body hurt.

"You should probably tell them you quit."

"I will. I just need a few days."

"No, Daniel. When we get home. You know, if you're involved in sports, stuff like this is less likely to happen, right?"

"Don't kick me while I'm down."

"I'm not kicking you. I'm just telling you...well, forget it. Dad should know, that's all I'm saying. He bought you those cleats and batting gloves that you had to have."

"Okay, I'll tell him when we get home. Just leave me alone about it."

We sat silently for the rest of the ride. I thought about how mad I was at Elliot. I thought about how I was going to extract revenge on Cliff and his cronies. I thought about all the wrong things.

And my hat.

"Alan, they stole my damn hat," I told him as we pulled into our driveway. I was closer to crying than I had been yet, but there was no way on this planet, or any other known planet in the galaxy, that I would allow myself to break down in front of him. No way.

"Well, that sucks. But, if you were playing in the game instead of doing whatever it is you were doing, maybe you'd still have it."

It's funny, the things you recall when you're drinking yourself stupid, trying to forget about the mysterious envelope - that a mysterious stranger - left on a pile of stuff that your recently deceased brother bestowed upon you.

I walked to the liquor store by my apartment complex and purchased a bottle of vodka, along with a balanced dinner of peanut butter-filled pretzels and a couple of Slim Jims. When I returned to my apartment, I placed one of the delicious sticks of processed meat on top of the envelope, then got to drinking. My initial plan was to get drunk enough to open the envelope, but I was sidetracked when I decided to call my ex-wife.

I told her about Alan and discovered that she already knew, and that she and my sister-in-law spoke fairly regularly. This really pissed me off and amplified the drinking by nearly double. I was able to remain calm, until she dismissed Neil and the government conspiracy as crazy talk.

"It's not crazy talk, Macy. Jesus Christ!"

"Are you still taking your meds?"

"Yes."

"Are you still seeing your therapist?"

"Yes," I lied. "God dammit, Macy."

"Well, I don't know. You sound unhinged. And you've definitely been drinking. Listen, Josh is waking up. I'm sorry about your brother but I have to go. Please stop calling me or I'm going to have to block your number."

"Josh. What a terrible name."

She hung up.

I sent my cellphone sailing against the wall, then sat at the kitchen table staring at Alan's corner. I started mentally referencing it as Alan's corner because I had built an invisible border around it. Like one of those fences they install for dogs. My neck would be zapped if I attempted to cross it.

There was a knock on the door. My phone screen read half past ten o'clock. There was no way that it was anything but trouble. I crept toward

244

the peephole and looked through to see a couple of men I didn't recognize. The taller of the two looked to be about my age. He was athletically built with a head like a LEGO block. The other was an older guy, maybe around his mid-fifties. He was out of shape and his clothes were disheveled. He reminded me of the time Robin Williams played the homeless guy. The Fisher King? That was it. The Fisher King was there to kill me. I was sure of it.

I shouted through the door, "Can I help you guys?"

"Hello, Mr. Trembly. We were close associates of your brother Alan. We have a few quick questions to ask you," the Fisher King explained.

"It's kind of late for a visit, no? Come back in a couple of days, I'll answer your questions then."

"We don't have that kind of time," LEGO Head added.

"Please allow us to come in and we'll be out of your hair," the Fisher King continued.

"Listen, guys. This all seems a bit sketchy," I told them. "I apologize, but y'all are not coming in."

"Open the fucking door," LEGO Head demanded.

My heart started to race. I felt dizzy. Through the peephole, I could see that the well put-together guy was digging into his pocket. "Who the hell are you people?" I asked.

"We told you already. We were your brother's associates and we're coming in whether you like it or not."

My buzz was long gone. I could feel my temples pulsating. I looked down and discovered that I had sweat through my shirt. For a moment, the fall from my window to the back porch seemed like something I could manage. As I took a quick seat on the futon to put my socks and sneakers on, the knob started to jiggle. "Daniel, we're coming in," the Fisher King said through the door.

Too many people that I had never met in my life knew my name. "I got a gun in here," I barked, pounding once on the door. I took the knob in my hands. "Listen to me, if you come in here, I'm letting a few off. I swear to God."

The men turned their backs toward the peep hole. Their muffled whispering led me to think that maybe they bought it, until they approached the door once again. I saw a flash of metal rise from The Fisher King's belt buckle just as the door swung open, almost smashing me in the face. I stumbled backward. The Fisher King aimed at me.

"Please, Mr. Trembly. Take a seat. Don't do anything stupid," he said, as LEGO Head closed the door, quietly, behind them. I put my hands up like I was under arrest and told them I didn't want any problems.

"If you tell us where they are, there won't be any problems," LEGO Head said.

"Who?"

"Neil. Marvin. Where are they?"

"Okay, listen." My legs felt like they were going to give out on me, "Neil was here, he left that envelope," then my ass hit the futon. "I told him to fuck off."

"Why would you do that?" The Fisher King asked, his gun still trained on me. His large friend was moving around the apartment, searching through drawers and cabinets. He stopped and hovered in Alan's corner.

"I don't want to be involved. I'm just a bartender. And a drunk. I'm of no use to anybody."

"He might be telling the truth," LEGO Head said, examining the envelope. The Fisher King asked why he would say that. "This envelope is still sealed." He put it in his back pocket.

"What can you tell me about Marvin?" The Fisher King whispered. His attention back on me.

"I know nothing about any Marvin."

"Neil didn't mention Marvin?"

"No. No mention of Marvin."

Because of my sheer ignorance, the situation started to seem less desperate. The men huddled up and whispered to each other again. The sloppy one dropped the gun to his side. I contemplated hightailing it out of the door, but I didn't want to give them any reason to think I was lying. Plus, I had only one shoe on. I stayed put as LEGO Head removed the wrapper from the Slim Jim.

"Don't eat that," I said, interrupting their hushed discussion.

"What's that?"

"It's for my brother. Don't eat it."

"I don't know if you've heard, Chief, but your brother is dead."

It felt like the right thing to say at the time and I was fresh out of inhibition. I figured if I acted unstable enough that they would take pity on me. "Have you ever left something by a grave?" I continued. "Same thing."

LEGO Head ignored me and snapped into it.

"It looks like it's your lucky night," the Fisher King continued, wiping sweat from his brow. "We've decided to leave you be. But listen to me, Daniel. We have nothing left to lose. So, if you're lying to us, we will be back, and we won't take it as easy on you next time."

There was something about the Fisher King's posturing that felt phony. It seemed like he hadn't spent too many days threatening people with violence. He was shaky and perspiring heavily. It's as if he traded in his pocket protector for a pistol. I wasn't about to test that theory, however. "I swear to God, man. I don't know anything."

Just like that, I was alone again. I locked the door, then killed what was left of the vodka. I hit the futon like a wrecking ball, hoping when I awoke, the rotten dream would be over.

Chapter 5

With all the alcohol in my system, I should've been incapacitated. Unfortunately, that wasn't the case. I had too many questions.

What the hell could Alan have been involved in, that led to a couple of guys tracking me down and threatening my life?

What the hell was a dying man named Neil rambling on about, this supposed night of noise and wonder?

Who the hell is Marvin?

I needed answers.

I decided to throw on a change of clothes and take Neil up on his offer.

The prints in the sugar sand led me down the trail, as the frostbitten hand of mid-December slapped me across the face. I used my cellphone's flashlight to navigate through the eerily quiet woods. When I reached the lot, I struggled to remember Neil's room number.

I started to worry that I finally put enough crap into my body that I was losing my mind. I panicked, walking up and down the outside hallway, counting the numbers as I went.

Eleven.

Twelve.

Thirteen.

Shit.

I recalled the front desk receptionist. A nice old lady, who I got to know a little bit when I was shuffling between residences. I tried to remember her name as I dashed toward the lobby.

Shirley.

Kathy.

Joan.

SHIT!

She was asleep on a couch in the waiting area while *Home Alone* played on the prehistoric television set in front of her. Kevin was in the process of booby trapping his house and I briefly considered the possibility of doing the same to my place. Or, at the very least, getting a chain lock. When she heard me get closer, she sprung up.

"Oh, Daniel. You startled me. Do you need a room?"

"No, I was just wondering if my friend Neil checked in earlier."

"Neil? No, I don't think anybody by that name has checked in. Let's take a look."

I paced the window while she slowly staggered to the computer. It would be Saint Patrick's Day by the time she reached it. Just when I started to think that walking to Taco Bell would've been the better decision, I spotted a shadowy figure across the lot. He walked in a familiar stride, the same one I watched from my apartment. "Thanks for looking," I said, "but I think I found him."

He somehow appeared worse than he did when I met him. He was wrapped in a comforter, ambling barefoot back to his room. His face was paler and more angular, his eyes were protruding from their sockets. I asked him what the hell he was doing out in the cold at midnight.

"Ice," he said, as he lifted the bucket up from out of the comforter. "My throat is dry."

"Okay, Neil. Let me help you, man," I took the bucket off his hands then clutched him by his arm.

In his room, there was a small, black suitcase by the bed, a backpack on the nightstand, and a plastic, dollar store evergreen sitting on the dresser by the TV. The tree was decorated with a string of battery powered white lights and a few cheap ornaments. I took it all in, as Neil collapsed onto the bed. "I need to know what's going on."

"I thought that you didn't want to be wrapped up in it?" he responded, pressing a handful of ice up to his forehead, letting a few chips fall into his mouth.

"Yea, well, when two guys break into your apartment and put a gun in your face, it could lead to a change of heart."

"Shit. They found you."

"Who are *they*?"

"They are Richard Arko and Dale Savage. And they are about to be the last living members of our *Mercury Seven*."

"That doesn't help me."

"Are you aware of the original Mercury Seven?"

"No, not really. Did they make cars?"

Another chuckle that quickly turned into a coughing fit. This time it was bad. I swear my sarcastic comments were accelerating this poor man's journey into the afterlife. He motioned toward the washrag draped over the bedpost. I picked the nasty thing up with my fingertips then tossed it toward him. He spewed a chunky, crimson mass into it. "Your brother always said you were funny." Bloody ice chips fell from his mouth.

"Dude, we need to get you to a hospital."

"No, Daniel. No hospitals. Please sit."

My adrenaline dipped. My legs were like rubber. I had no choice but to take a seat on the chair by the window.

"The original seven were a group of famous astronauts back in the sixties. Some of the first men in space. Great men. After your brother and I left NASA, we were eventually joined by five more scientists. Naturally, we borrowed the name."

"So why are these men looking for you? And who is Marvin?"

He stared at the TV screen. I turned to find Kevin reuniting with his mother in the foyer of their house.

"Can you turn it up? This is my favorite part."

It was always mine too, but I didn't tell him. I picked up the controller and did what he asked. We sat quietly for a moment and watched. Two strangers, in their own states of decay. I gazed upon his pathetic tree as the film's score filled the room and, in some bat shit crazy way, it felt like Christmas. More so than it had for many years.

"Before we talk about Marvin," he continued, softly, as the credits played on the screen. "I need you to help me with something."

"What's that?"

"You see my backpack? I need you to retrieve The Big Dipper and inject me with it."

"I'm sorry?"

"Please."

"What the hell is all this?" I asked, carefully digging through his bag. I've seen the belongings of a few junkies in my day. The hypodermic needles and rubber hoses, the cotton balls and tinfoil. This stuff was similar, but different. It was mixed up with vials and other unfamiliar medical supplies. "Most of it is what you would call serotonin receptor agonists. For my headaches. The Dipper though, that's something different." Sure enough, I found a syringe labeled The Big Dipper at the bottom of his bag. I held it up and asked what it was for.

"That's a cocktail of my own creation. Once injected, I'll feel a rush of adrenaline I haven't felt in some time. Then, within twelve hours, I'll die."

I flat out refused, then tossed the syringe back into his bag and began to pace the room. I paced so hard my feet almost set the carpet ablaze.

250

"Daniel, it's the only way," he persisted, as he watched me walk back and forth.

"It's not."

"It is."

"Nah. We can get you help. They treat everything nowadays. We'll find you some specialist somewhere and they'll fix this. I'm sure of it."

"Daniel, I like you," he laughed. "I wish we would've met sooner."

I managed to calm down, then take a seat on the bed next to him. "C'mon, man. It's always better to try to stick around."

"If I try to stick around, I will suffer. I don't want to suffer anymore."

That made sense. From the moment he showed up, Neil struck me as a man who wanted to do more than just stick around. He wanted to explore, to discover new things. You can deduce that within seconds of meeting him. I guess some people just have that type of spirit, even in the face of death. But, he was a damn NASA scientist. He knew better than me that to simply stick around, was a futile mission at that point.

"Okay, man. I'll do it," I said. "I need to know more though."

With my help, he sat up against the headboard and sipped the ice water. He battled through some stuttering and confusion, and did his best to elaborate further on The Mercury Seven and their impossibly secret project, Phone Home. He told me about the groundbreaking radio telescope that Alan invented. How it was able to scan the entire night sky, isolate strange signals from space, then focus in on them and communicate. How it was privately funded by the Arko family. Richard Arko being the heir to the Arko empire and sloppy bastard that broke into my apartment. Neil explained that he and Alan were the only true friends in the group, that the rest were selfish pricks, only involved for the notoriety that would come if their work was ever discovered.

He went on, and I could see him starting to fade when he got around to the night of noise and wonder. There was some kind of crash at the site of the telescopes. It caused the three men closest to it to die within months. Alan was next. Leaving Neil, who had one foot in the grave, and of course, the two assholes that threatened me.

"There was a radioactive element to the crash. Something we couldn't understand. It made us all sick. But, it also brought us Marvin."

"Neil, my next question is insane. Even in my head as I hear myself asking it. Insane. If I've lost track of what you've been telling me, you have my permission to laugh your ass off. Just don't hurt yourself. Anyway, here it goes. Is Marvin a Martian?"

"No. He's not from Mars."

"Right. Okay, good. Where's he from? Like Nebraska, somewhere? Perhaps the West Coast?"

"We concluded that he came from a planet in the habitable zone of the Proxima Centauri star. Your brother chose the name Marvin after his favorite cartoon character."

I chalked it up to a symptom of his disease. He was losing the last working parts of his mind. They were shutting down one by one, and random pieces of his past were firing through his thoughts, then colliding with the deepest parts of his imagination. I owed him enough to humor him. For the simple fact that he was my brother's best friend.

"Where is Marvin now?"

"He will reveal himself to you when he's ready. He'll communicate with you, but nonverbally. Because of the larger beings we pulled from the wreckage, we believe Marvin is a child. An incredibly intelligent child." He wiped a tear from his eye, then looked away. "Marvin seems to love Christmas."

"So, what do I do?"

"You inject me with the Big Dipper and be on your way. Take Marvin's tree with you."

"Right. I should've known the tree belongs to Marvin. The fucking guy loves Christmas." I was getting annoyed. "What about you then? You just rot away in room twelve of the Traveler's Lodge?"

"Absolutely not. I plan to meet my buddy in the ocean."

After some final deliberation, I assisted him with the injection, then departed. Our goodbye wasn't as emotional as I hoped it would be. Even though he was on the last stretch of a rollercoaster into madness, bonding a little bit with Neil felt good. Then again, maybe I didn't bond with him at all. Perhaps whatever radiation he spoke of from the night of noise and wonder had already killed him. The man I met was just a vessel, floating around until its mechanisms failed. I could've been a figment to him, just like his Marvin.

I thought of all this as I trudged through the trees once more. This time around, my travels were shorter by half.

I had the light from a dead man's Christmas tree to guide me home.

Chapter 6

Alan was always enamored with the notion of life on other planets and the possibility that they had already traveled to ours. Every time there was a little light up in the sky, or somebody went missing under mysterious circumstances, or some strange shit went down with cows, he went on and on about how it had to be the aliens.

The summer he acquired his driver's license, he carted us around South Jersey, from the Pine Barrens to the Shore towns, interviewing weirdos about their abduction stories. I followed him around with our mother's clunky RCA video camera on my shoulder, sweating profusely. He compiled the footage and produced a documentary called *Close Encounters of the Jers Kind* . You know, like the Spielberg movie, except we were from New Jersey. As the tape circulated, it garnered a pretty good amount of buzz.

The night it aired on our local station, our parents invited most of the street over and served plastic bowls of popcorn and cups of soda. Dad was the image of a proud father, smiling in his most formal *Panama Jack* as he welcomed guests. He thought it would be like a drive-in theatre if he rolled the television set out to the back deck and set up lawn chairs. The record hot temperature and invasion of mosquitoes didn't stop them from being awed, and a little scared, by the stories we filmed. Everybody seemed to be enjoying themselves, with the exception of Mrs. Fratelli, a grouchy Holy Roller from two houses down. About halfway through our production, she approached Dad and explained that our stories were ungodly. Stories of skinny grey beings snatching people from their homes. Disorienting beams of light and strange corridors. The unforgiving tables where painful experiments took place. I was more amazed at what I thought we had wasted the summer doing, turning out to be so good. The clever ways in which Alan added music and captions. By the time we reached the finale (a reenactment scene that consisted of a copious amount of homemade blood and questionable use of an aluminum foil probe) Mrs. Fratelli had already up and left.

At the end, after a rolling list of the interviewee's names, the screen read:

Written, Produced and Directed by Alan Trembly
Cinematography by Daniel Trembly

As my name flashed across the screen, I looked over to Dad. He was grinning and giving me a huge thumbs up.

Maybe there was a catastrophe at the site of the Phone Home project. Whatever it was, it made Neil and the others lose their minds. Maybe it was caused by simply being around the radio signals Neil mentioned. I wasn't sure.

What I did know was Alan and his crew spent their days wishing on a star for some contact with extraterrestrials, hunched over computer screens and listening into headphones, dedicating their lives to this crazy search. It made sense that, when the Mercury Seven became the Cuckoo's Nest, they all shared a delusion of an invisible alien named Marvin.

Still, I needed more answers.

My next move was to contact the person I should've contacted when I first received news of Alan's passing: my sister-in-law, Kate. It wasn't that simple though, and I needed to do some mental jousting to bring myself to call her. Kate and I had gotten along the handful of times we met; that's why, when I discovered that she was fraternizing with my ex-wife, on top of the fact that she failed to call me herself with news of my brother's death, it pissed me off. Then again, I made a promise and broke it. I chose a two-day bender with some loafer from high school over a Poconos trip with my family.

When she answered my call, she sounded like she had been crying. I told her who I was.

"Hey, Daniel. I knew it was you," she said. "I am so sorry you had to find out that way. I was planning to call you. It's just, things have been crazy."

"I would've liked to have known he was sick," I said, trying to conceal my aggravation.

"You would have? Well, he called you. Maybe you should've picked up."

I searched through my missed calls. Besides Rusty and the bartenders at the Foxhole asking me to cover their shifts, Alan was the only person that tried to contact me at all. This revelation made me feel like a tremendous asshole. It was time to make an offensive maneuver. "It's just really unsettling that the cheating bitch knew before I did."

"She never cheated on you, Daniel. Is this really what you want to talk about right now?"

254

It was. Even with all the life-altering events I was facing, my ex-wife still took up a copious amount of real estate in my thoughts. I desperately wanted to reiterate to Kate just what kind of succubus we were dealing with. But, just by the sound of her voice, I could feel the weight of my sister-in-law's grief. I told her I was sorry, then asked her how she was doing.

"We're taking it one day at a time. My sisters are staying with us. Gabbie and Jack are occupied with their cousins. How about you?"

"I'm hanging in." There was a moment of silence. A heavy silence. A silence that comes with the death of a loved one. A silence that has reflection, and regret, and sadness in it. "Listen, I have to talk to you about some stuff. Is now a good time?"

"Um, hold on," she put me on mute. I imagined that she was telling her sisters that she needed a few more minutes with her jerk of a brother-in-law. When she returned to the line, it sounded like she relocated to a quieter part of the house. "Okay, what's up?"

"Did you know Neil?"

"Oh, yes. Sweet Neil. He was Alan's best friend. I haven't been able to reach him."

"Oh. Uh, did you know he was sick? Like, the same as Alan?"

"That can't be."

"Something happened at that place. The place with the telescopes."

"What are you talking about? How would you even know about that place?"

I broke it all down for her. The Mercury Seven and their Phone Home project. Meeting Neil at the motel and injecting him with the Big Dipper. Richard and Dale breaking into my place and threatening me. The night of the crash.

"Jesus Christ. This is insane."

"I know. It makes me feel like I'm losing my mind just talking about it. But I felt like you should know."

"Daniel, those men you mentioned know where I am. Richard and Dale, they've been in our house for parties and stuff. Should I be worried?"

"I don't think so. It seems like the less you know, the safer you are."

"Well, then, I'm the safest girl on the planet, because I don't know anything apparently." She began to sob and I didn't know what else to say. I called for answers and it seemed like all I accomplished was making Kate's day go from bad to worse. "This is a lot, Daniel. I have to go."

The rhythmic sound of fists connecting with the leather of a heavy bag came from outside. It was Pedro, my neighbor, and according to him, the punching bag was one of the many ways he kept his mind and body right. If he wasn't hitting the bag or fixing some Spanish dish that made our whole building smell delicious, he was most likely painting. His work was always of one person, in an everyday situation. Sitting on the windowsill drinking coffee, strolling down a sidewalk in the rain, curled up under a blanket with a book. I asked him once why his subjects always seemed so lonely.

"There's something beautiful in loneliness, my friend. Something that reminds us that even when we find ourselves by ourselves, we aren't truly alone. We are connected as human beings," he explained, in his thick accent. Pedro was the only person in the world who I actually enjoyed hearing speak. He had two things I needed, empathy and insight.

"Daniel," he said, striking the bag. The cold air swirled from out of his nose and mouth, then danced around his face. He looked like a bull about to charge a matador. I used to think being an artist and a badass were mutually exclusive, until I met Pedro. "How are you doing on this fine day?"

"Eh, been better," I told him. He stopped swinging, then started to remove his gloves.

"Walk and chat? I need to cool down for a few anyway," he grabbed a towel from his back pocket, then wiped the sweat from his face.

"Sure."

"Cool, let's take the trail behind our place. It's beautiful back there."

The trail.

I never wanted to walk it again as long as I lived. I couldn't object, though. In Pedro's eyes I'd have no reason to. It didn't seem like the best time to tell him that this particular nature hike will forever be connected to what happened the night before. When I helped a man take his own life.

We set off through the woods. The sun was just starting to dip behind the top of the pine trees on both sides of us. The only prints left in the sand were mine from about thirteen hours prior. They were barely visible. Pedro noticed me noticing them.

I wanted to explain everything that had happened to me. I was desperate to feel like I had someone in my corner, someone who wouldn't judge me or jump to conclusions. The thing was, if I never saw another one of my brother's associates again, there was really no reason to let Pedro in on the fiasco. I chose to tell him about Alan and leave out the crazy parts.

"Daniel, my friend," he said, pumping the brakes. He rested his hand on my shoulder. I couldn't be sure if it was because of the weather or what I told him, but tears were running down his cheeks. "You've suffered too much loss. It's not fair."

He pulled me in for a bear hug. I felt rumblings from somewhere deep inside. A warm, relentless swell. The last time I was embraced by a man it was Alan, at our parent's funeral. The fight against my own tears was lost. Bursts of emotion left my body, making me jolt like I was on a gurney being resuscitated.

"Shit, man. I'm sorry," I whispered to him

"Don't be sorry, Daniel. Let it on out."

After I gathered myself, we continued our walk. I let the irrationality of current events drive the following question. "Do you believe in aliens?" He was caught off guard and a laugh squeaked out of him. I joined in. There we were, two madmen laughing in the woods.

"I mean, there was that movie," he said, catching his breath and wiping away his tears. A mix of sad tears and the tears that have no real meaning; tears reserved for life's absurd moments. "The one where the pretty white girl says it would be an awful waste of space if we were alone. That's how I feel." The more excited Pedro got about a topic of conversation, the more animated he became. "Have you ever seen that one picture from the Hubble?" He started to point to the heavens and move his hands like spaceships. "All those thousands of galaxies. Just imagine that."

"Do you think they've been here?"

"I think so," he kept watching the sky. I did as well. He held his hand still as if the ship stalled out. "There is this theory that says when the settlers first arrived here, the native people failed to see them. These huge boats sailing up to the coast were so alien to what they had experienced in their world, that they simply could not perceive what was right before their eyes." He read the confusion on my face, then continued. "I feel like maybe they're already here. So different from what we've experienced as human beings. So alien. We fail to see them."

His words reminded me of the ones Neil said about Marvin revealing himself. Suddenly, the quiet woods were alive with possibility. Every inch of the trees and undergrowth seemed foreign, almost strange. So much so, it was dizzying.

"Your brother was an astrophysicist, no? Are you thinking about getting into something like that yourself?"

His question and who I saw when we reached the motel's lot, was enough of a one-two punch to knock me back down to earth. It was Richard and Dale, getting out of a black BMW, with bags of Chinese takeout in hand.

"We need to go," I said, quickly turning back toward the direction we came from. Pedro saw my reaction to spotting the men and asked if I knew them. "Just cousins. You know, in town to pay their respects. I'm just not ready to see them."

When we returned to our place, Pedro gave me another bear hug and invited me to his family's annual holiday party.

"Good food, salsa music, and beautiful people. What's better than that at Christmastime? Please come." I told him I'd consider it, then we parted ways.

Janice was roosting on her decrepit lawn chair, observing our every move. Her mangy feline army was using her boney frame as a cat tree. "You," she cackled as I passed her. "I've seen your colored friend. Now you're gallivanting in the woods with the Mexican. Something is amiss here."

In a string of unexpected encounters, it was this particular run-in that I would've bet the farm on. I had told the cantankerous old queen of dirty looks and thinly veiled racism to kick rocks many times before. This particular time, I let her slide. Chalk it up to Pedro's compassion rubbing off on me, or perhaps the realization that there are things in the world far more important to worry about than a crazy lady barking at the moon.

"I'll write you a check for five thousand dollars right now. For the whole box," my landlord Joe said, as he fiddled with a lustrous, silver Rolex. We met in the community laundry room. It's where the bald, cement truck of a man liked to conduct business. When I first met him, *King Kong Bundy* came to mind.

"C'mon, there has to be at least thirty grand worth of watches in here," I snapped back, snatching the piece out of his hand and carefully placing it back into its spot.

"Then put them on eBay, or bring 'em to a damn pawn shop, I don't know what to tell ya."

"That seems like a lot of work. This is your forte. Imagine the profit you can bring in with these things. I'll tell you what. Give me five grand now, then five grand later, and they're yours."

He contemplated it for a moment. Joe has never been bashful about how he managed to take a fairly large inheritance from his father and triple it with a slew of savvy business ventures; my apartment complex being one of them. I knew he was just the guy to bring my brother's watch collection. I could almost see the wheels turning in his shiny dome.

"Fine." He removed a checkbook out of his back pocket.

"That's the spirit!"

"You owe December's rent still, by the way."

"Take it out of the second installment of the ten thousand."

"You sonuvabitch."

"Hey, I need a small favor while I'm here."

He dropped me off at my car. To my surprise, it hadn't been broken into or towed. Finally, a break. A Google search provided the directions to the nearest store that specializes in toy trains. It was about an hour away. A drive seemed like a good way to clear my mind and put some distance between myself and the lunacy of my new life as an unwilling participant in an episode of the *X-Files*.

My destination was one of the last exits off the Atlantic City Expressway, right before you get to Philadelphia. I found an infinite sea of cars, surrounded by a labyrinth of relentless capitalism. A perfect area to get lost in for a few hours. It didn't hurt that I was starving and my pockets were a bit fatter.

In the midst of newly built, swanky storefronts and an endless array of glossy chain restaurants, "Big Dave's" Train Emporium was planted like a monument to yesteryear. Inside, there were trains. Lots of them.

The middle of the store contained a ridiculously detailed mountainside village. The tracks that ran through it looked like veins, looping and intersecting from corner to corner. Right on time, a rotund man wearing overalls and a conductor hat approached me. Naturally, his plastic name tag read Big Dave. "Howdy. What can I do ya for today?" he asked. I told him I was looking for the most expensive train he had in the store.

"Well, okay then. Follow me right on back here." He took me to the back of the store, where an old-fashioned train set was displayed in a glass case. "This is a 1950 Lionel Freight Set. A rare, beautiful thing."

"How much?"

"It's gonna run ya about eleven hundred dollars."

"I'll take it."

He chuckled. "Well, okay. My wife is in the back. She does beautiful gift wrapping. No extra charge." About ten minutes later, Big Dave rang me up. "You are going to make someone very happy." He slid the large, perfectly wrapped box across the counter.

"I hope so. Thank you, Big Dave."

"You're very welcome. Come back again. And Merry Christmas."

Exhausted parents and their bellowing offspring surrounded me, as I glanced over Cracker Barrel's menu. It wouldn't have been my first choice but it was within walking distance of Big Dave's, and I hadn't consumed a real meal in days. A skinny blonde with a pixie cut and tiny crucifix hanging from her neck proceeded toward the table.

"Hey there, welcome to Cracker Barrel. Can I start you off with something to drink?" I told her vodka and cranberry, with a twist of lime, sounded fantastic.

"Oh, I'm sorry, sir. We don't serve alcohol here."

There was a Peg Game on the table. I recalled the time Dad and I proclaimed the thing was impossible, then Alan solved it. He rubbed it in our faces for the remainder of our road trip. To my right, there were two boys, each around ten, huddled close together in their booth. The bigger one was moving his tablet like a steering wheel, as the little guy shrieked, "Turn, Turn, Turn!"

"Sir?" The waitress whispered. I told her a sweet tea would be fine.

Bob Segar crooned about some barn animals "keeping time" as I devoured Country Fried Chicken with green beans, mashed potatoes, and an obscene amount of biscuits. With every bite I gained more energy. I was like Superman circling the sun. For reasons beyond my control, the place had me entranced. The brats misbehaving in the general store, the country bumpkin charm. I didn't mind any of it. I was a man without a job, a wife, or a family, but I had buttermilk biscuits.

For the first time since I was visited by his lawyer, I thought about Alan without any distractions. Not the astrophysicist, but the kid who could climb a tree faster than anyone I ever knew and beat *Mike Tyson's Punch-Out!!* without ever losing a round. The kid who taught me how to shave and shoot a jumper, and showed me my first X-rated movie. I missed him.

For many years, I missed my big brother. All it took was him dying for me to realize it.

When I returned to my place, I scoped out the lot to see if there was a Chrysler LeBaron with the last remnants of a Bush/Cheney '04 sticker clinging to its bumper. When I didn't spot it, I moved as quickly as I could through the front door, then up the stairs. I leaned the package against Glen's door. As I entered my place, I turned to see an old-world Santa glancing mischievously at me from the wrapping paper.

Neil's tree was lying horizontally on my floor. Most of the ornaments were scattered around the carpet. It may not have belonged to an invisible space alien but, if the thing belonged to Neil, it deserved better.

I stood it up on top of a vacant end table, then gathered the plastic balls of red, silver, and green. I hung them on the branches, one by one, making sure that they were evenly spaced. The last time I decorated a tree was with my ex at our condo, a half a decade ago.

When I finished with Neil's tree, I took a few steps back and sized it up. It was standing in the center of the windows that overlooked the lake. The glow from the string lights was reflecting off the colorful orbs. The final product, in front of the pink sky of dusk, didn't look half bad. Just one thing was throwing off the whole vibe.

The discarded Crown Royal bottle that Rusty kicked was still on the floor. I scooped it up, then tossed it in the trash can. I did the same with the greasy cardboard boxes of various sizes that once contained everything from chicken nuggets to extra-large pizzas. While I was at it, I retrieved the rest of the liquor bottles sprinkled about the place. It didn't take me long to fill the entire trash bag.

With momentum on my side, I finally fetched the cleaning products from the closet. My aunt had visited me and almost suffered a nervous breakdown upon entering. She fought with me about cleaning the place herself, until we reached an agreement that she would bring me the supplies, and I would use them. They'd collected dust, along with the rest of the apartment, until this night. I polished every inch of the place until I was a sweaty, sticky mess.

In the shower, I let the hot water wash off the remains of the filth that had festered in my apartment for much too long. The futon called for me and I imagined it was pretty surprised when I folded my blanket, placed my pillow on top of it, then took a seat. It had gotten so used to a sad sack of shit collapsing down on it and retreating to his *Fortress of Self-pity* underneath the blanket, that it probably thought a new tenant had moved in. I breathed in the fresh, lemony scent and took a look around. Night had fallen and the only light was coming from Neil's tree.

I closed my eyes.

Then wept.

Not like I did with Pedro. It was a softer, more concerted breakdown. This time, I wasn't sure it was entirely for my brother.

262

Do you ever try to recall how it felt the first time you saw something impossible?

I remember being on the beach with Alan, watching in awe as Dad flew a kite. A red piece of nylon, powered by an invisible force that someone, ages before we came along, named wind.

A couple of years later, I stood in front of a pane of glass at the Philly Zoo, with my mouth agape. A furry monstrosity known as a *Rodrigues Fruit Bat* hung from a branch, staring back at me with its beady brown eyes. Until then, bats were nothing but flying mice that occasionally got lost in our attic.

How about the way the roots of a tree can lift up the sidewalk and create a ramp for kids to bunny hop over on their bikes? Or, the way that Michael Jordan soared from the foul line?

The moon. A giraffe. Or you.

The mere fact that you exist and, at some point, you didn't.

As we get older, we take it all for granted. We deem it "everyday stuff" but, if you never had every day to get used to it, some everyday stuff seems pretty impossible.

Marvin first appeared as a two foot tall silhouette in front of the tree. His features gradually came into focus, like if I were looking through the lens of a camera. Although he was draped in darkness, I saw him.

Fucking impossible.

I sprung from the futon, out the door, then down the steps. When I landed, I missed the last few. My bare left foot went totally sideways. It felt like a bullet connecting with my ankle. I lost my bearings, barreled through the main door, and out into the cold air. The sharp indentations in the pavement stabbed the bottom of my feet. I hooked a left, toward the grassy area that separated our building from the neighbors' yard. When I reached it, I fell to my back and clutched my throbbing ankle.

A car pulled up, bathing me in headlights. It was the fornicators from around back. A Caucasian couple, both wearing some form of tie-dye. His was a Grateful Dead tee-shirt - hers, a head scarf. I'm guessing they had to be anywhere between twenty-five and sixty years old. I couldn't tell if they had never discovered shampoo or actually chose to style their long, dirty blonde hair into dreadlocks. They exited the vehicle with a couple of takeout bags. The guy, whose name I had forgotten, yelled toward me. "Aye dude. You okay over there?"

"All good," I quickly sat up and pulled both my legs underneath me. "Just meditating." The cold, wet, grass tickled me through my basketball shorts. "Nice night for it. Right?"

"Yea, bro. No doubt." He asked his girl if they should join me, as he started to remove one of his raggedy sneakers. She looked on, confused, holding both bags.

"I'm actually just finishing up," I said, quickly getting to my feet. "Gonna take a walk now."

"You got no shoes on, dude," he said with a goofy laugh. "Room number two is very bohemian. Who woulda thunk it?"

"Can you shut up and take these bags," his girl retorted. "Please."

As much as I wanted to limp aimlessly down the sidewalk for the rest of eternity, I eventually tired a few blocks down. The homes on both sides of the street were adorned with string lights. Reindeer and other whimsical creatures frolicked on front lawns. There was a Santa, made to look like he had crashed into the side of one house. The only sound I could hear was the air pump keeping a giant mug of hot chocolate inflated.

The lyrics, "All is calm, all is bright" came to mind. Problem was, the first flurries of the year had started to fall, and I was wearing nothing but basketball shorts and a Wu-Tang Clan tee shirt. When my adrenaline dropped a few notches, I realized how cold I was.

I had to turn around.

I had to walk back and re-enter my apartment.

I had to face the impossible.

I opened the door as slowly as I could. The apartment was still dark. I heard Nat King Cole singing his trademark number about chestnuts from the speaker of my phone. The alien was sitting by the tree, illuminated by the string lights. I closed the door behind me, then leaned back, using it to hold myself upright.

I looked him over, starting from the head. It was much too big for the rest of his slender, naked body. He had two large eyes, like Black Jasper crystals, almost taking up his entire face. They left only a small bit of room for his pinhole nostrils and a thin, shallow strip, which I'm guessing was his mouth. From what I could tell, he had no nipples or genitalia. His skin was light grey in color, smooth and hairless, almost amphibian like. The warm,

264

white glow from the string lights seemed to continue right into the darkness of his eyes. Like stars in the mirror of the ocean. Never beginning, never ending.

"Marvin?" I said to him. Like there'd be a different alien in my apartment. "I'm going to turn the lights on and music off. If that's cool."

He blinked. It took longer than a human, since his eyelids were much larger than ours. I flicked the light switch, then picked up my cell and closed the music app. I deduced that if he was smart enough to find Nat King Cole in my phone, he should've been smart enough to understand me. I spoke slowly to him, and emphasized each word, like I would with a foreigner.

"I can't help you. My brother, Alan. He was a scientist. I am nothing. Do you understand?" He blinked again. "I don't know why you are here, why anyone thought bringing you to me was a good idea. But I have to ask you to move on. Those guys, Richard and Dale. They - "

Something happened.

Like a chameleon changing its color. Except Marvin was drawing from everywhere around him. His skin became the color of the decorated evergreen behind him. The carpet. The walls. The kitchen table. Everything close to him. I was barely able to see him at all, except for the Black Jaspers, until they were gone too.

He was nearly invisible.

I said his name three or four times and received no response. The symptoms of some unknown bodily response came on like a tsunami. It could've been anxiety, or shock, or a full-blown heart attack, I wasn't sure. My ass hit the futon and I initiated some deep breathing techniques that my doctor had taught me in case of a panic attack. I tilted my head back, closed my eyes, and kept breathing slowly.

In through the nose, out through the mouth.

I reopened them, focusing on the spot he had just occupied. I couldn't see him. Not even his outline. Not a trace.

My apartment was laid out like a circle. Each of the four rooms led into the next. I vaulted off the futon, then checked the kitchen, the bathroom, the bedroom.

No luck.

I circled three or four times, until my head was spinning. I told him that was one helluva trick. I asked him to come back. Still I got nothing.

When I sat back down on the futon, I felt something slimy brush my elbow. Then watched in amazement as the cushion pressed down slightly. He materialized directly next to me. Although I was somehow expecting it, I leapt from a sitting position and almost pissed my pants.

"Listen, Marvin. Human beings, we're not ready for that kind of shit," I said with quiet intensity, trying not to tip off the neighbors. "I'm not ready for it. I'm on the verge of a nervous breakdown here."

The corners of the sliver where his mouth should've been were turning upward, and his oversized head was tilting, faintly, to one side. He was studying me, as I tried my best to unravel as quietly as possible. "No more magic. Please."

Pedro came to the door in nothing but boxers. Every inch of his muscular physique was either covered in tattoos or splatters of fresh paint.

"Hey, man," I whispered. "Were you asleep?"

"Sleep is the cousin of death, my friend," he lifted his hands up to show me his paint-stained palms.

"Hey, uh, I need you to see something. Upstairs."

"Okay, let me throw a shirt on."

He followed me up. When we reached my door, I turned around to face him. "Pedro, brace yourself."

"Jesus," he responded, with a burgeoning curiosity. "You got dead bodies in there?"

There was no sign of him when we entered. Before I left to get Pedro, I explained to Marvin that I had a friend that wanted to meet him. I thought it would be a way to stir things up. The alien and I had just sat there, quietly, for an hour.

"Marvin," I said, moving methodically around the perimeter of the room. "This is my friend, Pedro. He's one of the nicest human beings on Earth."

Pedro watched and waited, with a look of peak confusion painted across his face. From what I knew of him, Pedro was a pretty understanding guy, but a no-show from Marvin would make me the resident crazy person. As nuts as Neil appeared to me, I appeared similarly nuts to Pedro. It was a crazy train, and we were definitely off the rails.

"Is it a cat? I'm gonna be super pissed if it's a cat. I wanted a guinea pig last year and Joe wouldn't allow it." I was relieved to see that he was taking it all in stride. A few minutes passed and, still, no Marvin.

"I'm sorry. It is a cat. You guessed it." My voice trembled. "Little fucker is hiding." Beads of perspiration were starting to gather on my brow. I wiped them and observed the buildup on my fingertips.

"Daniel. Whatever it is you are going through, we can talk about it."

The door swung open.

Richard and Dale barged in. Richard was once again playing mercenary, brandishing the handgun in our direction. "Both of you sit down!" he shouted, as he shuffled the muzzle back and forth between us. Dale quietly closed the door, then positioned his large frame in front of it. Pedro and I did as we were told, me at the kitchen table, Pedro on the futon.

"Nah, big guy," Dale added. "Sit at the table with your amigo." Pedro indulged the man, and moved slowly to the chair next to mine. He hadn't broken eye contact with Richard. "Marvin, show yourself. Do it now or your new friends are going to die."

Pedro was soaked in sweat; his face was beet red. The veins were protruding from his neck and temples. I imagined him as Bruce Banner, just about to transform and smash these two guys into oblivion.

"He's not going to make it that easy. Find him," Richard said to his partner, his hand trembling from the weight of the gun.

"Listen Marvin," I said, loud enough that if he was hiding in another room, he could hear me. "These guys might not be your first choice. You know? They might not be like Alan or Neil, but they can help you. They can help you more than I can."

"You should listen to this man," Richard said, appearing pleasantly surprised at my comments.

"I'm not like you," I continued, my words now aimed at the intruders. "I'm not like my brother. You smart people think you can do whatever you want. You can mess with the natural order of things. Not me. I go with the flow. I need to get my life on track. Get my job back at the bar. I told you, I don't want to be caught up in it. I invited Pedro up here to figure this whole mess out for me." I was about to continue my rant, when Dale returned to the room.

"The bathroom window is open," he said. "It leads out to the roof, some trees. He could've fled." Richard let off a string of curse words, then dropped his gun by his side.

As fluid as one of his brushstrokes, Pedro was off the chair and headed toward Richard. The sloppy bastard tried to lift the gun back up, but was too slow. Pedro connected with a right hook, sending the man crashing to the floor. Dale dashed toward Pedro until I cut him off, as quickly as I could manage on a bum ankle. The two of us collided, crumbling to the floor in a mess of body parts. I watched as Pedro retrieved the gun, then aimed it at Richard's bloodied face. Then toward Dale, and back again.

"Y'all better be on your way," Pedro said, softly, to the men. I removed myself from atop Dale and limped over to my friend's side. Just then, there was a loud knock on the door, followed by Joe's voice.

"What the hell is going on in there?"

"Shit," I whispered to Pedro.

"It's okay," he whispered back. "Daniel and I had a fistfight, he said, louder. "We were at the bar, things escalated when we got back. It's okay now."

"Pedro? What the fuck? Open this door, man" Joe demanded.

Pedro whispered to the men as he placed the firearm on the carpet, then kicked it under the futon. "You two go into the bedroom. Close the door. You hold your face," he said to me.

"This is unacceptable. My family is sleeping down there," Joe barked, as Pedro let him into my apartment.

"Joe, it's all good," I said, figuring I should contribute something to this cover-up. "Can you believe Pedro is such a hot head? He treated me like that bag he's got outside." Glen popped his head in the door and asked if everything was okay.

"These two had a fight, Glen," Joe answered quickly. Even if he didn't buy our story, he rolled with it. The old man was prone to asking a lot of questions. "I think we're good now."

"Then I guess I'll ask, while I have you all in front of me," Glen said, and I was embarrassed already. "Do any of you know who left a present by my door?" I planned for it to be the opposite of a grand gesture but failed. I told him it was me. "Daniel? That's a very expensive item. I can't accept it."

"Yes, you can, Glen. You deserve it." He shuffled toward me in his flannel pajamas and wool slippers. Pedro smiled brightly while Joe looked on, completely baffled.

"That's very nice of you, young man," Glen said, wrapping me in his arms. "Very nice indeed."

Joe chimed in. "Pedro is a hot head. Daniel does a nice gesture for someone. What the hell is happening to my tenants?"

Pedro declared, "It's Christmastime, there must be something in the air!"

After some handshakes and pats on the back, Glen exited the apartment, followed by Joe. Richard and Dale emerged from my bedroom as soon as they heard the door shut behind the men. Richard was pressing one of my undershirts to his nose, as Pedro retrieved the gun from underneath the futon.

"I need you guys to get the fuck out of here," I said. "Marvin is gone. Do what you need to do and leave me out of it."

"You heard him. If I catch y'all around this house again, there will be big problems," Pedro added. He removed the magazine from the gun, without even looking down. It was like he'd done it a thousand times. "I've known men that are comfortable around violence. You are not those men."

He handed the gun back to Richard, who looked a lot like Neil the last time I saw him. It was as if he were using every fiber of his being just to stand and focus his eyes on what was happening before him. He struggled to hold the heavy steel in his hands. "I got it," Dale said, removing it from his clutches. On their way out, Dale, the larger, and healthier, of the two, admonished us with some parting words.

"Your brother would have been nothing without this man," he rested a hand on his friend's shoulder. "He had the intelligence, that's for sure. He just didn't have the resources, or balls, like Richard Arko. And, you're absolutely correct, Daniel. Marvin does belong with us. We still have much to learn from him."

"Okay, great. Go compare the size of each other's balls someplace else." I closed the door on them, then gave myself and Pedro a moment to soak what just happened in. After a few minutes, I spoke again. "You're pretty scary, bro. Any truth to that stuff you said?"

"When I was growing up in Los Angeles, my uncles were in a gang. That's how my folks and I ended up here, as far away from that life as possible."

"I understand."

"Cool. Now let's take a drive. I need to know that the hell is going on."

As we cruised the streets of Cedarwood, I filled Pedro in on everything, starting with the visit from my brother's lawyer, all the way to the scuffle back in the apartment. If I didn't live it, I wouldn't have believed a second of it.

"There must be a reason Alan chose you. He must have thought you were trustworthy enough," he responded. "And capable of handling it."

"What about his wife? Far as I know, they were as close as a married couple gets."

"Obviously there are dangers involved. He knew that. He couldn't bring himself to subject his wife and children to it."

My neighbor was making a little too much sense. I hooked a left, and pulled into a place where many great discussions have taken place at midnight. A 7-Eleven parking lot.

"I guess if he couldn't trust his colleagues and his best friend was dying, he had no one else but me," I said, trying to sort it out in my mind. "If that's really the case though, where are the instructions? He couldn't leave me with a damn recorded message or...fuck. Fuck!" I smacked the top of the steering wheel.

"What's up?"

"He left a letter with Neil. I got hammered and never opened it."

"Where is it now?"

"They took it. Those assholes took it."

"Okay, okay. Relax. We'll find them and get it back."

"It's too late. I abandoned Marvin because I thought I was in over my head, while this whole damn time Alan probably had it mapped out for me."

"Listen to me. We will find Marvin and we will get your brother's letter back. We just have to believe. That's all. Just believe."

I had stopped believing in anything the moment a drunk tractor trailer operator ran a stop sign and t-boned my father's station wagon. "If just believing got anyone anywhere, this whole assbackwards world would be a better place," I said. "I fucked this up, Pedro. It's what I do."

"Don't give up. Don't give up on your brother. Don't give up on Marvin. He's scared, man. He's far from home and scared."

"Richard and Dale will know what to do."

"Stop saying that! You know as well as I do that those guys are up to no good."

"Then, hopefully, someone better will get to him first. There's a lot of decent people out there."

"Yea. There's a lot of decent people. There's also a lot of ugly people. People that don't even want *me* here. How do you think they'll feel about Marvin?"

I didn't provide an answer. Instead, I put the Jeep back in drive and pulled away from the 7-Eleven. I took us back to the house as quickly as I could. Neither of us spoke another word until we pulled up. I thanked him for decking the dude and saving our asses, then said goodbye. He asked where I was heading, and I lied about needing to drive more to clear my head. My real plan was to find an open bar.

"Aye, man," he said as he exited, then stuck his head back in the passenger side window. "I know you try to give people reasons to hate you, like Glen's granddaugh -" I cut him off and asked how he knew her. "She was going through a rough patch and I took her out for some coffee. That's not my point though. It's a terrible way to live, pushing people away. But, I've never been in your shoes. You've faced profound loss and we all have different ways to cope. Since the day you moved in, though, you and I ain't been nothing but buddies. So, if you change your mind and continue to pursue this, I'm down. I'd really like to meet Marvin. Call me if there's any more trouble. Later, my friend."

He shot me a peace sign, then continued on his way.

Kate was sitting at the kitchen table. Her mascara had run down her face and dried. She looked exhausted.

A couple of other girls were at the table with her. They looked like an older and younger version of my sister-in-law. One was bouncing a cherubic toddler on her lap, while the other rubbed Kate's back. I tried to shout in their direction but couldn't. I was paralyzed.

I heard footsteps to the side of me. The urgent, rapping of a little girl's feet. It was my niece, Gabbie. She zipped past me holding a piece of sketch paper, then dove into her aunt's lap. I couldn't decipher the colorful arrangement of colors from where I lay.

"Look, Mommy," Gabbie said. "It's all of us with Daddy. We're in heaven. But we get to visit him and come back, like, with ladders that reach the sky."

"That's so sweet, baby," her mother responded, trying to keep the crying at bay. It was like she had mastered the technique.

"Who is that?" Kate's sister asked, pointing to the paper.

"That's Uncle Dan. Mommy, will Uncle Dan be coming to see us soon?"

"I don't know, baby. We'll see."

I glanced past them, through the window. There was nothing. No lake. No trees. Just a dark void.

Slowly, something came into the frame of the window, as if we were on a plane that dipped to one side. Some kind of gas, a million shades of pinks and purples, frozen in time. I caught a fleeting glimpse, deeper into the void. I saw clusters of stars.

My initial thought was that I had gone too far the night before and given myself alcohol poisoning. I believed that I was in heaven. Or hell. Or purgatory. Something didn't add up though. Alan wasn't there, neither were my parents. The people in my apartment with me were supposed to be alive.

I tried to call out to Kate again and couldn't. I couldn't do anything. I was stuck inside of myself.

In the corner (Alan's corner), the ceiling caught fire. It spread quickly, revealing the void as it burned. Within moments, the blaze engulfed everything. The wall was totally gone. Kate and her sisters floated from the floor, then through the opening, until I could no longer see them. Gabbie followed, but she wasn't scared. She kept clutching her artwork with her little hand as she flew into the void.

The flame grew closer to me. I felt myself rise from the futon. I was stiff, helpless, but I was moving.

Toward the darkness.

I awoke on the floor in front of the TV, sore and drenched in sweat. The blue light of morning was forcing itself through the shades. When I sat up, a sharp pain shot through my neck. My ankle was still tender from the stumble on the staircase.

Marvin was sitting by his tree with his legs crossed. His head was at the studying angle again but study wasn't a strong enough word for what he was doing. It's more like he was absorbing every fiber of me. The way I struggled to the futon. The way I rubbed my temples and belched. I'm willing to bet that this was his first time seeing a human being in such a state.

"Did you do that? Did you give me those visions? I said no more magic." His head tilted the other way, like a dog waiting for a treat. "I know you understand me. So, listen, if I'm going to help you, you're going to have to start helping me. And to do that, you can't disappear or run off. You have to stay here until I figure this shit out."

My insides coiled, then the back of my jawline started to tingle. That old, familiar feeling was back like it had never left. I sprinted toward the bathroom, stumbling a few times on my way there. As soon as the porcelain lid connected with the back of the toilet, I was on my knees. Vomit splashed in the fresh toilet water. If a clean apartment was some kind of symbolism for a new life, one hangover flips the script in a hurry.

Marvin appeared in the doorway. I don't know if he walked there, or teleported, or did the Cha Cha Slide. I didn't know what was up or down anymore.

"This is him," I said, sitting back against the baseboard. "This is the guy they left you with."

He followed me to the kitchen table, then mounted a chair belly first, swinging around to a sitting position. His movements were like a child's, only slower and more graceful.

There we sat. For a long time.

From the outside looking in, the situation couldn't have been more incredible. The existence of life on other planets changed everything. Forever. In the history of humankind. From where I was sitting, it was a comedy of epic proportion. Two confused, wildly different beings sitting at an IKEA table, giving each other the silent treatment.

I remembered what Neil told me about Marvin communicating non-verbally, then something occurred to me about the alien's mannerisms when we first met. It was a long shot, but I went for it.

"Let's try something," I whispered. "I'll ask a yes or no question. Blink if the answer is yes. Do you understand?"

He blinked. A surge of excitement hit me. I fired out the next question as if the moment would disappear if I hadn't.

"Were you involved in a crash?"

Another blink. We were officially in the money.

"Did my brother, Alan, help you?"

A third blink. His oversized eyelid took a bit longer to close on this question.

"Okay, um, do you have families where you come from? The others in the crash, were they your parents?" He stared at me. The gleaming black of his eyes was disorienting from that distance. I got caught up in the moment and asked a horribly inconsiderate question. I was about to apologize when he blinked twice.

With only his eyes, Marvin told me everything that I needed to know. He told me we had a lot more in common than I thought. I learned in that moment that loss spans light years. "Do you eat food? Are you hungry?" He blinked two more times. "What do you eat?"

He stared at me; his eyelids didn't move. I had to laugh when I realized why. My last question hadn't been a yes or no one. Marvin managed to answer it anyway when he held his hand up, pointing toward the Christmas tree. "You eat trees? No, like plants, right? Your kind are herbivores. That would make sense." He turned away, I think he had grown tired of my line of questioning.

My first order of business was to get him fed. I had to make a ShopRite run, but I wasn't about to leave him alone. I asked him if he could do his invisible trick and wait in the Jeep while I retrieved something for us to eat. He blinked. I opened the music app, then placed the phone in his hands. "I'm gonna get ready," I told him. "Enjoy."

Halfway to the bathroom, I turned to ask him a final question. "It is a pretty good song, ain't it?" He was too enthralled by what was happening on the cell's screen to answer but I took it as a yes.

In the shower, I felt reinvigorated. And, as the warm water washed over me, Nat King Cole sang about chestnuts once more.

Marvin went invisible before we exited the apartment and left for the store. On the way there, FM radio played a string of holiday hits: Frank Sinatra, Burl Ives, Thurl Ravenscroft. Marvin, who had materialized, sunk low in the back seat and enjoyed it all, the best I can tell.

It was Christmas Eve. The parking lot was jumping. Families were getting a late start on party preparations, racing in and out of the electric doors, their carts brimming with fat bags of groceries. I parked as close to the entrance as I could. "Here's my phone. Enjoy the playlist," I said to the alien, who had turned invisible again. "Lay low, I'm going to lock you in. See you soon." I kept looking back at the Jeep, as I moved quickly toward the store.

Although I felt pretty confident, it didn't stop me from limping through the aisles, grabbing what I needed, then darting back to him. When I was almost there, I heard my name. It was an old friend of my Dad's. A middle-aged guy, wearing a golf cap and black leather jacket. He looked and talked like an extra from *The Sopranos*. His name was Louie, maybe Tony. I had no idea.

"Danny Boy, I am so sorry about your loss," he said, coming in for a hug whether I liked it or not. He asked how I was holding up, and I told him that I was hanging in there. He followed it up with, "The silver lining here is that your folks are gone. They didn't have to bury their son." Something about the death of a loved one gives people a pass to skip the subliminal stuff entirely.

He was overstaying his welcome in my personal space, rubbing my biceps and breathing his tobacco-laced breath into my face. I kept looking over his shoulder at the Jeep. There was a little boy, about five, dragging his mother toward the back windows. I cut Louie/Tony off, then hurried over to them. The girl was from my graduating class. She was known for going through a pretty intense witch phase in eighth grade.

"Daniel." The way she said my name made me know that sympathies were in short order. I had no time for it, I needed to get her snotty nosed kid away from my vehicle. And fast. "I am so sorry about Alan," she continued. Her son kept tugging on her hand like a bell rope.

"It's okay," I responded. "I'm okay. I just need to get home." The kid finally got her attention with a string of "Mommies" that's probably still echoing across the North Pole.

"I saw a spaceman in his car, Mommy. It waved at me," he cried.

My heart felt like it had released itself from my chest cavity then descended down my rectum and out of my body totally, until it was nothing but a steamy pile of goo on the asphalt. I had just started to like Marvin; now I wanted to kill him.

"There's no spaceman, baby. Let me finish talking. Okay?"

I scanned the Jeep's interior through the driver side window. Marvin could no longer be seen. That didn't stop the kid from bellowing like a depraved banshee.

"I am so sorry," the mom said. "He never acts like this."

"It was in there! I promise! It was in there!"

The girl lifted her son up, as he took a couple of swings at her. People started to take notice. My knit hat suddenly felt like it was six sizes too small. Sweat started to pour down my face.

This was it. I failed. The cops would be there shortly, followed by news vans. Then nondescript, government vehicles. All pulling up to get a piece of Marvin. "Are you kidding me right now?" She grabbed him by the forearm. "Santa is not coming tonight if you keep this up! You hear me? I have to get in and out of this damn store. I have company coming over in an hour. Take care, Daniel."

"Good luck," I said, then removed my hat and wiped the sweat from my brow. "And Merry Christmas." She never took a second look at the Jeep.

I flung the bags into the trunk, jumped into the front seat, then shouted his name as we whipped out of the parking lot. He reappeared on the floor between the front and back seats.

"What the hell? You could've blown our cover!" I shouted, with a laugh. In spite of everything, it was the most fun I'd had in years.

I put together a leafy green smorgasbord. Lettuce, kale, Baby Bok Choy. Marvin answered any question I had, while I did my best to prepare it.

I tried not to chuckle as he picked each piece up individually, then slowly inserted them into his weird sliver of a mouth. They slid like a debit card into an ATM. About six pieces in total. When I pressured him on whether he was full, he insisted that he was, with three hard blinks in a row. I had to finish up the meal, which was bland, but much healthier than the hydrogenated nightmare I had lived on since my divorce.

After we ate, my neighbor in the house officially met our neighbor in the stars. It took a few minutes for Marvin to materialize once Pedro entered. When he finally did, Pedro approached slowly, then knelt down to the alien's eye level.

"It's so nice to meet you," Pedro whispered, with tears rolling down his cheeks. He turned to me. "This is the most amazing thing of all time." I nodded in agreement.

Pedro lifted his arm up, with his hand open and fingers extended. Marvin did the same, then they connected palms. I felt a tinge of jealousy that I wasn't involved in the moment.

Without warning, I heard a succession of airy blasts. The sound was followed by what felt like turbocharged bee stings on my chest and neck. The third shot - on my temple - made me collapse to the carpet. I wiped the side of my head where I felt the impact and expected to see blood; instead, my fingertips were covered in yellow paint. I tried to sit up, only to get bombarded again. This time, it was a relentless downpour of quick shots. Each one hurt more than the last. Not only was my body being drenched, the walls and windows, the table and chairs, the futon and television, all got painted over in a putrid lemony shade.

It was the return of Richard Arko and Dale Savage. They were coming in heavy again, only this time, they were packing something strange. The weapons were black, with long barrels. A canister jutted from the top, and an air tank from the back. It took me a minute to gather my thoughts and deduce that I was looking at paintball guns.

Pedro was hit a few times as well, but managed to shake it off and charge the men. He staggered Dale with a flying knee lift, then squared up with Richard, who tried to open fire. My friend grasped the gun by its barrel, yanked it from the assailant's grip, then punched him square in the face. Dale

278

advanced back on him fast. He flipped the gun over then swung it like a battle axe. It struck Pedro so hard across the back of the head that I thought it killed him.

Dale attempted to help Richard to his feet, but he smacked his hands away and shouted, "Forget about me, grab the alien. It's now or never!"

I frantically scanned the room for Marvin. When my eyes landed on him, they saw a helpless creature with half of his frail body wedged in between the radiator pipes. He was covered with splotches of yellow paint. Even if he turned invisible, the markings would not. They couldn't lose him now.

Dale bounded toward him. I rode a wave of adrenaline that put me between Marvin and the large man. We grappled, tearing at each other's shirts, trying to land small jabs. A couple rocked me. When he saw that I was on the ropes, he attempted a wide right hook. I ducked from the would-be death blow, leaving me wide open for a knee to the face. When it connected, I thought I swallowed my nose.

Marvin was trying his hardest to reach the latches on the window, but they were too high. In my dizzied state, I could do nothing but watch as Dale grabbed him from behind, then wrapped him in a bedsheet. On their way out, Richard brandished both guns in our direction, letting them pass. Marvin was trapped in Dale's grip, kicking his legs. One of his wiry arms broke free from underneath the sheet. He was reaching for me.

Pedro lifted me up by my armpits and brought me to my feet. "We are not losing Marvin, not today," he said, like we were co-stars in a war movie. We stampeded down the inside stairwell, then through the doors and out to the front porch. Glen's granddaughter was standing there. "Guys, what the hell is going on?" She turned to see the men peel out of the parking lot.

"We can't talk right now, Ali," Pedro responded. To my surprise, she (who now had a name) joined us in our mad dash to the Jeep.

"This is crazy. Why are you guys covered in paint?" she asked. "Who the hell were those men?"

Pedro ignored her and requested the keys. I had no recollection of grabbing them but, by force of habit, I must have on the way out. I tossed them to him, then we hopped in. Ali joined us in the backseat.

"Hey, uh. You should probably leave us be. I'm pretty sure what we're about to get into is pretty dangerous," I said, as Pedro threw it in drive. "Pedro, what the fuck?"

"Buckle your seatbelts, my friends," he said, tearing out of the driveway. "We've wasted too much time already!"

We were two cars behind them as they blew the first traffic light. When Pedro did the same, I asked him what the hell our plan was.

"We're going to trail them," he answered. "Eventually they'll get to their destination or run out of gas trying."

"Or we'll run out of gas trying," I said.

"You have a full tank. I'm willing to bet that they don't."

"Perfect. I guess we'll *just believe* then?"

"Now you're talking my friend!"

Pedro maneuvered successively enough that we managed to get behind them. He was keeping a couple of car lengths between our vehicles, but they noticed us. They hooked an abrupt left, cutting off two lanes of traffic heading in the opposite direction. Horns blared as we started to speed down a wooded road that stretched through Wharton State Forest.

"They're going to try to lose us in the Pine Barrens," I announced, clenching my butt cheeks together as Pedro floored it.

"This thing doesn't have the speed of their BMW, but it's all about the man behind the wheel," he said.

"Um, Pedro, have you done this before?" Ali inquired, clutching the grab handle. Pedro explained that he dabbled in illegal street racing for a few years and I started to think he was making this shit up as he went along.

The needle was pinned at about seventy miles per hour. Luckily, only trees and sprawling farmland zipped by our windows. When they blew a red light or stop sign, we had to as well. Each time, I waited to see an overzealous state trooper shoot from the edge of the woods, with their red and blue lights cutting through the New Jersey dusk.

After twenty nerve-racking minutes of hard driving, we entered Cedarwood's neighbor to the north, Pine Ridge. The town's famous Main Street was twinkling so splendidly that it managed to calm us down, as we leveled out at the speed limit of thirty-five. Occasionally, a car or two would come between us and Marvin's captors, but Pedro stayed on their tail lights like a fly on shit.

Up to that point, the topic of discussion in the Jeep had been focused on not getting ourselves killed. Ali finally felt safe enough to start asking the big questions. Pedro kept his grip on the wheel, with his gaze piercing the windshield, and I started explaining.

Alan's passing and his life's work. Neil and the Mercury Seven. Their top-secret project and crash at the site. I laid it all out in a descriptive, albeit frenzied, manner. Her expression changed when I got to Marvin. I saved mentioning him until last. I wanted it to be a big reveal. She sat back, letting go of the grab handle. "So, you're telling me there's a space alien in that car?"

"Yes," I answered. "Marvin."

"I think I'm going to throw up," she said, opening the window.

"I felt the same way," Pedro finally chimed in. "But then I met him, Ali. Wow. Just wow."

The residential area of Pine Ridge started to thin out. Log cabins and mom and pop shops made way for farmhouses and silos. Night was falling fast; their tail lights seemed to take on new life in the growing darkness.

Ahead of them, on the narrow two-lane road, was a tractor trailer. They sped up and began to pass it. Headlights were coming fast from the opposite lane. At the very last second, they turned, barreling across the forest edge, then through an opening in the trees. Pedro wasn't expecting their evasive action and was forced to slam on the brakes and cut the wheel. The Jeep went sideways and damn near toppled over.

We hit the dirt road and picked up speed again. I sensed that the three of us were bonding in some strange way. Ali had no reason to think I was anything but some asshole, but here she was knee deep in the batshit with us. I guess a perilous high-speed chase would have that effect on her. Or, perhaps, my brother was right all along. I thought about something he said to me the night of our parents' service.

The day had been long and sad and all around horrible. I smoked a joint in the gazebo while family members, friends, my father's coworkers, and everyone in between, mingled inside my childhood home.

"Had to get out of there, huh?" Alan said, scooping up a mostly deflated basketball and passing it to me. "*Cannabis sativa*," he continued, as he removed the joint from my mouth and took a hit. "It's no good for you."

"I guess these people ain't leaving until all the lasagna is gone," I responded, then exchanged the ball for the weed.

"Don't be like that. They cared about Mom and Dad. They care about us, man."

"Yea. Until we all go back to seeing each other once a year."

"Little bro. People are generally good. You should start noticing it."

"Sure."

"Anyway, they've all pitched in. In times like this, human beings tend to help each other out. They've helped me out a great deal this week."

"Us, you mean?"

"Yea, you know what I meant." I always knew when he was full of shit.

"Whatever." I flicked the joint into the woods.

"I'm just saying. You could come out of your room a little more. Wouldn't hurt."

"Don't start."

"Okay, Daniel. Just remember what I said. Especially now."

The dirt road led out to some undeveloped farmland. The captors zigzagged in the dirt, stirring up a dust storm. They were getting frustrated, perhaps desperate because of a dwindling gas tank. Pedro accelerated, getting close enough that we could've breathed on their car. He shouted about clipping them and sending them spiraling. I shouted in protest. Ali joined me. Before he made contact, we had to get back behind them on another dirt road.

They floored it again. Faster than ever. Our speedometer shot up, malfunctioning at about ninety.

We saw their brake lights. Then we didn't.

There was a jarring sound of glass, steel, and aluminum joining together in a nightmarish way.

We were following much too close to do anything. There was no way we weren't going to crash into them. We'd probably go up in flames. Like in the movies. I'd be forced to look around at my friends. Pedro. Marvin. Poor Ali who shouldn't even have been with us. Their limbs broken and bent, intertwined with whatever was left of the Jeep. I'd be the last to go. Burning to a cinder in the middle of a fiery nowhere, with no one to hear my screams.

I felt something.

I thought it was inertia from Pedro hitting the brakes so violently. Or wind had gotten under the soft top and picked us up a bit. The bewildering sensation was followed by weird noises from the Jeep. Like parts of the vehicle were suddenly moving and they weren't supposed to be. I looked *down* from my window. We were being propelled over the BMW. But it was a controlled flight.

We landed, safely, about ten yards in front of the car.

My first thought was Marvin.

Was he hurt?

Did he survive?

I sprinted toward the car in the hazy glow of its crushed headlights. A downed oak tree had decimated its front end.

"Marvin!" I shouted, turning on my cellphone's flashlight. Dale's fate was the first thing it illuminated. The driver side airbag had been deployed but did nothing to prevent his impact with the tree. His lifeless body was draped over the steering wheel. His face was punctured by a million shards of glass, a thick branch had impaled him through the chest, thumb tacking him to the seat. "Marvin, please. Are you there?" I asked frantically, aware that he couldn't answer, but I wanted him to hear my voice.

Pedro and Ali joined me on the other side of the vehicle, our cell phone lights converged on the bed sheet in the backseat. I tried to open the door but it didn't budge. Pedro saw me struggling and rushed over. With our combined strength we were able to dislodge it.

I yanked the sheet to find Marvin in the fetal position, bound at the wrist and ankles. I quickly realized it would be impossible to remove the cable ties without cutting them.

"There's a knife in my glovebox," I said.

"On it," Ali responded.

The ties were so tight that I couldn't fit my fingers underneath. I held both his hands in my own, then placed my other hand on the back of his head. His skin was slimy and warm, like it had been back in the apartment. When he felt my touch, his eyes opened.

"Marvin," I cried. "We're here. We're going to get you untied." Ali returned with the knife, then I cut him loose. I climbed in, cradled him, and took him out of the car. He was light as a feather. Literally.

"Give him to me. Find your brother's letter," Pedro said. I hesitated for a moment but carefully handed him off then turned my attention back to the car.

Richard was dead as well. There was no telling where the crooked, bloody branches ended and his mutilated body began. He had become one with the tree. My first instinct was to check the glovebox or front console, but they were destroyed. The only reachable area was the backseat where Marvin had been. I searched it with my light, turning up nothing but the paintball guns, some air canisters, and hoppers filled with extra ammunition. Anxious to get back to Marvin, I was about to give up, when my light caught the corner of the envelope sticking out of the backseat organizer. It'd been opened, but the letter was still inside and intact. I swiped it, then took one last, long look at the wreckage.

Whatever these men's intentions were, it had gotten them killed. Perhaps one day their bodies would be discovered. It would start an avalanche of investigations into the Mercury Seven and their work. Maybe the Arko family would hire some assassins to track me down. So many thoughts shuffled through my mind, but one took precedent. The well-being of Marvin.

I returned to the Jeep to find him in the backseat with Ali. They were holding hands, his large head rested on her lap. "Are you okay, buddy?" I asked from the passenger seat. He blinked. "How about you?" I said to Ali.

"I'm fine," she answered, "just a little shook up." She nodded toward Pedro, who was once again in the driver's seat; his head reposed on the steering wheel. I placed my hand on the back of his neck.

"Did you find it?" he asked, but didn't look up.

"I did. Dude, are you okay?"

"I'm just thinking about those men. Their families." We sat quietly for a moment. The only sound in the woods was the Jeep's engine.

"You should read it," Ali said, softly, from the backseat.

Pedro finally lifted his head off the wheel. "She's right," he said, wiping tears from his eyes. "Take your time with it."

I looked at both of them, then down at Marvin. His eyes were closed, but his chest was rising and falling. Just like ours.

"He's incredible," Ali said.

As winter's moon hung high over the woods, I sat in the glow of crushed headlights and read the last words my brother would ever say to me.

Dear Daniel,

If you're reading this, it means you've told Neil to piss off. I don't blame you this time. It's a game changer, for anyone. The existence of extraterrestrials is an amazing but incredibly frightening discovery. I assure you though, Marvin is nothing to be afraid of.

I know you're probably upset that I threw this all in your lap but, Daniel, you were the only person I knew capable of handling it. You're able to see the absurdity in life, more so than anyone else I've ever met. It allows you to take things in stride. It's something I've always envied about you. Not only that, but you're compassionate. You may not believe it, or even see it, but you are.

Marvin needs that compassion. My partners, Richard Arko and Dale Savage, if they come for him, act like you have no idea what the hell they are talking about. They'll believe you. I've given them no reason not to. It's why I've kept you and Kate in the dark for so long. They want to understand why Marvin was able to survive the crash. They want to examine him, until there's nothing left of him to examine. They don't want to end up like me and the rest of our group. And they're running out of time.

In my desk drawer at home, there are notes on everything, along with a second letter, for Kate. She should've found it by now but, if she hasn't, please let her know. They are coming back for him, Daniel. I've been able to communicate with others like him, and we've coordinated a landing on Christmas Eve. There's a clearing in the woods behind my house. Please bring him there. Only Kate should know of Marvin's existence. He will know what to do once you've arrived at my house. Daniel, tell my babies that it's Santa Claus if they see the lights.

I know I haven't been the big brother you've needed. There were times when I wanted to leave whatever stupid lab I was working in, get in the car, and come find you. We could've hit the boards, grabbed a couple of slices, and then looked out at the ocean. Just you and me. I understand why you pushed me away for so long and I want to say I'm sorry. I wish we had more time to be brothers.

You probably haven't bothered to open the comic book box yet but, when you do, you'll find a Christmas present in there. It's something small, but I know you've needed it for a long time.

I'll say hello to Mom and Dad for you. Take care, man.

- Alan

Chapter 12

We decided, as a trio, to keep going. It was already seven pm and we were still a couple of hours from Alan's house in Upstate New York. Ali put his address in her phone and we made our way out of the woods.

Pedro rang his mother to inform her that he wouldn't be making it to their annual Christmas Eve party. They debated about the "Pozole in the fridge" but worked it out in the end.

Ali made a call to her mom as well. She apologized for skipping out earlier, then went on to say that she and Steve are trying to work things out. She winked at me in the window's reflection when she said that part. This was both embarrassing (because she caught me watching her) and pretty exciting. It let me know that the "working things out with Steve" thing was bullshit, but also gave me a feeling that she was starting to forgive me for being such a dick.

As for me, it had been a few years since I'd spent the night before Christmas with anyone other than Foxhole employees. I had no one to call other than my sister-in-law Kate, to alert her to our arrival. She had found the note from Alan and was hoping to hear from me. I filled her in on everything that had happened since we last spoke: meeting Marvin, the chase, the demise of Richard and Dale. I also told her about the people accompanying me to her house.

"That's totally fine," she said. "To be honest, my sisters left this afternoon and I was dreading spending Christmas Eve without him. It was always his favorite night of the year."

"Yea, it was," I agreed, remembering how much Alan used to love visiting our grandparents' house. The bowl of walnuts with the silver cracker. The confusing perplexities of Pollyanna. Dad drinking VO and our great aunt wearing the same blinding red pantsuit every year. "I guess I forgot."

"I have a fridge full of leftovers," she continued. "Text me when you guys are close and I'll get it all out."

"You don't have to do that."

"I know, Daniel. I want to." She sounded much better than she had before, and I was in awe of her generosity and strength. She offered up hot showers and guest rooms and sofa beds. She also offered up her clothes for Ali, and some of Alan's for me and Pedro. "Daniel," she added, right before we were about to end the call. "What's Marvin like?"

"It's impossible to put into words," I answered.

Somewhere along the New Jersey Turnpike, Marvin came back to life. He sat up and peered through the window, surveying the industrial area on the outskirts of New York City. Beyond that, the lights of Manhattan were like the stars themselves. Cars and trucks zipped by us, trying to make it to their destinations in time for Christmas. I can't be sure, but I thought I saw a few people, mostly children riding in backseats, spot the alien in the window.

We stopped at the Vincent D'Onofrio Service Plaza. Or was it Vince Lombardi? I can't remember. The yellow paint was no longer visible on Marvin's skin. It somehow cleared up during the drive. When we hit the well-lit rest stop, he vanished in front of Ali for the first time. Needless to say, she was amazed.

The plaza consisted of a few fast food joints, rest rooms, and a gift shop crawling with miniature Statues of Liberty and *I Heart NY* apparel. Pedro gassed up the Jeep while I ran into the place to grab some pain relievers for my ankle. To my surprise, Ali joined me.

"So, I was actually looking for you today before the madness began," she said, as we waited in the checkout line.

"You were?" I responded.

"I wanted to thank you for doing that for my grandfather. You really made his whole Christmas."

"It's well deserved. He helped me when I needed it most." I found myself choked up. It was a stiff cocktail of everything going to my head at the worst possible moment. I turned my face away from hers, then wiped my eyes.

"Hey, you okay?"

"Glen is a good man. I failed to see it for much too long." I insisted on paying for her sparkling water and apple, then continued. "I wanted to apologize to you as well. You definitely didn't deserve what I said to you."

"Yea, well, that feels like another life after all of this. But, I guess I'll accept your apology."

For the first time, she smiled at me. A big, warm smile. Any man who received that smile on a daily basis would be a truly lucky man.

A long, flagstone driveway with lanterns on both sides brought us to my brother's Ranch-style house. It's a thing of beauty, nestled deep in the Hudson Highlands. And it was my first time there.

Kate greeted us at the door. It had been years since I last saw her but she still looked exactly the same. She wore an oversized NASA sweatshirt over her petite frame and Christmassy leggings. Her dirty blonde hair was up in a messy bun. Although she's a few years older than me, she could pass for a girl in her early twenties. I introduced her to Pedro and Ali. She seemed both excited to see us and shocked at our disheveled, painted up appearances. If the space alien we were bringing her was preoccupying her thoughts, I couldn't tell. Her main concern was getting us showered and fed.

About thirty minutes later, after washing off the sticky residue of a paintball attack, I found myself in the guest room. The world's fluffiest towel was wrapped around my waist as I stared at my brother's clothes, folded neatly on the foot of the bed. He and I were generally the same size, so his navy blue polo and gray trousers fit just fine. Maybe just a little snug in the midsection. Kate met me in the upstairs hallway as I was on my way back down.

"Hey, I just want to say that I'm so happy you are here. I've just been walking around aimlessly in his sweater for three weeks. When I found his note, it was like he was back for a minute." She burst into tears, then collapsed into my arms. I hugged her. As tight I could. "I'm sorry, Daniel."

"Don't be sorry. It sucks. I can't imagine how badly it sucks. But, you have two beautiful children sleeping right down there at the end of the hall." It was tricky terrain to navigate, and I wanted to cry myself, but I tried my best to comfort her. I rubbed her back, then continued. "They are pieces of him. His legacy lives on."

"Thank you," she whispered, with her head still resting on my chest. "Your girlfriend is so pretty."

"Oh. She's not my girlfriend. Just a friend. Actually, more like a neighbor, but, not really. A neighbor's granddaughter to be exact."

"Sounds like you might want her to be your girlfriend," she teased, then released herself from the hug. She backed up and grinned. "So, did you guys lose Marvin?"

"He sort of appears on his own schedule."

"Ah, I see. Well, let's go eat.

The house was still and bathed in a soothing darkness. There was no light at all except for the chandelier over the kitchen table where we sat, the Balsam and Cedar candle flickering on the mantle, and a flat screen in the living room playing *A Christmas Carol* on mute.

Opened Tupperware containers spread across the granite countertops as we enjoyed an array of leftovers. They didn't make much sense when served together, but were all equally delicious. The three of them were also putting a major hurting on my brother's wine fridge. I opted for a ginger ale and wallowed in the company getting looser at the table.

"This is all quite good," Pedro said, scarfing down forkfuls of Butternut Squash Pasta. "Did you make it all yourself?"

"My sisters and I," Kate responded. "Cooking is kind of our thing. It's like an outlet. So, as you can imagine, we cooked a lot these past couple of weeks."

"And your home is beautiful," Ali added. She was right. I felt at peace the minute I stepped through the front door. The place was pristine, but didn't feel like a museum. The kids' toys were scattered about, but it remained uncluttered. It smelled fantastic and everything seemed Hallmark movie level perfect. With the exception of the Christmas tree in the living room.

The huge Colorado Blue Spruce had been decorated with string lights to the middle and was surrounded by storage containers full of ornaments. It stuck out like a sore thumb in the rest of the incredibly tidy house. "Would I be able to take some pictures in here for my blog?"

"I mean, sure," Kate was caught a bit off-guard by Ali's question. "What's your blog called?"

"Just my name, Ali Bell."

"Wait a second. You're Ali Bell? I follow you on Instagram. Holy shit!"

"I'm sorry," I interjected. "You know her, Kate?"

"Uh, yea. Me and like a million other followers."

"A little under seven hundred thousand," Ali was starting to blush, "but I'm working on it."

Pedro's attention went elsewhere. His eyes were locked on the living room area. "Ladies, I'm intrigued by this development," I said, as my eyes followed Pedro's to the spot where he was looking. "But it's time for Kate to meet him."

Marvin had finally decided to reappear. He was standing behind the wraparound sofa, examining a photo gallery on the wall. A newborn Gabbie sleeping on her mother's chest. Jack dressed up as a Jedi, wielding a plastic lightsaber. The four of them in front of Cinderella's Castle. Marvin's head was tilted to the side as he ran his long fingertip across the largest frame in the middle. It was a professionally taken beach shot. They were basking in the golden hour. Alan was front and center, while his family doted on him.

Kate stood up from the table trembling so heavily that she could barely walk. Pedro jumped quickly to one side of her, then I did the same on the other. We held her by her arms.

"Marvin," I said, as we neared him. "This is the love of Alan's life. Kate."

His head tilted to the opposite side, then he extended his arm toward her and showed his palm, much like Pedro had done with him. She slowly went to her knees, then placed her palm against his. She started to laugh and cry and experience every human emotion in between. It was a bonding experience each time someone met Marvin. We knew what each other were feeling. A sensory overload; not of this world.

With their hands still touching, they connected foreheads. In an instant, every light in the place turned on, followed by an intangible force of energy circulating around the room. It was a similar feeling to the one I experienced when we sailed over the BMW. It's as if the house itself was alive and breathing. I could sense that there was some interconnection taking place between the two of them.

When they separated, it was dark again, except for Scrooge dancing on his bed, excited about his new outlook on life. A teary-eyed Kate backed up from Marvin and whispered something I couldn't quite make out. Pedro nodded toward me and we helped her back to her feet.

The three of us stayed locked by the arms, watching Marvin amble up to one of the storage containers. It reached him at about the chest, so he had to stand on his toes (he had three on each foot) to lift an ornament up out of it. At that point, Ali had joined us, taking Pedro by his other arm. We stood quietly, as Marvin began to decorate the tree.

"He loves Christmas," I said, gently, so I didn't embarrass him. Kate explained that Alan desperately wanted the tree up. They managed to retrieve it from the basement back in November but, by the time they started to decorate it, my brother was too weak to see it through. Pedro unhooked himself from the group and began to help. Then Ali. Then me.

Kate was the last to join. She wrapped herself in an afghan and went directly to a particular ornament. It was Gabbie's school picture floating in a mess of Elmer's Glue, ice pop sticks, and pom pom balls. "Is this not the ugliest thing you have ever seen?" she asked, then we all shared a laugh. The first one since our arrival.

The last touch was placing the star on top. Kate said something about grabbing the step stool from the closet but before she had a chance to leave the room, it was floating toward the top of the tree. We stood astonished, goggling at Marvin. What we already knew had been officially confirmed. He had saved us back in the woods. In the end, the tree looked truly beautiful. A sight definitely worthy of Ali's blog.

It started as a faint noise in the sky. A noise not much different than a crop duster passing in the distance. I wouldn't have given it another thought if Marvin hadn't followed it to the French doors leading out to the deck. At least six beams of light were scanning the trees beyond the backyard. They were like the searchlights of a helicopter, only they were a pale, cyan color and much wider. We scrambled to put our shoes on, as Kate grabbed a baby monitor.

Marvin scurried across the deck, then over the paved pool and fire pit area, past the garage, then through the back fence. A narrow aperture cut through the brush and I quickly discovered why. There was a small tractor, chainsaw, and other tools by the garage door. Alan had made the pathway fairly recently.

As we moved toward the bizarre light show, we discovered that it was coming from something huge above us. A shadow so dark that it blacked out the night sky. Strangely, the sound we first heard in the living room wasn't getting louder as we drew closer to its origin. Only now it was accompanied by a deep whoosh every time one beam crossed paths with another. I was amazed by how fast Marvin's short legs carried him to the spot that my brother mentioned in his letter. At times, it was hard for us to keep up.

The open land was about thirty yards wide and had a pop-up canopy to one side. It was covering a wooden table and a couple of folding chairs, a stack of industrial storage containers and a few heavy-duty crates with the words **Property of Arko** stenciled on the sides.

The craft lowered to just above the top of the trees as the beams joined at the center of the clearing. From what I could see through the light, the underside resembled tempered glass with optical fiber-like elements running across it.

Marvin turned to face us for the first time since we set out from the house. Starting with Kate, he connected palms with each of them one by one, letting the moment linger for a bit as he tilted his head to the side. He was studying the melancholy human beings standing before him.

He was always studying.

When he reached me, I couldn't stop myself from dropping to one knee and embracing him. I did it gently, recognizing how fragile he seemed to be. He reciprocated, as I felt his arms slide over mine and wrap around the back of my neck.

I was no longer in the woods.

I was on the beach with Alan. Except, I wasn't. I was everywhere. The ocean. The sand. The Ferris wheel towering high above Wonderland Pier. I could taste the salty air. The pizza. The caramel corn. It felt like twilight. Perhaps late August. The sky was every shade of orange and pink and blue.

"I'm glad we got to do this," Alan said. His voice echoed, vibrating through space and time. We were sitting on a blanket, our sneakers and socks were in a pile next to us. It was high tide. Soon, the waves would be crashing underneath the boardwalk, like when we were kids, before they brought in their machines and ruined the beaches.

"Alan," I responded. "Is this real?"

"As real as stardust, little bro." I glanced down the beach. There was no one else around. No one was strolling the boards. No one was dining at the eateries or enjoying the rides. "We don't have much time," he nodded toward the water. I could've sat there forever, with my toes nestled in the warm sand, listening to the sound of the ocean. He wrapped his arm around my shoulders, then I rested my head against his.

When he backed up, it was Marvin. We were back in the woods.

He walked to where the beams were intersecting. When he turned to face us again, the cyan light was showering him. It was like he was glowing. Tiny, luminescent particles danced on his skin as he began rising toward the craft. The sliver where his mouth should've been was as close to a smile as it ever got.

Then he was gone. Devoured by the light beams, right before they too disappeared. The fiber optics on the bottom of the craft began to glow brighter. Every color known to man (and some we didn't know) swirled above us. The whooshing sound became a song, some kind of otherworldly orchestration ringing through the sky as the craft began its ascent.

I didn't realize how much I was crying until I wiped a handful of cold tears from both my eyes.

"I have to go back," Kate said, showing us the *no signal* message on the screen of the monitor.

"I'll go with you," Ali added. "It's getting really dark out here, really fast."

As we watched them separate from us, Pedro rested his hand on my back. "You did it, my friend," he whispered. The craft was traveling higher with every passing second. "Let's go back to the house."

"I'll meet you there," I told him. "I just need a few more minutes."

"You sure? I could stay."

"It's okay."

"Cool. I'm freezing my ass off out here."

The lights elevated toward the heavens until they were nothing more than a pinhole in the vast darkness. I filmed the reminder of its travels on my cell phone. When it was no longer visible, I took a seat on the coarse sand that made up the floor of the clearing.

Who else on Earth besides me, Pedro, Kate, Ali, and my brother's Mercury Seven had met Marvin's kind? What if it was only us? It was a preposterous notion. A notion that hit me for the first time, just then, as I sat alone in the pitch-black woods.

Did I waste too much time? Being afraid of him. Being afraid that I wasn't enough. And would I ever see him again? My heart told me probably not. After a while, the cold started to penetrate my brother's clothes. I rose to my feet and headed back.

When I returned to the house, Pedro was reclining on the sofa with Ali's head on his lap. They were both sound asleep under the light of the evergreen. I felt a rush in my chest when I wondered if the two of them were closer than

Pedro had led on. Kate nudged me back to reality when she noticed me staring at them.

"Are you jealous?"

"No," I laughed. "But do you think they're a couple?"

"No," she laughed back.

"How do you know?"

"Girls just know."

I helped her retrieve presents from the basement and pile them up beneath the tree. Gifts of all shapes and sizes, some with pink and purple clad princesses dancing around the wrapping paper, others with dinosaurs and fire trucks. I was once again in awe of my sister-in-law's strength. She was determined to give her children as good a Christmas morning as possible considering their situation.

"Looks great," I whispered as we finished up.

"Thank you, Daniel." She looked at the screen of her cell. It was just after one in the morning. "And Merry Christmas."

I slept for a couple of hours, on the floor by the tree. When I awoke, the house smelled like coffee. Kate, Pedro, and Ali were sitting at the breakfast nook. Pedro and Ali were back in their clothes from the day before. The yellow stains had faded considerably.

"I did the best I could," Kate said, when she saw me notice. I wondered if she had slept at all. "Your outfit is on the bed in the spare room. I didn't think you guys were gonna camp out down here."

"Thank you. I think I'll wear this home though. If that's okay."

"Of course."

Over the finest toasted coconut coffee I ever tasted, we decided that everything should remain among us. The Mercury Seven. The car crash. Marvin. We swore to take it all to our graves, which made me feel like a kid again. All we needed to do was prick each other's fingers and rub the blood together.

Kate explained that her sisters would be returning that afternoon for dinner and insisted that she would be okay. She urged us to get back to our original Christmas Day plans. The problem for me was, I didn't have any to speak of. I was quietly hoping that we would end up celebrating the day there, assembling Barbie DreamHouses and eating delicious food. I could've finally met my nephew.

I examined Pedro and Ali from across the table, as they chatted about what the day would bring once we returned to Cedarwood. It seemed like their plans didn't include each other, which was a good sign, but it still depressed me that they had something to go home to. Kate must've sensed my sadness, because right on time she leaned into me and whispered, "Your niece is awake." I turned to see Gabbie on the landing in her flannel pajamas.

"Uncle Dan!" She sprinted toward me. I met her half way, scooped her up in my arms, then spun a few times until we collapsed onto the sofa. "I knew you'd come," she said, squeezing me as tightly as her little arms could manage.

"I have to show you something," I whispered, pulling out my phone. "It's the most amazing thing."

The lights of Marvin's ship sailed across the screen of my cell phone. "Is it Santa?" she asked, wide-eyed and giddy.

"You betcha."

"Mommy, Uncle Dan has Santa in his phone! Can you send it to Mommy? I'm going to show everyone. All day!"

"Heck yea little lady."

We walked out of the house just before sunrise. Kate and Ali did some last-minute sharing of phone numbers and photos. Pedro spoke on his cell, sternly and in Spanish. And I chatted with my niece - who had insisted that I carry her out - about the technicalities of making it around the world in just one night.

Some final hugs and kisses were exchanged at the Jeep. The four of us were basically strangers just a week before. Now, we were bound together by something incredible.

It was there. In the air all around us.

Impalpable, but definitely there.

"Hey," Kate said, as I handed Gabbie off to her. "I'm sorry you didn't get to meet Jack. You should text me when things settle down and we'll make plans."

"I would love that," I responded, with a lump in my throat.

"Look for the post in a couple of days, then let me know what you think," Ali added from the backseat. I couldn't help but feel like they were going to be pen pals of the highest order.

Gabbie leaned through the driver side window, waving her finger at me. "Now don't you be a stranger," she said in her most mature voice. It made all of us laugh.

Ali stretched out in the back seat and slept for most of the ride home, while Pedro and I conversed about everything from what Marvin's home planet was like to the possibility of returning to the crash site and giving Richard Arko and Dale Savage a proper burial. The radio played a countdown of the top one hundred holiday songs off all time. After a debate on the placement of the original "Last Christmas" by Wham! (his choice) over Jimmy Eat World's version (mine), I snuck in a question about something else entirely.

"Pedro," I whispered, glancing over my shoulder at Ali, who was still in the midst of a long winter's nap. "Are you guys an item?"

296

"Daniel, my friend," he chuckled. "Ali is smart, artistic, and beautiful. She deserves a good man. No doubt." He paused and I found myself anticipating his next words like a clueless schmuck. "But, I'm gay."

Just like that, I was Han Solo discovering that Leia and Luke were siblings. Pedro was officially out of the game. Good thing too, because the guy eclipsed me in any factor that made up a worthy suitor.

"Oh," I said. "I didn't know."

"It's all good. Listen, man, shoot your shot. Life is short."

He smiled at me, then we connected with a fist bump.

When we returned to the house, Pedro said his goodbyes quickly, explaining that his mother was going to kill him if he held up the preparation of Christmas dinner any longer. He hurried around back to his place, leaving me and Ali alone in the driveway. The sky was gray and the air brought the promise of snow.

"Well, it's been...I don't know," she said with a burst of laughter. "What would you call it?"

"I don't know. Interesting?" I answered, laughing as well.

"Definitely interesting." We stood silently for a moment. She waited for me to speak but I froze up. I was an awkward, gangling teenager again, wholly confused on what to say next. "Pop's car isn't here. He must be at my parent's house already. I should go."

"Okay." I was blowing it.

"I'll see you around, Daniel. Merry Christmas."

I said it back to her, then we hugged. It was quick. All business. I watched as she walked to her car.

"Ali," I said, probably a lot louder than I should have. "I was just wondering if you had any plans for New Year's Eve."

"I have a date," her answer killed me instantly, "with an older guy who loves toy trains." Her smile brought me back to life. I had no idea how to handle the mix of human emotions that I just experienced in a matter of seconds, so I stood there speechless. That same gangling teenager just got pantsed in the locker room. "The last couple of years, Pop and I have sort of made a tradition out of ordering Chinese and watching Hitchcock movies until the ball drops. Would you like to join? You won't have to travel far."

"That sounds perfect."

"Okay," she said smiling, just enough to show her dimples. "I guess I'll see you then."

"If not around here before then."

"Right," she giggled, then entered her car. I watched her pull out, waving my hand until she was no longer in sight.

Marvin's tree was still lit when I entered my apartment. The thought of Christmas coming to an end saddened me. Perhaps, I'd keep it up all year long. I hadn't been gone twenty-four hours but the place felt like uncharted territory. I saw bare walls in need of art. A bedroom in need of a bed. A kitchen desperately in need of a stocked refrigerator.

I removed Alan's red telescope from its box and set it up in the window by the tree. I looked through the eyepiece and saw absolutely nothing. A thought occurred to me that maybe one day I would become so proficient at using the thing that I would spot Marvin's ship with it.

A silly thought, I know, but it made me happy.

I put the dust caps back on both ends of the telescope then opened the next box. The comic books were lined up perfectly, in plastic sleeves with cardboard backings. Just like Alan always kept them. Where the books ended, there was a small box adorned in wild animal wrapping paper.

A sticky note was attached that simply read *Don't lose it this time* in my brother's handwriting.

I unwrapped it, then opened the box to find a North Carolina Tar Heels baseball cap. In place of their usual logo, read the word Tar Heels in graffiti.

It was the coolest shit I had ever seen.

LITTLE LIGHTS

Spencer

I should've listened to my son. I mean, really listened to him.

I heard him. His tiny voice whispered something as he leaned over the crib rail, with his finger pointed at the window. I didn't listen to him, though. I merely glanced toward the night sky before closing the shade and tucking him in.

Lila left the next morning for her fourth business trip since we became an item. They weren't a staple of our marriage yet, but it seemed the more successful she was getting, the more she was having to travel. It was just before dawn when I carried her suitcase out to our Jetta. As the car warmed, she finished a cup of coffee at the kitchen table.

"I can't believe I'm leaving him," she whispered. This was her first trip since George was born. "I'm so nervous."

The house was quiet, lit only by the recessed lights above. Her hair was tied up in a messy bun. She wore black leggings and swam in one of my extra large hoodies. Even at her most melancholy, my wife looked beautiful.

"He's in good hands, Mama," I said. "It's only for a few days."

She labored for thirty two hours the day George was born. A malpresentation forced the doctor to call an audible and opt for a cesarean section. I sat behind a curtain during the procedure, while something that sounded like a chainsaw rang out from the other side. I was in awe of her. She took every bit of it like a champ. Two sword like needles in the spine. Sawing and stapling. Being carted around hospital corridors, numb and exhausted. She wanted a vaginal birth, so when the lactation consultant entered our room post-operation, I knew the pressure was on. Lila wasn't going to let herself deviate from the plan again.

"See that, Mom. You got it. Nothing to worry about," the soft spoken woman said, after George latched on.

As I sidestepped the healthcare workers (pretty much getting in their way like I had all day) my wife smiled at me from across the room, with tears in her eyes and our newborn son at her breast.

"A few days away from my baby," she said, then took the last swig from her mug. George's chest was rising and falling underneath his cotton dinosaur pajamas. An array of multicolor stars and planets were swirling across the walls and ceiling. I kept checking the time on my phone, worried she would linger too long and miss her flight. "Maybe I should stay home."

She had worked her way up to assistant director of one of the biggest interior design companies on the East Coast. This particular project in Florida consisted of five multimillion-dollar resorts across the state. It was a huge deal. Staying home wasn't really an option.

"I'll turn the car off," I said, as I pulled her close by the waist, then kissed her forehead. "We'll get back in bed." She turned to me and our lips met.

There were a couple of grade levels between us in high school - might as well have been a couple of planets. She graduated third in her class and was a star field hockey player. I was a C student and set a new school record for consecutive beer funnels. I did manage to nab "Most Artistic" in the yearbook though. I was never much of an athlete. I tried to surf a few times before swearing it off forever. And, when my parents divorced, I took refuge in the only thing that I was ever good at.

My early work, the stuff I painted right out of high school, afforded me a life that I never thought was possible. It allowed me to live out my college years with my buddies in Philadelphia, without actually attending college. I spent most of my twenties mansplaining Van Gogh to art students before sketching them naked and taking advantage of the situation like Leonardo DiCaprio in *Titanic*. Except I was far from Leo. I was an insufferable prick. The kind of character I hated in the movies.

Until Lila made me better.

She pulled out of the driveway just as the sun was rising over our street. Our neighbor, Mr. Fratelli, was already in his yard staring at his lawn. It was only April, but there was a decent chance the old man would be out there willing his grass to grow for the remainder of spring and summer.

"Morning, kiddo," he said, from the other side of the fence that separated our driveways. "Lila leaving today?"

"Yessir," I answered.

"You boys going to be okay over there?"

"It's only a few days. We can't get into too much trouble."

"Well, you know where to find me if you need anything."

Mr. and Mrs. Fratelli were the neighborhood watch, trash picker uppers, and chroniclers all at once. The night Lila and I moved in, they brought us over an Italian lemon cake and filled us in on the unabridged history of our street. The house with the daughter and her substance abuse issues. The house with the cheating husband. The house with water in the basement.

George wasn't supposed to wake up for about an hour, so my plan was to fall back to sleep. I kicked my slippers off, then slid under the warm sheets, burying my face into my wife's spot. It smelled like Shea butter and oatmeal. It's not often I got our California king to myself.

As I spread out, I glanced over to the baby monitor and saw George standing in the black and white image, peering through the window above his crib. His body was stiff. There was none of the bouncing or head-first dives into the mattress that Lila and I had grown accustomed to. After a moment of hesitation, I turned the volume up. His voice was barely loud enough to hear over the white noise machine.

"Lights."

I brought the monitor closer to my ear.

"Little lights."

Lauren

For the first time in years, I felt nervous in a good way.

Excited?

Nah, couldn't be.

My bag was packed, waiting by the front door. The Monster's nightly cocktail was on the kitchen table. Cheap vodka and cranberry juice. When he threw up it looked like he was heaving blood into the toilet. He used to walk over from the garage and expect it at the end of his work day. If it wasn't mixed up and prepared, it gave him a reason to start in on us. I had no idea what he had been doing out there and I couldn't care less. What I knew was that he always walked in just after sundown.

Right on time, the back door creaked.

He was stumbling. I could smell his breath from a mile away.

"Well God damn. Look at this. Just like old times." I loathed the sound of his voice. "It's been too long since I've been taken care of. Thank you, baby doll."

I watched from the entryway as he slurped the whole thing down. His upper lip was shiny from the juice as he shook the glass. I wanted to puke. "So, what's the special occasion?" he asked, as he plopped down on the chair.

"It's my mother's birthday. Did you forget?"

"Well, shit. I guess I must have." There was a stretch of silence as he raised the glass to his mouth and let more crushed ice tumble into it, crunching the pieces between his teeth. One of the million tiny things that if someone else had done, it probably wouldn't have bothered me so much. "A lot going on."

About a year prior, my best friend Morgan and I swiped two tabs of Molly from her older brother. We planned to take them but never had the balls, so into his drink they went. It was taking longer than I anticipated for it to kick in.

"Your mom was a good gal." In the candlelight, he was more menacing than ever. His words meant nothing. "It's a Goddamn shame what's happened to her. This is some next level shit."

Maneuvering around his manipulation was a craft that I learned from my mother. It's a craft that kept the ass kickings to a minimum. I kept my distance and waited.

"Well, you gonna say something? You're supposed to be smart. Ain't ya? Figure this out. What the hell happened out there?"

"How am I supposed to know? It's not like we have the internet, or TV, or anything," I said, as my adrenaline surged.

"I don't think anybody has that shit right now. There's been a major event. We've been attacked if you ain't noticed!" His shouting sounded different. "Wake up!"

The pitch of his voice was rising, as his words became more and more slurred. I made him two more drinks, never allowing too much distance between myself and the knife set on the counter.

"How about we go on into the living room and you give me a back rub? Bring some of these candles with us. It'll be nice. Something nice for once."

He stumbled to one knee as he rose from the chair, grabbed the table cloth, then brought it all to the floor with him. Drinking glasses and bowls shattered on the linoleum. The salt and pepper shakers rolled down the hallway. "Man, I ain't been this buzzed in a long while."

My heart felt like it could jump from my chest. My temples were pulsating. For five endless years I dreamt about this moment.

"Help me up," he demanded. "Lauren, I said help me up."

He looked like a slovenly, helpless pig as he sat on his ass with his tattooed arms resting on his knees. Maybe it's the way the candles were lighting his eyes but they seemed absent of any white. Like two black holes in his skull. "Help me the fuck up you little bitch!"

It dawned on me that he didn't have the strength to rise or he would have and lunged for me. He'd grab my hair and smack me a couple of times across the face. Then, if I was lucky, he'd throw me to the floor. If not, if he was in a particularly foul mood, he'd yank me harder by my hair and let my head land into a cabinet or door jamb. Whatever was closest.

Not this time.

This time, he couldn't seem to find the ambition.

"What's wrong?" I asked. "Don't you feel good?"

"I don't know. I think I'm having a heart attack or sumthin'. Just help me up. Now!"

"Okay. Stand by." I grabbed a flashlight, then retrieved the baseball bat from the side of his bed. He "could've played for the Braves if it wasn't for his bum knees."

GTFO.

"What the hell are you gonna do with that? You fixing to hit me with it? Go right ahead. Swing for the fences."

I never hit someone in my life.

Well, that's not entirely true. I socked Randall Smith in the mouth junior year for informing me that I was "thicker than a Snicker." This would be the first time I used a bat, though.

"That first summer you and your mother moved in here, you was trying your damnedest to hit Carpenter Bees in the backyard with a Wiffle ball bat. You missed most of them. Swung that bat like your pussy ass old man."

I was too angry the first time I swung; the wood barely grazed the top of his head. It's the second one that caught him good.

It was gorgeous.

And funny.

The sound it made when it connected with his skull was like something out of a cartoon. There was a shit ton of blood. More than I expected. He was mumbling. I think there was a string of cuss words mangled up in there somewhere. I stood over him with the bat slung over my shoulder and a foot planted on each side of his waist. I felt like Harley Quinn with her hammer. He might've been dying, I couldn't tell.

The Monster's life was in my hands. I had ultimate power over him. But, still, there was a huge part of me that felt downright awful. As he croaked underneath me, tears started to fall. I dropped the bat. On the way out of the kitchen I grabbed the flashlight then, on the way out of the front porch I wrapped a scarf around my neck and scooped the heavy bag up off the floor. My mom was a backpacker for many years; her tattered old sack was able to fit all the worldly belongings I ever cared about.

The morning after everything went down, he buried her by the back fence. I watched from my bedroom window as he pressed a four way lug wrench into the ground. It didn't seem right, so I replaced the wrench with an actual cross that I carved out of plywood, roped together, then painted her name on, along with pink and purple flowers. My creation was broken into pieces and the lug wrench was back within hours.

"This isn't goodbye, Mommy," I whispered to the wrench as its chrome shined in the glow of my flashlight. "You'll be with me wherever I go."

A power walk took me to the end of the driveway, then to the stop sign at the end of the street. By the time I made it to the main drag, I was gasping for air. Except for the bulb in my flashlight and the moon, there was nothing to guide me but shadows. The stores and auto body shops, the train station and water tower, all colorless giants standing as still as they could.

Darkness and a suffocating silence is all that welcomed me into the changed world. I imagined it differently. I thought I might take a match to his house. To his dreadful town. I would dance around the blaze with the Gypsies and the vagabonds.

I guess it just wasn't meant to be.

Instead, I was off into the night with my life in my mom's old backpack. I didn't know what to expect in the wild. The beasts. The scary things not yet known.

All I knew was that I was finally free from the worst kind.

Walter

My beloved Helen.

It feels like only yesterday I sat on the front porch, swaying our Joseph on that old rocker. We would sip homemade iced tea as the sun set over our street. The train would howl in the distance. I whispered to him stories of the war. Stories of you and me. Then we'd take him in the house and rub some alcohol on his feet before bed. He had those terrible growing pains. I'd give anything to go back to that time. The happiest days of my life.

I had seen so much in the years you've been gone. I thought I had seen it all. Everyone had a telephone in their hands that told them everything they needed to know. I watched our nieces and nephews on a little screen just this last Christmas. I made faces and they laughed. You couldn't even imagine.

I was doing well at the home. It was boring at times, but we made do. They brought in a lot of guests. Singers and magicians. Things like that. Every Saturday we'd take a bus to a new restaurant. There was this place where the Oriental gentleman tossed a piece of chicken right into my mouth. You believe it?

Well, I guess that's all in the past now. They have us staying in a middle school gymnasium for the time being. The cots aren't ideal and the roof suffered some damage in the attack, but the staff that survived are good people. They've made a promise to stay with us until help arrives. Perhaps it's an oath they've pledged, or perhaps it's their way of making sense of our new reality. Whatever the case may be, I am eternally grateful for their loyalty.

I never thought I'd see the things I saw in war ever again in my life. But, at least, we were soldiers. We knew what we were in for. This time it was sudden. The sky fell and we were helpless. All of us. Man, woman, and child.

How much of the world has been affected?

Is there anyone left out there that can help us?

I try not to ask myself these questions, but there are nights I don't sleep and it's all I can do.

Well, I guess it won't be long now until I see you again, my love. And, I will see you again. My faith tells me so.

Spencer

Lila FaceTimed us from her sister's house in Orlando. We didn't get much of a conversation in before George pilfered my phone then darted around the house while screaming several variations of "Mommy" into it. Two years, plus a few months. That's all it took for him to completely understand that the face on that screen belonged to his person.

After the call, I decided to pull the boy to Mickey D's in his wagon. With Lila being gone, there was a fair chance that our balanced diet was put on standby for a few days.

It was unseasonably warm. A brother and sister were playing in a front yard while their father got an early start on trimming the hedges. A young couple strolled the sidewalk opposite of us, hand in hand, with a Golden Retriever leading the way on its leash. This was my town. The place where I was born and raised. You rarely know you love a place like Cedarwood, New Jersey, until you leave it for a while.

It was year five of living in Philadelphia, when I returned home for my grandfather's funeral service. The standard Catholic affair with a luncheon that followed. Mrs. Rossi, my high school art teacher, practically pleaded with me as I sucked down my third Captain and Coke.

"So how about it? A favor for your favorite teacher. As far as I can see, you can't say no."

Her newly opened cafe on Main Street wasn't doing as well as she and her husband expected and they needed something to draw in some business - spice things up. Apparently, I was that something.

It was a simple exhibit. About ten of my pieces surrounded me as I sipped delicious coffee and pretended to be ambivalent toward the fact that the people from my hometown adored my work.

Inside, feelings were stirring. Long lost feelings of gratitude and optimism. A few hours in, as the crowd finally started to thin out, and the stragglers began to mingle with each other and forget about me, I removed a sketchbook from my JanSport.

Things took shape on the page. A couple of figures. Their bikes. A curb. A house. The town's water tower. Light at first, but darker with each stroke. In those days, when inspiration hit, I had to ride it out or it might abandon me forever.

"Looks good. Do you always sketch something before painting it on canvas?"

When I looked up, I saw Lila.

She had come to check out the exhibit with her best friend and her best friend's beau. Months later, she admitted that it was with a purpose, but that night she played it cool. "Impressive turnout tonight. You're a pretty popular guy."

"Were you here long?"

"My apartment is across the street. I was spying on you." She had a constellation of dark curls and eyes with a splash of forest green hidden in them. Her smile was big and warm. I immediately sensed that she used it often.

Our conversation lasted about fifteen minutes. I was surprised, and a little bit jealous, to find out that she wasn't a scientist or some civil rights lawyer, but a fellow artist. A few weeks into our relationship, I discovered that she drew better than me. She could probably paint better too, but didn't want to hurt my self-confidence. I also discovered that a life without her was no longer a life that I was interested in.

We celebrated our one year anniversary on the floor of our new apartment, feasting on a ridiculous amount of sushi. Two years later we moved into our house. A one story bungalow built at the height of the Cold War. Its most unique feature being a bomb shelter a few feet away from the back door.

George ignored the apple slices and hamburger from his Happy Meal but was going to town on his French fries, and mine. I was toggling between apps on my phone (Tetris and Twitter) when something on my feed caught my eye. It was BREAKING NEWS from one of the various outlets I followed. News always seemed to be breaking. Bold, red fonts declaring the biggest story we've ever heard. Until the next biggest story we've ever heard.

This was different.

Lights were seen in the skies over most of the world. Strange lights. Moving. Disappearing. Following no pattern. Appearing on no radars. As I dug further, it became clear that the only thing people were discussing on social media were the lights. I hadn't checked my phone or looked at a television since early in the afternoon, the day before. After we put George to bed, Lila and I spent the rest of the night talking and packing and making love like two people who would never see each other again. As someone who prided himself on being informed, it was rare that I wasn't up on the events of the day.

I suddenly felt incredibly vulnerable. I glanced around the McDonald's to see if things felt off. I wondered if the conversations taking place between the other patrons and the workers were about the lights. George said "Dada," aware of the sudden change in my mood.

That's when it hit me.

George had seen them. He tried to point the lights out the night before and was still talking about them this morning.

"Hey, bud. Did you see some lights last night?" He ignored my question and continued shoving fries into his mouth. "Dada is sorry for not listening."

"Dada sorry," he repeated.

On the way home, I kept looking toward the afternoon sky as I called Lila. There was no cloud cover; it was endlessly blue. At first glance, it seemed as if nothing was out of the ordinary at all. I was finally able to reach her on the fourth dial.

"Hey, I'm at a meeting. Is everything all right? Is George okay?" She sounded a bit out of breath.

"Yea, we're okay. I'm just wondering if you heard about these lights."

"Lights?"

"In the sky last night."

"Oh. I guess. I think it's on the TV right now in the bar."

"You're at a bar?"

"Well. No. Not really a bar. It's like a country club. I don't know. Is that why you're calling me?"

She sounded slightly annoyed. Maybe for good reason. The lights could've been anything. A rare weather occurrence. A foreign government testing some newfangled aircraft.

"I'm sorry. Maybe I overacted."

"It's okay. I have to go. Talk to you later."

A pickup truck's horn startled me, as I was crossing the corner of our street in an anxious haze. I ignored my son's acknowledgment of the lights, then I almost killed us.

"Christ, Spencer. Get off that Goddamn phone and pay attention!"

It was my neighbor from a few houses down. A middle-aged guy. Pretty rough around the edges. Jack? Frank? I couldn't remember. He made up his mind early on that I was some artsy liberal and his mission was to subtly insult me every time our paths crossed. I apologized, then pulled George's wagon up onto the sidewalk, causing him to bounce around a bit and let out a belly laugh.

My grown ass neighbor peeled out like a senior leaving the parking lot on his last day of high school.

Lauren

In the years after my father died, I made a habit out of running away from home. I would sneak into bars with a fake ID or hitch rides with strangers, then talk them into giving me money. On occasion, I would stay a few nights in a seedy motel. The people I met on these excursions were mostly men. Fools, easy to take advantage of with a sultry look and feigned interest in whatever the hell they had to say. I wasn't scared, because I figured none of them would be half as bad as the one my mother met and decided to move in with.

Three days after the attack, a couple of soldiers came to the house. They were in dusty gear from head to toe with rifles slung over their shoulders. Their faces were covered in a thick layer of grime. I listened from my bedroom window as they explained to The Monster that the best thing to do was hunker down at home.

"I live off the land here," he explained, when they asked if we needed any food or supplies. "I'm a simple man. Grow my own stuff in the back. I've been ready for this for a long time."

This was all bullshit. The garden in the back was overrun by weeds. I had never seen it produce a single vegetable. He stockpiled goods in the basement, mostly beans and cereal, in case "the Commies ever decided to come for us."

It wasn't the Commies that came, but the endless supply of Ramen Noodles and Fruity Pebbles did come in handy. At least he was good for something.

The soldiers went on to explain that there could be another attack at any moment so we needed to stay vigilant. Get used to the idea of staying underground for long periods of time if necessary. It was then that I decided I would carry out my plan of escape. I figured if the military was out there, things couldn't be all that terrible.

I was starving. Food was a lot harder to come by than I anticipated, and the fifty bucks that I swiped from The Monster's nightstand before I fled wasn't going to be much help. Most stores and restaurants had been stripped bare already, if not completely destroyed. Cars filled the roads. Some piled up on top of each other. I promised myself I would stop looking in them after I saw a family decaying in a burnt minivan. The children were in their car seats, still hugging stuffed animals. The weirdest part was the disturbing lack of people around. I would go hours without seeing anyone except the dead.

On one side of the highway there was a heavily damaged Target and Home Depot. On the opposite, a strip of blown out fast food joints and a flattened movie theater. In every direction, plumes of smoke still rose. It was getting late in the day and I was exhausted. I dropped my mother's heavy backpack under the awning of a bus stop then collapsed onto the bench, trying to use my scarf as a pillow.

Maybe I should've stayed where I was. At the very least I had a roof over my head. A bed. Stuff to eat. I closed my eyes and focused on the sounds around me. Birds singing and the whoosh of helicopter propellers. Something that sounded like a series of deep, muffled booms in the distance. Echoes of indistinct voices getting lost in the breeze. And an engine. A running engine. And tires rolling over the pavement.

I sprang up and saw a vehicle approaching slowly. It was a beat up Lincoln Town Car, with a black man behind the steering wheel. He was stocky, with small curls of gray hair above his ears and a pair of huge glasses on his face. I tied the scarf around my waist, then scooped up the backpack. I was ready to dip if I had to.

He waved.

It was a friendly wave, like he had known me forever. I slowly made my way closer to the driver side window.

"Hey," he said. "I saw you from over there at the Home Depot lot. I ain't seen nobody else out here in a few days."

"Out where?" I asked.

"Out here. In the world."

His backseat was cluttered. Two suitcases. A plastic hamper full of non-perishable food items. A cooler and a saxophone. He also had a deer spotter, gas can, and camping axe on the passenger seat.

"What's that for?" I nodded toward the axe.

"Protection."

He explained that his daughter lived about forty miles up the road and that she worked as a nurse and how he hadn't spoken to her since before the attack. His goal was to make it to her before nightfall.

"If you'd like to join me, I wouldn't mind the company. My baby works at a huge hospital. They must have something set up over there."

A power nap seemed more likely in a moving car than spread out on an unforgiving bench.

"I don't know if I'd be much company. I haven't slept in days."

"You need to get in here and sleep then. Just to know another heart is beating is good enough for me." He relocated the stuff from the front seat to the back. Except the axe. He put that on the dashboard. "Throw your bag in the back and help yourself to whatever you'd like." I grabbed an unopened bag of Teriyaki Beef Jerky from the hamper and a Gatorade from the cooler.

"Are you sure?"

"Be my guest. It's warm. The last of the ice melted a while back. I hope you like The Drifters."

It had been so long since I heard music, that I welcomed the vibes. The way the men harmonized about being down by the sea with the sounds of a carousel hit differently.

"You okay?" he asked, when I turned my face away. "It's okay to cry. I been doing it a little bit myself lately."

So I did.

I cried.

The scent of old cigars filled my nose, while this beautiful music I had never heard before played from the car's busted speakers. I shuddered and sobbed until my face was a snotty mess. The man retrieved a roll of paper towels from his glove box, then put them on my lap. "Here, baby girl."

"Thank you," I said, with a deep sigh.

"What's your name?"

"Lauren."

"Lauren. I like that name. I'm Dwight. It's nice to meet you."

Walter

My morning routine at the school consists of waking up, then doing some light stretching. After that, I wash my medications down with a couple of swigs from a warm water bottle and get changed out of my pajamas in the boys' locker room. Breakfasts aren't much outside of dry cereal or protein bars, which I eat at a table we brought in from the cafeteria.

Most of the folks at the home didn't survive the night the sky fell. Even more perished in the terrible days thereafter, when supplies dwindled and the staff didn't have the resources left to tend to the wounded. I'm blessed to have made it this far. And to be in this good of shape. It gives me an opportunity to assist with the residents when I'm able. This helps the days go by a little bit faster.

It was late this afternoon. Most of the residents were asleep, so I used the quiet moment to step out of the gymnasium doors and look out over the parking lot. Things seemed pretty normal. None of the houses that border the school were destroyed. The only damage I could see from where I stood was a line of trees ripped from the ground and a decapitated water tower.

I imagined a time before, when herds of excited teenagers boarded buses. I could almost see them running across the lot, while others hopped on their bicycles, or played hopscotch, or got a jumpstart on their homework. I thought of you. And Joseph. Like most times.

Alberto, the Hispanic nurse snapped me out of it. "Mr. Walter," he said. "Come back inside. It could be dangerous out here." He has a tattoo on his neck and uses swear words a lot, but he's a good kid, far as I can tell.

"Alberto, what could be dangerous about this beautiful afternoon?"

"A lot of things, honestly, Mr. Walter. Your girl, Grace, is getting bored. Wanna push her around the hallways a little bit? I think she's got the hots for you."

"I told you already. I'm a married man."

Grace is five years younger than me but has terrible arthritis. We were lucky enough to salvage a wheelchair from the home, so once in a while I push her around the halls and we chat. Today she was telling me about how her youngest granddaughter was supposed to graduate from high school this year.

"So smart. An honor student. Not to mention a stunner," she explained. "Long legs. Blonde hair and this sun touched skin. She's a surfer girl. Can you believe that? Like Annette Funicello."

On our return to the gym, we heard a deep, unfamiliar voice. It belonged to a man. His words echoed off the gymnasium's walls.

"Y'all are in good hands with us. We are here for your protection. I promise you that."

"Oh my," Grace whispered. "Is that a military officer? Are we being rescued?"

He was middle-aged, with a beard down to his chest. His Kevlar vest was struggling to contain his girth and his fatigues were disheveled. There were more men behind him, five in total. An untidy tattooed lot, awkwardly holding their rifles.

"No, I don't believe so," I whispered back, as I scanned their matching insignias. *A skull wearing a gas mask, with two lines underneath it.* Our administrator, Whitney, spoke up. Alberto and another nurse named Jerry, a muscle bound kid with a couple of screws loose, stood on each side of her.

"With all due respect, sir, I think we're okay here for the time being." She's a tall, dark, drink of water. If there was ever a lady capable of handling herself around a handful of armed men, it's Whitney. "If you can get word out to any local government that we're here with six residents and three healthcare workers, it would be a tremendous help."

"Miss, there ain't no government out there," another man chuckled. This one was skinnier, with the flag of the Confederacy wrapped around his head and a thigh holster. "We're the only line of defense between y'all and the group of looters coming this way."

"Looters?" Whitney repeated.

The Bearded Man spoke again. "Yes, ma'am. There's a gang about ten miles north of here. If they come through, y'all are gonna be in big trouble."

The nurses glanced at each other, as a few of the residents gasped. I slowly approached Whitney, while the militia stared me down. We huddled in close with Alberto, who quietly explained that he and Jerry came across a young couple holed up in an apartment complex. The couple spoke about a group of depraved human beings, taking advantage of the desperate situation we're in.

"Why haven't you mentioned this before now?" Whitney asked. She grew more frustrated with each minute that passed.

"We didn't want to scare everyone," Alberto responded.

"What are these missions for if not to salvage supplies and compile other pertinent information?"

"I know. I'm sorry, Whitney. I fucked up."

"Excuse me, folks," The Bearded Man interjected. "All these secrets don't help nobody. You have something to discuss, you discuss it with us. Or, we can leave y'all right now. Much luck to ya."

Whitney was thinking on her feet. A specialty of hers, I witnessed firsthand hundreds of times back at the home. "Okay. What is it you need from us?"

"We got a guy with a major head injury here." Another man stepped up and removed his tactical helmet, revealing a crimson gash that ran down from his scalp to underneath his left eye. It was surrounded by a deep purple swelling and streaks of dried blood.

"My god," Whitney said. "How did this happen?"

The man hesitated, then mumbled, "I fell from my motorcycle."

"When?"

"A few days ago."

"Were you wearing a helmet? That one," Whitney pointed to the tactical helmet still in his hand. The man hesitated again. I know liars when I see them.

"I weren't wearing it at the time. Can you help me or not, lady?"

As Whitney and the nurses tended to the man's injury, darkness engulfed the gymnasium. I took it upon myself to light the candles and turn on the battery operated lanterns. Whitney found me when they were finished. She looked exhausted.

"How do you feel about our new guests? I saw your face earlier."

"Well, Miss Whitney, I don't like the cut of their jib," I told her. "They've already put a dent in our food supply. Now they're down there carrying on. But, if there are worse people roaming about, maybe it's not a terrible idea to keep them around for a while."

"My thoughts exactly. Great minds, Walter." She smiled. In the candlelight she looked a lot like Dorothy Dandridge.

All of us have suffered great loss. Some have lost everything. In spite of that, there are still rare occurrences like a smile, which let me know humanity remains.

Spencer

Talking heads were in the CNN studio, debating the origin of the lights.

The President spoke briefly from the south lawn of the White House, as he returned from a golf outing.

"We're doing everything we can to figure out what these lights are," he explained as the press shouted questions. "We have the best satellites in the world. It's tremendous what they are capable of. Absolutely tremendous."

I shuffled between a profusion of apps, searching for answers. Nothing much on my Facebook wall outside of old classmates posting about extraterrestrial invasion, and my parents' friends waxing eloquently on the coming of heavenly angels. Twitter provided nothing more than memes and the occasional half-baked think piece. I was becoming a sponge of electronic information. Until it went dark.

Everything at once.

George was asleep, so I had to move fast. I grabbed our emergency flashlight, then ran next door.

There was a cool mist in the air. A few stars tried to shine through the cloud cover. The family across the street was up to something, but I had no time to figure it out. Mr. Fratelli greeted me at the front door in his flannel pajamas, with his own flashlight in hand.

"Spencer, what the heck is going on around here?"

"I have no idea. I'm so sorry to bother you, but I was hoping for a landline."

"Of course. Right this way. In the kitchen."

I dialed Lila's cell number and got nothing. Three times. No busy signal. No mailbox is full message. Nothing. Mr. Fratelli sensed my anxiety.

"I'm sure she's okay. Must've been an accident somewhere. Why don't you have a seat? I'll put a pot of tea on."

"George is in bed. Thank you. I'm going to head back."

He walked me back out the front door. The couple across the street were on their front porch drinking wine by candlelight. They had five kids, four of whom were stretched out on a blanket on the lawn. The fifth was looking through a telescope. They were decked out in glow-in-the-dark jewelry and holding cardboard signs.

The lights in the sky had returned.

Mysterious, twinkling observers. As far as the eye could see, in every direction. One of the kids shouted. A precocious girl, maybe six or seven years old.

"The aliens are here! We're having a welcoming party!"

"Young people," the guy that almost ran me over earlier in the day said, as we met on the sidewalk. "Such idealists."

"They're having fun," I responded, trying my best to pass him.

"Fun? Nobody's been able to figure these lights out, brother. Not our people. No other country. Goddamn NASA. No idea. Satellites ain't getting a read on shit."

I stopped and looked up.

316

The lights were growing larger. Brighter. The sudden change in their characteristics was disorienting.

"You should probably get back inside with your boy."

For the first time, I was close enough to my neighbor to look into his eyes. They were a pale blue. He looked older than I made him out to be.

About a week after we moved in, he saw me struggling with a flood light over our front window. I tried to replace the bulb, causing the whole contraption to fall out and hang there by wires. "I'll bring over a taller ladder and fix that bad boy for you," he said. I insisted that he didn't but, fifteen minutes later, it was repaired. I thanked him as we shook hands. It was the last pleasantries we'd ever exchange until this moment.

Until the first rumble.

It was something like a whale song off in the distance, but powerful enough to shake the earth under our feet. He ran back in the direction of his house, patting me on the back as he went.

My thoughts were only of Lila and George. I didn't stop to think about rushing inside and scooping him out of his crib, or barreling through the back door as the noise reverberated around us. I didn't stop to think about the light. The blinding light that blanketed our backyard in such a way that it appeared as though it was a sunny afternoon. Only George, now in my arm, as I used my free hand to grab the handle of the heavy hatch. I never stopped to think about the absurdity of owning a home with a bomb shelter. The dumb luck that some builder, long ago, put it in place so a family would be protected from a possible attack by the Soviets.

A spiral staircase took us below the ground to a suffocating cell, where a musty smell of mold hung thick in the air. The walls and arched ceiling were corroded from the effects of time. Nothing inside but our mountain bikes, stored down there as a joke because Lila said we would never use the room.

Lila.

Our last words were not ideal. No I love you. Not even goodbye.

I sat on the hard floor, with my back against the wall and George tight to my chest as he fell back to sleep. The rumbling became more frequent but quieter. Muted by the deepness of the shelter. The thickness of the earth all around us.

Our wedding was on the hottest day of the year. We opted for a "first look" to get the technicalities out of the way and enjoy our cocktail hour together. I waited for her, staring into a hedgerow, as my back dripped sweat underneath my suit. Our photographer got into position as Lila tapped me on the shoulder. I turned around and saw her. This radiant woman I was about to marry.

I saw her that night in the shelter. It's all I could see. I dialed her number over and over again until my cell phone died.

Then it was dark. At some point the rumbling stopped and I began to concentrate on my son's breathing. It's all I had. Tiny breaths, warm on my arm. As long as I had that, the world hadn't gone away.

Lauren

I was dipping and diving. Flying again.

The night was so clear that the stars seemed close enough to yank from the sky. The soft glow of Jack-o'-lanterns sprinkled the street. My old street. The one I didn't know long enough. Costumed children towed heavy bags of candy back to their homes. I soared. My third year in a row as a witch.

When we got back, Mommy surprised me with a graveyard dirt cake. My most favorite thing in the world. The way the cookies and cream stuck to the gummy worms was magical.

Later, Daddy let me watch a little bit of Michael Myers. "It's edited for television," he told Mommy, as he winked at me. I fell asleep between the two of them on the couch. Our blanket was heavy and warm. The same blanket I kept for many years, until the scent of our old house waned from it and it wasn't much more than a dust rag. It was then I repurposed it as a scarf. The scarf I was wearing when I woke up to someone holding a handgun against Dwight's head.

"Do what I say and you won't get hurt."

The boy looked a bit older than me. He had a mound of messy blond hair with faded green tips. The way he leaned his thin frame over to see into the window made him look like some kind of dinosaur peeking in on us. "I need y'all to get out of the car." He pointed the gun at me. "You too!"

"Listen," I responded, trying to remain calm. "Whatever it is you want from us, you don't have to do it like this. Just put it down and we'll talk."

His hand was trembling so much that I thought he might drop the weapon. Dwight must've noticed too because he lunged forward and wrenched the boy's wrists. They wrestled, as the lanky stranger got pulled

318

further into the car. Fists and elbows were flying, hitting the horn. I grabbed the axe from atop the dash, tightened my grip, and sized up the situation. Dwight was able to push him back, creating enough distance between them to connect with a right hook. I was relieved to not have to swing the axe and possibly take a chunk out of Dwight's arm by mistake.

The aggressor dropped the gun and shimmied his way back out. Dwight rolled the window up, drowning out another tussle taking place. It sounded like a father reprimanding his son. The older man turned his attention to us.

"I am so very sorry!" he shouted through the window. He was tall and skinny, with long gray hair and goatee to match. He was holding a camping lantern. "My son is not well. I need that gun back. Please, sir!"

Dwight glanced over at me with something that resembled a smirk, then grabbed the gun and exited the car. The man jumped back and put his hands up even though Dwight never brandished the weapon.

"Don't hurt me. Please," the skinny stranger pleaded.

"What's your story?" asked Dwight.

"We're at the ShopRite. My wife and my son. And fourteen others. It's pretty well stocked. Join us."

"There's a hospital about a mile up ahead. I need to get there."

"It was hit in the attack. You won't find nothing much outside of rubble. I'm sorry."

Dwight appeared to be defeated instantly by the man's words. I was now out of the car, standing by his side, as he gathered his thoughts.

"Take me there. I have to see it for myself."

"I will, when the sun rises. You won't find anything down there in the dark."

He raised the lantern. Over the years, I had become a pretty good judge of character, just by looking at someone's face. He had soft features, with a scar running across his left cheek. The light reflected in his glossy, amber eyes.

"What do you think?" Dwight asked me.

A grocery store with stocked shelves sounded like a dream. I imagined planting my ass in the middle of the snack aisle and losing myself in it for a couple of hours. "I don't think it's a bad idea to wait until morning," I said. "Can we trust them, though? His son just attacked us."

"He's not well," the stranger said again. "He must've seen your headlights and panicked. I should have been paying more attention to my gun. I give you my word it won't happen again."

We decided to follow the man (who introduced himself as Albert) back to the store, under the condition that Dwight holds on to the gun. Inside, candles and lanterns lit the produce section by the entrance. The shelving units had been pushed off to the side and the group formed a semicircle on top of sleeping bags and blankets. They looked haggard but were making the most of their situation. A couple was playing monopoly, two children were lightsabering with pool noodles, another guy was strumming an acoustic guitar.

"Hey guys," Albert said, as their attention turned toward us. "This is Dwight and Lauren. They'll be joining us."

They bombarded Dwight with handshakes and introductions, as I grabbed a lantern and dipped off in the direction of the snack aisle. It's almost as if my eyes were adjusting to the darkness of the new world. I barely lifted the light to make my way around. The logos on the shiny bags of salty goodness greeted me like old friends. More than that, it was a reminder that they hadn't taken everything from us. I plopped down in the middle of the aisle and made a quick dent in a bag of Flamin' Hot Cheetos. Soon after, a voice startled me.

"I'm sorry," he said. I rose to my feet, folded the bag, then squared up like the world's worst amateur boxer. "It's okay. You don't have to be afraid of me."

"Oh, really? The gun in my face earlier was pretty scary."

"I don't mean to do some of the things I do." He seemed like a different person. I would've bet cash money that I was dealing with a set of twins. "What's your name?"

I told him.

"Hi, Lauren. I'm Orson. Most of these folks don't share our enthusiasm for junk food. May I join you?"

Maybe it was the delirium setting in. Not sleeping or eating correctly could do that. Or, maybe it was the fact that I hadn't been in the company of someone around my age in a long time. Either way, I told him it'd be okay. As long as he didn't try to murder me.

That made him laugh.

He explained that he and his folks had taken refuge in their basement for three days, until they walked over to the ShopRite, hungry and desperate. They were the first ones there until a young couple showed up. Another displaced family arrived a few days after that. And so on.

"We've taken them all in. Most of us are from here. This was our grocery store," he continued.

"Dwight and I weren't exactly welcomed with open arms."

"That's on me. Meds ran out a few days ago. My dad hasn't had any luck finding replacements out there."

"Crazy pills? I've been on a vast array of them ever since I turned thirteen. I feel for you, bro."

He laughed again. For a split second, I thought maybe he was cute. This was both alarming and sickening to me, so I did the only thing I could do, and joined him. Our laughter was cut short by another voice in the dark. It was a woman. Her hair was blonde with gray roots and she had faint wrinkles on her face. The kind of wrinkles that made me think maybe they were new to the scene. My mother was starting to develop the same kind right before my eyes.

"Orson, come back and join the group."

"In a little bit."

"No, honey. Now."

"I said in a little bit, Helen!"

She let her gaze linger on us a bit longer, then walked away.

"Is that your mom?" I asked.

"Unfortunately," he answered.

We rejoined the group a bit later, taking a seat between Dwight and a pretty girl with shoulder length, brunette hair. He laughed when he saw me sipping from a can of warm Coke, using a Twizzler as a straw.

"Find everything you need?" he chuckled. "Albert is going over some stuff with the group. Scavenging missions and what not. These people have lost everything." He paused for a moment and looked around. Bodies in the candlelight. Embracing. Whispering. They were tired. Clinging to each other. To whatever they could. "I guess we have, too."

"Not everything. Your daughter is out there. You'll find her tomorrow."

"I'm sorry," the pretty girl said. "I didn't mean to eavesdrop but Albert mentioned that your daughter worked at St. Joseph's. If you don't mind me asking, what's her name?"

"Whitney. Whitney Harris."

"Holy shit." The pretty girl's eyes widened. "Whitney is...well, was, my neighbor. She's been a really good friend of mine since I moved down here."

"Can you tell me more?" Dwight was downright giddy.

"Well, what I can tell you is that she was at work the night of the attack, but not the hospital. She switched over to a nursing home about a year ago." His giddiness turned to embarrassment, as he glanced over at me. He told me back in the car that they spoke regularly. Heck, maybe they did, just not about career opportunities. Who was I to judge? "I knew it was going to be Whitney. She looks just like you."

They were both crying and laughing. Dwight reached over and gave the girl a hug. I found myself laughing with some tears in my eyes as well. Dwight asked for her name.

"I'm Sophia. It's nice to meet you guys."

Walter

It only took these men a day to wipe us clean out of our supplies. Everything the nurses were able to salvage on their runs, pillaged and torn apart. Since then, they've been back and forth stockpiling for themselves, never sharing much with us at all.

Alberto and Jerry returned from a mission. It wasn't their greatest haul, that's for sure. Whitney was helping them transfer the items from the truck to the locker room we used for storage when we heard the familiar storm of motorcycle engines. They surrounded the truck. The Bearded Man and the guy whose head we fixed up entered the gym. Whitney stood firm, right in front of them.

"It's time for you to take your friends and leave," she insisted, with a quiet intensity.

"Now, why the hell would we do that? There ain't another building standing for miles. Besides, we like it here."

"I'm glad you're enjoying your stay but, if you haven't noticed, we've had to bury two people and another won't make it through the night. It's an impossible situation we have on our hands and you aren't making it any easier. At this point, we'll protect ourselves from any danger out there."

The men turned to each other and laughed. They were heavily intoxicated. Have been, nearly every day since they've arrived. Makes me wonder how many liquor stores and houses they've raided.

"Listen here, lady," this time it was the injured man speaking. Blood had leaked through the gauze wrapped around his head, staining it red. "You helped me out, good. Far as I see it, we ain't even yet. How about I take you down the hall there for some advanced sex ed?"

They laughed again, this time harder and louder. In my day, I would've socked him right in the mouth for talking to her like that. If there's one thing I don't tolerate, it's disrespect to women. I walked over and stood by Whitney's side. Alberto and Jerry made their way back into the gym with the rest of the ornery group followed behind them.

"It's a shame that you can make a nasty comment like that after I gave you the medical attention you desperately needed." She remained strong, but was shaken up. I placed my hand on her back. "You need to leave now."

"It's a joke. Travis don't mean nuthin' by it," The Bearded Man responded. "Let's start over."

"Nah," Alberto interjected. "There are people dying here. We are all they got. You guys have a whole world out there to be your playground."

"Look at that," the man now known as Travis said. "You people sure stick together."

"You people? What's that mean exactly? Alberto was seeing red and I understood. He started to move toward the disrespectful jackass when Jerry restrained him by the arm. A part of me was stirring that hadn't in a long time. I suddenly felt a bit dizzy.

"Okay, okay. Travis, go outside. Take the boys with you. Help them with the rest of the load."

"We don't need help," Alberto said, as he freed himself from Jerry's grip, stomping out of the gym doors.

"What did you say to me?" Travis asked The Bearded Man, as he stood face to face with him.

"Did I stutter? Take the boys and help these folks out." Travis did what he was asked, slamming the double doors shut behind him. The gymnasium fell silent as I and the rest of the residents watched, on edge, afraid to move. My dizzy spell worsened. I felt weaker than I had in a long time.

"Travis has always been a bit of a special case," The Bearded Man continued, "and now, because of his injury, he's downright fucked in the head. I realize we ain't been kind to you folks, so I'm fixing to make it up to y'all by patching that hole up there in the roof. Luckily, it's been dry, but if a strong storm comes through here, y'all are gonna have a mess on your hands."

"How do you plan on doing that, exactly?" Whitney asked.

"There's a Home Depot still standing down the road. They got what I need. We'll also be a lot better on sharing supplies. You got my word on that."

Whitney turned toward the staff, then me. I was compelled to speak, even though my nerves were racked and the gym was spinning faster than ever.

"If your buddy talks to her like that again, you boys go," I said. "No more negotiations on the subject."

"You got yourself a deal, gramps."

"My name is Walter."

"Okay, Walter. My apologies."

Night has fallen and my dizziness has subsided. For the first time since their arrival, things are quiet here. Their bikes haven't moved. There's no trace of them in the school. No commotion from down the hallway or hooting and hollering from outside.

It's a sad night, however. We had to bury another one of our people this evening. A quiet man named Harry. All I knew of him was that his wife passed years ago and he had a son in Florida. A doctor. Or, maybe a dentist. It's slipping my mind at the moment. They took him out to the baseball field with the others. Alberto made another grave out of a wooden pallet.

You and Joseph are in my thoughts on nights like these, my love. It's all that gets me through.

Spencer

After waiting an endless wait, George was hungry and irritable. His diaper was loaded, leaking through his pants. It had become quiet outside, long enough that I figured we were in the clear. I opened the hatch to find our home split in half. It was as if a tornado spun right through the center of it.

324

Everything Lila and I made together, everything we shared, torn apart like a piece of paper.

The driveway and kitchen were on the side of the house with less damage. A branch had fallen on the roof of the van, but other than that it was in good shape. I quickly collected what I could from the cabinets and fridge, filling a plastic bin and duffle bag. I did it all with one hand. I couldn't put George down. It was too dangerous. The only other necessities that came to mind were diapers and wipes. They were on the bad side of the house.

The hallway was without a roof. Smoke was drifting inside. I slowly made my way across heaps of debris. Charred drywall and a piece of Mr. Fratelli's fence was piled on top of George's changing table. I kicked it off. In the ruins of what used to be his bedroom, I changed my son.

On the way out, I took my first good look at the Fratellis' house. It was spared for the most part, but I had to check on them. I let myself in the front door, then shouted their names. As I searched, becoming more and more certain that I would find their corpses, I noticed that even though the exterior walls of the house were still standing, there was air coming in from somewhere. I followed it to the end of the main hallway. An opening had been seared, straight through the ceiling into the attic, aligned with a second one in the roof. A perfect circle, painted with the blue of the sky. This wasn't random like the rest. There was intelligence behind it. Profound intelligence. Mr. and Mrs. Fratelli were gone. This much I was sure of.

Fires burned in every direction. Roads were nearly impossible to travel. George was having coughing fits in his car seat. I looked for some kind of law enforcement or military. A shred of order amongst the chaos. If we were going to make it to Orlando, we needed to find my father first. I took the alternate route, through a dense forest, to my childhood home. My logic was, whoever did this, had no reason to attack the woods. It would be less dangerous to traverse. When we arrived, my heart nearly jumped from my chest. The house was unscathed.

"PopPop," George said, realizing his surroundings.

"Yea, PopPop. We're here to pick him up."

The place was a mess, but it was his mess. Work clothes hung on the back of chairs. Empty pizza boxes and water ice cartons were strewn across every hard surface. Old newspapers and scratch-offs were piling up on the kitchen counter. I called for him and received no response. A similar draft to the one at the Fratellis' house led me to the den.

"Hole, Dada."

"It *is* a hole, buddy."

It was the same size. Same precision. Same orifice opened to the sky.

In the garage, George swayed on a wooden rocking horse that used to belong to me, as I sat on a threadbare couch, listening to the faraway sounds of panic and destruction. I thought about my mother in Cape Cod, and wondered if she shared this fate. Being yanked toward the sky, her husband clutching her by the hand, using his other to grasp the shingles of their roof. I thought about my friends. Were they crushed or burnt like so many other bodies I had seen? I mostly thought about Lila. The most sickening thoughts. Thoughts that I was helpless against.

I loaded his hunting rifle in the van, as well a map of the United States, and three full gas cans. If I were never to see my father again, this was his final gift to me.

Lauren

The sun was barely up when we pulled out of the ShopRite parking lot. Dwight was driving, with Albert riding shotgun. Orson and I were in the backseat. Our destination was Red Oaks, an old age home about five miles from the store.

Albert, or "Big Al" as he insisted on being called by his friends (or people he's known for twelve hours in our case) recommended we take the back way. The attack had not only stopped time, leaving busy streets littered with cars, but it also inflicted a ton of damage on the roadways themselves.

We passed several farmhouses, surrounded by fields that were dead or beginning to die. Other houses were built every mile or so in the deep woods. These homes weren't like the ones I saw in neighborhoods. Smashed to pieces, like some giant went hard as hell with a mallet. These were mostly intact. Maybe the people in them were lucky, like me and The Monster.

About halfway there, we came to a ranch-style house that had a front window plastered with colorful children's drawings. Something drew my attention from the artwork to the second floor window. A streak of blonde hair, barely visible over the sill.

"There are people in there," I announced.

"Where?" Big Al asked, as Dwight slammed the breaks.

"In that house. I saw someone upstairs. A little girl."

"Are you sure?"

"I'm positive!"

"We should see if they need help."

"Wait a minute," Dwight said. "Let's get to where we're going first. Then come by here on the way back. We can't really take nobody with us right now anyway."

"Dwight is correct. Plus, the *Saurians* could be watching," Orson added.

"I'm sorry. The what, now?" I inquired, as Dwight put the Lincoln back in drive.

"The Saurians. The beings that did this to us. I'm connected to them in some way."

"Maybe now is not the best time for that," his father said.

"There is no better time," Orson snapped back. The wooded road let out to a cratered four lane highway. Some cars were being swallowed by large cavities, while others had been flipped over completely. A gas station had been decimated, along with the office building next door. I couldn't take my eyes off the disaster porn outside the window, but I listened as Orson continued. "Ever since the night they attacked us, I've been in their minds. I see what they see."

"Who?" Dwight asked.

"The Saurians."

"Yea, that part I got. Who are they?

"Beings from some other place."

"I knew it! Couldn't be another country did this. Or terrorists. Too much, too fast. I knew it had to be some damn spacemen."

"Well, we don't know that for sure. Orson has a penchant for telling stories."

"Fuck off, Dad."

"Son, what did I say about the disrespect? I don't - "

"They don't communicate like we do." He spoke louder and faster to drown out his father. "I can't get a good read on them. What I do know is that they aren't finished with us yet..."

Orson's words drifted off as the attention in the car turned to the approaching ruins. Seared walls sprouting from hills of ashy debris.

Dwight barely put the car in park before he was out, dashing toward the rubble. Big Al, Orson, and myself assisted with the search. We sifted through what remained of the old age home, moving charred pieces of furniture from one place to another, stumbling over hills of ash, silently acknowledging each mangled corpse that we came across. I never wanted anything more than for Dwight to not discover the lifeless body of his daughter in this horrible mess.

I'm the furthest thing you can find from a religious person but I prayed for it. I thought about a prayer that I used to hear my grandmother say. "Our father who does art in heaven" or something. I repeated it, over and over again. As we became sweaty in the morning sun and our faces and arms were painted by soot, I prayed.

Perhaps it worked. Two hours and a disturbing amount of death later, there was no sign of Whitney. Dwight collapsed backward with his head hung low.

"I give up," he said, as we gathered around him.

"I don't believe she's here," Big Al responded, placing his hand gently on the exhausted man's shoulder.

"What do I do now?"

"Well, Sophia said that their apartment complex was destroyed. That she was lucky to be out when it happened. So, she wouldn't be there. It's possible that she found a safe haven of some kind. Perhaps she's with good people. We'll continue to search, Dwight. We'll send groups out every day if need be."

On the way back, we stopped at the house where I saw the little girl. Dwight asked me what my plan was as he parked at the end of a long, stone driveway.

"I don't really have one," I answered. "I just want to see if she's okay."

"I'll come and watch your back," Orson said. About halfway up the drive, he continued. "Do you believe me about the Saurians?"

"I'd be an idiot not to believe in just about anything right now. Can I ask you something, though?"

"Of course."

"In the car you said they aren't finished with us yet. Does that mean they're coming back?"

"They're still here."

His words sent a chill down my spine, but our attention turned to the front door. I knocked and we waited. I wondered who she was with. I hoped it was her mother. The two of them drawing together in the days, and whispering ghost stories under a pillow fort in the long, dark nights. I knocked again, then examined her drawings: a rainbow, princess, unicorn, and sunflower.

"They're probably scared to come to the door. Let's head back." I didn't want to, but I followed him back to the car. The morning had produced no Whitney or girl in the window. I felt depressed, kicking stones as I walked.

"My little brother died of leukemia," he said softly, apropos to nothing. "It was the first time I felt the connection with someone. I heard his thoughts. I felt his pain. When he died, a little piece of me died with him."

"Jesus, Orson."

"Since then, whatever this affliction is, has grown. I don't control it. I can't. But it...it's like my mind reaches out and attaches itself with others around me." He towered over me, with broad shoulders and long, defined arms. But, in this moment, he seemed like a helpless, confused little boy.

My mind was spinning as we returned to the ShopRite. I sat on a checkout counter and looked out over the group. Big Al's wife welcomed him and Orson back with hugs and kisses. Sophia ran up to Dwight, inquiring about Whitney. I was sticky and disgusting, longing for a hot shower. I thought about how Dwight must've been feeling, as well as Orson's telepathic powers and the little girl in the window. Eventually, I stretched out on the conveyer belt and fell asleep. I dreamt of Halloween again. The graveyard dirt cake. My parents.

Dwight woke me up hours later. He was clean-shaven and wearing a different outfit. It was late afternoon, the sun was casting shadows throughout the store. It looked like a different place from the one I fell asleep in.

"Is this a dream?"

"Not at all, girl. There's a path behind the store, cutting through the woods. About a mile walk takes you to a swimming hole with a waterfall and everything. They've salvaged a gang of clothes. Most stuff got the tags still on. Soap and body wash in aisle four."

I told him I was so sorry that we didn't find Whitney.

"Thank you," he said with a sad smile. "She's out there, still. My baby is tough."

He took a long pause. Tears began to well up in the corners of his eyes. I knew he had more to say, so I waited.

"Truth is, I ain't never been much of a father. I've focused on the wrong things in my life. Always on the road. Chasing gigs. I failed her."

He broke down. I've never been good at dealing with crying adults. My dad cried a ton when we lost my grandmother. I remember just shutting up and putting my arm around his shoulders. I did the same for Dwight.

"Thank you," he whispered. "Now, I would see about that water before you lose daylight. You're stanky."

Walter

It was hot today.

Soon, the summer months will settle in, leaving the stuffy gymnasium like the inside of a pressure cooker. With water being as scarce as it's been, I wonder if those of us who are left will be able to stay hydrated.

Usually, I would've been pushing Grace in her wheelchair around the hallways, but today she didn't feel up to it. I'm worried about her. Ever since the militia showed up she hasn't been herself. She's anxious. Spends most of her time clutching rosary beads. I'd probably be doing the same, but I have a sense of duty to these people. To see them through this. As impossible as that may seem.

I came to an open locker. A denim jacket hung over a pile of binders and textbooks, with a mirror stuck to the inside of the door. The name *Kaylee* was stenciled on the wooden frame. I wondered what her fate was and it suddenly felt like an invasion of privacy.

"Walking around aimlessly again, old timer?" It was the man named Travis, coming out of the lavatory. He stunk like a honkey tonk at three in the morning.

"This locker has never been opened until today," I responded, sternly.

"You think I want to play around in some dead kid's locker?" I didn't get an answer out before he continued. "You know something? You been eyeball fucking me since we shown up here."

"I'm not going to dignify that with a response. What I will say is this. If it wasn't for Whitney, you'd be up the creek without a paddle. You should show her a bit of respect."

He loomed over me, his breath was warm and rotten. "Respect some coon? Why would I do that?"

The dizziness reared its ugly head once again. Rows of lockers appeared to be sliding back and forth like the coupling rods of a locomotive. It was too much. I used the wall to stay on my feet.

"What's the matter, Hoss? Having a heart attack?"

Another man shouted something that I couldn't decipher from the opposite end of the hallway. Everything was muffled and echoey. Before he walked away, Travis shoved me on the shoulder. I went down, hard, on my backside. A sharp pain shot up my spine. The last thing I remember is being eye level with his boots as they melted away.

I came to on my cot, with Whitney and Alberto standing over me. Whitney asked how I was feeling. Truth is, I'm in a considerable amount of pain, but I didn't want to worry her. Especially since there was another vacant cot. It belonged to Alice, a sweet lady who never stopped knitting and adored Elvis Presley.

"I'm okay. Just lost my wits for a second. I'm fine now."

Bert asked, "What's the last thing you remember, Mr. Walter?"

I had to lie again. Seems like I'm starting to make a habit out of it. "I was just taking a walk around the halls. That's all, really."

"Did you cross paths with any of the hillbillies?" Whitney flashed him a side eye. "What? That's what they are."

"No. It was just me. No need to worry yourselves any further."

"Okay, Walter. Rest up. Please let one of us know if you need anything."

They exchanged another worried glance. It was almost like they were hoping I would address the elephant in the room. So, I did.

"Has Alice passed?" Whitney answered with a nod. "Her medication?" She nodded again.

We were startled as the double doors swung open, letting the cool night air and the sound of crickets flood the gymnasium. The Bearded Man approached slowly, putting us on high alert. I tried to sit up, and in that moment, realized how much pain I was actually in.

"Don't get up, please. I just came by to say I'm sorry. I've seen you fellas burying a lot of bodies out there in that field," he gestured toward Alberto. His breath reeked of whisky and cigarettes. "I think we're gonna fix that hole up and make our way down the road tomorrow."

"So, that's it?" Whitney asked. "You guys come through here, scare the shit out of these folks, wipe us clean out of our supplies, then leave? Talk about looters."

"Them boys have lost everything too, ma'am. We're all dealing with this shit in our own ways. I ain't making excuses though. And, I can only speak for myself when I say I'm truly sorry."

It seemed like his words were coming from a real place. He didn't seem to have the same malice in his heart as his friend. Still, birds of a feather. I wasn't about to go fishing with the guy any time soon.

"Well, I guess that's it," he turned to leave.

"Excuse me," Whitney said. "What's your name?"

"Victor. Vic is fine." Whitney didn't say another word, just clutched my hand, then walked away.

Since then, I've been trying to lay as still as possible to keep my back from throbbing. I've been thinking about Alice, Harry, and the others. People I had gotten to know, then lost. It's like war all over again. Perhaps, in that way, I've been conditioned for this.

Spencer

I parked the van on the arch of a cul de sac, between the driveways of two houses. One had been reduced to rubble, nothing more than cinders, emitting smoke into the fading light of afternoon. The other stood mostly intact. Good enough shape to loot. I hate that word, but it's what I was doing.

Society was crumbling at an alarming rate. It was as if something nefarious had been lying dormant in the human race, waiting for the time it could crawl out of its hole and spread amongst us. Areas with grocery stores and strip malls were teeming with crowds - dangerous people, ransacking and setting fires. This left me with no other choice but to stay off the beaten path and try a residential area. The merit of this particular venture might be discussed one day in history books; it'll more likely be their history books (if they have them) than ours, but I had stopped concerning myself with right versus wrong.

Everything was wrong.

That's what I told myself as I filled a duffle bag with pricey bottles of Cognac and Scotch, along with a couple of unopened bags of Cool Ranch Doritos. These people had none of the supplies I needed for a two year old, but they knew how to party.

George was determined to take every single pot and pan out of the lower kitchen cabinet. As soon as he was mobile, he started making a habit out of this same thing back at our house. It was familiar and brought a fleeting moment of comfort, so I let him have at it. The junk drawer produced nothing useful outside of a flashlight, sandwich bags full of batteries, a couple of lighters, and a push button switchblade.

"Dada," George said, as he handed me a mesh strainer. He saw what we were doing and was either trying to contribute or wanted the thing because it had a handle and he could swing it around. Whatever the case was, I gave it back to him when he whined for it.

As I moved quickly through the foyer, with the duffle bag in my left arm and George in my right, I fought the urge to glance over at the photo gallery on the wall. Weddings. Vacations. Professional shots on the beach in matching outfits. Their eyes were locked on me. I could feel them.

I made it back to the van and strapped George into his car seat. He playfully whipped me in the face with the strainer.

"Dada," he chuckled.

"Don't hit, buddy." Parenting. As if it mattered.

Some motels were operating as safe havens. It seemed to me that there were a lot of displaced folks, looking for something that resembled a decent night's sleep. I hadn't had the nerve to check in to one yet, but a sleeping arrangement that wasn't a reclined driver's seat of a Dodge Caravan, with a toddler on my lap, sounded amazing.

I pulled over on the shoulder of a highway and inspected my father's road map. He was an old-school, "never ask for directions" type. Usually, you'd be risking your life in this spot, a few feet away from a nonstop stream of everything from motorcycles to tractor trailers. Not this night. On this night it felt like George and I were the only people left on Earth.

We pulled up underneath the canopy of a Holiday Inn Express. Some candles and lanterns led up to the front entrance. Night hadn't fallen yet but whoever was responsible for this establishment was getting a head start.

"Do you have rooms available here?"

My question sounded ridiculous as it came out, but the rotund man behind the front desk didn't flinch. He was in his mid-forties or so, with a balding head of slicked back hair and goatee. My gut told me he was okay, but there was no trusting anyone in the new world.

"I do, my friend," he answered softly.

"Is there anyone else here?"

"A couple of rooms are occupied. Is it just you and your boy?" He nodded at George, who was asleep in my arm with his head resting on my shoulder.

Why would he want to know that?

"Was this your place?" I asked, with a sinking feeling.

"I'm the general manager. We've seen better days. I'm not gonna promise a great breakfast bar in the morning."

He smiled, as tears welled up in his eyes. The guy seemed genuine but I wasn't about to let my guard down in a dark motel in the middle of nowhere.

"We just need a bed for the night. That's all," I said, stroking George's hair. If he was running a torture chamber out of the place, presenting myself as a loving father was the smart play. Perhaps he'd take pity on us. "What can I give you?"

"Well, if you happen to have any booze in that van, I'll take it."

Some things still managed to work out.

Lauren

It wasn't quite night yet, but the moon was high. This used to amaze me as a little girl. I would ask my mother how it was possible.

"It's in just the right spot," she would answer. "Enough light is reflecting off of it to make it brighter than the sky." I thought she was the smartest person in the world. Or, at least, had a way of explaining things to me that made her seem like it.

It took me a few minutes to gain the nerve to strip and submerge myself, with a loofah in one hand, and a bottle of body wash in the other. The water was cold. Almost freezing. I let it float me to a place that I never thought possible. Alone, naked. Listening to the waterfall. Nothing but trees, dancing in the wind. I wished that she was there with me. To warm me with a towel, then braid my hair while she gave me her best theory on what we were dealing with.

After, I dried off as quickly as I could, almost shivering to death in the frigid wind. The group's stockpiled clothing provided me camouflage leggings and a new Nirvana tee shirt. The kind of shirt Target sold to wannabe punks and dads that actually listened to the band a hundred years ago. I topped it off with my trademark scarf. I wouldn't be lighting the post-apocalyptic fashion scene on fire anytime soon, but I appreciated the clean threads.

The trail seemed to stretch forever on my trek back. The woods were slipping underneath a veil of darkness. I wondered if I somehow got turned around in the swimming hole and was heading in the wrong direction. I started to move quicker, but not fast enough that I would trip over a branch or lose my footing on the sand. It was taking much longer than it should have. Something was wrong. I took a seat on a downed tree to figure it out. Only one option presented itself to me, go back in the direction I came and start over.

So, I ran.

Night was falling relentlessly. The surrounding trees were closing in. It was as if the earth wanted to swallow me whole.

That's when I heard it. A noise that I couldn't quite comprehend. It was mechanical, that much I was sure of, but there was a pattern to it. A powerful whir, every five seconds or so, that ended with the crushing of the forest floor. I followed the sound, until I was off the trail and into the thick woods. Through the wide branches, I saw a lumbering Goliath. It took my breath away in an instant. I fell over and hid behind a thicket of bushes.

The machine was walking on two legs and guiding itself through the trees with two arms. It had a bulky midsection, with a cockpit of some kind. Instead of a head, there was a dome, made of something that resembled tinted glass.

I turned and sprinted in the opposite direction. Once I found the trail again, I started to move as fast as I had ever gone. A terrible cramp hit my side but I didn't slow, I kept going. As the woods became dark, my only goal was to put more distance between myself and the thing in the trees. That's when I saw two beacons up ahead. It was Dwight and Orson, flashlights in hand, shocked to see me approaching them full tilt. I screamed.

"We need to go now! Don't look back!"

They tried to ask questions but I blew right past them.

Back at ShopRite, the group gathered around me. They were concerned, offering up bottles of water and paper towels to wipe my sweat. I took both, then I took a minute to breathe.

Then puked.

In front of everyone.

The embarrassment would've been too much to bear in the old world. In this one though, the Nightmare Machine in the forest took precedence. As I was cleaning myself up, Big Al joined the group.

"Give her space, guys. We'll chat, then we'll fill you guys in on everything. Okay? Go back to what y'all were doing."

They dispersed reluctantly, with Dwight and Orson staying behind.

"What were you guys doing in the woods?" I asked, taking sips from a warm Ginger Ale Dwight handed me.

"You were out there a while, we were starting to get worried," he answered. I couldn't remember the last time anyone other than my mother gave a shit about me.

"Thank you," I said, then explained what I had seen - the best I could - trying not to sound like a crazy person. It was a robot. A cyborg. A mechanical menace. The Nightmare Machine. Just another symptom of a world gone mad. No more truths. No more fiction. It was time to dive head first into the whitewater and ride the wave of strange. "I know. It sounds crazy."

"We're living in a ShopRite darlin'. There ain't no more crazy out here." Big Al was starting to grow on me.

That night, four people kept watch, including Dwight. They walked around the perimeter of the building, scanning the surrounding area. It's an operation they had been running with a rotation of one person at a time, but Big Al thought it was best to up our numbers. Inside, the buzz was on. Because of my story, no one in the group could muster up any sleep. Being the most popular person in any setting was new territory for me, so I needed to break free from it for a minute. I called Orson over.

"Do you want to dip off to the snack aisle again?" I asked.

"Sure," he responded.

We took our seats at the same spot as last time, popping bags of all the best chips. We took turns slugging from a two liter of root beer to wash it all down. About ten minutes into our silent feast, my stomach began to hurt. Plus, I started to feel self-conscious.

"Orson, are you reading my mind?"

"Nope. Just chillin'. I like being able to hang with someone and not having to say too much."

"I never related to something so much in my life."

Here and there we chatted about the impossible things we had seen, but mostly we just sat there, deep into the night, while the rest of the group drifted off to an uneasy sleep. The only illumination besides ours were the flashlights of the lookout crew as they circled the building.

I found myself hoping that the Nightmare Machine wouldn't find us, hoping it wouldn't mess this situation up or hurt any of these people. Because as fucked up as the situation was, it was our fucked up situation.

Walter

Only two of them returned this afternoon. Travis thundered through the double doors, holding the other guy up. He had suffered a gunshot wound to the upper thigh. Alberto and Jerry assisted with bringing him in and laying him on a cot. Whitney calmly gathered the tools she would need for the procedure. It was like second nature to her.

"What happened?" she asked, as she applied pressure to the wound with a folded towel.

"We was rushed at the Home Depot. Them people we warned y'all about. Vic, Shawn, and Hickenbottom went and got themselves killed. Jimmy here got nipped but we managed to shoot our way out."

"Vic is dead?"

"Aw, how nice. Y'all were on a first name basis. Probably why he wanted to help you people out so bad."

She stopped what she was doing, removed the bandana from Jimmy's head, then tossed it at his friend's face.

"You want me to help your buddy or let him bleed out? It's your call."

"You know that Goddamn answer already."

"Then take your comments and get away from me."

As Whitney treated the injured man, I checked on Grace. She was in the wheelchair, with her beads dangling from her hands. "What happened to him?"

"He fell from his motorcycle. It's going to be okay."

I was lying again. This time it was to protect Grace from any added stress. The militia's occupation of the school has taken a very serious toll on the residents. Only she and I remain.

"How can we go on like this?"

Her question blindsided me. Throughout my life, I've prided myself with having the answers. Being there to comfort those in need. You and Joseph. My platoon. Even all those years ago on the farm, with my brothers and sisters. The true answer to Grace's question is we can't. This existence is unsustainable.

"Together, Grace. We'll make it through together."

A couple of hours later, I lit the gymnasium. With each nightfall, I feel we're closer to having the sun set on us for good. Whitney was sitting alone on the highest bleacher. I knew it would be quite the feat to make it up there, but I figured I could use the exercise.

"You fixed up another one," I said, panting, as I took a seat next to her.

"It pained me to do it, Walter. It really did."

Blood had dried all over her neck, face, and hands. Streaks of dark red painted the front of her scrubs.

"I understand."

"Do you believe their story about the attack?"

I don't. There's something rotten in Denmark. But, tonight, as I looked into the eyes of a woman that has taken such good care of me and so many others, I didn't have the heart. I lied again.

"They're rotten men, this much is certain. But, it's a dangerous world out there. I think I believe them."

"I guess I do too then."

"I hate to bring this up right now, Miss Whitney. We're running out of candles and batteries for the lanterns. And toilet paper."

She explained that with each run, Alberto and Jerry return with less food and supplies. They've been forced to venture farther away from the school. To make matters worse, the nearest gas station with working pumps just ran out of gas.

"Why are you staying?" I asked. "Grace and I are in the twilight of our lives. But you're young. You must have someone out there worth finding."

"My mother passed away five years ago. I haven't seen my father in a long time. Then there's my ex-husband floating around somewhere out there. I hope he blew up." I laughed, only after she did. "The truth is, I belong here. You guys are all I have."

We sat quietly for a moment and scanned the shadowy gymnasium floor. Grace slept on her cot just below us. A couple of drunk nurses played poker. And the injured strangers cuddled assault rifles at the far end, speaking quietly to each other about God only knows.

"Tell me about your son. If you want to. I mean, I know everything there is to know about Helen and practically nothing about Joseph."

It's hard for me to talk about our boy. You know that more than anyone. Perhaps, there's a bit of embarrassment there. Feelings of guilt. Resentment. Old feelings, scabbed over. Still, there's a part of me that yearns to talk about him.

"Well, my son was all the things I'm not. All the things I don't understand. He was an artist and a musician. He wrote beautiful poetry. He was sad, though. He let the problems of the world really get to him."

"Sounds like he was a very sensitive soul."

"Indeed he was."

On a normal night, that may have been the furthest I went into it. Besides, that's the gist of who Joseph was. The rest of his story are the ugly details. The ones that hurt coming out.

"He had demons because of it. Substance abuse. For years, I didn't get it. I believed he was weak. I believed it was a crutch. Then something changed. You see, he would have spans of time when he was clean. Weeks, months, even years. I saw life behind his eyes during those times. It's then I realized that he wasn't weak. He was sick. We did everything we could to help him. It nearly broke us."

I sighed deeply and forced myself to continue, as Whitney rubbed my back.

"I searched his eyes. In his darkest days, I prayed the life behind them would return. It never did. He overdosed at forty five years old."

"Oh my, Walter. I am so very sorry."

Everything slipped away in that moment. The night the sky fell. The death and hopelessness since. The impossible situation we are facing. To speak about Joseph was like I was giving my thoughts about him new life. It was as if my words were stirring up his spirit. I think maybe Whitney knew that would happen if she asked me about him.

I lie on my cot now, gazing up at the aperture that reveals the night sky. The aperture that Vic will never fix. A light rain is falling through, evaporating before it reaches the hardwood. My back is beginning to feel a bit better, but my dizzy spells are worsening.

Death is certain. How we arrive at it is anything but. My journey to get there has become quite peculiar. I imagine it'll get even more so. Tonight, though, our son is traveling with me.

I take comfort in that.

Spencer

There was a man that planned to make it to Orlando in two days. A naive man. A man I no longer recognized in the rearview mirror. He had grown a beard. His potbelly, from the comfort of his new life as a dad, was beginning to grow smaller. The altered landscape of the eastern United States was proving to be a more perilous journey than he could've imagined. Traffic jams frozen in time. Enormous craters tattooing the earth. The new world brought rare instances when he would cross paths with the living. People who had become indifferent ghosts, trudging across the wasteland. More than that, there was the dead. Each tangled, putrefied corpse pulled him closer to the inescapable reality that his wife was gone. But, mostly, there was the strangulating absence of man.

Although we were able to make it to Georgia on the gas cans my father left behind and two lucky pit stops at stations with generous owners and generators, the needle on the van's gauge was falling fast once again. This time, we were in the middle of nowhere.

George was down to his last diaper. Had been, for almost a full twenty four hours. He was hungry, but wouldn't eat. Irritable but didn't want to be soothed. I turned the dial to a random FM station on the radio and got nothing but static in return. I was hoping it would find some secret frequency with a loop of where to find a camp of survivors. Like you see in disaster movies. That never came, but the white noise seemed to be calming George.

I pulled over on the shoulder and let it play. The sound eventually lulled him to sleep. I watched him for a moment, snoring in his car seat. He was quickly becoming the bravest little boy I had ever known, simply by existing in this terrible situation. I began to sob uncontrollably, there was no use trying to stifle it. I relocated to the back and rested my head on the edge of his car seat, until I too drifted off.

When I awoke, I saw a pack of coyotes in the pale, blue light of morning. They were devouring a shredded carcass of something slightly larger than themselves. It wasn't much more than a skeleton when they finally dragged it back into the forest. I figured it was safe enough at that point to return to the driver seat and continue on our way.

Except, we couldn't. I had left the engine running.

The van was out of gas.

Lauren

"They're back!" Big Al shouted, as he charged through the entrance to the store. "The lights! They're back!"

The group followed him out to the parking lot, all of us, looking toward the dusk sky as we exited. We understood what this meant. Maybe no one more than Orson. I glanced over at him and our worried eyes met. Everyone was talking at once, questions circling like a funnel cloud. Orson and I gravitated through the crowd, toward each other.

"This isn't good," he whispered, never taking his eyes off the sky. "Not good at all." I asked him if he was reading their minds, if he could feel a connection like he had before. "I feel something, but it's different now. Chaotic and distorted."

"Listen up, guys," Big Al cried out, over the group's chatter. "If this is going to go down the same as last time, we have about twenty four hours to find a safe place. Maybe, underground somewhere. I'm open for suggestions."

A thin white guy in his mid-fifties spoke up. He had slicked back dark hair and a softball-sized Adam's apple. I thought he was some creep with a staring problem until Big Al explained that he was a rich business owner who had lost his wife and three daughters in the attack. He may have been battling symptoms of PTSD, or something. "One of my buildings is about five miles from here. It's mostly destroyed, but the entrance to the basement is accessible."

Big Al pondered our situation, pacing back and forth, then said, "Unless anyone else has an idea, that may be our only hope." The chatter sparked up again when Dwight's voice cut through it. Until that moment, I was convinced that he was physically incapable of being anything other than soft-spoken.

"Hold on just a minute now. It could take us damn near three hours to walk that distance. How do we know that they won't attack us in that time? Not to mention the machine Lauren ran into. We have no idea how many of them are out there. Or, what they can do to us. We'll be sitting ducks out on the road."

Dwight was right. The Nightmare Machine was pretty much all I could think about. The raw power of it. The way the woods were no obstacle. The possibility of more being out there, lurching about, searching for survivors to evaporate on sight, was enough for me to stay put.

"I agree," I said. "If any of you saw what I saw, the last thing you would want to be doing is walking around out here."

"We have a couple of cars," a woman added. She was scrawny, with a head of dark hair that she wore like a helmet. "The rest can ride in the bed of the pickup we found."

"It's just not safe," Dwight added. "I suggest we go back inside. Stay put. Ride it out. This store made it through once, maybe it'll make it through again."

Big Al stopped pacing, "Maybe ain't really enough," he said. "We got a target on us. They're coming back to hit what they missed the first time."

"No they aren't, Orson responded. "Dwight and Lauren are absolutely right. The store is the safest bet."

"None of your mind reading is necessary right now. Okay, Son?"

"I'm going back inside. Fuck this!" Orson whipped around, then stormed off. The crowd's anxiety grew to a fever pitch, as they continued to stare at the sky.

The night we were attacked, my mother and I had been fighting. It was an ongoing quarrel about me moving out, and her failure to defend me from The Monster. She was out by the back fence having a smoke, when I approached her.

"I'm leaving," I hissed. "Morgan and I have enough for a down payment on a little place, far away from him."

"Yea? And, how do you and Morgan expect to pay rent? She's at McDonald's and you're at a pizzeria. As far as I can tell, you two work a combined three days a week."

"We will make it work. Weren't you living on your own, waitressing at a diner, when you met Dad?"

"It was different, honey."

"Of course. The only difference is your mother wasn't married to the world's biggest asshole." She put her cigarette out on a picket, then turned to me with tears in her eyes.

342

"I am stuck. But you aren't. You know that."

About a month prior, she drunkenly admitted that she would escape with me if she wasn't so terrified. It was the first time I had ever seen her break free from the denial she was living in.

"You aren't stuck, Mommy. We'll just leave. Go somewhere he can't find you."

"He'll always find me," she nodded toward the sky. "Maybe, *they'll* come down and take me away." The lights from the night before were back. Bigger and brighter. I hadn't noticed them.

"We should go inside," I tugged her by the arm.

"No, stay," she clutched my forearm in return, then pulled me close.

"Mom! It's cold. There's some weird shit happening. I'm going inside!"

I traipsed through the living room. The Monster didn't budge, just continued to snore on the couch, with his hand shoved down the front of the raggedy blue jeans he wore every day.

As I tried to call Morgan, the room was deluged with a strange energy. Every hair on my body stood up. I dashed toward the window and saw my mother. She was still by the fence, bathed in a brilliant light. There was a noise. Quiet and deafening all at once. It was as if I wasn't hearing it at all.

A blast followed.

With it came another noise. This one shook the house. The mirror fell from the wall and shattered on my dresser. My legs gave out from under me. I managed to grab the windowsill on the way down, but I was disoriented. A few more explosions followed. Each slightly quieter than the one before. When I was finally able to use the base of the window to stand back up, I saw my mother again. She had flown about thirty feet from the fence. Her body was in an unnatural position and her face was misshapen and bloody.

I trailed Orson into the store and shouted "Hey!" when he ignored me. "Hold up for a second!"

"What is it?" he asked, reluctantly stopping in his tracks.

"We can't fall apart right now. We need each other."

"Who is we? I don't even know you."

His words stung a lot more than I thought they could. "That's fucked up, dude."

"What did you think was going to happen? We would live happily ever after in a ShopRite, shoveling Doritos into our mouths until we were old and gray? They are back and we are dead. You and Dwight should get into his car and go. While y'all still can."

"I'm chalking this up to your meds. You've run out and are talking nuts."

We stood without saying a word until the group reentered the building.

"We're leaving. Pack up whatever you still got," Big Al shouted. I glanced over at Dwight. He looked beaten into submission.

"What do you mean?" Orson asked his father.

"Exactly what I said. Mr. Brimley is leading a caravan of cars to his building. Pack your shit. Quickly."

"I'm not going anywhere."

"You are coming. If it means I gotta drag you by your hair, you are coming."

Orson's eyes let us know that his father meant what he said. Dwight gestured at me with his head. I followed him back outside.

"They've got a couple of cars and a pickup truck," he said. "There's room for you."

"Room for me?" My voice got weak and I began to cry, quickly wiping the tears with my scarf. It seemed like nobody wanted me around. "Whatever."

"What's whatever mean?"

"It means whatever. What are you going to do?"

"Well, I think the Lord brought me to this place for a reason. I'm gonna stay here. I gotta keep living. My daughter is still out there. I know it."

I didn't say another word, just bolted back into the store and grabbed my mother's backpack. On the way out, Orson ran up to me.

"Where are you going?"

"I'm out."

"With Dwight?"

"No. With myself. That's all I need."

"That machine is out there."

"I'll take my chances."

"Talk to my father with me. Please. Maybe if he hears it from both of us, he'll change his mind and let me stay."

"Stay and do what? Shovel Doritos in our mouths?"

"I guess if we're going to die, that's as good a way to spend our last moments on Earth as any."

344

My dad would always say that I was "stubborn as a bull" like he was. I never really knew what that meant until I got older. I wanted to stay, just like I wanted to sit on that fence with my mother and watch the skies until we were blown to smithereens together. My feelings were hurt, though. This meant I was going to do exactly the opposite of what I should have.

"No thanks. It was nice to meet you. Good luck."

I shot across the parking lot, trying not to look at Dwight, who was sitting on the hood of his car, smoking a cigar. He shouted my name as I raced by. Still, I didn't look over. I just kept moving.

As night fell, and harbingers of certain death hovered in the sky and lurked through the woods, I put one foot in front of the other and hit the road once more.

Walter

Today started with fire and ended with rain.

I followed Whitney and Alberto out to the ball field, just as the sun was beginning to rise. The militia men, along with Jerry, were standing around a blaze, clutching their rifles. It didn't take long for us to notice that it was the remainder of our supplies piled up, burning over a bed of wood. The wood Alberto had used to mark the final resting places of so many of our friends.

"Did y'all bring the marshmallows?" Travis asked sarcastically, as he tossed a roll of toilet paper into the flame. His bandage had been removed, revealing an infected, purulent scab. It was as if half of his face belonged to different species.

"How could you do this to us?" Whitney bellowed, holding herself up on Alberto.

"How? Well, our new friend used his key to the locker room. Led us straight out here. Y'all slept through your invite."

Alberto shouted in Jerry's direction, "You no good piece of shit!"

"Now, now. Let's not let our emotions get the best of us," he repositioned his weapon, letting us know he was in complete control.

Even though my heart was thumping in my chest, and the dizziness was back, I never took my eyes off of his. I learned many years ago that if you were able to look a man in his eyes, the fight wasn't over yet.

"Feeling froggy, old man? In case y'all forgot, this country belongs to us. No matter the current situation, this is the United States of America. It don't belong to no geezers, and it certainly don't belong to y'all." He gestured toward Whitney and Alberto, whose face was flushed with anger.

"Are you buying into this bullshit?" Alberto asked, in Jerry's direction.

"It ain't bullshit," he responded. "I'll be damned if I'm gonna waste another second of the life I got left tending to these folks. I ain't like you."

"That's for damn sure."

Whitney and I locked arms, using each other to stay upright. Alberto stood behind us, with his hands on our shoulders. I've seen terrible acts on the battlefield. Cruel acts. Acts of desperation. The ugliness of man rises to the top during war. This was something different. This was a pointless cruelty. A true evil that I never wanted to believe existed. Travis continued, this time aiming the muzzle of his rifle at us.

"The school is ours. We're giving y'all 'til noon to hit the road."

"We'll need the pickup truck. Grace won't get far in a wheelchair," Whitney said.

"That's a big no from me," Jerry responded. "I found that pickup. Peeled the dead guy right off the steering wheel myself. As of this afternoon I'm taking it up to South Carolina to find my family. What I should've done a long time ago."

"We worked together for six years, bro," cried Alberto, as he inched closer to the man he thought was his friend. "Don't do this."

Jerry turned his face away and stared into the fire until we went back inside. I've crossed paths with plenty of men like him. It's not that they are evil, but they're okay with evil just enough to take the path of least resistance.

Eventually they rejoined us, taking seats in the highest bleacher. They looked down on us gathering what was left of our belongings, cackling like some wicked gargoyles. I had nothing to take with me except three bottles of water, a Swiss Army knife, a framed photo of me, you, and Joseph at the beach, and this leather journal I write in now. I tossed it all in a salvaged gym bag, then waited with Grace right outside of the gym doors.

"Where will we go?" she asked, wiping her nose with a soiled handkerchief. She'd been crying all morning. I handed her a handful of fresh tissues, then answered.

"Alberto came across a ShopRite a few miles from here. The people there have a sign out front that reads *Safe Haven*. It's a hike, but we'll make it."

"I'm wheelchair bound, Walter. I won't do anything but slow you down. Have them push me to the end of the street, away from these men, then go ahead without me."

"Hush up, now. That's not going to happen."

We slowly made our way down the street. It was the first time Grace and I had seen the world outside of what surrounded the school. Houses reduced to sticks. Cars flipped over like children's toys. Trees uprooted and debris strewn about the roads. Alberto was finding it difficult to manage Grace's wheelchair over the unfathomable mess. What struck me most was the loneliness.

"Where is everyone?"

"This is pretty much how it is out here, Mr. Walter. We might come across a few folks, but for the most part, we on our own."

There were my days on the farm. Foot races and strength competitions with my siblings. Then came my military training and a lifelong devotion to physical fitness. This old man trudging along the wasteland is a far cry from that chiseled G.I. My legs began to weaken about a mile in. I collapsed to one knee soon after. Whitney and Alberto rushed to my aide with a water bottle.

"Drink slowly, Walter. Relax." Whitney instructed.

"We've been walking for a while and he's no spring chicken," Alberto added. It was like we were back in the home and I was overhearing them converse about some pitiful senior citizen. As terrible as it is to admit, I always laughed to myself and breathed a sigh of relief that I was doing better than most of the residents. This time it was me. I was mucking up the mission.

"I'm fine," I told them, lying. I was far from fine. My heart was palpitating. The world around us had been put on a swivel. Heat from the afternoon sun seemed to be gunning for me and me only. Perspiration drenched my clothing. "Let's keep going."

I tried to rise to my feet with every inch of my being and failed.

"It's okay," Whitney said. "Let's stay here for a bit. Right here." She sat beside me on the pavement. Alberto pushed the wheelchair closer to us, and took a seat himself. Grace's head hung lifelessly on her shoulder, her beads draped across her lap.

"Is she okay?" I asked.

"She's sleeping. I think the heat is getting to her," Alberto said, reaching into his bag. He removed a jar of peanuts, a box of fruit bars, and three cans of vegetables. "This is my private stash. Those assholes didn't find it. It's not like our lunches at the Olive Garden, Mr. Walter, but it'll do."

We ate. Savoring every bite. Eventually, Grace woke up. She barely had any appetite, but Whitney helped her consume a few green beans. Her thinning grey hair was caked with sweat on her forehead. She wasn't speaking. I knew from the anxious glances Whitney and Alberto were exchanging, that we needed to get her out of the sun. I scanned our surroundings. Beyond a field of grass was a lone, first floor apartment, wiggling off the end of a leveled townhouse like a worm on a hook.

"There," I said, pointing to the building. "Let's get her inside."

Like much of our movement since we departed from the school, we methodically approached the apartment, unsure of what problems could present themselves. Alberto knocked, which seemed strange given the circumstances. When no one came to the door, we let ourselves in.

After some deliberation, we've decided to stay the night. There's a putrid stink. Cigarette burns pepper the carpet. Flies swarm the kitchen. I shudder to think what other creatures have settled in the darkest corners of this place. Judging from the dusty set of dumbbells and the neon signs advertising beer, it was a bachelor pad, and its occupant had started to let it go long before the attack.

As I write this, Grace is sleeping soundly in her wheelchair. Alberto and Whitney have joined her in a rare, deep slumber. He's sitting on the floor with his back against a loveseat, while Whitney is spread out, with her head on his lap. I think maybe at some point in this burgeoning madness, these two young people have found comfort in each other's arms. Who could blame them?

Earlier, as we examined the place, I heard commotion from the direction of the bathroom. Whitney came charging out, slamming the door behind her. She and Alberto discussed something in a hushed, frantic tone, then she filled me in on their discovery.

"We found the source of the stench, Walter. I hate to ask this of you, but if you have to urinate, I would do it outside."

"Is it a corpse?"

"Yes. A young man. Suicide."

My curiosity got the best of me. As they slept, I took the lantern from Alberto's side and moved through the darkness as carefully as I could. Near the bathroom, the wretched stench grew stronger. I covered my nose and

348

mouth with the neck of my shirt, then slowly opened the door. The light from the lantern revealed a naked man submerged in a dark, thick water. His body was blistering, turning a greenish black.

I've seen the horror of human decay before. More than I care to admit. So it isn't the death that will stick with me as much as what surrounded it. The brownish powder on the sink. The cotton balls. The bottle caps. The shoelace and needle. A sad combination of things that I've been all too acquainted with.

As I turned to leave, my light caught a piece of lined paper taped on the medicine cabinet, with a message in black magic marker.

I'm leaving this world.
There's only darkness left here.

Before I joined my friends for some much needed rest, I stepped out of the front door, and into the blustery night. Except for a six foot radius of light from my camping lantern, the world was a limitless void. I lifted my face toward the sky, the sky that has unleashed its wrath upon everything underneath it, and felt the first few drops of cool precipitation.

Today started with fire and ended with rain.

Spencer

Lila would've made sure it never happened. She kept track of dentist appointments, saw that the bills got paid on time, kept the medicine cabinet stocked with children's Tylenol. She handled the million little things that kept the ship afloat. I imagined her hand in mine, "Let's keep going" she'd say, pulling us down the desolate highway. A never-ending trek under the hot sun.

I took nothing from the van. Not even my father's gun. It was stupid, but somewhere in my mind were naive visions of returning to it with canisters full of gas.

A stabbing pain ran from my feet up to my thighs, my lower back was throbbing from George's weight. No matter how many times I switched arms, it was like he was getting heavier as we went. The snapping of twigs and rustling of leaves came from the woods on both sides of us. Unfamiliar chirping and buzzing from species reclaiming their planet.

Fearing that I was on the verge of passing out, I stopped and put George down. It took him a moment, but eventually he started to walk. I followed behind his cumbersome gait and smiled, despite our desperate situation. Eventually he drifted to the edge of the trees and began searching for rocks and sticks like he would at the park by our house. I took the opportunity to sit on the underbrush, in the shade of the trees.

I imagined her again, helping him search, rubbing a finger against the smooth rock, and telling him how beautiful it is.

His pile started to add up. With each find, he babbled a description, although I could only decipher a few words. "Rock. Stick. Dada. Two. Three."

"Hey, George. We should get going, buddy. Why don't you keep your favorite rock, and Dada will pick you back up."

"Dada," he giggled.

His spirits were impossibly high. In his mind he was on some grand adventure with his father. I let him walk out a bit further from me. A scent of moss and burnt timber filled the air. The sun was descending below the treetops. Everything became a bit cooler and gray. The wind picked up, carrying with it a strange sound from the same direction as George's voice. Something caught his eye. He moved quickly toward it and the sound amplified.

A rattle.

A brownish-yellow viper was unfurling, poised to strike. I leapt to my feet and ran as quickly as my body would allow, then kicked it square in its head. My momentum took me to the sandy ground. It was ready to pounce again, but I crawled to where it was coiled, and yanked it down near the rattle, pulling it away from George. He reached for me. As I rose back to my feet, I scooped him up, then sprinted in the opposite direction of the snake. When I felt far enough away from it, I turned around.

I had let my guard down, and my son almost paid the price. I swore to myself from that moment on that George would have to stay in my arms at all times. The world was filled with dangers, both the extraordinary, mysterious kind from above and the kind that people with a much keener sense of survival than mine have faced for centuries.

After walking for another torturous hour, we came to an opening in the woods. A dirt driveway led up to an unadorned log cabin. Smoke was rising from the home's chimney, letting me know someone was there. As we got closer to the front porch, a man's gruff voice came from the window.

"Who are you?"

350

"My name is Spencer. This is my son, George. Our car broke down several miles back."

"Where y'all from?"

"Cedarwood." I took a long pause. "New Jersey."

"You're a long way from home, brother."

"My wife is in Orlando. I'm trying to get to her."

I saw his silhouette disappear from behind the sheer curtain. A moment later, he opened the front door. He was a potbellied, middle-aged man with broad shoulders and a handlebar mustache. He wore nothing but an open flannel and boxers. A faded tattoo of a crucifix ran down the middle of his chest.

"Howdy," I said, immediately realizing I've never said that word to greet someone ever in my life.

"Look at that boy," he responded. "That curly hair. Looks like mine when he was that age. Let me guess. A little under three?"

"Just about."

"Man, oh man, feels like just yesterday."

"How old is he now? Your son."

The question was unnaturally forward for me, and although the man had a presence that made you feel like you were talking to an old friend, he avoided it. "The name is Chuck. Come on in. We'll chat over supper."

Inside, there wasn't much more than a couch, wood burning stove, and bookshelves built into the wall. With a quick glance, I spotted a Holy Bible, *Encyclopedia Britannica*, and rows and rows of *National Geographic Magazine*. Three deer heads were mounted next to the library. Beautiful bucks. When George felt like we might stay a while, he wriggled from my arms and began to survey his surroundings, pointing to the heads.

"Doggies."

"No, buddy. They're deer. Look at the antlers," I mimicked them on my head with my hands. "I take it you're a hunter."

"I am. Mostly I hunt for food, but those are my three amigos. You boys look like y'all can use a bath. Especially little man. I have a three thousand gallon tank down the basement. Take some water on up and fill the tub out back. Take your time. Then we'll eat."

Doomsday preparation is a peculiar concept, until it's the end of the world and you run into a doomsday prepper. His hospitality seemed authentic, but I kept my guard up. A pit viper attack is one thing, getting taken hostage by a crazy man in his boxer shorts was a level of peril George and I weren't ready for. I spoke my next words out of nervousness, but also necessity. Every second we spent with this stranger, was a second away from Lila.

"Thank you for your kindness but, I would feel terrible using you for your water and food, then moving on."

"Y'all are wayward travelers in need. I wouldn't be able to live with myself if I didn't provide. Wash up. Eat. Then I'll drive y'all down to Orlando."

It took a few seconds for his words to register. "I'm sorry," I said. "You'll drive us?"

"Yessir. Now, let's bring some water up."

A large white tub was nestled in a grove of pines, sitting atop flat stones. On a stump next to us was a bottle of homemade soap and some washcloths. A symphony of bug noise circled us as I lathered George up. He frolicked in the soapy water, splashing and giggling. Chuck assured us our privacy, but I wasn't about to join in. The vibe was just a little bit too Old West for me. I could live with my grime for however long it took.

After, I wrapped George in a towel like a burrito and held him close to my chest, burying my face into the curve of his little neck. His damp hair smelled sweet, something like patchouli.

"Dop it!" he giggled, as I blew raspberries into his cheek. I backed my head away, then he took my face into his hands. His hair was a heap of dark curls. The setting sun glimmered green in his eyes. He looked like his mother.

"We're going to find Mommy," I whispered. "I promise you. We're going to find her."

"Mommy coming home."

"Yes, my little man. Mommy coming home."

Back in the cabin, candles had been lit around the living room in preparation for nightfall. Chuck was roasting something delicious in a pot, on the flat top of the wood stove. On the couch, there was a small piece of fleece cut in the shape of a diaper, with a safety pin stuck through each side.

"Did you just make this?" I asked.

"I did. Took me right back to my days as a new dad. Get some clothes on that boy and come eat. Rice, with tomatoes and peppers from the garden."

The meal was warm and incredible. Chuck and I washed it down with a bottle of homemade wine that tasted like blackberries. I felt compelled to thank him.

"You're too much, man. I'm extremely lucky we ran into you." We both glanced at George, who was passed out by my feet on a blanket, with a fresh diaper and a full belly. "Thank you."

"You're not a religious man, are you, Spencer?"

"How'd you guess?"

"All this talk of luck and what not. The Book of Revelation says God's judgment is always just, and we will only receive what we deserve. We deserved this. This was his wrath. Luck is nothing compared to that."

"So, you're saying God is responsible for all of this?"

"Is there any other explanation? We've become an ugly people. Hateful. Self-serving. Followers of corrupted, wicked leaders."

As I polished off a third bowl of rice and vegetables, I examined his words carefully. His theory was no more, or less, valid than my neighbors back in Cedarwood, with their homemade signs welcoming our alien visitors. The only indisputable fact was that the human race had been put through the ringer.

"My wife and son didn't survive," he continued. "If we were here, in our home, they would have."

"I'm so sorry."

"It's my fault. We were out for a walk. I felt like I needed it." He paused, glancing around the cabin. It was as if their deaths were registering all over again. "The tiniest things in life. Like a walk. Just a little walk on down the road. Mysterious ways, my friend."

The blinding light.

The deafening noise.

The sudden violence from above. Again.

Pieces of the log cabin scattered like matchsticks. Half of my face was sunburnt instantly. I draped my body over George, then closed my eyes and braced for impact from some piece of wreckage. A death blow, whipping through the air, then impaling us.

It never came.

I kept George cradled close to my chest as I rose to my feet and scanned the destruction. Fires burned. Smoke consumed everything. Through a cloudy, stinging haze I managed to spot Chuck. A piece of the roof had thumbtacked him to the floor.

"I'm going to try to get you out from under this," I declared, attempting to lift it with my free arm. George cried in the other.

"Forget it," he said. "In the garage. Keys in the glove box." He was choking to death on his own blood. "Find your wife."

"I can't leave you here like this."

He stared at the space beyond me. I spoke a few more words, but he was gone. There was an opening in the wall of fire that surrounded us. It wouldn't be long before it was lost. I sprinted toward it, holding George close. Whether it was luck, or Chuck's God, it was on my side once again. The garage had been spared in the attack.

I fastened George in the passenger side seat of the car as quickly as I could. The vehicle's interior reeked of marijuana and the hula girl dancing on the dashboard seemed silly considering our situation, but I knew from that moment on that I would be eternally grateful to have met Chuck.

I pinned it. The trees that seemed like they would devour us whole just hours before, zipped by the windows. Eventually, the road led to a neighboring town. I was so concerned with not killing us that I hadn't realized that the sky was filled with strange, silver ships. Glossy levitations behaving as if they were toy planes controlled by children. They flew in no pattern. No rhyme or reason. Defying the laws of gravity at every turn. Beams of dazzling light were projected, eviscerating everything they touched. I glanced in the rearview mirror and saw the vast wilderness being torched.

George was hysterical, tugging at the strap of his seatbelt. It rode up and was beginning to strangle him. I kept one hand on the wheel and reached over with the other, trying to adjust it. My eyes were off the road just long enough to miss a pickup truck heading straight toward us. We were almost in the clear when the truck connected with the tail end of Chuck's car. I placed my hand on George's chest as we spun out, crashing into a telephone pole about halfway through a rotation. Across the street, the other driver lost control, sending the pickup barreling through a storefront.

The light.

The unforgiving light.

I tried to look up but couldn't. I was paralyzed. I heard George crying for me, but his voice sounded miles away. Then I couldn't hear him at all.

My hand could no longer feel him. He was sitting there one second and gone the next.

And I was gone. Darkness. But, not really. An electric white. A gust in my face, both warm and cold, then a glimpse of the top of Chuck's car.

A man dashed from the pickup, his face bloody. He swung the door open. Shocked. He found no one.

Lauren

I was six when my dad died. I still remember seeing my mother's eyes through the little pane of glass in the classroom door. They were puffy and red, her makeup was dried in streaks on her face. The teacher welcomed her in, then I sprung into her arms. She carried me, down the hallway, out into the rainy afternoon, and into the car. I didn't know why she was sad but I knew she needed me.

Later that night, the house was quiet. It was dark and he wasn't home yet. My mother was lying in bed, sobbing. It was the first of many times I would find her like this. She pulled me close and explained that he wouldn't be coming home. She told me that he had gone away to heaven.

Why would he go away?

The answers to that question became when I failed a test, or when I acted up, or when Mommy lost a job. Those were the reasons why he chose to live in the clouds, rather than with us.

"Why would you ever think that?" she asked me, a couple of years later, as we visited his grave. I told her what I had deduced. "No, no, baby. Daddy didn't choose to leave. He was taken from us."

"How?" I asked, even though I wasn't ready to hear it.

"Well," she hesitated, staring into some other place. A place where she didn't have to tell her nine-year-old daughter how her father died. "He was out on his bicycle and a drunk driver hit him. He didn't suffer. He died instantly."

Suffer? Die instantly?

These are words that haunted me. For a long time. They ramped up in the days after we moved in with The Monster. Eventually, with the help from therapy and some self-medication, I was almost able to make a tiny bit of sense out of them. Maybe my abandonment issues stemmed from those years of thinking he had some choice in the matter of life and death. Could've been.

Or, it could've been the couple of shitty boys I got myself wrapped up with in high school. Whatever it was, it had me cussing Orson and Dwight aloud as I followed the railroad tracks.

It was the edge of night. The deep purple sky was speckled with the lights. Halos had formed around them, making me wonder if they were getting brighter, or closer, or hadn't moved at all. It was a dizzying, tantalizing sight. Quite beautiful, even if it brought along the possibility of another ambush from above.

The tracks eventually ran across a downtown area. A gun shop was wedged between a laundromat and check cashing place. This piqued my interest.

I climbed through the broken front window and learned quickly that the place had been ransacked to an almost comical level. I was searching the empty shelves and display cases in search of a gun, or even a stabbing weapon, when I heard engines from outside. The familiar howl of motorcycles. My instinct was to jump behind the checkout counter, and peek over.

Two men parked across the street. I could only manage to see one, with the other behind a crushed box truck. He was jabbering away, as he removed his helmet and a bottle of Southern Comfort from his backpack. He glanced over at the store, then limped in my direction. I ducked down and prepared myself to flee if need be.

The skinny, bearded man scanned the store, methodically, the way someone does if they have the feeling of company in their midst. He had a rifle slung over his shoulder, and wore a Rebel Flag bandanna and leather vest with familiar patches.

My stomach sank.

An air of familiarity started to grow around him. I had seen him before, hanging around The Monster's garage. *It couldn't be*, I thought. *The other biker could not be him. There's no way. I killed him.*

My thoughts were in a tailspin. I felt like puking. Right there, behind the checkout counter. I contemplated making a run for it, but they would give chase, there was no doubt about that. My only other option was to act like I was in serious trouble. I doubted that he would remember me. In fact, I was certain, I hoped, that he had never spotted me as I spied on him and The Monster from my bedroom window.

"Don't shoot," I said, softly, as I rose from behind the counter.

"Hot damn, girl," he said. "You trying to get yourself kilt? What the hell you doing back there?"

"I'm hiding. There's a group of men. Like fifteen of them. Mexicans. Or, maybe black. I don't know."

I was smearing it on heavy.

"The hell? A group like that ain't no good. We know that. You're in good hands now, though. Come outside and meet my friend."

"What's his name? I mean. What are your guys' names?"

I messed up. I spoke too frantically. I stuttered. Lying was always second nature to me, but the thought of The Monster being alive, not more than a hundred yards away, took me off my game.

"Do I know you from somewhere?"

"No. Of course not. I was vacationing with my family when we were attacked. I'm from California. Los Angeles."

"California? What you do out there?"

He was creeping closer with every word. I hadn't realized I was slowly back pedaling away, until I brushed up against the edge of a trash can.

"I'm a makeup artist. For horror movies. Like zombies and shit. I'm pretty well known. There's a group out there looking for me right now. A big Hollywood studio sent them. SEAL Team Six, I think." I was throwing as much information at his peanut-sized brain as I could. "My uncle is a big time actor. You might know him."

"Who?"

"Dwayne Johnson."

When he started laughing, I hightailed it toward the exit sign at the back of the store, leaping over the counter, then smashing through a door. A quick dash through a storage room brought me to an alleyway. I hooked a quick left, then took the alley to a parking lot.

I thought I had put enough distance between them and myself, until I heard the engines fire up. I turned it on again, cramping, sucking wind, looking back in the direction of the motorcycles. There was a fence up ahead, at the top of a steep hill. I climbed, then scaled the chain links. At the other end, I dropped prematurely. A pain shot through my ankle, and I fell to the ground. After managing to get back my feet, the pain proved to be too much. I collapsed after a few steps.

Night had fallen, bringing with it the sound of engines. They grew louder, until I was shrouded by their headlights.

"Well, God damn," The Monster said, as he removed his helmet. Half of his face was pretty much gone. It would have given me some satisfaction, if it wasn't so scary and disgusting to look at. "Hardly anybody left in this fucked up world, but here you are. My darlin' little girl."

I shouted, "Fuck you!" then spat at his feet. If I was going to die, I was going to go out swinging.

"Still as prim and proper as always, I see." He returned the favor by hocking a loogie of his own. I fought the urge to cry with everything in me, as I wiped the warm, wad of phlegm from my neck. "Should I tell my boy, Jimmy, our story? The night you decided to drug me, then hit me in the head with a baseball bat. That one?"

"I don't care. Just get it over with. Kill me. I'll be back with my mother."

"Nah. We ain't gonna make it that easy for you, darlin'." He staggered toward me. I instinctively threw a kick, as he yanked the scarf from my waist.

"Give me that back."

"I always hated this thing. I tried throwing it out once, then I had to hear your mother bitch about it." He swung it around like a dance ribbon. "I gave in. Like always. You two took advantage of my kind hearted nature."

I don't remember much of what came next. I know I was hit in the head with *something*. Not sure if it was a fist, or a rock. I don't really remember how I was flipped over to my stomach, or how he was able to straddle me, then wrap the scarf around my throat. I don't remember what I was thinking about, if anything, other than death. I felt my favorite blanket, the blanket I napped under, the blanket my dad and I shared on movie nights, wrapped tight around my neck, choking the life from me.

I don't remember how I heard it, or when. But, I heard it. Another engine. This one was somewhat familiar. The thing I do remember, the thing I can still see in more than just fragments, is Dwight's Lincoln mowing over The Monster's friend. I definitely remember the dirt bag squealing, as he was crushed between the front of the car and his toppled motorcycle.

The Monster jumped off of me, then leapt for his rifle. He opened fire in the car's direction, as Dwight was exiting. The noise from the gun, and the bullets connecting with the hood of the car, were the worst things I had ever heard in my life. While The Monster's focus was off of me, I ignored the pain in my ankle, ran in his direction, then tackled him backward over his bike. He landed awkwardly over his handlebars. I pressed the gun and his hands

358

into the ground above him, then sank my teeth into the cartilage of his nose. The unexpected bite made him loosen his grip. I grabbed the rifle, then hurried toward Dwight.

He was keeled over by the driver side door, clutching his stomach. His hands were drenched in blood.

"Oh, no!" I cried, bending down, placing my hand on his back.

"I was hit. Got me good."

The Monster rose to his feet. "You sick bitch," he grumbled, wiping the fresh blood from his crusty mess of a face.

"Shut up," I said, as I stood and aimed the heavy gun at him. "Just shut your mouth."

"You've done a number on me, that's for sure. Give me my damn gun back, and I'll let you and your boy head on down the road. No more trouble."

"Yea, right. The moment we turned our backs, you would shoot us, because you're the world's biggest scumbag."

"The world's biggest scumbag," he chuckled. "You don't know the half, girl. Your mom never knew this. Shit, nobody did. But the way I figure, ain't no better time than now to come clean."

Dwight's eyes were glazing over. The puddle of blood grew beneath us. "We have to get back to the store," he croaked. "There's medical supplies there."

"That day your daddy died," The Monster continued. The mere mention of my father sent a jolt through my chest, my finger slid over the trigger. "He weren't killed by no drunk. I clipped him. Didn't mean to. Just weren't paying attention. The rain and everything."

I didn't think I could hate him more than I already did but, in that moment, I hated him with a fire that could've scorched what was left of the Earth. Whether it was true, or not. Whether he was using it as Kryptonite to weaken me and make his move, it no longer mattered. I saw red, then pulled the trigger.

It wasn't the first time I shot that gun. He had forced me to many times in his backyard. The first go around, I was a skinny little girl, with the sound of the rifle ricocheting around my head, and the pushback damn near blowing my arm from its socket. He got a good laugh out of it, all the way up until I hit my late teens. That's when he stopped laughing. Probably because I grew into a better shot than he ever was.

I thought about how differently I would've turned out if my dad wasn't killed. Maybe, I would've been one of those pretty girls at Starbucks, bent over a laptop, sipping a steamy Macchiato. Or, a perfectly tanned little thing, going viral for some silly dance. I'm almost certain I wouldn't have been the girl that murdered a man, then stood over him and interrupted his death wheeze by dumping another round into his carcass. Or, the girl that fixed a sweet little cherry on top by turning and popping his dead friend a couple of more times on principle.

Dwight willed himself around the back of the car and slumped into the passenger side. I tossed the rifle to the backseat, then joined him up front behind the wheel.

"You drive, right?" he asked.

"Once or twice with my friends," I answered. "Never really owned a car."

"Just take it slow and follow the headlights."

I did just that, navigating as carefully as I could through the eternal darkness that surrounded us. I was feeling every emotion at once, and none at all. It was like some kind of outer body experience. My main concern was Dwight. I was far from a medical expert, but he appeared to be bleeding to death right before my eyes.

"Dwight, stay with me," I said, like they did in the movies. He acknowledged my words with slight nods of his head until we reached the ShopRite lot. I threw the car in park, then shook him gently. His eyes were closed. He didn't budge. I rushed around the front of the car, opened his door, and shook him with a little more force. Still, nothing.

He was gone, and I didn't even have the chance to thank him.

Walter

Grace passed this morning.

I woke up first and found her slouched over in her wheelchair. This desperate situation proved to be too much. As the only resident left, I can't help but feel like my time is coming. This is not a place for the old.

Whitney knew of a church about a mile out of our way. Although they argued that we should keep on our path to ShopRite, and that deviating from our plan could put us in further danger and waste vital energy, I insisted on taking her there.

360

We walked a few blocks through a ramshackle development, which brought us to a highway. We crossed it and arrived at a stretch of road that cut through a wooded area. I pushed her the whole way. Even when Alberto pleaded with me to take over, I refused.

It was a quant, antiquated church at the crisscrossing of two dusty roads. Behind it, there was a field that seemed to stretch as far as the eye could see. An untampered ocean of green, basking underneath the cloudless sky. It made me forget, if only for a moment, what has happened to the world.

"So, what should we do, guys?" Alberto asked, after a stretch of silence. "I didn't bring the shovel with us."

"Walter?" Whitney responded.

"She was a person of faith. She belongs in the church."

I wheeled her in, then placed her before the crucifixion. Our presence stirred up specks of dust. They danced in the light of the sun, shining through the stained glass windows.

We stood side by side, as I said a silent prayer for our friend. When we were ready, Alberto lifted her from the wheelchair, then wrapped her lifeless body in a blanket he found in the antechamber. Her final resting place was on the chancel, underneath our Lord.

"You should let us push you," Whitney said, guiding the wheelchair toward me by the hand grips. "Just until we get to ShopRite."

I'm not ready to give up and become somebody else's burden. I'm my own man. If I perish out here in the wild, I will do it on my own two feet.

"No, thank you," I said.

"Mr. Walter, it's a couple more miles. It'll be easier for you," Alberto added, right on beat. It was like they discussed it already.

"I will walk. If I can't make it, I can't make it."

"Then what? We keep going and leave you behind?"

"If that's what it takes."

Whitney spoke again. This time, she was sterner.

"Walter, we don't have time for this. We have a single flashlight that's going to die any minute. If we get stuck out there at nighttime, we'll be as good as dead."

She was absolutely right.

They've been beyond good to me. They've brought me this far. If angels exist here on Earth, Whitney and Alberto are a couple of their names.

"Fine," I said. "Just don't bump into anything."

So, now I sit. I scrawl in my journal as Alberto pushes me across the uncertain land. Just like that, I've become one of those useless old people. The kind that barely exists at all.

Spencer

I dreamt of late afternoon.

The sun was setting over the ocean, as ribbons of color splashed across the sky. Lila sipped an iced coffee as we watched George play with his plastic trucks. His jeans were folded at the ankles. His chubby feet were covered in sand. The waves crashed and the seagulls crooned, mixing perfectly with the faint laughter of children frolicking on the boardwalk. A breezy, beautiful dream. Ice cubes in Lila's cup. People mingling. In crowds. Laughing. Food being served. The promise of another day. Another sunrise.

It soon became feverish. Pitched in an awkward way. At first, I thought it was a lucid dream. I crawled on my hands and knees on the burning sand searching for George and Lila. They were nowhere. There was no boardwalk. No ocean. Just sand. And thirst. And loneliness.

Then, I was naked. A jagged tube was stretched down my throat. The sharp end wedged itself into the pit of my stomach. Its slimy, warm texture, made me think it was connected to a living thing. I was weightless. One of many, floating in a chamber, gently colliding with each other.

George and Lila. That's all there was. Everything began and ended with them.

I took the strange tube in my hands and pulled. Vomit. Blood. Pieces of my insides, floated in front of my face like bubbles. I swam upward, causing something to snap behind me. With it, came a sharp pain in my anus. Another tube whipped slowly around the first, like the tentacles of an octopus. More of my bodily fluids filled the hollow chamber. I climbed the naked bodies toward a hazy, blue light, gleaming at the top of the chamber. Somehow, I managed to breach the side of a corridor, crashing to the floor with a thud. My attempt to walk became nothing more than a painful lurch forward that ended with me vomiting again. Bile splashed below me. Unlike the chamber, there was gravitational pull in the long corridor.

The hall was narrow, with walls made of something like flesh. Light blue fiber-optics ran through them, leading me to a large door. Mechanical in nature, but connected to the walls and tentacles. All living. Breathing. In the center of the door was an interface. Symbols beyond my comprehension were glowing on the screen. I placed the tip of my finger on the largest one. The color of the fiber-optics changed from blue to orange, along with the symbols. They liquefied and changed their configuration on the screen.

"How are you here?" A voice in my head. But, it wasn't mine. "This is no place for you."

"What?" I said. This time aloud. "Where are you?"

"Beyond the door. You dare approach us?"

"Where is my son?"

"Your offspring is very much where it should be."

"Let me see him."

"It's peculiar that you were able to regain consciousness."

"I need my son back."

"One of the most remarkable aspects of your species is this notion of love. Do you love this creature?"

I balled up my fist and brought it down as hard as I could against the screen. The symbols liquefied again, getting stuck between the two colors. The voice in my head no longer spoke to me. I frantically rushed down the adjacent corridor, panicking that I lost communication somehow. It was more of the same. Fleshy walls. Fiber-optical veins. One false move and I would've lost myself in the otherworldly labyrinth. This much, I was sure of. I centered myself in front of the door, then struck the interface again, this time with my foot.

"Let me the fuck in!" I shouted, then kicked it again.

"What do you expect to achieve beyond this door?"

I had no answer. There was nothing more I could say. There was nothing I could do. I was at the mercy of the unknown. The incomprehensible. I was naked and lost. Something broke inside of me and I fell to one knee. I began to sob, and plead for my son.

The door slowly rose, as the fiber-optics turned red.

The room was a command center of some kind. There were more screens, with more strange symbols. Once I was clear of the door, it closed behind me. Beyond the hub was a huge window. I climbed a small ramp, up to a platform, then looked out.

We were in space, hovering right above Earth. There was an endless fleet of the ships. Opals in line formation, with systems of lights on their undersides. The sight took my breath away. I shut my eyes and fell, sliding down the glasslike window. When I reopened them, a creature had appeared at the center of the hub.

A half-man, half-squid monstrosity. A twisted mollusk. The nonsensical bane from midnight movies and horror marathons. Its tentacles unfurled around it, as it looked upon me with the twitchy, unsettling eyes of a curious insect. It spoke to me in my thoughts once again.

"Do I frighten you?"

"I'm all out of fear. I just want my son."

"You're weak. As is your planet. An incredible waste of our resources."

"Then leave. Give us back who you've taken and move on."

"Do you take pity on your ants?"

"What?"

"Ants. *Formicidae*. As your species destroyed all that was before you, then built upon that destruction, did you once consider the ants?"

I had been abducted and violated. Stuck, in an inescapable nightmare world. If this was its attempt at taunting me, it wasn't working.

"Your words mean nothing to me," I told it, as I rose to my feet, then inched closer. "My son."

"Did these ants ever try to appeal to your species? If they had, would you have heard them?" A viscid tentacle slid up my back, then wrapped around my chest and underneath both arms, lifting me off the platform. "Lucky for you, we are empathetic." I hammered the tentacle with the edge of my hand. To no avail.

It brought me close to its eyes. My reflection glimmered in a million tiny photoreceptors. The tentacle tightened, crushing my rib cage. As I gasped, another whipped out in front of me, then lodged itself back down my throat.

Lauren

I sat on the checkout counter with Dwight's saxophone on my lap. The brass shone in the light of the only lantern left with working batteries. The candles had burned out. The shelves had provided us almost all they could. Our salvaged supplies were nearly wiped clean. A grocery store, in some Bumblefuck town in Georgia, would be the place I died. I was sure of it.

I rubbed my fingers over the area of my neck where the scarf tightened. The skin was tender to the touch. Bullets, ripping through The Monster's flesh, played over and over again in my mind. It was a vision I wouldn't soon forget. Did it make me want to vomit or laugh hysterically? That part I wasn't sure about. I felt mad. Like the last lunatic alive. Feelings of guilt began to multiply as well. A guy I barely knew - a good guy - was dead because of me. Because he decided to save my life, he would never find his daughter.

A gleam of light washed over the interior of the store, pulling me away from my thoughts. I ran toward the front windows and looked out over the parking lot. There were more flashes of light in the distance, followed by explosions. I was so frightened by the chaos, I hadn't noticed a pickup truck swerve into the lot. Big Al was behind the wheel, with an old man I didn't recognize riding shotgun. Big Al's wife, Orson, Sophia, and two others were in the bed, holding on for dear life. They parked the truck, then moved like a stampede toward the entrance. Orson shouted as he grabbed me by the arm.

"We need to get to the freezer!"

The ShopRite survivors had formulated a plan to use the freezer as shelter in the event of another attack.

"Wait," I said, then removed my arm from his grip and bolted toward the checkout counter. I grabbed the saxophone, then handed the rifle off to Orson.

"Where'd you get this?" he asked.

"It's a long story," I responded.

Big Al led us to the freezer with a hunting spotlight. Once inside, he slammed the heavy door shut. The plan was a hodgepodge at best. With each muffled boom, we looked into each other's eyes, reaching an unspoken consensus that we were nearing our demise. Eventually, though, they grew softer. More sparse. One by one, we felt comfortable enough to loosen up and sit on the plastic Adirondack chairs that had been placed in the freezer. Sophia was hugging one of the strangers.

That's when I knew.

She looked just like him.

Something about her eyes.

"You're Whitney."

"Yes," she answered. "That's his," she gestured toward the saxophone. I didn't have the heart to answer. "He's dead. Isn't he?"

I could only nod my head.

She cried, but there was no emotional outburst from somewhere deep. No sobbing into Sophia's shirt. It was a quiet cry.

I looked around at the faces in the room with me. A tattooed guy rubbing some old dude's back. Orson sitting between his parents. Sophia and Dwight's daughter sharing a Kodak moment. I felt like the odd one out. That old familiar feeling that everything was my fault had returned.

"Why did you come back?" I asked, glancing at Orson.

"We never went," Big Al said, before his son could get a word out. "My boy convinced us to come looking for ya, so we split up. We went one way, Dwight went the other."

His words made me feel even worse. A whole damn search party could've gotten themselves killed because of me. I excused myself, then headed for the door. I needed to get out of the freezer.

"Whoa now," Big Al said, "we don't know if it's safe."

"I'll take my chances."

"Take this, at least," the tattooed guy tossed me a flashlight from his backpack. The quiet darkness beyond the door was a welcomed sight. It let us know that we weren't directly involved in the attack. I turned back to the group as if to say, "I told you so."

The checkout counter (my special apocalyptic place) was right where I left it. Fires burned in the distance, but the ShopRite and its surrounding area had been spared once again. Just like Dwight's Lord intended.

Whitney's voice arose from the darkness behind me. "Hey," she whispered, as I turned around.

"Oh, hey." I dried my eyes with my sleeve.

"May I sit with you?"

"Of course."

I nervously scooted over. I'm not sure how much older she was than me, but she was beautiful and her body was incredible. Jealousy still reared its ugly head in even the direst of circumstances.

Whatevs.

She asked me how her father died, and I explained, starting from the beginning. I mean, all the way from the beginning. My dad. My mom. The Monster. The attempted murder by baseball bat. Right up to how he found me.

"He saved my life," I said, beginning to sob. "He shouldn't have. I'm not worth it." She took my head in her arm, then I leaned into her chest. "I'm sorry."

"Don't be sorry, baby girl. Let it out."

"He wanted to find you so badly. He was never going to give up. I promise." She was embracing me with both her arms now. Emotions poured out of me in heaps. I'm not even sure who, or what, my tears were for, but I was soaking the front of Whitney's shirt. "You just lost your dad and I'm the wreck."

I gave her a moment. When she didn't respond, I figured she was processing everything. We were two lost souls, in the light of a burning world.

"Lauren," she whispered. "We need to go."

I picked my head up.

The Nightmare Machine was standing outside the window, looking right at us.

Walter

Something was wrong.

It was taking too long to reach our destination. I was in and out of consciousness, trapped in a warm, sweaty sleep paralysis of some kind. Dehydration. Exhaustion. Maybe whatever was causing the dizzy spells had finally decided to take my life.

"Have we taken a wrong turn?" I asked, from the seat of the wheelchair.

"The ShopRite is a little bit further than I thought, Mr. Walter. Go back to sleep," Alberto said.

His voice sounded different. So did Whitney's. They were arguing about distance, and time, and ships hovering in the heavens high above us. Thousands of silver flecks, scattered like glitter across the twilight sky. I was too tired to make sense of it.

I was starting to believe that feelings of joy could no longer grow in the infertile fields that our souls had become. I submitted to the notion that human beings would suffer a loveless plunge into the abyss. I mourned, not for me, but for the children that will inherit this new world. I mourned for the people we've lost along the way. I mourned for Whitney and Alberto. It was over. We were out of food. Out of time. Headed for a place that might be abandoned. Or a trap, set by sick people primed to take advantage of us.

"Leave me," I said. "Just leave me."

"I'd leave Alberto before I would ever leave you, Walter," Whitney said.

I opened my eyes. Through a dreary haze, I saw the road we were on, stretching uphill. Tall pines on both sides, reaching up to touch the merciless sun. It was then that a pickup truck appeared like a mirage. A figment of our collective imagination. We moved to the shoulder and let it pass. A boy with green hair waved to us from the bed. The dreamlike moment escalated, as the brake lights came on and the passenger side door swung open.

"Sophia," Whitney said, under her breath, when she saw the pretty brunette exiting the vehicle. "Sophia!"

They landed in each other's arms, hugging so tightly that they became one. My heart fluttered with something that resembled joy. Perhaps, I was wrong in my line of thought.

"I think they know each other," Alberto said, with a laugh. It made me want to laugh, too. On the way to the church, he asked me what I missed most. I was too tired to speak, but I thought about vanilla milkshakes. Wheel of Fortune. Christmas parties back at the home.

"This," I finally answered, as we watched the reunited friends continue their embrace. "I missed this the most."

A tall man with long, gray hair tied back in a ponytail, and an air of military about him, introduced himself as Albert. He explained that he and his family were responsible for the ShopRite safe haven and that Whitney's father, Dwight, was there.

"He was looking for me," Whitney said to her friend, but it was more like a question. For a fleeting moment, the impossibly strong woman seemed like nothing more than a little girl, searching for reassurance that her father loved her.

Introductions were made quickly. "Oorahs" were exchanged by myself and Albert. The things in the sky would not wait. Our powerless reality took precedence over anything else. When my insistence to sit in the bed failed, I knew that I wasn't about to both kick someone out of the cab and take up room in the bed by hauling the wheelchair along with us. Being in the company of a fellow Marine gave me the shot of adrenaline I needed to rise to my feet, then push the wheelchair straight into the woods.

"Mr. Walter, you might need that," Alberto said.

"Forget it," Whitney chimed in. "Get in the bed and let's go."

A few minutes into our drive to ShopRite, I broke the ice.

"So, your name is Helen," I said to the lady sitting between me and Albert.

"Yes it is."

"That was my wife's name."

"Oh, I'm sorry. Has she passed on?"

"About fifteen years ago. Almost to the day."

"Do you think it means something?"

"What could it mean?"

"Well, there's almost nobody left on Earth, as far as we can tell. And you just happen to end up in a truck with a lady that shares your wife's name."

Albert interrupted. "It's a damn coincidence, sweetheart. Don't mean nothing. Leave the man alone."

His heavy foot took us to a four lane highway. Banks, fast food joints, liquor stores. Some destroyed, some left halfway standing. He had to slow down when we reached a graveyard of parked cars. He weaved in and out of a few before taking a hard turn up over the curb, across a grassy area, then back down on a paved lot. The boy with green hair shouted from the back.

"Dad, what the fuck? A little warning next time!"

As the sun dipped below the horizon, the ships began to make their descent. They shot out in every direction, zigzagging, circling, leaving no trail in their wake. No sign that they were traveling at incomprehensible speeds. There was a dangerously precise pattern to their movements. Beams of light touched down all around us, followed by huge explosions. Bigger than any I had ever seen on the battlefield. Albert was shouting through the rear window.

"The ShopRite! Twelve o'clock! We need to get to the freezer as quickly as possible! No looking back!" He turned his attention to me, then lowered his voice. "How fast can you move, soldier?"

"Fast enough," I answered.

Spencer

When I came to, I was naked.

Every inch of my body ached. My throat was sore and inflamed. I could barely swallow. The sun was rising, ushering a damp, chilly air from the forest. As I rose to my feet, the area where the second tentacle entered me, throbbed to the point where it pained me to walk.

My head felt hollow. The squid creature no longer communicated with me, although traces of its voice still lingered. I thought about the way it spoke of pity and empathy. I thought about how it could've killed me at any moment. A strange gratitude filled my heart. Especially when I heard George cry out.

He was sitting on his butt, in a pile of leaves. When I rushed toward him, he stood up, then stumbled to meet me with his arms extended. His naked body was cold and wet. He was trembling.

I cradled him close, then buried my nose in his hair. A cry from the deepest parts of me rumbled through the trees, causing birds to take off from the highest branches.

"I'm so sorry, buddy. Never again. I promise. Never again."

Sharp twigs, pine cones, and the jagged edges of rocks decimated the bottoms of my feet as I trekked through the forest, clutching George against my chest. The deepest depths of my imagination couldn't provide an explanation for the slimy substance dripping down the back of my thigh.

We came upon the backyard of a large warehouse. I entered through a garage door, shouting for help. The building provided no answer. Nothing but a cold, dusty emptiness. George had stopped crying. He nestled himself further into my chest, as I marched across the paved driveway that connected the parking lot of the warehouse to a highway.

For unearthly reasons I'll never understand, I was given a second chance at finding Lila. I had no idea what it meant. What, if any, consequences my actions in the ship had when it came to the bigger picture. What I did know - what I was certain of - is that we had been attacked again. New fires were burning. New levels of destruction dished out by the beings above.

The highway ran through an industrial area. A soulless, gray district of stone and steel and barbed wire. One of the large buildings was ablaze, while others were in the process of collapsing on themselves. With every step, I was weakening, leaving bloody footprints on the concrete behind us. The rawness of the world was beating us down. It felt as if we would leave it the same way we entered. Naked and afraid.

I longed for the million things I had taken for granted. The good. The bad. The little arguments that seemed like nothing. Lila hated that I left kitchen cabinets open. She kicked me out of bed most nights because of my snoring. She was prone to leaving piles of paperwork around the house.

Paperwork that I would store away in a safe spot, then promptly forget where that safe spot was located. There's a rhythm to marriage. We didn't always play it perfectly, but we managed to make beautiful music most of the time. I swore to somebody, perhaps Chuck's God, that if I were to see her again, I would never waste another second.

Had I been a good husband? Father? Man?

I wasn't sure.

These were the questions reverberating around my head when the military vehicles arrived. Two jeeps, followed by a larger cargo truck. They came to a stop about twenty feet away from me. Two soldiers hopped out of the first vehicle. A Caucasian and an African American. Both were camouflage clad and muscle-bound. George stirred in my right arm, while I instinctively shielded my man parts with my left.

"Are you okay?" the African American soldier asked.

My throat pulsated when I answered. "I don't know. Where are we?"

"Florida. About five miles out of Orlando."

His words clobbered me. I grasped George, then fell to one knee. They rushed to my side, trailed by a third soldier carrying a heavy blanket. A young girl, with red hair thrown together in a bun and freckles across the bridge of her nose. She draped the blanket over my shoulders.

"Thank you," I whispered.

She led me to the back of the cargo truck. Inside, there were twelve people - all ages, shades, and sizes - underneath blankets, trying to warm up. Some were in shock, while others sobbed. I immediately felt some kind of kinship with them.

"We found you guys all today," the red headed soldier explained. "Mostly in the last two hours."

"Where are you taking us?" I asked.

"We've set up shop at the Wide World of Sports complex. We've been there since the first attack. It's in pretty good shape. We even have power, as of this morning."

"Is Lila Wells there?"

"So many people have been displaced. The arena is beyond swamped. But, if she was in the area, it's possible."

Once we got moving, she took my blood pressure, then checked my temperature.

"Are you a nurse?" I asked.

"Yes," she answered.

"Oh. The camo and everything. I wasn't sure."

"I'm an Army nurse."

"They have those?"

"Yes," she chuckled. "They have those. We need to get the bottoms of your feet cleaned and bandaged when we reach our destination."

"That's fine."

She checked George next. There was no outburst. No meltdown. No protest at all. I was worried that everything he had been through was having some adverse effect on him.

"Is he okay?" I asked.

"His vitals are fine. We'll examine everyone further when we reach our destination."

She took a seat on the bench next to me.

"Hey," I whispered. "Thank you again."

"Don't mention it. Do you remember anything? Anything at all about how you arrived on this highway?"

I thought about speeding through the chaos in Chuck's car. The truck that almost killed us. I thought about the ship. The walls that seemed to breathe. The strange fiber optics, and screens, and symbols. The half-man, half-squid beast and its musings on choosing Earth. "A weak planet" as he put it.

"I remember everything," I told her.

"They're going to want to talk to you."

"Who are they?"

"The people in charge."

"Well *they* can kindly fuck off."

We shared a laugh. A couple others joined in. Maybe the simplicity of two human beings having a discussion in front of them was enough to begin to thaw whatever frozen shock they were in. It was enough to let them know that they were back.

"Is Lila your wife?"

"Yes."

"Mommy," George added.

The empathetic Army nurse placed her hand, gently, on his head.

"Well, I hope you guys find her."

Lauren

The front windows rained down in shards. Checkout counters were torn from the ground like they were nothing more than weeds. It swatted shelving units out of its way like minor annoyances. Big Al and Orson exited the freezer and met us in the storage room. Big Al was brandishing The Monster's rifle.

"May I use this?" he asked, as we watched through the small window in the door. The Nightmare Machine was methodically destroying the ShopRite. "It moves slowly," he continued in a hushed frenzy. "If we exit through the loading docks, then head around the side of the building, we can get back in the truck."

"What if there's more out there?" Orson asked. "What if they attack us from above?"

"We have to take that chance, son."

"Okay. Let's move, then." They turned to flee. Whitney and I followed.

Suddenly, a cable, with a claw at the end, buzzed by our heads. It had traveled through the pane of glass in the door, then clenched Big Al by the ankle. He withered in pain as Orson jumped on top of him. They both slid on the floor toward the machine, as it smashed through the wall. In a storm of debris, Big Al managed to readjust his body so he was lined up with the machine's torso, then trained the rifle at it. He fired a direct hit that went through the thing's dome. The clawed cable recoiled back into the machine's palm. The shattered glass of the dome revealed an impossible sight.

Whitney screamed "Holy Shit!" as a horrifying squid man used its tentacles to climb up out of the machine, scale down the front, then plop on the floor. It pirouetted toward Big Al, as he hit it with a few more shots. The bullets tore through its flesh, bathing its body in a lime green substance. I could tell from the way it started twitching, that it was injured. Whitney and I leapt to the floor when several of its tentacles stretched out straight, like spears, piercing wherever they landed. Orson bellowed. A noise that I'll never forget. He was impaled. When it dislodged, he crumbled to the floor in a heap.

Whitney and I rolled to where he fell. I pulled him close. A gaping hole was left in his midsection. There was blood everywhere.

"What can we do?" I asked Whitney.

"He's hurt bad," she said. "Orson, can you hear me?" He didn't respond. Life was fading from him fast. "Lauren. The thing is coming toward us."

The wretched creature loomed. Its body was a slimy wilderness of veins and contusions. A funnel cloud of tentacles surrounded us. Whitney got to her feet, then squared up with it, landing blows to its head and body. She blocked incoming tentacles with her forearms and elbows. It was like watching a superhero, only there were no panels neatly arranged on a piece of paper, displaying the action. There was nothing glamorous. This was real and raw. Just a human being deciding to fight when there were no other options left.

"Lauren," Orson gagged. His head was heavy on my lap. "Go back."

"Go back? Where? Talk to me, Orson!"

"The house in the woods."

I shook him out of fear and frustration, more violently than I wanted to. It didn't matter. He was dead. Right in front of me. Like my mother, and Dwight. A rage twisted and contorted somewhere deep in my stomach. My face burned with anger. I rose from the ground, feeling like I had stepped outside of my body, then lunged at the creature. A web of tentacles intercepted me, wrapping around my limbs and throat. Whitney and I were lifted off the floor, the tops of our heads reached the ceiling. I tried to yank at the oily appendage, to loosen the grip on my neck. It smelled like gasoline and a million dead hermit crabs.

From high above, something like a Viking war horn sounded. The tentacles unfurled, dropping Whitney and me to the floor. The creature crawled away from us, over the crumbled wall, back out across the ShopRite, then through the shattered windows. I grabbed the rifle off the floor near Big Al, then chased after it, still seething from having my mother and friends taken from me. If the fucker was weak, I was going to see to it that I finished the job.

Outside, hundreds of Nightmare Machines were being pulled toward the ships by iridescent tractor beams. The squid man hitched a ride on the nearest one, while the ones further from us were nothing more than shadowy forms, ascending in the rays of light. It somehow took me back to summers at my old house with my parents. The way fireflies would rise from our lawn at dusk. "What a cool planet we live on," my dad would say.

374

I wasn't ready to go back inside and face what had happened. I wanted to take off running right then and there. But, I wasn't going to fail to thank Whitney like I had her father.

She met me halfway, wrapping me in her arms. Sophia came up from behind her and did the same. I don't know who was comforting who, but I definitely needed it.

"Thank you," I cried, as we continued our triple hug. "Thank you."

In the shadow of the malfunctioning Nightmare Machine, looming like a monument to our invaders, Big Al and Helen held their dead son. They were sobbing uncontrollably. The others had exited the freezer and were taking in their surroundings as I approached the family.

"I'm so sorry," I said.

"Don't," Big Al responded. "Just leave us be."

Perhaps I should've expected that type of reaction. They didn't know me. I was some stranger that walked into their ShopRite. Some little mess that their son liked to eat snacks with. If they didn't decide to come looking for me, maybe Orson wouldn't have been killed.

Then again, he had a gift. A gift that they didn't want to understand. It could be that they never recognized it at all. To silence that kind of power out of fear was to fail their son. At that moment, I made a promise to myself that I wouldn't do the same. I would heed his final words to me.

I snuck away, leaving behind Dwight's saxophone and The Monster's rifle. The tools of love and hate. Of creation and destruction. Only my mother's backpack would come with me. It's all I ever needed anyway.

The night air smelled as if the entire world was burning. The Lincoln was in one piece. Through the window, Dwight looked like he could've been sleeping peacefully in the passenger seat.

"Lauren," Whitney said from behind me. "Where are you going?"

"You wouldn't understand."

"I don't understand anything anymore."

"I guess none of us do."

"He's in there. Isn't he?"

It clicked that she hadn't seen her father yet. "Yes," I said. "I'm going to leave you two alone."

"Listen, Lauren. Whatever happens from here, please, don't blame yourself. For Dwight, or Orson, or your stepfather. None of this is your fault.

You are beautiful and smart and stronger than you realize. And, you are going to be okay."

Her words made me cry.

I heard my mother in them.

"Thank you," I said, then hit the dark road.

Walter

I awoke to light. Not just a flashlight or a battery operated lantern but fluorescent lamps, in the ceiling above me. A catheter was running into my arm. Alberto was asleep in the chair at my bedside, his snoring was falling in line with the beeps of my heart monitor.

The last thing I remembered was being in the freezer. Whitney had gone out to check on the young girl. A ruckus started. Loud, close. Not like the faraway explosions. This was right outside the door. Albert grabbed the rifle and headed out as well, followed by his son. The green haired boy.

That's when the discomfort in my chest started. It traveled between my shoulder blades, then down my arm. Dread surged inside of me. I tried to stand, only to fall over, flipping the Adirondack chair on its side. Alberto called my name from miles away.

"You had a heart attack," Whitney explained, wearing fresh scrubs. Her hair had been washed and pulled back. She smelled lovely. "The surgeons here put a stent in. You're going to be okay."

"Where are the other people?"

"The boy died in the attack. His folks took him in the pickup truck. Sophia is downstairs helping out. There's a soup kitchen."

"What about the other girl? The one with the scarf."

"She went her own way," I could sense sadness in her voice. "She'll be okay."

"How did we get here?" I grimaced in pain, as I tried to reposition myself in the bed. Whitney held me by the arm, then wedged a pillow behind my back.

"All your questions will be answered in time. You need to rest for now."

"I made sure to grab this, Mr. Walter," Alberto said. "I know it's important to you."

He handed me this journal.

376

Spencer

The arena was a hive of activity. Families were in the stands, huddled close. Injured people were stretched out on the hardwood, some on cots, and others on blankets. Medical personnel took vital signs, while soldiers handed out bottles of water and trays of food. People with clipboards asked questions.

They ushered us to a row of folding tables, where piles of clothing had been arranged by gender and size. I swapped some for George and myself, then stepped behind a curtain working as a makeshift dressing room. The Army issued sweats felt miraculous against my wind-burnt skin. George's were a bit big on him, but he was relieved to be in clothes, and a fresh diaper, which they supplied as well.

When we stepped out, I scanned the building once more. It was a sea of exhausted strangers, easing into the possibility that the world hadn't ended. I waded through, cradling George. My feet throbbed as I stepped down on the hardwood. It reminded me that the Army nurse wanted to tend to them. I looked around for her. She was nowhere in sight. None of the group that I arrived with was in sight. They were swallowed up by the crowd. Even if she was there, locating Lila seemed like an impossible task.

A spindly, middle-aged woman with a pixie-cut approached us. She was holding a clipboard, with a megaphone under her arm, as she explained that she was working with the Red Cross. I was probably shorter with her than I should have been, but I had to cut right to the chase.

"Do you have Lila Wells on your list?"

"Wells. Let me see." She flipped through the pages. It was taking an eternity. "I don't see a Lila. I'm sorry. There are a few more of us collecting names. Follow me."

"Wait a second. Let me see that." I gestured toward the megaphone.

"Excuse me?"

"The megaphone. Please."

She reluctantly handed it over.

"Daddy have a gun," George said, as we cut through the crowd, toward the stands.

"Not a gun, buddy. A really loud thing we're going to use to find Mommy."

"Find Mommy?"

About halfway up the second section of seats, I turned around and peered out over the throng. It wasn't until then, that I realized just how many people were packed into the arena. Some of whom were already looking up at me, including the aggravated Red Cross worker, who was now flanked by some other well-doers.

"Lila" I said, into the bullhorn. My voice bounced off the stadium's walls. George took it out of my hands.

"Mommy," he said, but I wasn't pressing the button.

"Try again."

"Mommy!"

He jumped when his little voice erupted from the speaker.

Eventually, people were able to give their loved ones proper memorial services. Homes were rebuilt. Kids went back to school. Farmers tended to fields and construction workers took to roads. Through the detritus, the world would begin to appear once more. For George and me, our world appeared on the basketball court that morning.

Lila ran through the crowd, practically knocking folks over. She waved her hands while screaming our names. From afar, my wife looked crazy. I imagined what she must've been feeling at that moment. When all hope was gone. What it must've felt like to hear our son's voice on that megaphone. To see us in the stands. I screamed her name in return, then shuffled down the steps, almost losing my footing. George was cracking up.

Crazy, indeed.

We collided at the base of the steps. Falling into each other's arms. I freed George from my grip, then he wrapped his arms around her neck.

"I thought I lost you," she cried. "This can't be real." She backed up and took a good look at me. "How can it be real?"

"It's real, Lila. We're here."

We held each other again, sandwiching George between us. I wasn't sure we'd ever let go.

In the months that followed, human beings began to find their place once more. It wasn't a broad reclaiming of the planet, but a quiet, slow process. People helped their neighbors pick up the scattered remains of their lives. Brick and mortar stores found their footing and eventually **Back in Business** signs started to pop up on doors. Governments realized how powerless they truly were, as they ignored petty differences and aided each other in the relief efforts. Our neighborhood threw a huge block party on

Main Street. We celebrated the return of our loved ones, and mourned those we lost. The Fratellis brought a huge Italian lemon cake, which I washed down with way too much booze.

Our house proved to be unsalvageable, so we decided to destroy what was left of it and start over. In the meantime we moved in with my father. He was one of the millions like me. Except, much like all of them we heard from in the news, he didn't remember anything between the moment he was taken and the moment he returned. It was like a long, deep slumber for most of the abductees. The men in suits came asking questions eventually, only to find the same answers from me that they had from everyone else.

I spoke of what happened only once.

It was that first Thanksgiving night.

My father was snoring in his recliner. "The turkey does it to me," he said, then dozed off.

George was asleep as well, snuggled between Lila and me on the couch. The soft glow of the Christmas tree's string lights washed over the room as we finished a bottle of wine.

When I neared the end of my story, a story more spectacular than any tale of science fiction, I started to shudder. The memories of the ship, the creature, the realization of how helpless we were, was too much to bear. I couldn't finish.

"It's okay," Lila whispered, as she took my hands into hers. "We are together now. You found me. You protected George."

She picked him up, then placed him into my arms. Our chests met. Our breaths became one.

The three of us cuddled close together under a thick, fleece blanket. Our combined body heat warmed me to my core. The trembling ceased. The bad memories melted away.

"You guys were with me on that ship," I said, as I kissed my wife's forehead.

"And we'll be with you forever," she responded. "No matter what."

As George shifted to a more comfortable position on my chest, I glanced out the window beyond the illuminated evergreen.

The night was still and the sky was clear.

Lauren

I waited at the entrance of the driveway until the sun came up, relieved to see the house hadn't been damaged or destroyed. If there were people in there, I didn't want to knock in the darkness.

I thought about all the people it took to get me there. My folks. Dwight. Orson. Even the Monster. The fact that they were all gone was both sobering and terrifying. The chances that Orson was just some troubled dude with a fondness for storytelling were high. It was likely that the streak of blonde hair I spotted in the upstairs window was simply a hallucination brought on by hunger and stress, that I would only face more death if I saw this plan through.

The rainbow, princess, unicorn, and sunflower were still in the window. Along with something else. A new drawing, added after my first visit to the house.

An array of dark blues and purples depicted the night sky. Something that resembled the Nightmare Machine was soaring high above the treetops. Whoever the artist was saw our invaders retreating into the heavens, just like I had in the ShopRite lot.

The addition meant there was life inside those walls.

I dropped my mother's bag to the ground and dug my pocket mirror out of it. I blotted my face with a cleansing wipe, then used blush for approximately the third time in my life. For some reason, I was compelled to remove my nose ring, then pull my hair back into a neat ponytail.

When I looked back up, a man was standing in the front doorway. He was thin, with a salt and pepper beard growing on his square jaw. He wore glasses and a navy blue Polo shirt. A young teacher trying his best to be cool came to mind.

"Hi," I said, suddenly feeling like I could combust right where I stood. "I'm sorry. I should go."

I swung around. Prepared for takeoff.

"Wait a second," the man said. "You were here the other day. With a boy. We watched you guys from the window."

I was about to respond when a woman approached from behind him. She was slightly taller than me and physically fit, with shoulder length strawberry blonde hair. They were both pale and exhausted. If they were unnerved by my presence, they were doing their best not to show it.

"Are you alone?" the woman asked.

"Yes," I answered.

380

My gut told me that the couple had already discussed the possibility of mine and Orson's return.

"What happened to the boy?"

"He died."

"Oh no. Where's your family?"

"They're dead too."

They shot each other a disquieted look.

"I'm so sorry," the man continued. "What's your name?"

"Lauren."

"I'm Michael. This is my wife, Lena. Our daughter, Ruby, is inside. Are you hungry, Lauren?"

"I'm starving."

They looked at each other again. This time the woman took him by the arm.

"Would you like to join us for breakfast?" she asked.

"I would love to."

I stood there for a moment, unsure of what to do next. Orson's final words opened up a world of impossibilities. On my way to the house, I catalogued them, each one more implausible than the last. His mysterious affliction. The stuff of magic and wonder, made little sense. Then again, sense had gone extinct in the new world.

The window to the side of the front door slid open. Ruby pressed her nose against the screen. She was no older than five or six, with a heart-shaped face like her mother, and the blonde hair I was hoping to see for days.

"We thought you were the a-wee-ins," she said. Her parents snapped their heads toward her.

"Ruby, what did we say about hanging around the windows and doors?" her father asked.

"Is Lauren our new friend?"

"She's going to join us for breakfast. If that's okay."

"Of course it is! Lauren, do you like princess stories? How about blowing bubbles? Drawing? Do you like to draw?"

"Okay, Ruby, calm down. We have all been through a lot," her mother added.

"It's fine," I said. "Hey Ruby, have you ever had gummy worms?"

She shook her head no.

"I have some in my bag. Maybe we can have a couple after breakfast. If it's okay with Mom and Dad."

"Mommy, can I? Can I try the worms?"

"Sure, baby. Let's have Lauren come in and get cleaned up first. Then breakfast. Then worms. Okay? Lauren, you coming?"

I was so enthralled with the cute ball of energy in the window that I forgot they invited me in. On my way up the front steps, I held my scarf and turned to gaze toward the sky.

"Do you think they are gone?" Lena asked, placing her hand, gently, on my shoulder.

In the time between the two attacks, the place beyond the clouds felt heavy and ominous. Like there were a million eyes on my every move. That morning, as a symphony of bird calls surrounded us, carrying the warmth of the sun along with their song, things felt different.

"Yea," I answered. "I do."

"Me too. Let's go in and talk about it."

Walter

Behind the hospital there's a footpath that follows a lake. The song of summer sang to me through my room's window this morning, so I decided to head outside for a walk.

A sweet smell of honey, mixed with the faintest scent of distant firewood, hung in the air. Peach blossom trees lined the trail, their pink blooms led me to an old wooden bench in the shade of a red cedar. I took a seat and watched the occasional overactive fish splash in the water.

None of us know what the days ahead will bring; the future is uncertain. But, it appears as if mankind has made an unspoken pact to revel in that uncertainty. Those of us in the hospital. The folks on the news programs. People all over the world are seeking refuge in each other. They're singing on balconies and dancing in the streets. They're discovering the things that make us all the same. The human things.

I keep thinking about the boy in the tub. The words on his note.

It's not all darkness. Not anymore.

I wish he had stuck it out a bit longer to see it for himself.

Whitney and Alberto are going to stay at the motel up the road, until they find a more permanent situation. They've asked me to join them. I think

I will. It's not like I have many options but, even if I did, I couldn't think of two better people to live out the rest of my days with.

I feel okay, Helen. I have some metal scaffolding in my heart now but I feel okay. Perhaps it'll be a little bit longer until I see you again.